FROM LEGENDARY TALES
TO CITY FANTASIES. . . .

From the jazz clubs of New Orleans to the nation's capital, from city tenements to private mansions, the seventeen stories included here transplant everyone from the Big Bad Wolf to the Pied Piper to the Beast and li'l Red herself into our modern-day world and urban settings. And though the perils may be different, the magic is still the same. See for yourself as you discover your childhood fairy tales given new life in such memorable stories as:

"Trading Fours with the Moldy Figs"—Would the New Orleans music scene prove the salvation for a Big Bad Wolf on the run?

"If You Only Knew My Name"—She'd taken on a tech job way beyond her skills, but would the little man on the help icon bail her out or destroy her career?

"The Rose Garden"—A witch's curse had made him an immortal Beast. Time had transformed him, at least outwardly, to something more human. But would he ever find the key to freedom from this spell?

More Magical Anthologies Brought to You by DAW:

FAERIE TALES *Edited by Martin H. Greenberg and Russell Davis.* In twelve original stories, some of today's finest tale spinners—from Charles de Lint, Kristine Kathryn Rusch, and Tanya Huff to Jane Lindskold, Elizabeth Ann Scarborough, and Michelle West—open the hidden pathways between the human lands and the kingdoms beyond time, allowing elves to exchange changelings for mortal babes, letting those with the Sight see things and meet beings beyond most humans' wildest imagining, rescuing those who prove worthy and tricking those who do not.

CONQUEROR FANTASTIC *Edited by Pamela Sargent.* From such masters of the genre as Michelle West, Pamela Sargent, Jack Dann, Ian Watson, James Morrow, and George Zebrowski come these thirteen original "what if" tales about famous, infamous, or legendary figures, and the paths their lives—and the world—might have taken. The stories range from the ancient world to the modern, from legends to historical people . . . from Alexander the Great, Genghis Khan, and Saladin to the Indian leader Metacomet, an Aztec princess, Napoleon, Hitler, John Wayne, Lyndon Johnson, and the Kennedys.

THE SORCERER'S ACADEMY *Edited by Denise Little.* Fifteen original tales of the perils and pitfalls that await students of the magical arts in a very private, spell-guarded school. . . . Includes stories by Josepha Sherman, Laura Resnick, P. N. Elrod, Michelle West, Rosemary Edghill, Robert Sheckley, Jody Lynn Nye, and more.

Little Red Riding Hood
in the
Big Bad City

Edited by
Martin H. Greenberg
and John Helfers

DAW BOOKS, INC.
DONALD A. WOLLHEIM, FOUNDER
375 Hudson Street, New York, NY 10014

ELIZABETH R. WOLLHEIM
SHEILA E. GILBERT
PUBLISHERS
http://www.dawbooks.com

First Printing, July 2004
1 2 3 4 5 6 7 8 9

DAW TRADEMARK REGISTERED
U.S. PAT. OFF. AND FOREIGN COUNTRIES
—MARCA REGISTRADA
HECHO EN U.S.A.

PRINTED IN THE U.S.A.

ACKNOWLEDGMENTS

Introduction © 2004 by John Helfers.

"Mallificent" © 2004 by Nina Kiriki Hoffman.

"The Last Day of the Rest of Her Life" © 2004 by Russell Davis.

"Jack and the B.S." © 2004 by Tanya Huff.

"Panhandler" © 2004 by Thranx, Inc.

"Trading Fours with the Moldy Figs" © 2004 by Jean Rabe.

"Signs Are Hazy, Ask Again Later" © 2004 by Fiona Patton.

"Puss in D.C." © 2004 by Pamela Sargent.

"A Faust Films Production" © 2004 by Janeen Webb.

"Brownie Points" © 2004 by ElizaBeth Gilligan.

"After the Flowering" © 2004 by Janet Berliner-Gluckman.

"Little Red in the 'Hood" © 2004 by Phyllis Irene Radford.

"Exterminary" © 2004 by Patricia Lee Macomber.

"The Nightingale" © 2004 by Dena Bain Taylor.

"Meet Mr. Hamlin" © 2004 by Bill Willingham.

"If You Only Knew My Name" © 2004 by David Niall Wilson.

"Keeping It Real" © 2004 by Jody Lynn Nye.

"The Rose Garden" © 2004 by Michelle West.

CONTENTS

INTRODUCTION

by John Helfers

EXACTLY what is it that allows the fairy tale, a story archetype that by all rights should have disappeared with powdered wigs and petticoats, to survive, and even thrive, throughout the last millennium?

If one examines the first fairy tales (and by fairy tales I mean the ones told and retold from generation to generation long before the good Grimm brothers collected and published the old stories, in the process editing out of them much of what would now be called "local color," you would find many of them to contain a decidedly nasty tone. Babies being thrown on fires to see if they were changelings. Children punished by being forced to wear red-hot iron boots, or face, alone, all kinds of fearsome monsters that would just as soon eat them as look at them. A dangerous world inhabited by the likes of the fearsome Slavic spirit Baba Yaga, who dwelled in a hut that perched on chicken legs, was ringed by a fence made of human bones, and lived to eat mortal flesh whenever she could.

And these stories of pain, torture, and death were often told to children. Why? There are several reasons. Aspects of the unknowable, such as disease, death, and nature, were often given human forms or attributes to lessen their mystery. Fairy tales often contained warnings, morals, or instruction in their macabre plots, and were a way of passing down the ac-

1

crued wisdom of one generation to the next. And, since many fairy tales deal with people encountering hazards and trials while traveling, perhaps some tales were spun to keep wandering children closer to home, rather than traipsing off to see what lay beyond that hill on the horizon.

Whatever the reason, fairy tales themselves are still enjoyed today. Whether it's classics collected by Grimm or Perrault, or new tales, such as Charles de Lint's Newford stories or Neil Gaiman's wonderful novels *Neverwhere* and *Stardust*, fairy tales, stories of fantasy, myth, and legend, are still creating wonder and magic for people around the world. And perhaps that is why they survive, because no matter when or where a fairy tale is first told, they embody universal images and truths that, over the centuries, have passed beyond time or place, and become one with the vast tapestry of human consciousness.

Naturally, as times change, the stories people tell also change. During the Dark and Middle Ages, families often lived by themselves, or clustered together in small villages for protection. In today's society, the world has become urbanized, with its own attendant joys and terrors. The modern city would dumbfound a fourteenth-century peasant, much as trying to live in the Middle Ages would most likely be the quick death of a twenty-first century person. But there is one thing these two very different societies have in common—the stories they tell.

Cities have given rise to their own types of stories— the urban legends that make the rounds from time to time, stories that utilize elements of the old ways, but with a metropolitan spin on them that just didn't exist until the modern city was created.

Of course, that does not mean that the basics have been forgotten. After all, variety is the spice of life, so they say. And what better way to celebrate the fairy tale's survival than by setting it in the very place that creates new ones as well—the city?

That was the challenge we posed to seventeen of

today's best fantasy writers, and they did not disappoint. Classic elements of traditional fairy tales have been plopped down in the middle of the hustling, bustling city. The resulting stories take twists and turns even I didn't expect. Russell Davis illustrates one haunting, chilling night in a girl's life that leads to revelations she never expected in an update of "The Little Match Girl." The Big Bad Wolf makes his well-deserved appearance in Jean Rabe's tale of jazz and jive in New Orleans. Dena Bain Taylor takes "The Emperor and the Nightingale" into the far future with her story about a human songbird who just yearns to be free. And Michelle West rounds out our collection with a poignant story of love, hate, death, and forgiveness—all the great tropes of fairy-tale fiction—in her own inimitable style in "The Rose Garden."

It's a world where Little Red Riding Hood doesn't walk. She rides the subway, and if any wolf comes sniffing around, she's got the street smarts to put him in his place long before she gets to Grandma's tenement building on the Lower East Side. The places and names may have changed, but the stories are, well, almost the same, just updated for the times. So come see what new creatures lurk in the big bad city, and enjoy this all-new collection of fairy tales—with an urban twist.

MALLIFICENT

by Nina Kiriki Hoffman

Nina Kiriki Hoffman has sold more than two hundred stories, five adult novels, three short story collections, and a number of juvenile and media tie-in books. Her works have been finalists for the Nebula, the World Fantasy, and the Endeavor awards. Her 1993 novel, *The Thread That Binds the Bones*, won a Horror Writers Association Bram Stoker Award. Her fantasy novels include *The Silent Strength of Stones*, *A Red Heart of Memories*, *Past the Size of Dreaming*, and *A Fistful of Sky*. Her other work includes the short story collection *Time Travelers, Ghosts, and Other Visitors* and a YA fantasy novel, *A Stir of Bones*.

GWEN stood by the bus stop in the parking lot and stared at the front entrance of the mall. It had a windowed facade three stories high, with arches above the entrances studded with red neon teeth. Beyond the frosted windows, the lights of the food court beckoned in the twilight: green, red, orange, yellow, blazing blurred names that promised tacos, pizza, cinnamon rolls, pretzels—all sorts of high-fat, high-sugar treats nobody cooked at home. Teenagers and young mothers pushing babies in strollers went in through clouded glass doors that slid aside for them, but no one came out.

Somewhere inside this monster was her little brother, and she had to go in and rescue him.

Hollis was supposed to come straight home after school every day, but school had let out four hours ago. Hollis had missed not only the supervised afternoon homework period Mother made them both endure when they got home from school, but supper.

Missing supper was serious business.

Gwen hated the mall. It had eaten her three best friends when they were all in sixth grade, and even though it threw them up later, they had come back partially digested by shopping acid and were never the same. Also, they kept going back, letting the mall work its magic on them until they had fallen deeper and deeper under its spell.

In the two years since she and her friends had moved on to middle school, Gwen had avoided the mall the way she muted commercials during her one-hour-a-night TV ration, and tore stinky perfume ads out of magazines. Mother had taught her and Hollis to shun the clutches of all things wrapped in advertising.

It wasn't always easy. Gwen's three ex-best friends were still her lunch friends—the friends didn't know that Gwen had drawn away from them because they had fallen under the consumer spell and talked about things like clothes and makeup all the time; they had just learned never to invite her to the mall anymore. It seemed like the mall was the only place they went outside of school.

The best friends often had strange food in their lunches, which they sometimes offered to Gwen. She resisted as well as she could. She said she was on a special diet, which was true. Mother supervised her and Hollis' food the way Mother supervised everything they did; she said they were special children, meant for great things, and they deserved special treatment.

Gwen resisted offers of Twinkies from Brenda and Pop Rocks from Tiffany and Ding Dongs from Frankie, but once she had eaten a quarter of a Cinnabon, and she had never been able to forget the sweet sticky taste that made her long for more, a Cinnabon bigger than her head, bigger than a bread box, a Cinnabon as big as she was—it haunted her dreams and showed her the wisdom behind Mother's prevention tactics.

A car backed toward her, taillights red, backup lights white. Gwen jumped out of the way, though the car didn't even slow. Maybe the driver hadn't seen her. She wore a blue denim smock with long sleeves, blue jeans, and black leather boots, and her blonde hair was hidden in a black knit cap; not very visible at night. But still. The parking lot was lighted, though the light was a weird orange.

The car zoomed off into the night. Gwen walked past the tail ends of large lumbery cars toward the mall.

Something clattered against the toe of her boot and skittered out into the road. She glanced down and saw something shiny and plastic, about the size of a grapefruit, but not as round.

Just then another car cruised down the aisle toward her, sniffing for a parking place. Gwen saw that the plastic thing was about to be crushed beneath the car's wheels. She stepped out into the street and spread her arms wide. With the headlights shining full on her, she should be visible, shouldn't she?

The car almost didn't stop. Maybe the people inside it wanted to get to the mall so badly they didn't care what they ran over on their way. But brakes screeched. The car stopped. A window rolled down, and someone cursed at her.

Gwen stooped and picked up the plastic thing, then jumped out of the way. "Sorry," she called. The car continued cursing at her as it nosed into the space left vacant by the other car that had backed out.

Backed out. Gwen clutched the plastic thing to her stomach and went on toward the mall. Someone had driven away. That meant people could get out of the mall once they went in. Well, she knew that anyway:

hadn't she seen her friends after they'd been to the mall?

But they weren't like her friends used to be. The mall had changed them.

What if Hollis wasn't even here?

Davy, the kid next door Hollis walked home from school with every day, said Hollis had gone to the mall. Mother had fed Gwen supper, armed her with a credit card, and given her a sack of peanut butter cookies to sustain her on her journey, then sent her here on the bus to find Hollis. "You're old enough to face the mall alone now," Mother had said as she smoothed a wrinkle from Gwen's sleeve. "If I've done my job right, you should be safe."

"Yak. Yak yak yak!"

Gwen looked down. The thing she had rescued moved in her hands. It was a red plastic animal, with green ears, arms, and legs. It had lighted green eyes and a shining red tongue. "Yak!" it said.

Gwen lifted it, stared into its glowing eyes. "Yak?" she repeated.

"Yak yak."

She crossed the final road and stood face-to-facade with the mall. She examined the plastic thing in the light that leaked through the clouded glass. "Electropet," jagged lightning-bolt yellow letters said over its rear flank. It wasn't shaped like any animal she had ever seen, in person or in photographs, though it wasn't too different from some of the weirder dog breeds. It had a clip-on hook attached to the top of its head.

"Yak," Gwen said again.

"Yak yak. Yak yee," said the pet, waving its arms, its eyeglows blinking on and off, its triangular ears flipping up and down.

"Well, hi to you, too. What were you doing out here in the road? Did somebody lose you?" Her heart pinched as she thought of Hollis, lost in the mall's maw.

"Yes," said the pet.

"What?"

"I was lost, but now am found."

"What?" Gwen couldn't believe a plastic toy could talk back to her. She'd seen various e-pets other people at school carried around, things that moved and made noise, but she'd never heard of one that could have a real conversation.

"Yak," it said.

"Ah." She must have been hallucinating. "Well, Yak, I don't know how to find the person who lost you. Right now, I have to find my little brother. I'll worry about you later." She clipped the Electropet to her purse strap and crossed the sidewalk to one of the mall's three tall doors. It whooshed aside, letting out the smell of foods her mother would never let her eat and a tinkle of tinned music.

She took a deep breath of outside air, clutched the strap of her purse, and stepped into the mall for the first time in her life.

Mind-numbing music. People talking. Smells: a Cinnabon smell that made her mouth water, the smell of meat cooking, spices she didn't know; and some sort of fake pine-and-flowers smell, like air freshener she'd sniffed at her friends' houses.

The music was a syrupy version of a rock song so awful she tried not to remember what the original version had been like. How could people spend so much time here?

She breathed out the last of her free air and breathed in the air of the mall.

Something silkened in her throat and soothed her. Something warmed beneath her skin, until she felt light, almost as though she were floating. She looked around and saw smiles on most faces, and thought, *Oh. Oh, good.*

Then she thought: *Hollis. Where is he?*

She plunged past the jigsaw pieces of the food court, each counter with its lighted menu above showing pictures of different kinds of food to order, the people behind the counters in their varied uniforms and pointed hats, rolling food into pieces of paper and selling it to people who took loaded colored trays to the scatter of tables and chairs in the center of the area ringed by restaurants.

Hollis had missed supper. A glance around convinced Gwen that he wasn't in the food court. She moved past, deeper into the mall.

Storefronts lined the corridor, wares beckoning behind glass. She made it safely past "As Seen on TV" and a camera shop, a kitchenware place and a luggage store. She slowed at the open front of a toy store.

Mechanical dogs and cats danced in an elevated playpen, pausing to lift their heads and bark or mew, then march again. When they came to the fence around their playground, they bumped, backed, turned, and marched more.

An army of Fairy Princess Barbies in pink boxes stood in a second bin, all of them in brown and gold velvet dresses and rhinestone tiaras, all wielding wands tipped with pink glitter stars.

A green pile of stuffed crocodiles, turtles, and frogs filled the third bin in the front of the store.

Gwen stopped. She had never seen such a huge number of toys all in one place before.

"Yak," said the Electropet dangling from her purse.

Hollis would like this store. One of his favorite toys was a plush frog Gwen had given him for Christmas five years before. Mother favored educational toys— a toy had to teach them three different things before Mother would even consider buying it, and she only shopped from catalogs—so neither of them had many stuffed animals. Gwen had found the frog at a drugstore.

Maybe these toys had pulled Hollis into this store.

She stepped off the gray stone tiles of the mall corridor and onto the streaked brown and white linoleum of the toy store.

"Yak! Go back!"

Gwen put her hand on the Electropet's plastic back. Did they sell Electropets at this store? Maybe she could find an instruction booklet, or at least read the description off the box. Maybe the salesgirl knew how many she had sold lately and could track down the Electropet's owner with credit card receipts so Gwen could return him.

"What a cute toy!" said the girl behind the counter. She came out and knelt beside Gwen to stare at the Electropet. The girl had her hair in two ponytails that stuck out of the sides of her head, and her cheeks and lips were bright and pink like a doll's. She wore a white top with black polka dots on it, black suspenders, a stiff pink skirt that stuck out like a ballerina's tutu, sagging white socks, and black MaryJane shoes. "Where did you get it?"

"I found it in the parking lot," Gwen said. "I was hoping you could tell me about it."

"I've never seen anything like it."

"Yak!"

"Oo! It moves and talks! Ooo! Cool!"

"But you don't have an instruction book?"

"Ooo! No. We have lots of other cool stuff, though. Let me show you our latest e-pet, the Lively Monkey."

"But my brother—"

The store girl dragged Gwen down an aisle crowded with hanging packages of toys and stopped in front of a special display. The cutest furry monkey Gwen had ever seen sat on a little throne. He had wide bright eyes and dark fur, and the fur of his face and palms was lighter. He had such an engaging smile. The store girl touched a button on top of his head, and he stood up and bowed.

"What's your name?" asked the store girl.

"Gwen," said Gwen.

"Oh. Hi, Gwen," the store girl said. "Watch these features. He responds to twenty-six different commands. Monkey, dance!"

The monkey whirled as he wagged his arms up and down. Music tinkled from his stomach.

"Monkey, kiss!"

The monkey kissed his hand and blew the kiss to

Gwen. She felt strange and warm, as though sunlight bathed her face. She leaned closer. The monkey's eyes were bright, their irises yellow-brown and their pupils dark behind a layer of glass. The pupils looked deep. As Gwen stared into the eyes, the pupils flared wider, and the monkey nodded his head. She nodded back to him.

"Monkey, tell Gwen hello," the store girl said.

"Hello, Gwen," said the monkey in a warm, friendly voice.

"Hello, Monkey," Gwen whispered.

The monkey held out his hand, and she shook it. He smiled. He seemed so alive. His eyes were warm and full of approval. She realized she had always, always wanted a friend like him.

"How much?" she heard her voice asking.

"Only a hundred and ninety-nine dollars," said the store girl. "He comes with all kinds of really cool accessories, too. He has three outfits, upgradable to lots more, and he has several intelligence modules, with lots of room for improvements when they come out with them. And the great thing about him is that no matter what you tell him, he'll never, never tell anybody else your deepest secrets. He'll listen to you as long as you like, and he'll support you in anything you do. You can't find a better friend for any price."

"Yak!" said Electropet.

"Sure," said the salesgirl, this time with a hint of disdain in her voice, "but you're not soft and furry. You're not something a girl wants to hug at night."

"Gwen's brother," said the Electropet.

Gwen shook her head and woke up. "My brother!" she said. The whole reason she had come to the mall. "Have you seen a blond boy about eleven, this high—" she held her hand up to her collarbone, "—wearing jeans and an orange and black windbreaker?"

"I think he was in here before," said the girl vaguely. "I don't know. What about Lively Monkey? Wouldn't you love to take him home?"

Gwen stared at the monkey. "Hello, Gwen," he said. He kissed his hand to her and smiled.

She had her mother's credit card in her purse. "Only use this if you need it," Mother had said when she handed it over.

Lively Monkey danced. Gwen knew she would be happy if she could take Lively Monkey home. He would make the long afternoons of homework bearable, the evenings with the rationed hour of TV and the other hours she was supposed to spend playing educational games or reading improving books less tedious.

"Brother," said Yak, waving his arms up and down.

She didn't need Lively Monkey. She had Electropet. "No, thanks," she said.

"We've got a few more in the back if you change your mind," said the store girl.

"Thanks." Gwen took a quick look through the store to make sure Hollis wasn't there. Other kids were in the aisles, grabbing toys and filling baskets. Some whined to reluctant parents and tugged on shirts and hands, begging for this doll or that truck.

She left.

The instant she stepped out of the store and back onto the tan tiles of the mall proper, she felt a weight lift from her heart. Lively Monkey? Who needed it?

She glanced back. The monkey blew her a last kiss, and she felt a small quiver of want, but she turned away.

Three corridors converged by the corner of the toy store, and escalators led up and down nearby. Gwen sighed. Hollis was somewhere in here, according his friend Davy. What if Gwen never found him? What if she went one way and he went the other, and they missed each other for the rest of their lives?

Technically the mall was supposed to close at nine PM. Gwen checked her watch. It was barely seven-thirty. Anyway, just because the mall was *supposed* to close at nine didn't mean it would. Maybe people wandered around in here twenty-four hours a day because they couldn't find their way out.

"Where could he be, Yak?" she asked.

"That way." Yak's arms waved up and down, but she couldn't tell which way he pointed.

She unhooked him from her purse and set him on her palm. "Please tell me better."

He whirled and pointed to the corridor that branched right.

"Thanks." She hooked Yak back on her purse strap.

People—mothers with babies in strollers, teenagers in a whole range of clothes from goth to jock to hippie renaissance—wandered all the corridors to and away from her. Men swaggered around, too, post dinner, guys in rugby shirts and football jerseys and jackets, some wearing ball caps facing forward, some backward. Many had glazed eyes. They stopped, trapped by things behind store windows.

Gwen pushed past them, heading in the direction Yak had pointed her.

"Yak!" said Yak, just as Gwen's sort-of best friends, Brenda, Frankie, and Tiffany, swept up to her with glad cries.

"Gwennie! What are you doing here? Oh, my *gawd!* I never thought we'd run into you here! We're going for a sundae! We're all going to share. You want a bite? Oh, my *gawd!* We have to get you into WildLife! There's this perfect red dress in the window—you never get anything new! Come on!"

"My little brother—" Gwen said, but Frankie and Tiffany grabbed her arms and swept her along with them, right into a store with a red dress in the window.

"You know you have no fashion sense," said Tiffany. "You have the greatest hair potential of any of us, but you never do anything with it—you should let us take you to Regis while we're here and get you the perfect cut—"

"But this dress, wasn't I just saying this dress would be perfect for Gwennie, guys?" Brenda said.

"She did. She goes, 'Wouldn't Gwennie look great in this dress?' " said Tiffany. "And we all thought so. You always wear those boring denim things, Gwennie. No color sense!"

"What size are you?" Frankie asked. "I bet you're a six. All that weird food you eat, at least you stay thin." Frankie wore a size fourteen and often worried about food before she put it into her mouth, but ended up eating it anyway. "Let's get a six and see if it fits."

Somebody grabbed a dress off a rack of red dresses and they all swept Gwen into a fitting room. Brenda went in with her, and before Gwen could mention Hollis, Brenda had jerked Gwen's purse, with Yak, from her shoulder and set it on the bench. The purse's denim covered Yak, who emitted a few stifled squawks no one paid attention to. Brenda grabbed Gwen's knit cap and tossed it on the purse, pulled Gwen's denim smock off over her head, revealing the simple cotton bra Gwen wore, and then grabbed the snap-and-zip front of Gwen's jeans, opened it, pulled the jeans down to reveal white cotton underpants. "Okay. Take off your boots and step out of those damned jeans, Gwennie," Brenda said.

Dazed, Gwen sat and tugged off her boots, then stepped out of her jeans.

"Come on, Gwennie. Hold up your arms. I've been dreaming of this for so long!"

"Dreaming of what?" asked Gwen. Why was Brenda dreaming about her? Was this one of these weird relationships her mother had warned her about? But Brenda hadn't stripped her just to look at her; Brenda was more interested in the dress than in Gwen. Gwen held up her arms, and Brenda slid the dress down over them, guided Gwen's arms into the short puff sleeves, settled the tight bodice over Gwen's torso, tugged the wide skirt out to flare from Gwen's hips, moved behind Gwen to zip the dress shut.

Then she got a comb out of her purse, unclipped Gwen's barrettes, and combed Gwen's hair.

"There!" Brenda said, hands on her hips as she studied Gwen. A smile lit her face. "Oh, yes. I am a genius." She flicked one of the sleeves, then gripped Gwen's shoulders and turned her to face the mirror.

"Oh!" Someone Gwen had never seen before stood there, hesitation in her eyes, but the rest of her gorgeous and surprising. The red dress made her look like a princess. Her hair, loose around her head and shoulders, was pale blonde and fell in waves. Her face—she'd never spent much time looking at her face. Above the red dress, her face floated, heart-shaped, the cheeks bright and lips pretty, her eyes blue and fringed with dark lashes below slender dark brows.

"We have *got* to get you some decent shoes," Brenda said.

Gwen's gaze dropped to her boots. She had never actually been on a horse, but she liked these calf-high black leather English riding boots. She had bought them at Goodwill with her allowance, and Mother had allowed her to keep them.

"No." Gwen sat and pulled her boots on, then stood and studied her image. She thought the boots looked good with the red dress. Like she was the kind of princess who might jump on a horse and ride off to save the kingdom if necessary.

Brenda sighed, shrugged, smiled. "Let's show the others." She opened the fitting room door and dragged Gwen out by the wrist. "Look, you guys! Am I not a genius? Salute me!"

The other girls gasped and made noises of total awe. Compliments flew.

Gwen posed. The others hadn't said anything nice about the way she looked since they were all in sixth grade. Frankie had admired a hat Gwen wore. Last compliment. That was before the mall ate her friends. Since then, she only heard sneers about her clothes and hair, if she heard anything at all. Mostly she heard them dissing her when they didn't know she was near. Gwen's eyes prickled. She had missed this.

A saleswoman approached. "Would you like to wear it out, young lady? I'll just take the tags off, shall I? You couldn't choose a better dress to suit your coloring and shape. It makes you look like a princess."

"Thank you," Gwen whispered. Sometimes at home

with Mother and Hollis, she had wondered if anybody would ever say anything nice to her about the way she looked again—someone besides Mother, who picked her clothes except for the thrift store finds. She looked like a princess. She wasn't the only one who thought so.

"Now you look like a movie star," said Frankie.

Gwen ran her hand through her hair and smiled. She could walk out of here in this dress and watch people's faces as she passed them. If her friends and this saleswoman were right, she would see smiles of admiration. Red. A color she had never worn before. An exciting and scary color, blood and valentines. She went back into the fitting room to get her purse.

Brenda had flung her old clothes on the floor. Gwen stooped to lift them. A note rustled in the pocket of her jeans. She took it out. "Hollis," it said.

What was she doing? She had to find Hollis!

She couldn't reach the red dress's zipper.

"Gwennie, what are you doing in there?" Tiffany asked. "You have to come strut with us! Wait'll all those high school boys at the food court get a load of you!"

Gwen gave up trying to reach the zipper. She grabbed her clothes and purse, but as she whirled to leave the dressing room, she knocked Yak on the wall. "Please!" he cried. "Forget your mission if you must, but don't hurt me! You must have saved my life for *some* reason!"

Gwen dropped her clothes and sank down onto the bench. She cradled Yak in her hands and stared into his glowing green eyes. "I'm sorry," she said. "I'm sorry. I didn't mean to hit you, Yak."

"My name is not Yak." His ears flapped.

"What is it?"

"Charles." His eyes glowed and faded, glowed and faded. His tongue lit up.

"I'm sorry, Charles," she said. She sat back. "Hey. You can talk!"

"What do you mean? I've been talking to you since you picked me up."

"Not in words I can understand."

"Oh. That. It's part of the enchantment I'm under. I can't make much sense if you're with anyone else."

"Enchantment? You're not an Electropet?"

"Well, I am at the moment."

"What are you when you aren't?"

"I can't tell you, Gwen. I *can* tell you that if you care about your little brother, you better find him soon. He's in danger."

"Oh, God! Hollis! I keep forgetting Hollis. I have to get out of here!" She slid her purse strap over her shoulder, making sure this time that Charles hung safe without hitting anything, hugged her old clothes to her chest, and left the fitting room. Hollis was in danger? What kind of danger? Horrible images from newscasts flooded her mind. "I have to go," she told her friends.

"Please pay for the dress first," said the saleswoman.

"Oh, yeah. Sorry!" Gwen dragged her mother's credit card out of her purse and followed the saleswoman to the cash register. The dress cost two hundred dollars, four times as much as the most expensive piece of clothing Mother had ever bought her. How much was that in real money? In an evening of baby-sitting, with a really good tip because the kids were obnoxious or the father felt guilty, she could make maybe twenty dollars. Ten long nights of baby-sitting with really bratty kids would pay for this dress. How often was she going to wear it?

Oh, well. She was going to wear it now.

She tucked the receipt into her wallet and put her wallet back in her purse. The saleswoman gave her a plastic bag with handles to put her old clothes in.

Her friends followed her out into the corridor, chattering about her new look, asking if she wasn't enjoying the mall? Didn't she just love it? Wasn't it to die for? Wait till she saw what they had in this other dress shop, the Gilded Lily—

"You guys, I came here to find my little brother. Have you seen Hollis anywhere? I have to find him!"

Three heads shook no.

"But you have to let us come with you and watch what people do when they see your new look," Brenda said. "I can't wait to see Jason's face. He was here before, with that skank Sandy. Wait'll he sees you now!"

"You guys—" Gwen began. How could she talk to Charles when her friends were around? All he said when anybody else could hear him was "yak." She had to find Hollis and save him, but from what?

She unhooked Charles from her purse, set him on her palm, and said, "Which way?" Even if he couldn't speak, he could point.

"Yak yak!" said Charles. He shifted his legs, turned on her palm, and waved ahead of them down the corridor.

"Oh!" Tiffany said. "What a great toy, Gwen! Can I see him?"

"No," Gwen said, but Tiffany snatched Charles from her hand.

"God, he's great! I want one! Where did you get him?"

Tiffany had a habit of acquiring other people's belongings out of sheer persistence. She kept at you and at you until you gave her what she wanted just to shut her up. Sometimes Gwen couldn't remember why she was friends with Tiffany. They were so used to going around as a group; maybe that was all there was to it.

"You can't have him, Tiff," Gwen said. "I'm putting my foot down. He's mine. Give him back."

Tiff stared at Gwen's face, laughed, and ran down the corridor, dodging between other people and disappearing way too quickly for someone in a lime-green top and purple pants.

"Charles!" Gwen yelled.

"Sheesh, you named your plastic dog Charles?" Frankie asked.

"I need him back!" Gwen said. "I'm not letting her

get away with this!" But what about Hollis? Did she have to rescue Charles *and* Hollis?

First things first. She had to get Charles back so he could help her find Hollis. "Here." She handed the bag with her old clothes in it to Brenda, and raced down the corridor in search of Tiffany.

The corridor opened out to another branching of the ways, three broad corridors and another nest of escalators, plus a waterfall and tall fake trees in pots of real dirt. Gwen paused to look everywhere. Lime and purple, where are you? She ran to the railings and looked below; no sign of Tiffany going down the escalator. She moved the other way and checked the up escalator—

Yes! There she was, riding up, almost to the next floor now, holding Charles in front of her face and shaking him. Gwen plunged up the escalator, pounding on the ribbed steps in her riding boots and pushing past people who didn't feel like being shoved aside.

Tiffany stopped running. She stepped off the escalator and wandered out of the stream of pedestrian traffic, holding Charles at face level and staring at him.

"Tiffany!" Gwen yelled. She grabbed Tiffany's shoulder.

"What?" Tiffany jumped about a mile. "Oh, jeez, Gwen! Did you hear what this stupid toy said to me?" She lifted Charles above her head and leaned over the railing.

What if she dropped Charles? The floor was three stories below.

"No!" Gwen jumped up and grabbed Charles from Tiffany's hand. As she landed, her ankle turned under her. She ended up sprawled on the floor, but she had Charles safe, tucked tight against her stomach, bounced into nothing but her upper thighs.

"Don't ever do that again, Tiffany," Gwen said in a low tight voice she almost didn't recognize as her own. "Don't you ever take anything from me, and don't you ever even hint you're going to hurt him if you do. Do you hear me?"

"Well, excuuuse me," said Tiffany. She turned and marched away.

"Are you all right?" Gwen asked Charles.

Even though they were sitting on the floor in the middle of people going in all directions, except for three boys over by the sports memorabilia store, who were pointing at her and talking—Gwen realized she had landed with her skirt hiked up so her white cotton underpants were visible, so she pulled her skirt down—even though they were in sight of all kinds of people, Charles answered her. "I'm okay." His eyes glowed steady green. "Thanks for saving me again, Gwen. I owe you another big one."

"I'm sorry she got hold of you, Charles."

"It's okay. It's over now."

"Except I have to find Hollis. Can you tell me where he is?"

"He's in the Fun Zone."

"And he's in danger? What kind of danger?"

Charles' ears flopped, and his arms wagged up and down. "Just get there," he said.

She clipped him on her purse, climbed to her feet, and hopped for the escalators. It wasn't until she was riding down that she realized she didn't know where the Fun Zone was, or even where she was, or how she was going to get out of the mall once she found Hollis.

She tapped the shoulder of a man standing on the escalator below her. "Do you know where the Fun Zone is?"

"Do I look like a cruise director?" he asked as he shrugged away from her.

Gwen glanced up and down the escalator, but everybody looked closed-faced. She lifted Charles. "Where is it?"

"You're asking a toy?" said a woman behind her.

"Do you know where it is?" Gwen asked the woman.

"Where what is?"

"The Fun Zone."

"Sure, it's way at the end of the Sears arm of the mall, second level. That way." She pointed.

"Thank you!" Gwen pushed past more people to escape the escalator, and ran in the direction the woman had been pointed.

A few stumbling steps convinced her how stupid that was. Pain shot through her sprained ankle with every step. "Ow, ow," she muttered. She tried to run, but found herself flat on her face. She pulled herself up using a bench, then hobbled along clutching the railing. Whatever kind of danger Hollis was in, she hoped it would wait until she got there before it killed him. She couldn't figure out how to go any faster.

"Hey, Gwen!"

She turned. Jason Seabrook, the guy she had loved hopelessly and one-sidedly since they had shared a desk in second grade, was standing there looking tall and handsome, with beautiful, totally built, dark-haired Sandy at his side.

Gwen clutched the railing and looked down at her new dress, which was rumpled and dusty and a little flattened from her encounters with the floor, though still mostly red. She brushed at it. It didn't help. "Hi, Jason." She stared at the floor.

"Great new look," he said. "Don't you think so, Sandy?"

"Anything would be better than what she usually wears," said Sandy, gazing off into the distance.

"It's kind of beat up," Gwen said. Two hundred dollars just because she couldn't undo a zipper on her own, and the dress was a wreck already. God. On the other hand, Jason said it was great. Which proved boys didn't know what they were talking about. "Do you know anyplace around here where I can rent a wheelchair?" she asked. "My little brother's at the Fun Zone, and I have to go find him, but I hurt my foot."

"Not our problem," said Sandy.

"Let me help you," Jason said. He came and put his arm around her, much to Sandy's apparent disgust.

With Jason's help, Gwen could hobble much faster. "I love the Fun Zone," Jason said. Sandy trailed behind them. "They have the coolest of all possible video games there. You play any video games, Gwen?"

"No," said Gwen. She had seen advertisements for them once in a while on Saturday morning TV, which she occasionally sneaked a look at when Mother had to be out of the house. Mother sold real estate and sometimes managed weekend open houses for people. Gwen felt guilty about watching unrationed TV with the sound on during the ads, but she couldn't stop herself sometimes. All this normal life she was supposed to stay away from. All her friends who knew what everyone else was talking about when Gwen lived in total ignorance, and looked stupid most of the time. Every once in a while, she had to do something Mother had told her not to do.

In ads, video games looked wild and strange; most of them seemed to involve killing as many people as you could. How could Hollis possibly be interested in that?

"There's this one game, Future Doomfest, where you get to kill not only Irks and Quirks and Quibbles, but hippies—they bleed rainbows when they die—and old people—they turn to dust—and you get extra points for taking time out to breed. If you have six babies at once, you win the game."

"Wow," Gwen said.

Jason walked faster. "I want to play it now!"

"Jaaaaaay-son! You promised we'd go to Sears and check out furniture," Sandy said.

Gwen had forgotten Sandy was there.

"Oh," Jason said, his step faltering. "Yeah."

Sandy slid her hand through Jason's other arm, the one that wasn't around Gwen's waist to help her walk.

Getting to the Fun Zone seemed to take forever. Gwen liked the feel of Jason's arm around her, the way his hand gripped her waist, and his smell, which was part chocolate—he had a stain on his shirt, so she suspected he and Sandy had had sundaes already—

part crushed grass, and part man. She liked the warmth of his side against her, and the strength of his support. But she was worried about Hollis and the mysterious danger Charles had warned her about. How long could a mall corridor be?

"There it is," Jason said at last. Big, brightly lit windows in primary colors, a giant triangular sign with FUN ZONE in clown letters on it.

"Thanks," said Gwen. "Thanks for your help. I couldn't have made it without you."

"Aw," said Jason, "my pleasure. Let me help you inside. Your little brother's here?"

"Yes. I need to get him out—"

"You're not going in there," Sandy said, pulling on Jason's arm. "We are *not* stopping here. I've waited long enough for you to drag Gimpy Gwen all this distance. Now we're doing what *I* want. Come on."

Before Jason could let go of Gwen, Sandy dragged the three of them on past the Fun Zone and into the wide entrance to the Sears store.

"Wait—" Gwen said, but Sandy was unstoppable, and Jason didn't seem to want to let go of Gwen.

Her dream had finally come true. Jason had his arm around her, and he even knew her name. But what about Hollis?

"This is the one I want, Jason," Sandy said. She pulled Jason into a display set up as a bedroom: a king-sized bed with a pink spread, pink pillow shams with white ruffled edges, a big puffy pink quilt folded across the end, and headboard and footboard of wooden spindles. There was an overstuffed reclining armchair in shades of brown and beige, a giant-screen television, two spindle-legged bedside tables with ruffle-shaded pink crockery lamps on them, and a dresser and vanity table that matched the bed and the tables, the vanity with a quilted-topped, ruffled-edged pink stool in front of it.

"This is it, Jase," Sandy said. "My dream bedroom. We could live in this room, don't you think? It's got everything we need, except I guess we'd need a kitchen." She detached Jason's arm from Gwen and shoved Jason down into the recliner, then tripped the lever so his feet were up and he was almost flat on his back. "Isn't this great?"

"Huh? Uh, yeah. It's comfortable."

Sandy put an unexpectedly gentle arm around Gwen's shoulders and led her over to the bed, where she sat her down. "Wait here a sec, Gwen." Sandy went over to the television and turned it on.

"For true comfort in your new home, you will want to buy the latest in air filtration equipment, and a whole line of ergonomically designed furniture. The recliner in this display module is designed to keep you happy for the rest of your life, and the bed will take care of all your sleep needs," the TV said. It showed animations of the furniture: the recliner reclined, then unreclined. The bed was adjustable, too. "Special features of our Eternal Dreaming bed include a soothing subliminal hypno sound-and-massage unit that will give you the best sleep of your life."

"Lie down," Sandy murmured to Gwen.

The bed hummed. Under the hum, Gwen heard a lazy summer day, with birdsong and the ripple of a little stream somewhere nearby. She lay back on the bed and felt the tingle of fingertips against her spine through the fluffy pink bedclothes. Soooo nice. She was tired after all that running, fighting, and falling. She angled her ankle so it rested against the vibrating surface of the bed, and the ache was soothed. This probably was good for her. Maybe it would help her heal. Maybe it would iron her new dress. A little nap would be so great—

"Yak!" said Charles at her hip.

Gwen jerked awake.

"Yak! Yak yak yak!"

She sat up. Where was she?

Jason lay in the recliner next to the bed, his gaze fixed on the giant TV, which was talking about built-in vacuum cleaners and vinyl siding now. Sandy was curled in his lap, her arm around his shoulders, her hand toying with his hair as she whispered in his ear. She glanced lazily over at Gwen and smiled.

"God! How long have I been here?"

"Does it matter?" Sandy said. "Don't you want to live here the rest of your life?"

Gwen contemplated the secret dream of her future. Here was Jason, and here was furniture. Well, Sandy was here too, but she didn't seem mean, for some weird reason. Here they were, closer to being in a home of their own than they ever had been before. It was almost perfect. Except Jason was watching the moving images on the TV screen. He wasn't paying attention to her *or* Sandy.

For a second she saw another image of Jason overlying him: older, almost bald, with a watermelon beerbelly paunch, his gaze fixed on the television, empty of spirit and thought.

"Yak!" Charles said.

Both visions shattered. Gwen wasn't sure what she wanted to do with her future, but she didn't want to end up trapped in a recliner staring at a TV with a husband who was doing the same thing. She had to get out of here!

Gwen stroked Charles' smooth, cold back. "You're right. I have to find Hollis!"

"So go." Watching Gwen, Sandy kissed Jason's cheek, but he never stirred. Sandy smiled a contented cat smile.

The bed still murmured against Gwen's legs and butt. It felt so good! She slid over and put her feet on the floor, then tried to stand, but crumpled. Her ankle felt worse than ever.

She sighed and pulled herself up using the bedspread, then hobbled carefully out of the bedroom set toward the exit. On the way she saw a display of wooden canes, and she bought one. It helped, though it took her a little while to figure out whether to hold the cane in the hand opposite her sprained foot or next to it.

The Fun Zone was right by the entrance to Sears. She caned her way inside and found a vast, dark hall lit by the screens of ranks and ranks of video games, most of them sending out trills and exciting music and the sounds of car crashes, punches, kicks, and grunts of effort. Boys stood in front of many of the games, light playing over their absorbed faces. Some of the machines were shaped like cars or helicopters you could climb inside. On the far wall were games that took more active participation, games where you shot pistols or threw beanbags and won tickets.

A quick scan of the room didn't reveal Hollis. Oh, God! What if Charles had lied? She unclipped him from her purse and brought him up to eye level. "Where is he?" she asked.

"In the spaceship."

She looked again. In the far corner of the room sat a silver saucer-shaped spaceship with a bubble dome on top. She hobbled toward it. As she approached, she saw that there was a head inside the bubble, and a viewscreen the face was turned toward. The hair on the head was Hollis-blond.

"There's nothing wrong with him," she muttered as she walked toward him with the aid of the cane.

"He's been in there for hours. If he stays another three minutes, the clock will strike nine, and the mall will own him forever," said Charles.

Gwen dropped her cane and ran, her ankle shrieking with pain every time she put her foot down. She collapsed across the spaceship and scrabbled for the dome, trying to figure out how to open it. "Charles!" she yelled. "Hollis! Hollis, come out! God, how do I get this open?"

Hollis turned blank blue eyes toward her, then returned to contemplating the screen in front of him. He held a joystick in his lap. With his right hand, he manipulated it while he watched the action on the screen.

"Charles, what am I going to do?"

"Go around the other side."

Gwen pushed up and edged around the spaceship,

still searching the dome for a catch she could release. She stumbled over a twisting black cord.

"Find the outlet and unplug the game," Charles said.

Gwen followed the cord to the wall and found a big silvery junction. She tugged at the big three-pronged plug, but it seemed welded to the wall. She couldn't budge it. "Charles!"

He remained silent for an agonizing ten seconds. Then he said, "Let me see it."

She unclipped him and held him so his eyes faced the plug. The green glow played over the silver of the socket and plug.

Charles sighed. "Let me lick it," he said at last.

She set his plastic mouth against the plug. Lick it! Short circuit it with saliva? Should she lick it herself? How could a toy have saliva? Charles' tongue glowed red, though, and then a rage of sparks shot up from the join of plug and socket, and the plug jerked and jumped. Gwen dropped Charles, leaped on the cord and jerked it, separating socket and plug.

Just then a tone sounded over the mall's public address system. "Ladies and gentlemen," said a friendly, amplified voice, "the mall is now closing. We appreciate your patronage. Please finish your shopping and enjoy the rest of your night. We'll be open again tomorrow at nine for all your shopping and entertainment needs."

Had they been in time? Gwen struggled to her feet and looked at the top of the spaceship.

The dome had popped open.

Hollis sat, gaze on the dead screen, hand working the joystick.

"Hollis!" Gwen stretched across the upper level of the saucer and reached for her little brother. "Hollis!"

His head turned slowly toward her. His blank eyes blinked. Then blinked again. "Gwen?"

"Hollis!" She was crying. She reached toward him. Slowly he lifted a hand from the joystick and stretched it toward her. She grabbed his hand. His fingers were curved and stiff from clutching the joystick for so long. She massaged them until his hand opened to grip hers.

"Gwen," he said, his voice rusty.

"Hey," said a deep, gruff-voiced someone. It was a grown-up in a bright purple tunic with the Fun Zone logo printed in pink on the front. "You kids, we're closing now. Come back tomorrow."

Hollis dropped the joystick and stood. He turned. Shallow footsteps down the back of the saucer let him walk off it. "Gwen. Let's go home."

"Just a minute." She slid off the saucer and knelt at the outlet, picked up Charles.

Nothing. No blinking eyes, no glowing mouth, no yak yaks. She hugged him to her stomach, felt tears slide hot from her eyes to cool on her cheeks.

"If you're not going to stay forever, get out of here!" said the Fun Zone man.

Gwen clipped Charles to her purse and hobbled around the spaceship to join Hollis. They walked side by side, Gwen limping, Hollis stiff and hesitating. He swung his arms and kicked with his feet as though waking from a long sleep.

The Fun Zone man rounded the spaceship to where the socket was and yelled, "Hey!" as Gwen and Hollis headed for the exit. Gwen stooped to pick up her cane on the way, and then they went faster.

Outside, they joined a flow of people heading somewhere. Gwen felt lost. She didn't know how to get back to the bus stop. But maybe everybody else knew. She didn't care where they went, so long as they made it outside.

Lights winked off behind store windows. Chain fences flowed across the storefronts that didn't have walls along the mall corridor. Store workers waved good night. Objects in the windows tugged at Gwen's attention: a silver purse, a pair of shiny turquoise boots, a white fur hat. She gripped her cane and Hollis' hand and walked past.

Finally, they reached the exit. It was the same one Gwen had come in earlier: frosted glass that looked dark now because of all the width of night beyond it, with a few fuzzy orange moons from the parking lot lights.

When Gwen and Hollis approached the sliding glass doors, the doors stayed shut. Gwen tugged Hollis, and they went to the next door, which opened to let someone else out and couldn't shut fast enough to keep Gwen and Hollis in.

Out on the sidewalk, Gwen took deep breaths of cold damp air. Non-mall air! No strange fake pine-floral scents! No cloying music! The bus stop was in sight. Gwen rushed as fast as she could on her bad ankle.

They caught the last bus of the night. Gwen had enough money for both of their fares. Once they found seats, Gwen pulled her purse into her lap and looked at Charles. He had scorch marks on his snout, but there was no light in his eyes or mouth. She hugged him. "Thanks, Charles," she whispered, though she knew he was dead. "Thanks for all your help." Tears leaked from her eyes again. She kissed Charles' nose, tasted the scorch of his final act to save Hollis.

The plastic toy shook and shivered and rattled. She held tight. "Charles?" she whispered.

"What's happening?" Hollis asked.

"Charles?"

The toy changed in her lap, shifted and grew heavier and larger and different. When it finished changing, a boy sat in Gwen's lap. He wasn't much bigger than she. He wore black high-tops, jeans with frayed cuffs, and a black T-shirt with a line of white piping around the neck and sleeves. He had spiky brown hair and a strong chin, and he wore round, wire-rimmed glasses over his green eyes. Gwen stared and stared at his mouth, thinking it was the most beautiful mouth she had ever seen, soft but strong. He leaned over and kissed her. He tasted sweet and fiery at once.

"Charles," she whispered, when he stopped kissing her. She put her arms around him to see what that felt like. It felt good.

He leaned his cheek against hers and sighed in contentment. "Gwen," he said.

"Gwen?" Hollis said beside her. "What? Who? What just happened?"

"It's a long story," said Gwen. "Some of which I don't know. Charles, where did you come from?"

"My aunt's a witch. She thought I was getting too into computers and video games, and that I had no people sense—"

"Video games," Hollis said. He shuddered. One hand curved tight into a joystick fist.

"I had to be a toy until I could help someone," Charles said. "Thanks for being my good deed, Gwen."

"Thanks for helping, Charles."

He sighed again and fell asleep in her arms.

THE LAST DAY OF
THE REST OF HER LIFE

by Russell Davis

Russell Davis currently lives in New Mexico with his wife Monica and their three children. His short fiction has appeared in numerous anthologies including *Sol's Children, Single White Vampire Seeks Same,* and *Villains Victorious.* His most recent novel is *Touchless.* In addition to writing, Russell is an editor for Five Star Publishing, running their romance and women's fiction line as well as supervising their speculative fiction series. He's currently hard at work on several novel projects.

> *"You wish you could change places*
> *with that child who warmed herself*
> *with small fires . . ."*
> —*The Little Match Girl,* Jane Candia Coleman

SHE left home on Christmas Eve. Eight days ago. Eight days of a Minnesota cold snap that could strip skin from bone, and suck the air—and the pride—right out of a person's lungs. It had been snowing when she left. As she'd stepped outside, big, wet flakes stuck to her curly blonde hair and Salvation Army clothes, touching her face like the cold, white kisses of the dead before disappearing in wet trails down her cheeks. She knew when she left what the forecast was:

snow, followed by extreme cold, followed by yet more
snow, with no real sign of a letup until after New
Year's.

Thinking back, she was surprised she'd heard the
forecast clearly enough to remember it. At the time,
she'd been lying on the dirty linoleum floor in the
kitchen and trying to crawl under the table while her
father screamed and cursed and kicked at her with
his boots.

She'd decided to leave that night, the weather be
damned. Better to face the elements and the uncertain
streets of the city in winter than her father's rage for
one more night. When she was born, he'd given her
the name Angel, and up until her mother had died—
four long, dirty years ago—that's what he'd called her.
His little Angel. A blessing from heaven itself. But
that had died along with her mother in a downtown
car crash.

Angel didn't have a winter coat—just a denim
jacket with a hooded sweatshirt underneath. It wasn't
heavy enough for a normal Minnesota winter, but any
money that might once have been spent on season-
appropriate clothes was now being spent to feed her
father's despair. He was addicted to matchsticks—thin
strips of pure crack that dissolved into the skin and
produced an extraordinary high. They looked like
matches and users were easily identified by the
similar-sized stripes that marred their skin. Everything
they'd once had—a nice home, clothing, vehicles,
security—had been sold off and invested in his addiction. Angel's breath had trailed white behind her as
she headed for downtown, hoping that she might find
space in a shelter somewhere, though on Christmas
Eve and in the frigid cold, she'd had her doubts.

It had turned out that her doubts were well placed,
and that, for a change, the weatherman had been
dead-on accurate, too.

Eight nights is a long *time*, Angel thought. She stood
across the street from her house and stared through

the falling snow and the clouds formed by her her breath. The ratty curtains over the living room window were open and she could see inside. It looked warm. Maybe not safe, but safe hardly mattered to her. It looked warm, and eight days out in the cold was enough to make her think that maybe her father's rages weren't so bad—it was never cold during a beating.

Why is it, she wondered, *that all things begin in blame?* Not responsibility, but blame. She had no one to blame for her current, half-frozen condition but herself. She could have stayed. Her life with her father, *their life,* such as it was, he blamed her for. Perhaps rightfully so. She'd been driving the car the day her mother died.

They were on their way home from a shopping expedition—just the two of them, a girls' day out—when the accident happened. The police said it wasn't her fault. But that didn't stop him from blaming her, or her from blaming herself.

But she was past that now. Blame didn't matter any more than safe did. Not when she was this cold, this hungry. Not when she was missing her mother, missing the times when her father had picked her up by the arms and swung her about the living room, laughing and saying, "Fly, Angel, fly!" She wanted to go back to those times, before the blame and before the despair, and laugh with the joy of an innocent. She'd been innocent then. Now, she was among the guilty.

In the living room, she could see her father. He was sleeping in his battered recliner, the floor lamp casting yellow slats of light and shadow across his tired face. He'd probably been watching the television, waiting for the ball to drop in Times Square like he did every year. "A new year, Angel," he'd say every year, "is like wiping down a chalkboard of our past. A clean slate." This was the first year she'd missed watching it with him. How she'd prayed over those words, hoping that *this* would be the year he'd get clean.

She wondered if he'd let her come in, maybe warm

up a little, or even have a cup of the tomato soup she knew was in the cupboard.

He would, Angel knew, if she gave him the handful of matchsticks in her pocket. At least for a night. But how long would it be before he hit her again, or worse, forced her to get more? A day maybe, or two, until he ran out of matchsticks and wanted her to get him some the only way she could—by offering a free blow or a lay to one of the dealers. That's how she'd gotten the twelve that were in her pocket right now, by letting that thug Julio have his way with her.

At the time, she'd thought to give them to her father so she could come home. Angel had learned the hard way that addicts will do anything to get their fix, and dealers will accept all forms of currency, but now . . . did she really *want* to go inside? The relief of warmth and food would be temporary at best—and she'd be feeding his addiction and their mutual slide into despair.

She wanted to go in, but hated herself for it. It was New Year's Eve, and Angel would give almost anything to be warm again, even if it only lasted a night. She crossed the street and walked through the heavy snow on the front lawn, taking the straightest path to the window. Her pants and sneakers were soaked through, and her feet nearly frozen, so wading through more snow now was not going to make a difference.

Looking through the window, Angel realized that her father *looked* old—his face dominated by fine cracks and lines that told of a life hard lived and painful. The years since her mother's death, his addiction, their mutual despair, even her futile attempts at resisting their inevitable slide, had taken a horrible toll.

She couldn't go in. If blame didn't matter—and it didn't—then responsibility did. Not all the bad choices were his.

On the side of the house there was a small, somewhat sheltered space next to the garage that she thought would provide at least some protection from the wind. Nestling down between two overflowing trash cans, her body shaking from the cold, Angel considered her remaining options. She could try to sneak inside—he was sleeping, after all—but she quickly dismissed the idea. The risk wasn't worth what he'd likely do if he caught her. At best, he'd take the precious matchsticks and kick her out. At worst . . . Angel shuddered. The worst was unthinkable.

Angel removed the slender matchsticks from her pocket and looked at them carefully in the dim light. They appeared harmless enough—off-white, with faint swirls of brown and black. She'd never used one, never done any drugs. By the time she was old enough to consider it, she was all too familiar with the damage they could do. If she couldn't go in the house, couldn't sneak in, what did that leave her with? Not a whole lot.

She was sitting outside slowly freezing to death. It had been two days since her last meal that had consisted of a piece of ratty toast and a Styrofoam cup half filled with cold chicken broth from the food wagon. Maybe the matchsticks were her only real option. Perhaps by trying one now she'd at least *feel* warmer. Perhaps she'd live until morning, and the first sunlight of a new year would bring warmth and hope, a clean slate, as her father had said, or at least a place to stay.

She selected one of the sticks and wet it delicately with the tip of her tongue, as she'd seen her father do, then placed it on the inside of her left arm, just above the wrist. Her hands, which had gone numb a long time ago, shook in the cold and the tips of her fingers were bluish gray. She pulled her feet underneath herself, trying to warm them or at least keep them from freezing entirely. When the first hint of the drug hit her system, Angel leaned back against the wall and slowly exhaled. She felt herself relaxing for the first time in . . . days? months? She didn't know for sure, and strangely, she didn't care. Angel felt herself begin to float, and her face tingled vaguely—the way it would, she was certain, if she went into the house and the warm air hit her icy skin.

And then she heard it. Her mother's voice. For a moment, Angel looked around wildly, then she realized that it must be an effect of the drug. She'd missed that voice, soft and confident, the binding that held her world together. . . .

"Do you want to stop for a bite to eat before we head home?"

"That sounds great," Angel said. *"Sit or spin?"*

Angel's mother thought for a moment. "Let's sit. Your father will still be puttering in the garage anyway."

"Good deal," Angel said. *"How about Hooligan's?"*

"Perfect," her mother said.

Angel turned left at the next set of lights, and neither of them saw but the briefest flashes of silver light before the car coming the other way blew through the light and slammed into them.

Our last good moment, Angel thought, coming out of the haze. She realized that she felt warmer than she had in days. She could almost hear her own heart beating, and suddenly understood why her father had fallen into using the matchsticks so easily. They made the pain distant and tolerable, while at the same time . . . she hadn't felt this good since . . . she couldn't remember a time she'd felt this good. And she drifted some more.

Angel woke with a start. How long had she been in the clouds? She looked up, but the sky was still dark. The neighborhood sounds of night were still present. Not long, she decided. A half hour perhaps, maybe a bit longer. There was still a long time before the sunrise.

She selected another matchstick, wet it, and laid it on her skin. It had been nice seeing her mother, feeling warm and loved. She didn't want another high, but it had been *sooo* nice. And she was getting cold again. The drug acted fast, and this time, she saw her father. Was it eight years ago? Longer?

"Ang, hand me that socket wrench, will you?"

Angel took the socket wrench off the worktable and handed it to her father who was buried beneath the hood of his car. "What's doing, Dad?"

"Changing the plugs, Angel," he said. The squirr-click sound of the wrench being turned. The rotation of his elbow. His sweat and grease-stained work shirt. She'd always felt comfortable here.

"Why?"

"It keeps the car running smooth, Ang," he said. His voice was deep and mellow. "When you take good care of things, they take good care of you." He paused for a moment, then added, "Or they should."

She knew he meant more than the car. She'd gotten into a fight with her mother and said some things she shouldn't have. "I know, Dad."

"Do you, Ang? I wonder sometimes." He returned to his task. Squirr-click. Squirr-click. "You know," he said, his voice a metallic echo from inside the engine compartment, "it's easy to get mad at someone who's telling you things you don't want to hear."

"I know, Dad. It's just . . ." Angel said, her voice trailing off.

"It's just that you don't want to hear her."

"It's not that," she said. "I know she means well. She doesn't like anything about me."

"That's not true, Ang. She likes you just fine. She doesn't like what you do sometimes. That's different."

"Why is she always judging me, then?" Angel said. "It's not fair!" She heard the whine in her voice and tried to ignore it.

"It's a parent's job to judge, Angel," he said. "If we don't, someone else—maybe someone who doesn't love you—will." Squirr-click. Squirr-click. "And whoever said life was fair?"

Angel shrugged. "No one, I guess. Life isn't fair."

Life isn't fair, Angel thought. Easy to say back then, wasn't it, Dad? Back when we had a nice house and Mom was still alive. Back when you loved me. Back when I wasn't sitting next to a pile of trash and freezing to death on New Year's Eve while you sleep in a drug-induced haze in a *warm* house. Oh, to hell with it. Angel could feel her body shaking. If one match-stick was good, could bring back warmth and memory, wouldn't two or even three be better?

She prepped them and laid them on her arm. The slight burning sensation she ignored. The racing of her heart, beating so fast that it felt like she was running a marathon, provided a pounding accompaniment to her descent back into the haze. Her breath, passing in quick gasps over her blue lips, rose in puff clouds of frost around her, looking like small ghosts of memory, before fading into the subzero air.

It was autumn. The leaves on the trees surrounding the lake were gold and red and yellow. A wind, not too strong, stirred the water. Angel sat on the dock, her feet swinging carelessly over the water. She was tossing bread crumbs to the scavenging ducks that swam around the dock looking for a free handout. She won-dered when they would fly south.

"What are you doing, Angel?" her mother asked, stepping lightly onto the dock.

"Just feeding the ducks, Mommy. Look how fat they are."

Her mother came up beside her, placed a hand on her shoulder. "They always are this time of year. Too many people feed them, I guess." She laughed lightly, and Angel smiled. She loved the sound of her mommy's laugh—like wind chimes in summer.

"Think they're too fat to fly?" Angel asked.

Her mommy pondered the ducks for a moment. "Maybe so, Angel. They don't look like they're in any hurry to leave anyway."

"They sure don't," Angel said. She threw the last of the bread crumbs into the water, creating a brief frenzy of quacks and flapping wings.

"It's about time to leave, Angel," her mother said.

"I know, Mommy. Do we have to?" Angel loved spending time at the lake. The cabin was small and some-times crowded, but she loved the two weeks a year they

spent here—one in late spring, one in late autumn. It was a treat.

"Yes, we do," her mother said. "Aren't you about ready to go home?"

"Home," Angel said. "I guess I have to, don't I?"

Her mother smiled. "Everyone has to go home eventually, Angel. Even the ducks."

"Okay," Angel said. "Let's go home."

Is that where she is? Angel wondered. She knew she wasn't thinking clearly. Her mind wandered in the haze. *Did my mom go home?*

She realized her whole body was shaking. The remaining matchsticks were scattered over the frozen snow around her. She must have dropped them. Carefully, she picked them up. Her fingers didn't want to move, much less try to tweeze the tiny drugs off the ground. She dropped several before she managed to gather them all.

If I freeze to death, Angel thought, *does that mean I get to go home, too?* At least her teeth had stopped chattering—and even though her body was shaking and her hands felt strangely disconnected from her arms, she didn't feel too cold. The matchsticks must be helping, she thought.

In the alley across the street, a dog barked rough and hoarse. On a street a block or two over, a car horn honked. Life in the big city went on. It was still night. Inside the house, Dick Clark had probably gone off the air and her father had probably stumbled to bed, his clean slate thoughts tucked in with him beneath the blankets. Did he wonder where she was or was he too far gone to care?

Angel giggled. It didn't matter. She had the matchsticks and in the morning, when the sun rose, she'd walk downtown and maybe find space in a shelter. She tried to count the matchsticks in her hand, but her eyes wouldn't focus long enough for her to complete the task. She was tired and the thought of sleep, warm with the dreams of a past she'd never know again, beckoned. She could go back there, she realized. The matchsticks were like a magic carpet that could take her anywhere.

Angel wanted to go home.

One by one, she licked the small strips and placed them on her arm. How many did her father take in one sitting? Did it matter? What if she ran out before sunrise and had no way to keep warm? No, Angel decided, shaking her head. These would be enough to carry her through until the sun returned.

She leaned back against the wall. The drug hit her system like a lightning bolt, racing through her bloodstream on a path to her already pounding heart. Her breath came in little gasps that sounded like a very fast socket wrench: *squirr-click, squirr-click, squirr-click.* It rattled in her lungs.

"Angel!" *her mother's voice yelled.* "Come inside! It's going to rain buckets!"

"Yes, Mommy!" *Angel dragged her feet on the ground, slowing the speed of the swing a little bit at a time. She looked at the horizon and saw the storm coming in. Minnesota was pretty flat and the dark clouds were rolling over each other in a rush of purple and blue and black. The other side of the sky was yellow-gold with sunset.*

"Angel! Now, please!" *her mother said again.* "We'll make cookies for your father."

"Yes, Mommy," *she repeated, stopping the swing. She turned away from the vision of the storm and headed for the back porch. In the field behind her, cicadas sang their song of oncoming night, unaware they were about to take a major bath.*

Her mother met her at the door. "What were you doing, lollygagging out there?"

"Just watching the sky, Mommy. There's a storm coming in."

"A big one," *her mother said.* "Guess we'll have to keep the radio on, but it doesn't feel humid enough for a tornado." *She tousled Angel's hair, the little curls bouncing and springing like fresh flowers.* "Want to make some cookies with me for your father?"

Angel grinned. "Do I get to lick the bowl?"

"Always, Angel," her mother said. "Always."

Together they went inside, and when the rains came, they kept on baking and to Angel, everything was just about perfect.

Perfect, Angel thought, coming out of the haze for the last time. *I'm perfect. At least now I'm warm.* She drifted off to sleep, and when her heart stopped, she never felt a thing.

The policeman stopped his car on the street, stepped out of his door, and pulled his Maglight from his belt. He hoped what he thought he'd seen was a mirage of garbage. In the growing light of sunrise, it was hard to tell. He walked up the short drive, cursing under his breath at the snow seeping into his shoes.

He turned on the flashlight and saw her. A girl—barely more than a teenager, he was certain—was sleeping between the trash cans. He stepped closer. Damn homeless kids would curl up anywhere when it was this cold. The lighting back here was poor. He'd wake her up and move her along. Hell, it was New Year's Day—maybe he'd even give her a ride to the shelter.

The sun chose that moment to break over the roof and illuminate her face.

Oh, God, the policeman thought. She's sure as hell not sleeping. Only then did he realize that he should have been able to see her breath in the cold morning air. He knelt beside the dead girl, thanking God that *his* daughter was home safe in bed.

The girl's face, blue and frozen—and should it have been that small?—was marked with faded bruises, but her expression was almost angelic. A faint smile showed on her lips.

The door on the side of the house opened. "Saw your car, officer," a man's voice said from behind him. "What's the problem?"

The policeman stood, shaking his head. "Looks like a homeless girl chose your walkway to take a sleep in. She's dead."

The man was wearing a ratty-looking bathrobe, but stepped out anyway. "What?" He looked at the girl huddled there among the trash, saw the marks on her arm. "Oh, Jesus," he said.

The policeman nodded. "A hell of a way to start the New Year, huh?"

When the man didn't reply, he said, "Sir? Do you know her?"

The man shook his head. "No, officer," the man said. "I . . ." He paused, then managed to say, "She sure looks like a little angel, though, doesn't she?"

"She surely does," the policeman said. "I'll call it in. Sorry to disturb you."

For a long minute, the man said nothing, just stood there staring at the frozen girl, an unreadable look in his eyes.

"She's got a clean slate now, doesn't she?" he finally whispered. Then turning, he trudged back inside, looking like a puppet coming off its strings.

"It's a new year," the policeman said. "We all get a fresh start, don't we?"

The man didn't answer, just kept walking. The policeman shook his head. Something was odd here, but he'd wait for backup before he pursued it.

A moment later, when the shot rang out from inside the house, he realized what he'd missed—the uncanny resemblance between the man in the tattered bathrobe and the girl. But it was too late now. Whatever troubles they'd had were over and they'd gone to their final home.

Maybe it was as close to a fresh start as anyone ever really got.

Author's Note:

This story is based, somewhat loosely, on Hans Christian Andersen's classic story The Little Match-Seller. *It is one of the earliest stories I can remember reading, and one of my personal favorites.*

JACK AND THE B.S.

by Tanya Huff

Tanya Huff still lives and writes in rural Ontario with six cats (as I type) and a dog (who could care less). Her latest book is *Smoke and Shadow,* the first novel in a three-book series spinning Tony off from the Blood Books. (This is *not* a sequel to the Blood books.) (Really!) In her spare time, she's learning to play the guitar. Fortunately, the nearest neighbors are half a kilometer away.

ONCE upon a time, a young man named Jack lived with his band in a dilapidated third-floor walk-up on what would have been the wrong side of the tracks had the city actually contained tracks. As it didn't, the boarded-up storefronts, uncollected trash, and debris-filled vacant lots were a fairly good indication of the local socio-economic condition.

Not good.

Jack and his band were determined to move up and out, and so they practiced day and night. Unfortunately, they were a thrash metal group who didn't so much play as assault their instruments in an era of breathy boy bands and vapid blondes. No one wanted to hear their music: not the producers who signed bands for the major record companies, not the DJs at the local radio station, not the guy who booked bands at the club on the corner, not even their neighbors. . . .

"Would you shut up! It's three in the morning and you suck!"

"Come back to bed, babe. No way they hear you over the damned reverb anyhow."

"They're always fucking practicing; you think they'd get it right occasionally!"

"Word."

Jack slammed his way through the G7(sus4), went back to the C, slid through the Em6th, and came down hard on the F# added 9, really leaning on the strings for all he was worth. They were in the space; his ax was screaming, Gustav's bass was rattling the windows two freaking rooms away, and Maitland was leaving bruises on his skins. They should've been making music, but something was wrong.

He stopped playing. After a couple of minutes, he stepped back and turned off Gustav's amp. The bass player kept going for a couple of bars then he frowned, stared down at his fret board, and finally turned toward Jack. Who pointed at Maitland.

Gustav pulled a ballpoint pen out of his dreads and threw it at the drummer's head.

"Fucking OW!" In the sudden silence, Maitland rubbed at the blue dot in the center of his forehead with the end of a stick. "That hurt."

Jack ignored him. "I couldn't hear Angela."

All three turned to face the skinny blonde in the center of the room. She shrugged bare shoulders, her butterfly tattoo rising and falling. "So?"

"If I can't hear you and I'm standing right next to you, how the hell can they hear you?" He nodded toward the "audience"; on this particular night made up of the usual imaginary crowd and a cockroach investigating the top of the toaster.

"Pretending I care; you got two problems. First, your lyrics blow and second, you play too damned loud."

"Sing louder."

"This is as loud as I sing. Look at this." Angela held out a pale arm Jack could have circled with his thumb and baby finger. "I'm still vibrating. You guys have to play quieter—and when I say play, I mean that in the most general sense."

Maitland stopped scratching down the crack of his ass long enough to frown. "Was that a burn?"

"Yes, you idiot! I am *so* wasting my time here." Heavily kohled eyes narrowed. "Gustav, let's go." As she reached the door, she realized she was alone. "Gustav! I mean it! Me or the band."

"Cheer up man, she wasn't that good."

"Maybe not at the whole singing thing," Gustav allowed. "But she sure looked fine in all that leather underwear."

"Word." Maitland stroked a brush over a cymbal. "What do you call that red thing she had?"

"A corset, man."

"Guys!" Jack cut the reminiscing off cold. "We don't need a skinny fetishist, we need someone with pipes. It doesn't even have to be a chick."

"Dude!"

"For the band, Maitland, you neb. We got the sound, we just need a voice."

"And some food."

"What?"

Gustav stepped back so that the other two could see into the fridge. "The cupboard is bare, Jack."

"That's not a cupboard, man, that's . . ."

"Shut up, Maitland." Jack stepped carefully through the web of wires spread out over the floor. "What about the packets of plum sauce?"

"Ate them."

"And those three olives?"

"Them, too. Man, we are down to tap water and toaster leavings."

Jack glanced over at the cockroach and mentally stroked the toaster leavings off the list. "Tomorrow, we'll buy . . ." His voice trailed off as Gustav slowly shook his head. "We're broke?"

"Totally. And I am not scooping coins out of that fountain again; I almost got pneumonia last time."

"Well, then we can . . ."

"No."

"You didn't even hear . . ."

"I don't want to hear another dumb ass idea, Jack. Face it, you got to sell the cow."

Jack turned to face the closet and his leather trench coat hanging black and supple over the top of open door. "No."

"You have to."

"I can't." The coat made him feel tough and sexy and powerful and talented and tall.

Gustav draped a supporting arm across his shoulders. "It's all we've got left, man. You don't sell the cow, we don't eat."

And so the next day, Jack set out with the coat over his arm, heading for the pawnshop on Seventh. There were pawnshops closer—some days it seemed like they were the only growth industry around—but the pawnshop on Seventh was next to the closest store selling food. Besides, Jack wanted to spend as long as he could with the coat. The weather was cool and he could have put it on, but he was afraid that if he caught sight of his reflection striding along, if he smelled that distinctive aroma of tanned cow hides, if he felt the leather flapping around his calves one more time, he'd never be able to part with it.

About to walk past the park—because as depressed as he was about pawning the coat, he wasn't suicidal and that's what it would take for a sane man to actually walk into that junkie/mugger-haven-with-trees— he heard the wail of a guitar rising up over the ever present roar of traffic.

Drawn by the sound, he stepped off the sidewalk.

Jack found the ax-man under the skeletal remains of a swing set; a barrel-chested dude with long gray hair and a short gray beard, he was just standing there, pulling the most amazing music out of an old Martin. It was an acoustic, a folkie guitar, but it sounded like Eddie Van Halen and Joe Satriani and Chris Impellitteri all rolled up in one. Incredible sounds. Impossible sounds.

With the coat over his arm and his mouth open, Jack stood and listened. The music pounded through him, vibrating blood and bone.

After a final, amazing chord progression—chords Jack couldn't even identify, the sausage-sized fingers moved so fast—the old man stopped playing, looked up and frowned. "What?"

"That was like wow. And loud. Like, really really loud! I never heard a guitar played like that. I never knew anyone *could* play like that!"

The old man snorted. "You don't get out much, do you? What's your name, boy?"

"Jack. I play. Not like that; but you know. I have a band."

"Of course you do."

"I got a demo disk!" He pulled the tiny MP3 disk out of his back pocket. "We already pawned the player, but I got a disk. I carry it everywhere because, like, you never know."

"You never know what?"

"What?"

The old man sighed. "Never mind."

"Man, if I could play like you . . ."

"You'd sound like a crap imitation." He let the guitar slide around on its strap until it hung upside down along his back, tangling with the long gray ponytail. "Play like yourself," he growled, turning away.

"Don't go! I need to know how you do that! Please . . ."

The scuffed motorcycle boot, raised to step away, settled gently back onto the packed sand. "Ah, the magic word. You really want to know how I play like I play?"

"Yes!"

"It's these." And the old man reached into the pocket of his faded jeans and pulled out three neon green picks.

Jack looked down at the plastic triangles and then back up at dark eyes. "Picks?"

"Magic picks."

"Are you shitting me?"

"I wouldn't think of it. These picks will let you pull the music in your soul out of your ax."

"I don't do soul. Or country or R&B. I do metal, man."

"And does anybody actually listen to you? I thought not," he continued, raising a hand to cut off Jack's sputtering rationalization. "Use these picks and I guarantee people will listen. You give me that coat you're carrying, and you can have all three of them."

"The coat?"

"Yes."   .

"That I'm carrying?"

"Yes."

"For three magic picks?"

"Yes."

"Totally a deal, Dude!"

So Jack ran back to the dilapidated third-floor walk-up, past the boarded up storefronts, and the uncollected trash with the magic picks clutched tightly in one hand. He couldn't wait to hear what the rest of the band would say.

"Are you fucking nuts, man?" Disbelief—and possibly hunger—made Gustav's voice more than a little shrill. "We sent you out to buy food and you came back with fucking guitar picks?"

"Magic guitar picks," Jack explained, holding out his hand, the three picks piled on his palm.

"Can we eat them?"

"No, but . . ."

"Then I don't care if they make you sound like Mike Fucking Nesbit. You traded the only thing we had that was worth anything for them and they're crap!" Gustav slapped Jack's hand aside.

Frustration added force to the slap.

The picks flew up, turned slowly through a beam of late afternoon sunlight, and disappeared out the open window.

Jack searched until long after dark but the picks had disappeared into the debris that filled the vacant lot.

They didn't practice that night. They went to bed early listening to the rumblings of their empty stomachs and Maitland complaining about having to return to work for the finance department of the municipal government.

Jack usually woke up when the beam of sunlight spilling in through the curtainless window had moved far enough across the room to fry his face. On cloudy days, he slept in. On this particular day, after having rolled over and gone back to sleep twice, he finally sat up and peered across the room at the window. Either his internal clock was way, way off or the pollution levels over the city had gotten seriously out of hand.

He scrambled into the clothes piled on the floor beside his mattress, and, holding his shoes, padded barefoot across the room. If he turned on the lights, he'd wake the guys so, considering how pissed they already were about the whole food thing, he decided he'd just do a little checking first.

The window opened almost quietly.

The total lack of light beginning to seriously freak him out, he leaned through the opening and almost immediately cracked his head against another building—a building that definitely hadn't been there when he went to sleep.

A building about fifty stories tall and exactly the shape of the vacant lot, Jack discovered standing out on the sidewalk a few moments later. It looked like it had been made from sheets of gold-colored glass and, gleaming in the sunlight, it seemed to promise that, inside, dreams could come true. Written in shiny black on the big front doors were the words B. Stalk Productions.

He could see a security guard sitting at a desk in front of a pair of doors. One was the elevator, the other bore a sign saying EMERGENCY EXIT. On the wall between them were about a hundred gold records. At least Jack assumed they were records; he'd never actually seen one up close and personal. After scraping a bit of crusty plum sauce off his T-shirt with the edge of his thumbnail, he pushed open the door and shuffled across the polished marble floor.

"Dude?"

The guard looked up from his monitors, dark eyes locking on Jack's face. "Yes?"

Jack opened his mouth, closed it, and opened it again. "Do I, like, know you?"

Inside his short, gray beard, the guard's lip curled. "No."

"Are you sure because . . ."

"I'm sure. What do you want?"

"What do I want?"

"What. Do. You. Want?" the guard asked again, very slowly.

And Jack remembered why he'd come into the building. "What does B. Stalk Productions, like, produce?"

"Music, boy. Mr. Stalk is a giant in the music business. Sitting up there in his offices at the top of this tower, he decides what gets heard."

"I've never heard of him."

"Has he ever heard of you?"

"Not yet, but . . ."

"Then I'll have to ask you to leave the property."

"Yeah, but . . ."

"Now, boy, or I'll . . ."

Jack never found out just what the guard was about to do because at that very moment a stretch limo pulled up outside the building and four faceless minions in suits herded a girl out of the back and into the lobby. She wasn't the kind of girl he'd ever expected to see coming out of a car like that. She amply filled both jeans and tank, an electric pink mouth seemed curled up into a permanent sneer, and a tattoo on one rounded arm read, "BITE ME!"

She looked angry.

Jack loved that about her. He loved everything about her. He really loved the way she'd totally drawn the attention of the guard. Backing up slowly, he headed for the emergency exit and slipped through as his new love used some very, very bad language and was even more distracting.

And what a voice! It sounded just like Jack had imagined it would. It sounded the way she looked, strong and edgy and different.

He hated to leave her, but this was his big chance.

He'd climb all the way up to B. Stalk if he had to and force him to listen to the demo.

He reached back into his pocket, touched the disk for luck, and started climbing.

By the sixth floor, his knees hurt.

By the tenth floor, he started singing to keep up his spirits.

By the twelfth floor, he stopped singing because all those bottles of beer falling off the wall were making him thirsty.

On the twenty-third floor, a skeleton wearing a white jumpsuit and rather a lot of tacky jewelry leaned against the door. Jack had seen freakier art on disks so no real big. "Dude, I guess you never *did* leave the building," he said thoughtfully as he passed.

He felt as if he'd been climbing for days when he finally staggered up the last flight of stairs and stood staring at the gold number 50 stenciled onto it. For a moment, he didn't realize what it meant, then, his heart beating like a double drum kit, he very carefully pulled open the door.

He was standing at one end of a long hall. At the nearer end, a huge window let in the light. At the far end was a double door, the right half slightly open. To his immediate left was the elevator. Along the other side of the hall were half a dozen closed doors. He could hear voices and, logically, they could only be coming from one place.

His shoes sinking deep into the plush beige carpet, he made his way toward the open door.

The cream-colored walls were covered in laminated posters of half a dozen interchangeable boy bands— where the word boy had been stretched to its limit and beyond—and three different blondes. The "oh look at me I'm a bad girl but not really" poses were all slightly different, so Jack *assumed* they were different blondes. He'd never considered himself overly imaginative, but he could've sworn the eyes on the posters followed him as he passed.

"Look, I don't know about this, Mr. Stalk."

It was the voice of the girl. She sounded like she was still angry although a hint of uncertainty had begun to soften her edged tone.

"But I do know, my dear. I've handled a hundred young women, worked them like clay, made them into what they are."

"I guess, but . . ."

"You want to be a star, don't you?"

"Yeah, but . . ."

"Trust me."

Trust him? Jack shuddered as he peered around the edge of the door. He'd trust that deep oily voice about as far as he'd trust Maitland to maintain a certain minimum standard of personal hygiene. Which was to say: not very.

The room behind the door was incredible. The desk, the leather sofa, the bookcases, the poster of the current flavor of the month covering the wall behind the desk; they all looked like they'd been super-sized. The minions looked dwarfed by the furnishings. In the center of the room, perched in a chair so overwhelming the thick, ridged rubber soles of her boots barely touched the floor, was the love of Jack's life. The moment he saw her, all thoughts of having B. Stalk listen to his demo fled.

She was . . . blonde!

And somehow, she looked . . . thinner!

"Packaging, my dear, is everything."

Jack's gaze jerked over to the music mogul. He was kind of a little guy actually; short and skinny and going bald. The cigar clenched between his teeth was probably bigger than his . . .

"We'll work the tattoo into the design of something a little more marketable. Something like a butterfly or a unicorn. Won't be any trouble at all, will it, boys?"

"No, sir, Mr. Stalk!"

Given the harmonies in their unison answer, Jack had a horrible suspicion he knew what happened to boy bands when maturity won out over marketing.

She chewed on her lower lip, no longer electric pink but softer, glossier, and said, "I . . . I . . . I need to take a piss."

"Tinkle."

"What?"

"From now on, you tinkle."

Jack shuddered.

Her fingers gripped the arms of the chair so tightly the leather squeaked a protest. "Whatever. I gotta go."

"First door on the left."

Jack flattened against the wall as she came out into the hall remaining hidden safely behind the open door and exposed again as it closed. Fortunately, she didn't look back.

"The girl's got potential."

"Yes, sir, Mr. Stalk."

"As soon as we change the way she sings, and pierce that navel, we'll have ourselves another . . ."

As the bathroom door closed behind him, it cut off the name of the blonde they were planning to copy. Jack was just as happy not knowing.

He'd never been in a girl's bathroom before. It was cleaner and it smelled better and instead of a condom dispenser there was a . . .

Eww.

"Hey! What the hell are you doing in here?" Oh,

yeah. That was the rage he loved! He ducked her
swing, backed up against the sink, and raised both
hands in surrender. "I'm here to rescue you!"

"Are you tripping?"

"No! This Stalk guy, he's trying to . . ."

"To make me a star, fuckwad."

"OW!" Hopping sideways, rubbing his shin, Jack
tried to watch her fists and her feet simultaneously.
This wasn't easy given that he was being to feel a little
faint with hunger. "He's not trying to make you a star.
He's trying to make you a *pop* star."

"That's a lie!"

"Don't take my word for it, look in the mirror."

Straightening cautiously, he watched her face as understanding dawned.

She reached out one trembling finger and touched
her reflection. "Oh, my God. I'm almost . . . cute."

Grabbing the hem of her tank, she hauled it up,
bent forward and scrubbed the soft glossy coloring off
her mouth. Just as Jack began to wonder what she
was going to do next, she reached into the depths of
her cleavage and pulled out a silver tube. In half a
heartbeat, her lips were electric pink again.

"Man, that's better."

And it was, although Jack was too busy watching
her put the lipstick away to say anything.

"Well don't just stand there with your thumb up
your ass, let's haul it!"

"Right." A raised hand held her back as he peered
out into the hall. The coast was clear and the elevator
was still at the top floor. "Come on!"

Holding his breath, Jack led the way. The door to
B. Stalk's office was still open and something about
the music mogul suggested his life would not be pleasant if they were caught. Fortunately, the carpet muffled two sets of footsteps as easily as one. Jack had
begun to breathe normally again when, suddenly, the
posters lining the walls cried out, "Master! Master!"

Jack froze. The girl froze. They looked at each
other. They looked at the walls.

"Okay," Jack muttered. "Didn't expect that."

"Master! Master! A dirty metal head is helping the new girl escape!"

From the far end of the hall came an enraged roar. "Fe, Fi, Foe, Justin! After them!"

"Yes, sir, Mr. Stalk!"

All at once, standing still seemed like a bad idea. "Run!"

The posters were shrieking, the minions were yelling but they were at the elevator and Jack jabbed the button. The door whooshed open. He dove in, hit the close door button, grabbed his love by the arm, and dragged her inside.

"That's for bleaching my hair, dipshit!" she screamed back at the minion sinking slowly to his knees, both hands clutching his crotch.

Then the door closed and they were moving. It took a few floors for that final word to stop echoing within the stainless steel enclosure.

Mouth open, Jack stared in admiration. "Man," he said when there was a chance of being heard, "have you got a set of pipes."

She spread her hands, the gesture somehow taking in not only the tower but her reason for being in it. "Well, duh."

"I'm uh, Jack. Jack Grimm."

Her eyes narrowed. "Stage name?"

"Yeah. But not the Jack part." He waited.

After a long moment, she sighed. "Lyra Gold. Not a stage name. Dumb ass parents."

He nodded sympathetically. "Rough."

"No shit."

They watched the numbers fall on the digital display.

"So now what?" Lyra asked as they passed the halfway mark.

"Well, there's only the one elevator, so the minions'll have to take the stairs."

"Yeah, but there's a security guard on the first floor; they'll just call down and he'll be waiting for us."

Jack had a strong suspicion that one elderly security guard would be no match for Lyra's boots, but he kept it to himself and pressed the button for the third floor. "I flop next door," he explained. "The building's three stories high, but the stories, they're not so high. Not so high as here, I mean. Because they're high enough for themselves. Anyway, that oughta put the window on the third floor hall right over the roof."

"What?"

"We're going to jump out the window to the roof of the building next door."

"Right."

The elevator chimed softly and the door opened to an empty hall; plainer than the hall on the fiftieth floor and poster free but otherwise identical.

Jack listened at the stairwell door. He could hear the minions descending, moving fast. "Oh, sure," he muttered, joining Lyra at the window. "You guys get to come *down* the stairs."

He could see his roof, his peeling tar paper, his fine patina of pigeon shit, only an easy four-foot jump away.

"It doesn't open!"

"No problem." Taking a deep breath, Jack moved back a dozen paces and ran at the window as hard as he could. The noise he made on impact wasn't quite splat, but it was close.

"Move your skinny ass out of the way," Lyra snapped.

It seemed like a plan, so he did and then watched amazed as Lyra took a deep breath—he was definitely in love now—and sang. One note. One very high, sustained note.

The window shattered.

"You okay?" she asked as the glass fell to the roof below.

"Thrash metal band," he told her. "I got calluses on my eardrums an inch thick."

"Sweet." She gestured out the jagged opening. "Age before beauty."

"Pearls before swine."

"Together?"

Her hand was warm and dry.

"Together."

They stood shoulder to shoulder on the roof and stared up at the tower. As impossible as it seemed they could clearly hear the footsteps of the minions still pounding after them, prodded on by screams from the fiftieth floor.

"YOU BELONG TO ME, LYRA GOLD! WE HAVE A CONTRACT!"

"You signed a contract?"

"I was desperate!"

Jack raised both hands. "Say no more. Been there."

"I'LL GET YOU! I'LL GET YOU AND YOUR LITTLE BAND, TOO!"

"I think he's confused," Lyra muttered as Jack ran for the door leading down into his building. "Hey, where you going?"

"I've got an idea."

The door was never locked, but then again the wood was so rotten there wouldn't have been much point. Jack ripped it open and stuck his head into the moldering stairwell. "Gustav!"

Down below, the door to the apartment opened and Gustav peered out into the hall. "Dude?"

"Up here!"

"Dude!"

"My ax, man. Throw me my ax!" After a moment he added, "And an amp and an extension cord!"

The tower threw the first note back at him. Jack smiled. He was just warming up. By the third note, Gustav was plugged in and playing beside him. By the . . . well, after a while, Maitland had his set up and was pounding out a rhythm on his skins. Chording right up at the base of his fret board, Jack turned to Lyra and nodded.

"Dude!" Gustav bellowed into his ear. "She doesn't know the words!"

"Yeah, she does!"

"But . . ."

"Trust me!"

And Lyra sang. They weren't the words as written but that didn't matter.

Two angry verses later, nothing had happened.

Jack threw everything he had at the lead-in to the chorus. Knew the guys were doing the same. He watched Lyra draw in a deep breath—worth watching regardless.

Last verse.

The tower began to shimmer.

The gold coloring in the glass began to pick up an oil slick on a puddle kind of iridescence. It began at the edge of the broken window and worked its way out. It shimmered and moved faster, growing brighter, chasing itself from floor to floor until it finally caught itself and . . .

Jack had been on stage at the community center once when they were testing the lights. This was a thousand times brighter. This wasn't community center lighting or bar lighting—this was stadium lighting!

Although they couldn't see, they played on to the end of the song, Lyra's final note hanging in the air until it became the distant sound of a police siren over on Harris Street. Clutching his guitar, blinking away afterimages, Jack shuffled to the edge of the roof; pretty much exactly as far as his cord would let him go before he tipped over his amp.

He wasn't surprised to see that the tower was gone.

The grocery store with the bins of fresh fruit out front, that surprised him a bit.

As Lyra joined him, an old gray-haired guy with a guitar hanging down his back stopped in front of the apples, picked up a granny smith, and tossed a coin to someone just out of Jack's line of sight.

"Thang you, thang you very much."

The old man didn't look up; he just shoved the apple in his pocket and walked on.

Except that Jack was ninety percent certain it wasn't an apple by the time it reached the pocket. He was ninety percent certain it had become a handful of bright green picks.

He was ten percent certain he'd suffered irreparable brain damage at some point over the last couple of days.

"Dude?"

He turned to face the band. Maitland was scratching his ass, but Gustav seemed to have a few questions. One question, actually.

"What the hell just happened?"

Lyra slipped her hand into his and Jack smiled. "We just made music."

Continuing to make music, they all lived happily ever after.

"Dude! I said no red M&M's! What kind of a dumb ass stage manager are you? Man, this show's been a total crap fest since Carson Daly left!"

More or less.

PANHANDLER

by Alan Dean Foster

Alan Dean Foster was born in New York City and raised in Los Angeles. He has a bachelor's degree in political science and a master of fine arts in cinema from UCLA. He has traveled extensively around the world, from Australia to Papua, New Guinea. He has also written fiction in just about every genre, and is known for his excellent movie novelizations. Currently, he lives in Prescott, Arizona, with his wife, assorted dogs, cats, fish, javelina, and other animals, where he is working on several new novels and media projects.

HARBISON folded the back flap of the overcoat's thick, heavy collar up against his neatly trimmed hairline so that it shielded the fuzz and the bare skin on the back of his neck. With the passage of time, the morning's icy rain was turning to sleet as the incoming storm layered the city with a cold, damp mucus. In response to the glooming clouds, lights over store-fronts and on billboards were coming to life automatically. Some flickered uncertainly in the murk, as if confused by stalking weather masquerading as night.

The park lay to his right, an oasis of dull green even in winter. Awaiting still distant spring, trees slept in silence, wooden obelisks scarred by switchbladed hieroglyphs. Bundled up like trolls, old ladies scuttled along the slick sidewalks, heavy woolen mufflers making their necks wrestler-thick. Businessmen preoccupied with affairs of the ledger long-strided between the heated hobbit holes of favorite luncheon spots and the blandness of dead-end lives they knew no longer had meaning. At this time of midday you could tell which ones were going to lunch and which ones were returning to work, Harbison knew. Those who had already eaten were blushing from the effects of having consumed too much rich food and looked depressed at having to repopulate their myriad cubicles in the tall buildings, while those on their way to indulge their expense accounts at fancy restaurants exuded anticipation like sweat.

He was on lunch hiatus, too, but it wasn't food he was after. Prowling the clammy streets, he sought satiation of a different sort. Striving to maintain as much anonymity as he could, he tucked his own muffler up over his chin and pulled the brim of his fedora lower on his forehead. That way, little more than his eyes and mouth showed. Both were eager.

The boys hung out on Eighteenth Street, opposite the park. There weren't many of them, but there were enough. Practiced at pretending to be waiting for the bus, for friends, for a pickup game of basketball or street hockey, for anything but the tricks who sought them out, they worked hard at avoiding the attention of the police. As a general rule, the local cops didn't bother them. In a city plagued by the activities of genuinely bad people, hookers of any gender tended to be overlooked by the police until and unless some fool of a news reporter decided to guerrilla some video with a shaky, handheld camera so he or she could fill three minutes of the six o'clock report with human interest of the shameful kind. It was a cheap and easy way to sensationalize the news, maybe grab a few bored channel surfers, and push those boring reports about thousands dead of starvation in Ethiopia to the late-night last minute. Following the occasional roundup, executed to show the powers-that-be that the boys in blue were On Top of the Situation, those boys and girls unlucky enough to be apprehended promptly got out on bail and went back to work. The cops (the ones of good sense and duty, anyway) went back to actually trying to protect the public.

Harbison didn't need any protection. He knew his vices and how to slake them. He was their prisoner, and the boys on Eighteenth Street were happy to fulfill his needs and take his money. Usually he found someone quickly, terms were agreed upon much faster than in his law office, and it was all over and done with in time for him to still grab a relaxed meal at Carrington's.

He didn't have to approach anyone. All they needed to come flocking was to see the need and the hunger in his eyes. Impatient, he checked them out one by one, like a farmer evaluated prize sheep at a country auction. This one too old, that one tweaking, the next too needy, his friend too sunk in depression. He ran through them by walking past them, having long since mastered the ability to ignore the filmy haunt that veiled their old-young eyes. They were nothing more than fruit in a market, and he had the time and the money to pick and choose the fresh from the rotting.

He was about to make a deal with a lanky recent immigrant from the heartland, all soulful brown eyes and agile Midwestern hands, when he saw the boy in the back.

He was leaning up against the stone wall of the office building, one knee raised, foot propped against an early twentieth-century granite outcropping, and openly smoking a joint. He was short, maybe five-five or -six, lean but apparently muscular beneath his jeans and too-lightweight black leather coat. The icy slush dribbling down from the sullen sky didn't seem to bother him. Atypically, he was gazing off into the distance, ignoring the two or three other johns who were cruising the street offside the park. His eyes were a striking arctic blue. Wavy blond hair peeked out from beneath the brim of the backward cap that covered his head without warming it.

Harbison was drawn to him immediately.

He didn't put out the joint, but he did look over as the lawyer approached. His attitude was an intriguing mix of bottled arrogance and heartrending vulnerability. The latter Harbison was used to encountering in the boys he used, but the former was not. He immediately got down to business. He had to, if he was going to finish and still make lunch.

"How much?" he asked offhandedly. Those eyes. His own eyes strayed elsewhere. The boy didn't object to the blatant inspection. It was expected.

"The usual?" The kid's voice was high, sweet, girlish. Natural, not a put-on. Better and better. Harbison nodded. "Twenty."

Good, the lawyer thought. He wouldn't have to waste time bargaining. "Needs to be quick. I've got a lunch appointment." He indicated his wrist without exposing his watch. This was neither a sensible street nor location to flash a Piaget. "You got a place?"

The boy nodded. Flicking the remains of the joint onto the street, where the gathering cold slush instantly extinguished it, he turned his head toward the nearby alley. Harbison hesitated.

A grin creased the childlike face. It bordered on the angelic. The boy looked even younger than he doubtless was, Harbison mused. What a delightful discovery. "Got a little box in back. Propane heater. Mattress, chair. Real private. I'm okay spending the night there. You don't have to, but it'll do fine for what you want."

Harbison wasn't convinced, but there was no way he was going to pass this up. Lunch beckoned. And the boy was small, couldn't weigh more than one-ten, one-twenty. An adorable kid. Remarkably, his skin was as pale and unmarked as a baby's. Not something one encountered every day on a city street. Especially on this street.

"Okay, but no funny stuff."

The grin lingered, humorless. "You ain't payin' enough for funny stuff."

Smart, too, Harbison decided as he followed the boy into the alley. Not that he was paying for smarts. "What's your name, kid?"

"Peter."

Harbison choked something akin to an amused response.

"No, really," the boy told him. "Ironic, huh? Or poignant. Depends on your point of view, I guess."

Something about the response struck Harbison as out of the ordinary. Natural suspicion being a hallmark of his professional as well as his private life, he slowed. "Just out of curiosity, kid, where'd you learn how to use that word?"

The boy stopped too and turned to face the curious lawyer. "What word?"

"'Poignant.'" Turning slightly, Harbison indicated the street behind them. "The kids I meet here usually can't get a handle on anything with more than four letters."

Blue eyes narrowed slightly and hands rested challengingly on narrow hips. "You want to fucking talk or you want to get it on? I thought you were in a hurry." The pose reminded Harbison of something, but he couldn't decide what. Then he saw the green shirt peering out from behind the battered leather jacket. It had a fringed edge. His gaze dropped. The shoes. They hadn't registered at first. Now they did.

"Your toes must be freezing in those."

Looking away, the boy muttered something obscene under his breath before his gaze returned to meet the lawyer's. "What the fuck do you care about my friggin' toes, jack?"

"You're an actor, right?" Harbison wasn't sure why he continued with the questions. Maybe because he'd always been one to act on hunches, even in court. "When you're not on the street picking up a few extra bucks for rent, you're in a play." He smiled reassuringly, confidently. "I think I know which play."

"Oh, shit," the boy muttered. His expression twisted. "Yeah, that's right. Only, you know what, jack? I'm gonna tell you something. Because every once in a while, for some reason, I just feel like telling somebody. For the hell of it. I'm not an actor, see, and it's not a play. Not that it means anything, but my last name is one you already know. From the 'play.' "

Harbison's guard went up immediately. Either the kid was toying with him, and before time, or else he was going to prove difficult. The latter didn't concern Harbison overmuch. He'd had to deal with rants before. They rarely interfered with what he came for. Like all the others, the boy would eventually settle down. Because in the end, no matter how pissed off he became or for what reason, he would still want his money.

"It's all right," he said soothingly. "I don't care what you do once we've concluded our business. I just thought, seeing the shirt and the shoes and all . . ."

"Turns you on, does it?" The boy was watching him steadily.

"A little, maybe, yeah."

"You don't believe me, do you?"

"Sure I do. Hey, I think it's great. Stay in character when you're offstage. Ought to be good for business, anyway. I know a couple of guys who'd pay double just to have you do them in full costume."

"I bet you do." Raising one arm, the boy gestured to take in the alley, the street beyond, the vast, uncaring city. "You know why I'm stuck here, putting up with this shit?"

"It doesn't matter." Time's a-wastin', he mused. He could still do this and make lunch. Assuming the kid knew his business.

"It's all the fault of a certain fucking jealous little bitch. Since you're so confident of what role I'm 'acting' in, I'm sure I don't have to name her. Not the Brit twit, that's ancient history. But last New Year's I was in Times Square, and there was this little Puerto Rican chiquita and her friend, and they thought the hat and shirt and shoes were like, oh so cute, you know? Yeah, I'm bi. That bother you?"

"No," Harbison admitted honestly.

"So we like, went back to her place, and I showed them how to fly, in a manner of speaking, and that mini-bitch I can never seem to shake no matter where I go or how hard I try showed up at just the wrong moment. Being kind of preoccupied at the time, I'd forgotten all about her. I thought she'd be out boogying with the fireworks—that's one of her things, you know? Man, was she pissed! So, no more fairy dust. I'm grounded until she gets her tiny little panties out of a knot." He looked around at his cheerless surroundings. "This was months ago, and I'm starting to wonder if she's ever coming back, and like, even an immortal's got to eat, you know? I'm fucked if I'm gonna sling burgers for minimum. And with this not growing old thing, this fucking permanent youth, turns out I'm a boy-magnet to perverts like you."

Harbison bristled. "Calling clients names is bad for business."

"No shit?" Bold and completely unafraid, the boy approached until he was standing right up next to the older, bigger man. "You a lawyer or something?"

Harbison nodded. "Right now I need your services, but if you ever need mine . . ."

The lithe young male body spun around and back, a startlingly agile pirouetting leap that might have sprung straight off the stage at the city's main venue for ballet. "Oh, right! That's it, that's the solution! We'll sue her! Haul her blonde little ass right into civil court. Give new meaning to the term 'small claims.' With you and her together there, facing each other, there'd be two fairies confronting the judge." His tone darkened, like the weather. "Wouldn't work, dude. And you ain't licensed to practice where I come from." His gaze rose skyward. "Damn, but I miss the place. Forest, mermaids. No fucking snow. No pathetic, lonely bastards like you to have to squeeze for enough wampum to get a decent meal. Even that miserable homicidal son-of-a-bitch nemesis of mine's got his crew to help him out."

Despite having begun with promise, this encounter was souring rapidly, an unhappy Harbison saw. As a lawyer, he knew when to pursue a case and when to settle and get out. It was time to get out. Plainly, the poor, beautiful kid was seriously disturbed, maybe strung out on crystal or ecstasy or who knew what. He'd concealed it just well enough to fool Harbison. Until now. Regrettably, the lawyer decided he would have to take a pass on his pleasure today. But there was still lunch to look forward to. And the street, with its ready, accommodating, doe-eyed urchins, would still be here tomorrow. And the next day, and the day after that.

"On second thought, Mr.— Peter, I think we've wasted too much time talking and not enough doing. Now it's too late. I've got an appointment I have to keep." He turned to go.

He wasn't sure what they hit him with. It might have been a stick, it might have been a brick. Too early anticipating the night, stars filled his vision. He hit the alley pavement hard, his head bouncing off the wet asphalt like a mud-filled sock. Blinking, trying to clear his vision, he saw them standing over him. There were four, maybe five. A couple of them pretty big, all of them armed with potentially lethal detritus scavenged from the alley's battered, oversized Dumpsters. Reaching around behind his throbbing head, his hand came back bloody.

"Don't hurt me," he mumbled weakly. "I've got money."

The boy was bending over him, unsympathetic, thoughtfully checking his face. To the others he snapped, "He'll be all right. Joey, Arturo—get his wallet. Just the cash." The lawyer felt grubby fingers fumbling at his pockets. "Don't forget his watch." Crap, Harbison thought. Insurance would cover part, but not all, of its replacement cost.

He saw the boy straighten, open the ostrich-skin

wallet, and pull out the few hundred bucks Harbison always carried with him. Another boy admired the glint of the Piaget on his own dirty wrist. His face flush with contempt, Peter tossed the wallet down on Harbison's face.

"Come to my home, you self-important, condescending fucker. I'll turn you over to our local felon and his crew. They'd use you up. But you'd probably get off on that." He gestured to the other members of the gang before sparing the man on the ground a last, disdainful look. "I don't want to see you here again. Meanwhile, me and the local version of my homeboys are gonna go and get us something to drink and something hot to eat."

Turning sharply, he and the other kids, laughing and joking, headed for the street. Pushing himself up on one elbow, a dazed but still gratefully alive Harbison watched them go, sniggering and cursing and shoving one another playfully in the manner of arrogant street kids everywhere. Superior and self-confident in the shadowy, misty murk, their leader seemed to float along just above the ground.

Slowly, painfully, Harbison picked himself up. His clothes were a mess, smeared with street grit and dirty snow, but the red oozing at the back of his head seemed to have slowed. He needed medical attention. Any legitimate doctor or hospital emergency room would demand the details of his encounter. As he staggered toward the street, his afternoon trashed, he was already hard at work putting together the lie he would have to tell.

He could hardly confess to having been mugged by a boy named Peter.

TRADING FOURS WITH THE MOLDY FIGS

by Jean Rabe

Jean Rabe is the author of eleven fantasy novels and more than two dozen short stories. Among the former are two DragonLance trilogies, and among the latter are tales published in the DAW anthologies *Warrior Fantastic, Creature Fantastic, Knight Fantastic,* and *Guardians of Tomorrow.* She is the editor of two DAW collections, *Sol's Children* and *Historical Hauntings,* and a Lone Wolf Publications CD anthology, *Carnival.* When she's not writing or editing (which isn't very often), she plays war games and role-playing games, visits museums, pretends to garden, tugs on old socks with her two dogs, and attempts to put a dent in her towering "to-be-read" stack of books.

MUSIC bombarded Bigbad—rock, pop, new age, rap, heavy metal, country, and jazz. Mostly it was jazz, with its muted trumpets and thrumming basses. And some of that was blues, some of it Dixieland, a hint of fusion and ragtime thrown in for good measure. It came at him from every open door and window, pulsed through the brick sidewalk to vibrate in three-quarter time against the pads of his aching feet.

Bigbad loved music, and he'd expected plenty of it here. This was New Orleans, after all, and the beginning of Mardi Gras. He just hadn't thought there would be quite so much. It was all so painful to his sensitive ears.

Nor had he counted on the so-garish-it-made-your-eyes-hurt-rainbow-clad crowd, all highlighted by the glaring streetlights and flashing neon signs that held the night at bay. He'd anticipated tourists, just not the shoulder-to-shoulder-to-shoulder laughing, shrieking, singing, pressing, smothering, swarming mass surging like an inexorable wave down the Bourbon Street sidewalk and sweeping him along in its wake.

Women leaned over black iron railings and waved at him, some wearing little more than strands of plastic beads and several layers of makeup. Vendors hawked their wares on every corner—urging him to buy T-shirts, lemonades, flowers, and more—but their pitches were lost in the pandemonium.

Costumed folk with overlarge masks jiggled and danced and drank beer and bumped annoyingly against him. Fortune-tellers waved to him from shadowy archways. An occasional policeman threaded his way through the press—and these Bigbad worked to avoid.

So many, many people. Too many.

So much noise and color and odor. Too much!

So hard to think!

Bigbad set his feet against the wave and tried to ask directions to a jazz club from an old woman selling roses. Fortunately, she seemed to understand what he wanted, jabbering back and nodding, pointing. Bigbad couldn't separate her words from the rest of the ruckus, but he followed her finger, seeing a flickering sign halfway down the nearest side street. He would've missed it! He grinned wide, and the rose-woman stepped back, frightened by all his sharp-looking teeth.

"It's just a costume," he said, though too softly for her to hear.

Indeed, he seemed to be attracting surprisingly little notice despite all his fur. Perhaps, because Bigbad walked on his hind legs, the throng took him for one more costumed reveler instead of the wolf he really was. That had been his hope, after all.

He struggled through the crowd and narrowly dodged a horse-drawn carriage to reach the narrow side street, where the lighting was poor and where there were thankfully fewer people. He leaned against a wall and took a deep breath, told himself to relax—the building he was looking for was only a dozen yards away. The taste of the salty ocean air filled his mouth.

"Compose yourself," he said.

Put on a dignified front. Make a good first impression.

He closed his eyes and shut out all the riotous colors of the people and the buildings and the neon. Away from the bulk of the horde, Bigbad could smell more than sweat and the warring fragrances of cheap cologne. He picked up the delightful scent of fried clams and something spicy he couldn't put a name to. His stomach rumbled; it had been nearly two days since he'd stopped for something to eat. Or had it been three? Little time to eat when you're on the run.

Only a dozen yards away, the building.

He'd go there, take care of business, then get something to eat. Find a place to stay. Lose himself in New Orleans. Be safe. Really, really relax.

He allowed himself a brief pleasure, rubbing his shoulders against the wall. The bricks still held some warmth from the afternoon, and the roughness felt good. After a few moments he opened his eyes and looked down the street again and up at the flickering sign the flower woman had indicated.

Les Lupes, it read. Wolves.

Music came from that building too, a slow and familiar ragsy piece.

Rock-a-bye your baby with a Dixie melody, a craggy voice sang.

Bigbad wouldn't call it a "good" voice, but it was engaging like Louis Armstrong's had been. It had a touch of a French accent, and it settled in his ears just fine.

When you croon, croon a little tune from the heart of Dixie!

Al Jolson, Bigbad thought. Jolson recorded that tune back in . . . oh . . . 1918 if his musical memory served. He had it on wax at his old place, two copies. Had a lot of albums there—33s, 78s—all left behind when he fled. Maybe in time he could replace the collection. Certainly he could buy some of the old stuff in this city. This city, where he could be safe.

Just hang that cradle, Mammy mine, On the Mason-Dixon line, And swing it from Virginia to Tennessee with all the pull that's in ya.

Rock-a-bye your baby with a Dixie melody.[1]

Bigbad let the rest of the tune wrap around him and tug him into the establishment. The room was fairly small and crowded, only two vacant seats that he could see. Intimate, a Yellow Pages ad for the place might read. The lights were low, mostly stubby candles in glass jars burning merrily, and a spotlight on the band. It was a four-piece group, all wolves—a saxophonist, piano player, drummer, and someone handling the clarinet and flute and currently playing the latter. A weathered placard near the stage proclaimed the group the Moldy Figs. Once upon a time there were five of them, but Bigbad had learned that something unfortunate had happened to the bass player a month or so back. Fortunate for himself. He was here to fill that vacancy.

He shuffled toward the empty seat nearest the stage; the couple occupying the table didn't seem to mind the intrusion and paid him the slightest attention, only a brief nod of greeting, their eyes riveted on the musicians, their fingers drumming in time on the edge of their plates.

His stomach growled again.

The Figs started another piece, one Bigbad hadn't heard before. The saxophonist—he played a tenor sax

[1] "Rock-A-Bye Your Baby with a Dixie Melody" by Jean Schwartz, Sam Lewis, and Joe Young. Transcribed from vocals by Al Jolson and recorded March 13, 1918.

with a breathy, fat sound—was on vocals. He was a big gray wolf, fur tinged silver from age and his left ear ragged as if it had been bitten in a fight. Between riffs, he threw back his head and howled.

The couple finished their wine and left, and Bigbad hefted a leg across one of the chairs to discourage others from joining him. A waiter appeared and cleared the dishes.

"Shrimp Creole," Bigbad told him. "And a beer. Make it a Heineken, and make sure it's very cold." He had enough money in the pouch at his side to cover it, and hopefully the deposit and first-month on a shabby apartment, a little left over for a day or two of groceries. He'd upgrade his digs after his pay from the band—and from other sources he would develop—started rolling in. He eased back and continued listening. The Moldy Figs were better than he expected, and they performed three more tunes.

Silver-gray told the audience the band was taking a break and would be back in fifteen minutes for its final set. Even speaking, his voice had a hoarseness to it, a whisper cocooned around its French edges. He bowed his head to acknowledge the applause, then he and the pianist, a smallish black wolf with a patch of white fur on his throat, threaded their way through the tables and toward Bigbad. The other two wolves disappeared into the kitchen.

"Bigbad Wolf," Bigbad said as an introduction, offering his right paw in a handshake and taking his leg off the seat.

Silver-gray and the black slid into the empty chairs.

"Didn't 'spect you till the end o' the week," Silver-gray said. "Name's Gautier. This's Jamie-Lou. Says you can stay with him till you find a place o' your own." The black nodded. "Jamie-Lou's on keyboards and plays trombone from time to time. He's known from 'The Wolf and the Man.' Skip and Buzz in the kitchen, drums and woodwinds . . . they's from 'The Wolf and the Seven Little Kids' and 'Gossip Wolf and the Fox,' respectively."

"Grimm tales, all of them," Bigbad observed.

"Jacob and Wilhelm Grimm," Gautier said to make it more formal.

"The Grimm brothers got our stories mostly right," the black said. "What's your tale, Bigbad?"

Bigbad didn't answer right away. So Gautier did the talking for him. "Bigbad here's from Kentucky. Ain't that right? He's got a hankerin' for le porceau. Me, I favor coq au vin followed up with crème brûlée."

"Porceau," the black snickered. "Piglet. You's the wolf from 'The Three Little Pigs.' And speaking of dinner, I'm gonna get me a bite if you don't mind." He shook Bigbad's paw and headed toward the kitchen.

"Didn't 'spect you till the end o' the week," Gautier repeated. "Your letter said you'd be comin' on Saturday, most likely."

"Change of plans," Bigbad said.

"Not that I mind. We really need a new bass player, and the demo tape you sent showed you sure can play. It's the bass what really holds the sound together, I think. Good for us you were lookin' for a change o' scenery. None o' the wolf bass musicians in town were lookin' for work. Already had gigs. Got us a bevy o' wolf clarinetists, though, out o' work. Regular Pee Wee Spiteleras and Pete-gushing-Fountains."

There were dozens of questions Bigbad wanted to ask Gautier. Pay, hours, were there gigs on the side— things he certainly would have covered in the last phone conversation had he not been in a rush. Did the police frequent this place? Was the band in any trouble with the law?

"Good for me you put that ad on Wolf-dot-Net," Bigbad said. "I was getting tired of playing bluegrass in backwoods bars to good ol' boys soused on moonshine. No way a wolf could land a solid job with a city band in Lexington or Louisville. Not even in Paducah. City people in Kentucky wouldn't accept it. But wolves seem to be accepted here. Is it because of Mardi Gras?"

Gautier shook his head. "Can't rightly say what it

is that lets us walk freely. We play every week to a full house. And there's another all-wolf band, plays rag only, on the north side. Two on the south are into country." He spat the last word out like it was a piece of spoiled meat. "Must be about fifty or so o' us in the musicians' guild here. We have no trouble walkin' in the open in broad daylight. Oh, we all get occasional looks from the tourists, but nothing to ruffle our fur. Maybe folks expect a strangeness here. Somethin' different. We're accepted, is all that matters. 'Spect that's why you're interested in the job."

Bigbad drew his lips into a thin line. "Yeah. I guess I need to find a good fit." A place to hide in the open and play music.

"Lots o' wolves here," Gautier continued. "And lots o' music. You'll like it, an' you'll fit well."

Bigbad knew that most people, including the police, thought all wolves looked the same. It might be impossible to pick him out from the pack in New Orleans.

Did any policemen frequent this place? And how expensive were apartments? When would he get his first check? Would there be an advance? Did the Moldy Figs have a recording deal in the works? He'd have to change his name if something was going to appear in print. Did the Figs write any of their own pieces? Did they have any "ins" with the local black market? And, if so, could they arrange some introductions so he could establish a second income? There were so many questions he wanted to ask Gautier.

"How long you been in New Orleans?" Bigbad asked instead. *Ease into it,* he thought. *Be all friendly at first. Don't seem desperate or panicked or greedy.*

"Long? Nah, not long. Only 'bout a hundred years," came the raspy reply. "I came to N'awlins . . ." Gautier pronounced it Naaaaawlins like a native, the word drawn out nice and deep like a contrato clarinet holding a note, ". . . just before the Great War."

"Is that when Red dumped you?" Bigbad immediately regretted that question. Friendly! he cursed at himself. You need to keep this gig for a while!

Gautier's eyes narrowed. "Me an' Red . . . Bernadette . . . split long, long before that. Jus' after we started living together on the outskirts o' Paris." He laid his head back against the chair railing and let out a deep breath. "Bernadette broke with me right after that Charles Perrault fellow penned my tale."

"Little Red Cap. Little Red Riding Hood," Bigbad supplied.

A nod. "Yeah, that be the one. She broke with me because o' a typographical error."

Bigbad raised a hairy eyebrow.

"A typo, can you believe it? When I was dictatin' my story to Perrault, I told him I was walking with Red in the woods one day an' told her I wanted to meet her grandmother. Bernadette an' her grandmother were real close, you see. I figured if I was going to marry Bernadette, I should get to know her family."

Bigbad's expression urged Gautier to continue.

"Well, Perrault was getting on in years, and his hearin' must have been failin' him. He didn't write that I wanted to 'meet' her grandmother. He wrote that I wanted to 'eat' her grandmother. And when Bernadette's grandmother turned up missin' . . . and then Perrault printed my tale with that typo . . . that would be in 1697 . . . well, Bernadette figured I'd offed the old lady an' really did eat her. An' she got so angry that she split on me. Found out several years later that Grandma had run off with some German woodworker named Gepetto. I tried to get back with Bernadette then, when all the truth came out an' Perrault admitted his mistake, but she'd found someone else an' had moved to Switzerland. Last I heard she was workin' as a waitress to help pay the mortgage 'cause her husband couldn't keep a full-time job. Pity. Me an' Red were good together."

"That is a pity," Bigbad agreed.

"So I traveled a bit, heartbroken natu'lly. Finally came to the States an' eventually settled here. I like

Naaaaawlins. Fits me. It'll fit you, too. My favorite color is this city."

"Color? I don't . . ." Bigbad started.

"Color, my man. There's a color to this city, an' it's the blues." Gautier laughed. "Naaaaawlins is a blues town. It's the Wolverine Blues, Dippermouth Blues, Jackass Blues, Wildman Blues, Farewell Blues, Basin Street Blues, Tin Roof Blues, Beale Street Blues, Dallas Blues, The Jazz-me Blues, Sidewalk Blues, Sobbin Blues, St. Louis Blues, Tishomingo Blues, and the Weary Blues. That latter being one o' the best that Mort Greene an' his friends wrote before the Great War. Oh, but I love the blues.

"Beats bluegrass," Gautier said. "You can start with us tomorrow night. Seven o'clock. Get here a few minutes early so you can get accustomed to the bass. You said you weren't bringin' your own, right?"

Bigbad looked sad, thinking of his polished six-string bass fiddle in the house he abandoned. "No, I didn't bring my bass. Had to leave a lot of things behind."

Bigbad got directions to the piano player's apartment and left halfway through the Moldy Figs' final set. Gautier was singing scat on "Stompin' at the Savoy." Bigbad asked one of the bartenders on the way out if policemen frequented this club and was relieved to hear they were noticeably absent. Coming here, to this musical city, had been the right thing to do.

Bigbad got up early the next morning, intent on exploring his new home before starting work. He'd concentrate on the narrow streets and secluded courtyards of the French Quarter today, branch out in the days after that and test Gautier's claim that wolves were accepted in broad daylight. Indeed, he drew only a few looks as he made the rounds, taking in the folks dancing in the middle of the street and singing off-key. Gautier had slipped him an advance of two hundred and fifty, so he figured to spend some of that during his explorations.

A soulful, seductive city, Bigbad decided, a sensuous spot of civilization surrounded by swamp. He watched an elderly couple sway beneath a massive oak tree. He noted that five-star hotels on Bourbon Street were not far from strip joints. That men in suits and ties partied alongside shabbily-dressed college students. Sensory pleasures abounded everywhere on this piece of crescent-shaped land that had been carved by the Mississippi River. A passionate, friendly city, dressed up in mansions and flowers and restored historic buildings, dressed down in quaint jazz spots. An insouciant city, though a respected, dignified one with southern good manners and playfulness, and fun around every corner.

Crescent City, Isle d'Orleans, The City that Care Forgot, The Big Easy, wrapped up with the motto "Let the good times roll"—*Laissez les bon temps roulez.*

Bigbad hoped he could find an apartment he could afford in the French Quarter, or Vieux Carréé, as some of the natives called it. Old Square. A brochure told him the Quarter was established in 1718 by the French, intended as a military outpost and a commerce port. That it became a place filled with so much food and music . . . and life, amazed him.

Food . . . he was hungry again. Bananas Foster, Shrimp Remoulade, Oysters Rockefeller and more were invented in this city. Cajun and Creole dishes, French, Italian, African, and other cuisines begged to be sampled. He could smell a variety of dishes cooking as he walked, could hear music still coming from every open window and door. But he was learning to send the sounds to the back of his mind, so he could truly enjoy this place.

On Decatur Street he stopped at the Café du Monde for breakfast and had café au lait and beignets, small puffs of fried dough covered with powdered sugar that ended up dusting the hairs on his chest and stomach. Lunch was at the La Marquise Patisserie de Roi on Chartres Street. For an early dinner he feasted on Pompano en Papillote at Antoine's, then he went for a drink back on Decatur at the Marie Laveau Voodoo Bar. He made mental notes to try the Clover Grill on Bourbon Street and the Pelican Club Restaurant and Bar on Exchange Alley later in the week.

In between meals he visited a fortune-teller in Jackson Square for a tarot reading, and made an appointment for next Thursday with a tasseomancer, a tea-leaf reader at the Bottom of the Cup Tea Room on Royal Street. On Rue Conti he stood outside the Musee Conti Wax Museum, and decided he'd take a look some other day. It was said to depict wax figures of legend and the supernatural.

Bigbad paused outside of a café to hear an old black man play a trumpet. It was improv and sounded more spiritual than straight jazz. At another stop, he listened to a trio play tunes made popular by King Oliver's Creole Jazz Band in the early '20s, and some of the Hot Five and Hot Seven pieces Louis Armstrong had recorded a few years later.

By luck, he caught a "jazz funeral" on the edge of the Quarter, then heard some unscripted ensemble work. Bigbad would have pursued more music, but an antique street clock showed it was past six and time to head toward Les Loupes.

"My favorite color is this city," he said to himself, as he ambled along. "Lord, why hadn't I thought to come here before?" Like Gautier, he figured he might never want to leave.

"This city is incredible," Bigbad told Gautier. The two wolves were in an alley behind Les Loupes. It was the only place Gautier said they were allowed to smoke . . . the establishment's ordinances and such. "All the music. The food. It's . . . amazing."

"So you fit," Gautier said.

"Like an expensive leather glove," Bigbad returned.

"We'll play some traditional stuff tonight and some improvisation. Make things easy on you."

"The Big Easy," Bigbad said, still caught up in the city.

"Get you some sheet music you can go over tomorrow. An' you can get us a list o' pieces you already know."

"I want to see the bass," Bigbad said. His claws were itching to play.

The candles were burning merrily and the spot was on the band. The silver-gray wolf stepped forward.

"Ev'nin' ladies and gents. We are the Moldy Figs, an' we aim to please you tonight."

Bigbad scanned the crowd. People were seated at every table, and a few he recognized from the previous night. The Moldy Figs evidently had a following.

"We's moldy for certain," Gautier continued. "Oh-so-very moldy. Moldy Figs is a borrowed term, one the beboppers a couple decades past came up with. It be a derisive term for folks who favor the old style o' jazz, particularly the moldy traditional stuff. Moldy means you're not up to date." He let out a low snarl that stretched to the corners of the room. "Come get moldy with us."

The audience applauded, and Gautier began to sing, the first several words of "Do You Know What It Means to Miss New Orleans" drowned out by the clapping. There was a rightness in the rhythm that made Gautier a real "monster," a master jazz musician who when he wasn't singing could lay down a perfect line with the sax between the bass and the main melody.

Next came the "Basin Street Blues," and "It Don't Mean a Thing," both thick with improv. The Figs traded fours among them. The drummer started, playing a four-measure section, then turning it over to the wolf on clarinet, then to Bigbad. Gautier and Bigbad traded back and forth in a chase for two choruses before everyone joined in for the finish.

Bigbad thought the night was as close to heaven as he'd ever get, especially when he was handed large sections of an 1883 piece, "My Ragtime Baby," and then "Crazy Blues" from the 1920s. They were fairly obscure pieces, he thought, and wondered if the Moldy Figs were testing his repertoire. Between sets he either went into the kitchen for a nibble or out in the alley to talk with the rest of the Figs.

"So what's your tale?" the drummer asked.

"Told you," the black wolf growled. "He's from the Three Little Pigs."

"So what's your tale?" the drummer repeated. "The Grimms got us mostly right, but not completely. What got messed up with your story? Any tragedies stemming from typos?"

Bigbad didn't tell them the first night, or the first three weeks for that matter. He had to know them better, know for certain he was going to stay, that this "fit" was truly perfect. He didn't need the sheet music Gautier provided, he knew the tunes well enough. Bigbad could play by ear when he wanted, a trait many wolf musicians possessed.

The days passed with trips to a smattering of Creole and Cajun restaurants, where Bigbad sampled seafood dishes he'd seen mentioned in *Food and Wine*. There was time for the wax museum, a trolley ride, and a tour of the City of the Dead, the famous cemetery where the voodoo queen Marie Laveau was buried. After the band was finished some evenings, he spent a few early mornings looking for Marie's ghost in the ten-hundred block of St. Anne Street, where sightings had been recorded. In the afternoons he sampled various imported and local beers, made time to walk by the grand homes in the Garden District, and toured the D-Day Museum on Magazine Street, though he balked at the seven-dollar admission price. He met a young wolf one Sunday night on Decatur—the Figs never played on Sundays. She gave him a gris gris, a voodoo good luck charm, and they passed a few hours at what she called a 'fais do-do, a Cajun dance party.

"This city is amazing," he told Gautier, while the pair sat on crates in the alley behind Les Loupes. "I'm going on a riverboat ride this weekend."

Gautier smiled. "Told you wolves're accepted here, Bigbad. Should've come here years ago."

"So true."

The Figs didn't repeat a single tune during a three-week stretch. There were enough moldy songs to keep everything seeming new. Bigbad became a fan-favorite because of his flashing grin and snazzy presence, and he watched the nights melt quickly by, playing "All of Me," "Blue Skies," "Can't Help Lovin' Dat Man," and "Gee Baby, Ain't I Good to You." His world became "Have You Met Miss Jones?" "How Deep Is the Ocean," "Mood Indigo," and "Moonglow." He lived for "My Romance," "Solitude," "When I Take My Sugar to Tea," and "You Took Advantage of Me."

"So what's your tale?" the drummer asked again one night.

"It's not the 'Three Little Pigs,'" Bigbad admitted. "Well, not pigs in the *les porceaus* sense. More in the *les gendarmes* sense." He'd learned a few French phrases and was proud to show them off. "Police . . . pigs."

The drummer scratched at his face. "What about all the huffing and puffing you were said to do?"

"The only huffing and puffing I did was when I took trumpet lessons about eighty years ago. Didn't have the lips for it. Don't know where that huffing and puffing and blowing your house down thing came from. Maybe a typo or misprint, as Gautier is fond of saying. Oh, don't get me wrong, in my younger years I treasured roast pork, especially in fried rice dishes. But I bought it in restaurants and at the grocery store. No way would I skin and cook pigs myself."

Gautier joined them and pulled up a crate. "So if not three little pigs . . ."

"It was three *gendarmes* . . . police . . . in Henderson, Kentucky, just a stone's toss south of Indiana." Bigbad put on a sad face, thinking of his record collection and his prized bass fiddle he'd left behind. "Me and my friends weren't making enough playing the backwoods spots. So we did some other gigs on the side . . . running booze into some dry counties . . . peddling a little of Kentucky's number one cash crop."

"Pot? You mean you sold marijuana?" The black wolf sounded incredulous, a rare naïve.

"Only in the summers and sometimes into the fall," Bigbad continued. "We grew it in some of those abandoned barns, ones where the roof had fallen in so the sun could get to the plants. Most of the cops looked the other way. Heck, some of the sheriff's deputies were in on it, particularly the liquor running."

"So what about the three policemen?" The black couldn't hold his curiosity.

Bigbad laughed. "They were rookies."

"*Les porcelets,*" Gautier supplied. "Piglets."

"They were so new to the force the tags were still hanging on their uniforms." He chuckled. "Anyway, it was a small force, Henderson being a little place to the west of Owensboro and sort of north of Paducah. They kept dogging me, these three newbies, trying to catch me in the act and make a name for themselves. Well, I caught them."

The black wolf sat on the edge of his crate, eagerly waiting for the rest. A strand of saliva spilled over his lip and stretched to the alley floor.

"They were working on a report late one night, were the only ones in the tiny station house from what I could gather. I got them—and all the goods they had on me—in that proverbial one fell swoop. I guess I really did huff and puff and blow their house down. You see, I'd managed to get my paws on some plastique, and it leveled the place. Yep, I blew their house down but good." He leaned back against the wall and put on a self-satisfied expression.

"Wow," was all the black could muster.

"Wow, indeed," Gautier said.

The drummer scratched at his face, and the clarinetist sputtered.

"But if you got rid of the cops," the black started, "why'd you come here? Why didn't you keep your business going as usual?"

Bigbad's expression clouded. "I got rid of one problem only to find myself in a worse one. Seems there was a witness to the bombing, a night dispatcher heading toward the place. Next thing I know, my mug's plastered on the front pages of the Henderson *Gleaner* and the nearby Evansville *Courier*. The Feds were called right away. Them backwoods cops didn't take kindly to me offing three of their own, even if the three were piglets."

"So you fled." This from Gautier.

"Yeah. And it was a good thing I'd seen your ad on Wolf-dot-Net the day before I'd lit the fuse. I sent out the demo tapes I had made on a lark several months ago, then cleared out of my place before the Feds came into town."

The black shook his paws. "But aren't you worried. . . ."

"That they'll find me?" Bigbad let out a deep breath. "Not in *this* city. I fit in here, and there are lots of wolves."

"We all look alike to most people," Gautier said.

"Got that right," Bigbad said.

That night finished with "You're My Everything," followed by two encore numbers—"Any Ice Today, Lady?" and "Did You Ever See a Dream Walking?" Bigbad was "in the pocket" for all three, playing flawlessly on his bass in the center of the beat.

The next night was not so smooth.

There were policemen in the audience, for the first time in recent memory of the establishment. A dozen officers sat at tables in the front row, and nabbed Bigbad before he could entirely realize what was happening.

"Why?" Bigbad hollered, as the gendarmes ushered him out the door.

"Shouldn't've told us your tale," the black wolf snarled. "We's a group that keeps our noses clean. Don't want our music tainted."

It was nearly a month before the Moldy Figs found a new bass player, one who was even better than Bigbad. It was the first woman the group had accepted, a large brown bear who never missed a note when trading fours on "Who Will Take My Place When I Am Gone."

"What's your tale?" the black asked her in the alley during a break after the second set.

"My baby bear grew up and went to college," she said. "Papa, he ran off to the far north with a polar bear he'd met while surfing some site on the Internet. The den seemed kinda big. And I was feeling pretty blue."

"My favorite color is this city," Gautier sighed. "It's the Rooster Blues."

"The James Street Alley Blues," she traded back. "It's the Deep River Blues, Dying With the Blues, Minor Blues, Shake Man Blues, Squabbling Blues, Hard Luck Blues, and 'Fore Day Blues. It's the Bitin' Fleas Blues, Evil Man Blues, the Twelfth Street Blues, and Mama's Got the Blues."

"You gonna fit here just fine," Gautier said.

SIGNS ARE HAZY;
ASK AGAIN LATER

by Fiona Patton

Fiona Patton was born in Alberta and grew up in the United States. In 1975 she returned to Canada and after a series of unrelated jobs including electrician and carnival ride operator moved to rural Ontario with her partner, one tiny dog, and a series of ever changing cats. Her Branion series which include *The Stone Prince, The Painter Knight,* the *Granite Shield,* and *The Golden Sword* have all been published by DAW Books, and she is now working on the first book of a new series tentatively entitled *The Silver Lake* for DAW as well.

THE ice storm had raged across the county for three days and nights. When it finally moved out across Lake Ontario, the streets of Greenville glittered like ribbons of silver in the afternoon sun, the ten-foot-high snowbanks—polished to a marblelike finish—and the overhanging, ice-clad tree branches transforming the small, industrial town into a wintry fairyland.

The Rink Pirates Memorial Hockey Arena parking lot, however, resembled the aftermath of a demolition derby, with snow-covered cars and pickup trucks jammed in wherever they could find room regardless of actual space. The wooden sign nailed above the side door reading: "Super Jackpot and Progressive Bingo 3 PM, February 17," explained why.

"Bee-four. Bee-four."

The arena canteen was so smoky the three-hundred-odd players seated along both sides of the dozen chipped and burn-scarred tables could barely see the bingo caller, but the two young men who'd just entered never broke stride. Their eyes wide and dark, they scanned the room swiftly, then made for a central table where a wizened old woman, cigarette clenched in her teeth and bright pink bingo daubers clenched in each fist, was busily working her own three twelve-game sheets and the single six-game sheet of the heavyset man beside her. As they approached, he looked up, red-rimmed eyes watering.

"Brandon? Fred? Is that you?"

The older of the two men, his own eyes returning to their usual blue, lit a cigarette before pushing up the brim of his Mill Valley Co-op cap.

"Hey, George. What the hell are you doing here?"

"Eye-nineteen, eye-nineteen."

The man gave a helpless shrug, indicating the woman who showed no sign of breaking concentration even as she knocked the inch-long ash from her cigarette with a practiced jerk of her head. It landed in the general direction of the overbrimming ashtray beside her. "I offered to give Cousin Maude a ride into town, Brandon," he explained weakly.

"That was dumb."

"Yes, well, you know, she's *family*."

George Prescott, sixty-four years old and a retired Toronto tabloid journalist, had come to the county over a year ago, ostensibly to prevent a fourth heart attack, but also with the hopes of discovering his grandmother Dorothy Mynaker's "rural roots" in the archives and newspaper offices of the small, local town that served the half dozen surrounding villages. What he'd found instead was a tight-knit four-family clan of two hundred or so people with a host of metaphysical abilities only hinted at by the magazines he'd worked for—abilities tempered by their complete lack of ambition. Once they realized he was not going to jeopardize their lives by telling anyone about them, the families, headed by his young cousins, Brandon and Fred Geoffries, had accepted him, lending a hand with the various, unfamiliar hazards of country living such as wasps in his drive shed, pigeon dung in his side porch, and foot-high quack grass in his garden. They could not, however, protect him indefinitely from the exploitive clutches of the older members of the clan.

"Eye-sixteen, eye-sixteen."

Now, as Fred took a seat beside them, he made a fruitless search through his pockets for a cigarette before slipping one from the old woman's pack.

"Hey, Aunt Maude."

"Hey, yourself. Get outta there."

She aimed a distracted slap in his direction before returning her attention to the sheets.

"En-thirty-seven, en-thirty-seven."

"Ah, shit, George, pay attention. You've missed another one."

Her right-side pink dauber slapped down onto the sheet in front of him and only the four of them noticed she hadn't bothered to direct it with her hand.

George started. "Maude! Um, sorry." He glanced sheepishly up at Brandon. "I never will get used to that," he explained, "in public, I mean."

"No one's looking even if they could see it," the younger man replied laconically, before drawing up a chair. "But I thought you couldn't take the smoke, George?"

"I can't ordinarily, but well, Maude will need a ride home and the storm's closed down half the town, including the library. I understand they have a special room where you can wait at the Mill Valley Hall, but Maude prefers to play in Greenville."

Brandon snickered. Fred laughed outright.

"That's 'cause they won't let her play in Mill Valley anymore," the younger of the two brothers scoffed.

George bristled at his tone. "Why in heavens not?"

Brandon shot him a raised eyebrow. " 'Cause she's a Frawst, George."

"So?"

"So . . ." Fred glanced over at the old woman who pointedly ignored him, then swore as en-forty-three only elicited eight daubs out of thirty-six games. Rheumy gray eyes suddenly very dark, she smiled as bee-six found a home on twenty of them.

"She cheats."

She turned an annoyed glance in his direction while her daubers flew across the sheets. "Why don't you make yourself useful and get your Great-*Great* Auntie Maude a beer?" she snapped, the steel in her voice belying the frailty of her body.

" 'Cause they don't sell beer in bingo halls?"

She gave him a disgusted look. "Not from the snack bar, fool, from the cooler. Down there." She jerked her chin toward her feet, liberally scattering ash across her light pink sweater.

"Oh."

As Fred fished two doctored Pepsi bottles from the cooler beneath the table, Brandon glanced over at the piles of discarded ink-covered bingo games.

"So, who paid for all this?"

"Well . . . um." George looked sheepish.

"Oh-seventy-five, Oh-seventy-five."

If you must know, George treated me," Maude sniffed. "Not that it's any of your business, anyway. *He's* a proper gentleman. The Mynakers always are, unlike the Geoffries. Get your arm offa that, you're blockin' my game."

"With the Mynaker Sight, you'd think he'd be smarter'n that."

George shrugged modestly. "It was only eighteen dollars."

"Per book, plus the specials . . ." Fred flipped

through the games until Maude smacked his hand
away, ". . . and the super jackpot."

"I hope you're gonna split your winnings, Maude,"
Brandon said sternly.

George waved his hand at him. "It was my pleasure.
Besides, your Aunt Maude hasn't won at all this afternoon despite what you think. The actual odds of win-
ning are . . ."

"Oh-sixty-six, Oh-clickity-click, Oh-sixty-six."

"BINGO!"

Maude's hand shot up into the air so fast her cigarette went flying.

"That the monthly five grand progressive?" Brandon asked dryly as he retrieved it.

"Nothing else worth mojoin' the bingo machine
for," she answered out of the corner of her mouth.
"Here," she handed him the sheet. "Take this up
there and get me my winnins."

He frowned at her. "Is the sheet legit?"

"Of course it's legit! Get going!"

"In the old days she used to wipe the ink off the
sheets an' reuse em," Fred explained. "But they put
a stop to that by puttin' code numbers on 'em. Now
she just mojos the machine by levitatin' the right
balls."

"Only from time to time," she corrected stiffly. "At
the end of the month when I need a little extra cash.
You know how it is when you're on a fixed income,
don't you George?"

He smiled weakly. "Um . . . not quite yet."

"Oh that's right, you're just sixty-four, aren't you?
Well, you'll learn."

"What," Fred scoffed. "That every month you don't
die the government sends you more money?"

"And how much do you get, Mister Keep-a-job-just-
long-enough-to-collect U.I?"

"Not as much as you get."

"Damn right."

They continued to squabble as the people around
them began to pack up. "Don't forget your Hospital

Auxiliary contest applications," the caller shouted out as he scribbled Maude's name on the five thousand dollar check for Brandon. "Deadline's tomorrow."

"No."

"Aw, c'mon, George, it'll be fun. C'mere, rat-dog."

Stretched out on the dining room couch in George's century-old farmhouse, Fred lifted Lucky, his cousin's very spoiled Chihuahua, onto his lap before waving the form at him. "We'll win for sure."

The older man rubbed a towel through his thinning hair—Lucky had refused to come near him until he'd showered the overpowering smell of cigarette smoke away—before shaking his head again. "It's one hundred dollars per application," he replied. "And I'll soon be *on a fixed income*, you know."

"The three of us can go in together, then it'll only cost twennie bucks or so."

"Thirty-three dollars and thirty-three cents."

"Whatever."

"No. Remember the last contest you talked me into entering? That walleye derby? All I caught was a cold."

"That's 'cause you was fishin' in the wrong spot," Brandon interjected. He reached absently for his cigarettes, but at Lucky's indignant bark, dropped his hand again. "Told you that at the time."

"Yes, I know, I wasn't fishing where Ike Frawst had just stocked the lake, and as it turned out Ike Frawst won the derby anyway, so why did we bother competing at all?"

"For the beers," Brandon answered.

"Oh, yes, I was forgetting."

"Look, first prize is a two thousand and three sport ute," Fred insisted, poking at the application. "Wow, fully loaded, too: four by four, air-conditioning, CD player, woo cup holders," he added sarcastically. "It's gotta be worth a fortune."

"I already have a perfectly fine sport utility vehicle," George sniffed. "It's practically brand new."

"That's 'cause you never take it off road."

"No, *you* take it off road. And you'd better not be poaching *anything* with it either."

Fred grinned. "Hey, Bran, does rustlin' count as poachin'?"

His brother considered the question seriously as George's face went dangerously red. "Can't see how it would," he said after a moment. "You can't poach somethin' if there's no season for it."

"That's not funny," his cousin retorted.

"So, who's offerin' the sport ute, anyway?" Brandon asked, winking at Fred.

His brother peered down at the paper again. "Uh-oh. Looks like Gary Wallace."

"So, basically, it's got cup holders an' a big burned-out block of crap where the engine should be."

"Likely. But, hey, it's nothing Art can't mojo better," Fred argued, holding up his father-in-law Art Akorman as an argument on the pro side—the Akormans could magic any machine back to perfect working order no matter how old and battered it was.

"It's probably a tax write-off," George said charitably.

"Whatever. We can always sell it an' buy three used cars instead."

"I don't need a used car," George insisted.

"No, but you could use a half-decent pickup truck. 'Sides," Fred continued as he watched Brandon glance out the window at his '86 Plymouth station wagon slowly rusting in the driveway. "Bran could. And so could I."

"I suppose."

"It's settled, then. We win it, we sell it."

"Fine." George raised his hands in defeat, settling himself in his armchair by the window. Lucky immediately launched himself off Fred's lap and into George's arms. "So how do we win it?"

"What?"

"The contest or whatever it is, how do we win it?"

"Oh. It's a scavenger hunt."

Brandon took the paper. "Old license plate, Coke bottle, skeleton keys, square nails; shit, Dad's got most of this crap up top of his drive shed," he noted. "Duck decoys an' Tetley tea figurines?" He scanned the paper. "Thought so," he said in disgust. "Look here. All objects judged become the property of the sponsoring body."

"Who is?"

"Fuckin' Wallace Antiques. This is just a scam to get more shit to sell the tourists in that rat bag flea market of his. Antiques, my ass."

"Still, takin' a sport ute off him for the price of a few bottles and nails'd be worth it," Fred argued.

"Maybe. Final item: most unusual object priced under five dollars."

His brother frowned. "What the hell does that mean?"

"And most unusual according to whom?" George added.

"There's a panel of judges. The Greenville Business Association. Figures."

"Who are?"

"Gary Wallace's fuckin' cousins." Brandon tossed the paper onto the table next to George's computer. "That's it, then."

The older man glanced up with a confused frown. "Why?"

" 'Cause the Wallaces don't get on with the four families," Fred explained. "They're from the same part of the county and there's old land disputes between us that go back a hundred years. They hate us all, Frawsts, Akormans, Geoffries especially, an' even the Mynakers, as hard as that is for you to figure."

"Oh."

The three of them sat in silence for a few moments until Brandon scooped up the paper again with a slight frown. "Okay," he said after a few moments. "We use George's name."

"Hello, what part of the word Mynaker don't you get?" Fred sneered.

"The part where his name's actually Prescott. Gary Wallace doesn't know shit about incomers, he'll never figure it out."

"Someone'll tell him."

"So?" Brandon's eyes went very dark. "We'll make this fuckin' item look so special he won't be able to screw us."

"It'll have to be pretty fuckin' special even with a Geoffrey illusion thrown on it to convince that lot, an' where we gonna get something like that around here?"

"We'll have to go to the city, I think," George answered, the gleam of competition suddenly darkening his own eyes and giving his face a very Mynaker expression despite his urban upbringing.

"Toronto again?" Fred suggested with a grin. "Last time we went you came back with a little pisser of a psychic Chihuahua. You can't get much more unusual than that, can you?"

Lucky squeaked at him before scratching at George's hand for a pat.

"I'm not so sure he's psychic," George replied modestly, rubbing the dog's wide, expressive ears. "He's just very intelligent, aren't you, boy?"

"He knew Bran was gonna smoke."

"Brandon chain smokes. It wouldn't take much to remember that. Anyway, back to the subject at hand. Given the weather, I was thinking a little closer to home would be more appropriate. Kingston, perhaps? There are a lot of unusual antique stores around Queens University."

Brandon nodded. "Okay, then, we'll get the rest of this shit together an' meet you back here first thing tomorrow morning."

"Are you sure you don't need more time?"

"Naw, what Dad hasn't got, Art or Ike'll have."

"And Cheryl doesn't need help with the baby?"

Brandon shook his head. "Her mom's stayin' with us right now. Kaley's got a cold an' Cheryl says I fuss too much to let her sleep."

"Well, all right, then. First thing tomorrow, it is. We can drop the application off on the way."

"You want me to borrow Art's truck again?" Fred asked, grinning as George blanched. The last time he'd ridden with Fred in Art's old one ton he'd been sure they were all going to die.

"No, that's quite all right," he replied. "We'll take my car. I'll drive," he added firmly.

Fred just laughed.

The next day dawned sunny but cold. The brothers spent the cigaretteless hour-and-a-half drive along the ice-covered lakeshore complaining about George's lack of speed and telling him how silly Lucky looked in his brand new burgundy sweater with its matching harness and forty-dollar dog boots. After squeezing into a very narrow parking space on Princess Street, George set the Chihuahua carefully down on a patch of shoveled sidewalk as his cousins spilled out beside him. Brandon immediately lit a cigarette with a grimace.

"You'd think after an ice storm the place'd smell better," he noted.

"I'm surprised you can smell anything other than smoke," George retorted. "But I agree, it's amazing how fast one loses the ability to breathe in the city. Oh, well, we won't be here long." He checked his watch. "All right, it's ten o'clock now, and the meter's good for, let's see, two hours for two dollars—that's a bit steep. Anyway, what say we split up and meet back here at noon. We can have lunch and compare treasures." He paused. "That is if you're sure you'll be all right on your own."

Fred frowned at him. "Why wouldn't we be?" he demanded.

"Well, er, Brandon told me once that you hadn't been anywhere bigger than Greenville before."

"Yeah, well, Brandon lies. We were here when we were kids. How much can it have changed, eh?"

George looked alarmed. "Er, maybe we should stick together."

Brandon just shook his head. "Relax, George. We came up here with Art last fall to buy a trailer."

"What?"

He grinned. "Fred lies, too, ya know. Meetcha back here in two hours."

As the two brothers headed off, George exchanged an exasperated expression with Lucky.

"So, I think we may have to admit defeat, boy," he said an hour and a half later. "We've haven't found anything suitable at all, have we?" From deep within his jacket where Lucky had climbed after the first ten minutes, the Chihuahua let out a faint, uninterested snore and George sighed.

They'd visited at least a dozen antique stores that morning, all of them vastly overpriced, and all of them selling disappointingly normal objects. Now, as he glanced up at the darkening, slate-colored sky, he shivered slightly. His feet were getting cold. And wet. He was half inclined to give up and spend the final half an hour in a nice, warm café—after all he hadn't wanted to join this silly scavenger hunt in the first place—but the thought of Fred and Brandon returning with moon rocks or radioactive dust or some such other exotic item steeled his resolve. "All right," he said resignedly, "one last street. But you're walking for a change. It's time you peed, anyway." Hoisting the sleepy-eyed dog from his jacket, he turned the corner. "Let's see." He glanced from one side of the small street they found themselves on to the other. "Convenience store, probably not, map shop, wish I had the time, used bookstore, again, no time, we should have come alone last week, eh, boy? Café, café, café. Well, let's follow along that way, shall we? Yes, you can so walk, it's all shoveled along here. Come on."

They made it past a shoe store, an army surplus store, and an unusually large toy store before Lucky suddenly stopped dead. George tugged gently on his leash, but the tiny dog simply sat down and fixed him with a big, round-eyed stare. George sighed.

"You can't possibly be cold yet," he admonished.

Lucky continued to stare at him.

"Oh, very well." As George bent to pick him up, he came face-to-face with a green plastic dog-shaped plant sitting in a golden pot. As he straightened, Lucky under one arm, he saw it was actually a Chihuahua topiary, great green ears stretching almost three feet wide. Lucky immediately began to bark at it.

"Hush," George said absently as he glanced up. "The Laughing Chihuahua Knick-Knack Shoppe," he read. "I don't remember seeing that before. Wasn't this an auto parts store last month?" He smiled suddenly, all hint of his earlier weariness vanished. "Still, that's a bit of good luck for a change, isn't it? I bet we'll find something very unusual in here, and if not, you could always use a new coat." Laying a finger on Lucky's nose to quiet him, he headed inside.

The Laughing Chihuahua Knick-Knack Shoppe was warm and bright and smelled of dog biscuits. The tiny puppy-shaped bell atop the door tinkled musically as he entered and he stopped just inside and gawked.

The front showroom was crammed to the rafters with Chihuahua-themed objects of every size, shape, and description, from the usual pint-sized dog beds, sweaters, chew toys, and bathing products to Chihuahua-shaped teapots, cream and sugar sets, and salt and pepper shakers. Dog-decorated flags, tapestries, and wind chimes hung from the ceiling while racks of Chihuahua-embroidered sweaters, T-shirts, hats, sock, ties, and scarves marched down the center of the room. One wall was dedicated to a very familiar brown deer-type Chihuahua whose face was plastered on everything from mugs to buttons to mouse pads to stationery, and the other was made up of a special holiday display carrying dog-festooned Christmas stockings, ornaments, and lights, beside Chihuahua figurines dressed as pilgrims, bats, and leprechauns set in front of a collection of stuffed dogs wearing hearts, maple leaves, and Easter eggs on tiny little knitted sweaters. What space was left on the walls was covered in Chihuahua photographs, plaques, paintings, and drawings, beside a wide shelf of what were probably Chihuahua-themed books and videos. The woman who came around the glass-topped counter was equally decked out in a bright blue sweatshirt emblazoned with a white Chihuahua in a jester's hat. She smiled widely when she caught sight of Lucky tucked in the crook of George's right arm, one leather-booted paw braced against his shoulder.

"And who is this little darling?" she asked.

"Um, Lucky, that is Lucky Charm," George replied, suddenly inexplicably shy.

"Well, aren't you adorable?" She tickled Lucky under the chin. "Is he an only chi?"

"Hm?"

"Do you have more than one dog?" she explained. "Many chi owners have multiples."

"Oh. Um, yes, there's just him."

"Well, now." She turned her head. "Ashley? Ashley, come here, girl. My little one is an only chi, too. Why don't you set him down just there. . . ."

George couldn't help but raise Lucky a little higher. "Yes, well, I'm not so sure that's such a good idea, I mean Lucky hasn't met that many other dogs."

"Oh, don't you worry about that. Chis are very clannish, you know. They may not be too fussy for other breeds, but they're usually extremely fond of each other. They bond instantly most of the time. Ah, there you are, Sweetie. See, he does want to meet her."

Lucky had begun to wriggle frantically in George's arms as a small, reddish female Chihuahua came out from around the counter, and rather than risk having him leap to the floor and break a leg, George set him carefully down on the carpet. Ashley immediately began to sniff his muzzle and ears very aggressively while Lucky stood stock-still, shivering with pleasure.

"I told you," the woman beamed. "I'm Wanda, by the way," she said, sticking her hand out.

"Um, George."

"Hello, George. Always nice to meet another chi-parent. Were you looking for anything in particular today?"

"No, I mean, well, that is, yes, sort of . . ." He explained about the scavenger hunt, and Wanda nodded sagely.

"Well, you've come to the right place, I'd say. Let's see what we can find, shall we? Oh, don't worry about them, they'll be fine."

She led him around the store, offering various items for his consideration as Lucky continued to suffer Ashley's thorough inspection with a beatific look on his face. George considered and discarded a Chihuahua-shaped cookie jar, wine bottle, and a bumper sticker that read, *"My Chihuahua is smarter than your honor student,"* before pausing at the new age section. Wedged between a deck of Chihuahua tarot cards and a book entitled *Discovering Your Chi's Chi*, was what seemed to be a kind of Aladdin's lamp. On closer inspection he saw that it was etched with several of the distinctive little dogs wearing turbans and sitting on tiny flying carpets.

"What's this?" he asked.

"Oh, that. That's a lamp," Wanda answered. "Don't rub it."

George smiled a little self-consciously. "Why, will a little chi-shaped genie pop out?"

Wanda gave him a noncommittal shrug. "Could be," she said with a serious expression. Taking it out of his hands, she very carefully set it back on the shelf. "Besides, it's six ninety-nine. I thought you said your item needed to be under five dollars."

"Oh, yes, yes I did." George turned away from the lamp with an expression of real reluctance before picking up a somewhat more prosaic looking object. "What's this?"

"Ah. Now that's really unusual," Wanda said with a smile. "And it's only three-ninety-nine."

"So, you bought a plastic *dog* figurine?"

Hunched over a large, black coffee in the Sleepless Goat Café, Fred eyed George's purchase with disdain.

"No, I bought a fortune-telling plastic *Chihuahua* figurine," George retorted, moving his mocha latte out of Lucky's reach before fixing his cousin with a reproachful stare. "You ask it a question and then you turn it over and read the answer."

Brandon nearly choked on his own drink, a cinnamon mochachino with chocolate powder sprinkled on top that George had insisted he try.

"You bought a plastic dog figurine that tells the future through its butt?"

"Oh, yeah, that'll win for sure," Fred scoffed.

"Just try it. Ask it a question."

"Okay, fine." The younger man snatched up the figurine. "Is this going to be the lamest item in the scavenger hunt, or what?" he demanded. Turning it upside down, his eyes narrowed, then he grinned.

Brandon and George leaned forward. "Well?"

"It says, 'No way.'" He turned it right side up again. "Okay, is it going to *win* the scavenger hunt?" He checked the bottom again and chuckled. "'Chances are.' Right, I'm sold, it's kinda like a magical doggie eight ball."

"There, you see?"

"But it's still not as unusual as mine," he scoffed, dropping a strange looking contraption that resembled a copper spider onto the table.

Brandon frowned. "What the hell is that?"

"The guy at the store called it a homemade brain wave machine."

"A which?"

"A brain wave machine. You put it on your head and move it up and down and it kinda scratches your scalp. It's supposed to have magical healing powers."

"That's the stupidest thing I've ever seen."

"Is not. George's is way stupider."

"Yeah, but at least George's works. This thing's way too small to stick on your head."

"That's 'cause it's the kid's version. The adult one cost ten bucks."

George lifted it up to examine it more closely. "It certainly is . . . um, unusual," he said finally.

"You mean it's just plain weird," Brandon retorted. "Tell the truth, Fred, you found some wire in an alley and built it yourself."

"No way. The guy said it's for real." He jerked his chin at his brother. "What'd you get?"

Brandon placed a small, black box in front of them and George started.

"Is that what I think it is?"

"I dunno, what do you think it is?"

"Well, it looks like a Fuzz Buster."

"That's what it is."

Fred turned a skeptical expression on them both. "What's that, some kinda weird lint brush?"

"No, it's a radar detector, for keepin' the cops off your tail on the highway. Found it in an auto parts store down the road."

"No shit? Why's it called a Fuzz Buster?"

"Dad said that's what they used to call cops in the old days: fuzz."

"Were they fuzzy?"

"How the fuck should I know, Fred."

"George?"

The older man looked down his nose at him. "You wouldn't understand even if I explained it to you," he answered haughtily. "It was a sixties thing."

"Oh." Fred winked at Brandon. "You mean it's an *old guy thing*."

"Exactly."

"Will you quit screwin' around with that? You're gonna break it."

"Am not." Leaning against George's car, Fred

glared down at the Chihuahua figurine. "There's something really weird about it, Bran."

"You mean besides it telling the future through a dog's butt?"

"Yeah. Until we got to the car it only said things like, yes, no, and signs are hazy, ask again later, but now . . ." He held it out and Brandon frowned.

"Shit."

After setting Lucky on the passenger seat, George glanced over. "What?

"It says, 'Check your oil.' "

"Well, it's obviously an advertising gimmick. I just had the oil topped up."

"So, you're not gonna check it?"

"I wasn't going to, no."

"Well, okay, but don't say it didn't warn you."

The oil light came on a block later. His face red, George pulled over in a warehouse loading zone.

"There's a can of oil in the back, Fred, if you wouldn't mind," he muttered.

Fred undid his seat belt with a snicker.

"What's it say now? Anything about the traffic?"

Turning onto Major Mackenzie Boulevard, George glanced over at the figurine until Lucky yipped at him, and he returned his attention to the road.

"I dunno," Fred answered, shaking it with a frown. "The little thing inside seems to be stuck.

"Told you you'd break it," Brandon said dryly.

"I didn't break it, it's just . . . oh, fuck me."

"What?"

The younger man shoved the figurine into Brandon's hand. The letters in the tiny white triangle were so small they could hardly read them but once the older brother made them out, his face whitened.

"Kaley's in hospital."

"Shit."

"Get us home, George."

                    *   *   *

They made Greenville hospital in just under half an hour. George drove like a man possessed, only dropping his speed once when the Fuzz Buster began to beep. The police cruiser carried on past them without hesitation, which was just as well since neither Brandon nor Fred were in any condition to cast the distinctive "hide from the cops" illusion that made the Geoffries ability so popular. When they reached the emergency entrance, Brandon was out of the car before it stopped moving. By the time George and Fred had found a parking space, money for the parking meter, and Kaley's hospital room, he was pacing the halls with his crying, four-month-old daughter held tightly in his arms while Cheryl and her mother argued with the doctor. Illusionary rainbows, butterflies, and teddy bears were already beginning to spin about the child's head and George very quietly guided the distraught father into the empty wardroom. Cheryl joined them a few minutes later, her pale face flushed a deep, angry red. She deftly lifted Kaley from Brandon's arms as the sound of raised voices continued to filter in to them.

"Bastard says it's just an ear infection, but he won't give her anything for the pain till he knows for sure," she snarled.

The baby began to wail even louder, the vein on the left side of her temple throbbing dangerously. Fred elbowed George in the ribs.

"How about we use the brain wave thing," he suggested in a whisper.

George frowned. "I don't know, Fred. The doctor . . ."

"Is a dickhead. It can't hurt her and it might help her."

Brandon turned to them, his eyes gleaming like black marbles. "Do it."

A few minutes of very careful treatment later and Kaley was sitting up in the cell-like hospital crib, trying to grab Lucky through the bars and chortling happily. Cheryl headed for the nurse's station, a martial gleam in her darkening eyes, while her mother reached for the child's snowsuit.

"It had better be the Fuzz Buster, I'm thinking."

Sitting in Brandon and Cheryl's kitchen later that evening, the older of the two brothers finished his third beer before staring down at the three "unusual items."

Fred and George shared a surprised look.

"You're kidding, right?" Fred protested. "We've got a magical doggie eight ball here and you want to put in a radar detector?"

"You want Gary Wallace to get his hands on somethin' that really tells the future?"

Fred opened his mouth, then closed it again. "Okay, but what's wrong with the brain wave thing, then?"

"Kaley might need it again."

"Oh." The younger man slumped. "Okay," he agreed gloomily.

"I don't know," George said, turning the black box over in his hands. "I think they might be illegal."

Fred straightened. "Yeah?"

"Yes. I seem to remember reading something about that before they disappeared off the market."

The two brothers shared a grin. "That might mess up Gary Wallace's plans to resell it," Brandon noted.

"Fuzz Buster it is," Fred crowed.

They met back at George's a week later to wait for word on the contest. Brandon had brought a case of beer and Fred, the latest copy of *Auto Trader*. But when George set the phone down, his face said it all and Fred threw the magazine onto the table in disgust.

"We didn't win."

"Clara Wallace tied us with a bobble-headed calico cat from the dollar store."

"The bugger just doesn't want to give up that sport ute," Brandon growled.

"Fucker."

"No, it's all right. I said she tied us, which means we still have another chance. One more unusual item by tomorrow evening."

"That doesn't give us much time."

"No, so I was thinking," George began, wondering at the sudden fluttering in his stomach, "we go back to the Laughing Chihuahua Knick-Knack Shoppe. We're bound to find something unusual there right away."

They arrived just as Wanda was opening up. The store owner was as thrilled to see George again as Ashley was to see Lucky and while the two dogs played tug-of-war with a brightly colored knotted rope, they huddled over a glass case containing Chihuahua pencil toppers, erasers, zipper pulls, and jewelry, trying to ignore Fred and Brandon's unhelpful suggestions.

"How about a bongo drum with a picture of a dog takin' a crap on it?"

"No."

"A garden dog dressed as a gnome?"

"No!"

"*The Chihuahua Lovers' Cookbook*. Shit, these people cook Chihuahuas?"

"What!"

"Can't be feeding too many people."

"Will you two please shut up?"

George glared at them as Wanda plucked the cookbook from Fred's hands and set it back on the shelf. "It has perfectly normal recipes inside," she scolded. "And the proceeds go to the Chihuahua Rescue League. Now if you don't mind . . ."

"What's this?"

"A lamp, don't rub it." It was also returned to the shelf. "Here, I think this might do." She set a small plastic toy on the counter.

The three men peered down at it skeptically.

"A Pez Dispenser?" Brandon asked finally. "What's so unusual about that?"

"Well, it's not exactly a Pez Dispenser, rather it's a dog treat dispenser."

"Okay, what's so unusual about a dog treat dispenser?"

She turned it around to show them a battery door and a tiny button lodged in the back of the large brown head. "The eyes light up."

The brothers laughed. "A demon dog treat dispenser?"

"Go for it."

"Whaddya mean, we tied again?"

About to knock the snow off his boots in George's side porch a week later, Fred stopped dead, staring at the older man in frustration.

"Clara submitted a sleeping Persian cat made of rabbit fur," his cousin explained in a strangely excited voice. "Are you going to come in or not?"

"What? Yeah, sure." Kicking his boots off, Fred stomped into the dining room and threw himself down on the couch. Brandon followed a few minutes later after tossing his cigarette butt into a snowbank.

"This is gettin' lame," he muttered.

"No, it's all right. I'll just nip back to Kingston and pick up another item. Um, there's no real need for you to come with me," he added.

Brandon raised an eyebrow at him. "Nip?"

"Well, yes. It's supposed to be a nice day tomorrow and Lucky and I were planning another visit anyway. He needs, er . . . flea treatment."

"Flea treatment?"

"Um, well, yes. And . . . other things," he trailed off weakly.

Brandon poked through the pile of new Chihuahua-themed items on the table. "How many times have you *nipped* back there since last week?" he asked.

George straightened. "Once or twice. Maybe. All right if you must know, Wanda and I are seeing each other." He glared at the two men, daring them to make a smart-ass remark, but Fred just grinned at him as Brandon picked up the Chihuahua eight ball figurine with a distracted expression.

"Buy the lamp."

"What?"

Brandon looked up, his eyes wide and dark. "The lamp, buy the lamp." He tossed the figurine to George. "It says it's on sale. Just don't rub it."

"Bee-fourteen, bee-fourteen."

The Greenville Arena parking lot had been finally cleared of snow although the cars and pickup trucks were spaced no better when Brandon pulled his new '98 Taurus wagon up next to Fred's shiny new '99 Dodge Viper. The canteen was remarkably free of smoke when they entered. Scanning the three-hundred-odd hunched figures they easily spotted Maude, George, and Wanda at the central table and ambled over. The old woman pointedly ignored them, but the others paused to indicate a couple of chairs. Brandon shook his head.

"Can't stay. Just wanted to tell you Gary Wallace got outta hospital this mornin'."

George smiled. "That's a relief."

"Yeah, well, I knew it was preyin' on you. He'll be stayin' pretty close to home, though. He's still tellin' folks a giant blue dog in a turban attacked him. Hey, rat-catchers." Brandon bent to scratch Lucky and Ashley behind the ears as George frowned at him.

"It's not funny," the older man admonished. "It brought on a heart attack."

"Bull shit. His crappy eatin' habits did that," Fred retorted, raising an eyebrow at the sight of Wanda's Chihuahua-shaped bingo dauber. "But it took him off the judges' panel long enough to win us our sport ute." He glanced around. "So this is what you spent your share on? Bribin' the bingo hall to go no smokin'?"

"No, the arena decided that all on their own. The law's coming into effect in May anyway."

"Fuckers," Maude growled, stuffing a piece of nicotine gum into her mouth.

"En-forty-one, en-forty-one."

"I gave half of my share to Clara Wallace," George

continued. "Her meowing cat clock really should have won. And the rest, well . . ." He smiled at Wanda, "I've spent that on gas and bingo cards."

"Didn't think you cared for the game that much," Brandon observed, lifting the Chihuahua eight ball figurine from its position between them.

"I don't, but it turns out Wanda enjoys it almost as much as Maude, so I imagine I'm just missing the finer points of the game's entertainment value." He shrugged. "I've never been lucky enough to win anything," he admitted.

"Oh-sixty-six, oh-clickity-click, oh sixty-six."

"You sure about that, George?"

"Hm?"

Brandon turned the figurine over and George started, then looked down at his sheet in surprise.

"Oh, um, Bingo?"

"See you, Maude."

Her dark eyes amused, Maude waved them away, as the two brothers headed back outside.

PUSS IN D.C.

by Pamela Sargent

Pamela Sargent has won the Nebula Award, the Locus Award, and has been a finalist for the Hugo Award. She is the author of several highly-praised novels, among them *Cloned Lives* (1976), *The Golden Space,* (1979), *The Alien Upstairs* (1983), and *Alien Child* (1988). Gregory Benford described her novel *Venus of Dreams* (1986) as "one of the peaks of recent science fiction." *Venus of Shadows* (1988), the sequel, was called "alive with humanity, moving, and memorable" by *Locus*. *The Shore of Women* (1986), one of Sargent's best-known books, was praised as "a compelling and emotionally involving novel" by *Publishers Weekly*. The *Washington Post Book World* has called her "one of the genre's best writers."

Sargent is also the author of *Ruler of the Sky* (1993), an epic historical novel about Genghis Khan. Her *Climb the Wind: A Novel of Another America,* published in 1999, was a finalist for the Sidewise Award for Alternate History. *Child of Venus,* the third novel in Sargent's Venus trilogy, called "masterful" by *Publishers Weekly,* was published in May 2001. Recent work includes the anthology *Conqueror Fantastic.*

I was trained to be discreet, to keep my extraordinary abilities to myself, but still retain my dreams of public glory, of being openly acknowledged for my accomplishments. Perhaps one day, I muse to myself while grooming my fur or lying about on my favorite pillow, I'll be able to dictate my memoirs and see them set down on paper.

Given the stories I have to tell, there's no question that my book could fetch a large advance from a major publishing house. I can hardly watch television lately without imagining myself matching wits with Charlie Rose, or responding to Larry King's amiable goofball questions with answers that would shame him with my eloquence. Surely Oprah would be interested in a guest who would most likely be the first ever to sit on her lap during the interview, and if Bill O'Reilly got excessively argumentative, a snarl and a display of my front claws should be enough to calm him down. As for book signings, my paw print on the title page ought to serve as well as an autograph.

I would, of course, insist on certain amenities during the rigors of any book tour: a personal assistant to help with grooming and running errands; a comfortable carrying case with ample cushioning; shrimp and crabmeat at least once a day; bottled spring water and the occasional bowl of cream; first class seating instead of consignment to the luggage and cargo hold; and a good workout chasing mice at least two or three times a week. I dream of it all—being number one on the *New York Times* and Amazon lists, being offered a fat chunk of cash for the movie rights to my story and, most important, finally receiving the credit that I deserve for all I've done.

Not that my life is so bad as it is, and there are certain impediments to full disclosure. There's my knowledge of certain Agency operations, for one thing, although I would happily make an agreement not to give away any classified information. And Maury, in spite of his gratitude for everything I've helped him accomplish so far, probably wouldn't want the world to know exactly how much he owes to me, especially now, with more victories assuredly lying ahead of him. There's also the matter of my legal rights, since as a cat, I currently lack the status to sign contracts and make any binding agreements, and wouldn't care to spend the rest of my life in court being a test case for animal rights.

So perhaps these musings of mine should be regarded as mental notes for a memoir I'll probably never be able to write.

The Agency was where my life truly began, with Maury's father, Charles Carabas, as my caretaker and mentor. I have no memory of my life before Mr. Carabas found me, an abandoned kitten, outside his house in Georgetown. Moved by my piteous meows and my plight, he took me in and gave me a home. As a widower who lived alone, he was grateful for my presence, since his son Maury was in law school at the time and came home only for holidays.

Not long after Mr. Carabas had given me shelter, he discovered that I had the ability to speak when I, tiring of my usual fare, politely requested a can of tuna for supper. A lesser person might have been convinced that he had gone mad, and run to a psychiatrist; a more fearful one might have regarded me as a freak of nature and disposed of me somehow. It was my good fortune that Mr. Carabas not only welcomed a feline companion with whom he could carry on a conversation, but also enabled me, with his example, to acquire a verbal facility I might otherwise never have attained. He was an erudite man, a graduate of Harvard and Oxford and occasional lecturer in political philosophy and foreign affairs at Georgetown University. He read voraciously and spoke several languages, which is how I managed to pick up French, Spanish, German, some Japanese, and even a decent command of Arabic. Because he had been employed by the Agency for almost forty years, he had also been well schooled in secrecy and discretion, and taught me to follow his example. I concealed my conversational abilities from other human beings, even from Maury when he was home between semesters.

Often Mr. Carabas brought me to his office at the Agency's headquarters in Langley, Virginia; his fellow intelligence officers tolerated this eccentricity out of their esteem for the old man. I knew how to conduct myself, was soon roaming freely from the seventh-floor offices of the chiefs down to the cubbyholes on the floors below, and quickly became a kind of mascot. Analysts, operatives, and directors welcomed me into their offices, offered me toys stuffed with catnip, fed me treats fetched from the building's dining room, allowed me to nap on their desks or in chairs, and marveled at my ability to perch on toilet seats in the rest rooms in order to relieve myself, thus sparing anyone from having to maintain and clean a litter box for me.

Mr. Carabas had named me Angleton, after James Jesus Angleton, the legendary chief of counterintelligence during the Agency's glory days, and it was a more suitable moniker for me than any of his colleagues realized. As I prowled the hallways and perched on desks, I overheard a good many tidbits, and passed the tastiest of them along to my human companion. Learning how to read, which presented fewer impediments than mastering speech, also enabled me to surreptitiously peruse many a highly classified document; as a result, Mr. Carabas cemented his reputation as someone who knew all, could never be deceived, and was to be feared and respected.

My mentor and caretaker often thought of retiring. For well over a decade and a half, the Agency had endured scandals, humiliating Congressional hearings, ruined careers, and rules that had made nearly everyone overly cautious and suspicious. Operatives who might be required to support covert operations took out liability insurance, foreseeing the day when they might have to face committees of angry politicians demanding answers, along with heavy legal bills. Analysts who reported to the chief of counterterrorism sifted through their data to the point of obsessiveness, fearing that they might miss important clues and thus have to live with being responsible for the deaths of fellow citizens, deaths they might have prevented. All of them were deeply suspicious of a government that promised them support one day, yet might leave them all hanging out to dry the next.

The atmosphere in Langley was not a healthy one, and Mr. Carabas had been warned by his doctors that stress was taking its toll on his heart. But he was a patriot, and devoted to his craft. He would do what he could for his country for as long as possible.

I often think of the last operation he dreamed up but was never able to carry out, the one in which I would have had a crucial role to play. This was during the time a certain Middle Eastern dictator had gone from being a thorn in our side to becoming a knife aimed at our nation's throat. Mr. Carabas, dismayed at the increasing likelihood of war—he had always regarded warfare as a massive failure of intelligence in both senses—had come up with a plan.

He spoke of his scheme one evening when we were by ourselves. His catering service had dropped off several prepared meals for his consumption on those nights when he wasn't out dining with friends or at Washington's better restaurants, while the cleaning woman who came in three days a week had left late that afternoon. "I'd need your assistance, Angleton," Mr. Carabas said to me as I dined on chopped chicken livers and he sipped brandy. "It would mean blowing your cover and risking your life, so I won't hold it against you if you decide not to volunteer."

I felt my whiskers twitch. "Go on, sir," I replied, feeling that I owed it to Mr. Carabas to hear him out.

His plan, to put it simply, was to smuggle me into the dictator's country with a couple of operatives who were working with that nation's resistance movement. A fast-acting and deadly toxin would be applied to my claws, and I would be turned loose near whatever palace was currently housing the tyrant. My mission was to locate that disagreeable fellow, administer the powerful and inevitably fatal poison with a few scratches of my claws, and then make my escape.

"That's the beauty of it," Mr. Carabas continued. "Whatever suspicions might be aroused afterward, no one would be able to prove that it was an assassination. If we're lucky, the evildoer's cronies might begin to think that a usurper among them had found a way to administer poison, and never suspect an outside intelligence service at all. And there wouldn't be any of those blasted hearings with all those windbags in the House and Senate." He peered at me over his snifter. "But it's a lot to ask of you."

"I might have a problem getting close to the man," I said. "He's extremely paranoid, heavily guarded, and has a fetish for personal hygiene." I had picked up those details while eavesdropping on some roundtable discussions at Agency headquarters.

"All true enough, but he also has a great fondness for cats. Magnus Ritchard confirmed that with one of his deep cover contacts just the other day, that's what gave me the idea. Apparently there are cats in every one of the dictator's palaces and hideaways at all times."

"No doubt doubling as his food tasters," I murmured.

"That was also in the report given to Magnus," Mr. Carabas said.

"My biggest problem might be getting past the other cats without engaging in a territorial dispute. If I end up clawing one of them in a fight, and the cat keels over, that would give our whole game away."

Mr. Carabas set down his snifter as I leaped into his lap. "As I told you," he said while scratching me behind the ears, "this has to be your decision. I'll understand if you refuse."

Actually, it wasn't the dangers of the mission that gave me pause. If my human handlers could get me into the country and anywhere near the target, I knew that I could accomplish my task. What worried me more was what might happen to me afterward. My accomplices, and probably others in the Agency, would have to be informed of my abilities if they were to trust me to carry out the mission. Could I rely on all of them to keep my secret? Would I, instead of being rewarded for my success, end up as a prisoner, a caged experimental subject at a government laboratory? Even worse, how could I be sure that the Agency would want to keep me alive after the operation was over? I would, after all, be a loose thread that could tie our intelligence service to the assassination of a foreign leader.

Another danger, however remote, was that some counterspy planted within the Agency by a foreign power might learn about me. Such a mole might try to do away with me, or might even be foolish enough to think that I could be "turned" with bribes of lobster, live mice to chase, and other such luxuries, but in any case, my life would become much more precarious.

I said as much to Mr. Carabas.

"If I could take you on this mission myself," he replied, "I would, but I've been out of that game for too long. I can promise you that I will only send you in with people I trust implicitly."

That was good enough for me. "I'm in, Mr. Carabas." I curled up on his lap and settled in for a nice long nap, dreaming of my eventual triumph.

A week later, just before Maury was to receive his law degree, Mr. Carabas suffered his last heart attack. He was already dead by the time two fellow officers found him in his office, slumped over his desk, his ever-present cup of black coffee spilled across his papers. Had he brought me to the office that day, perhaps I might have saved him; a resonant and persistent repetition of meows might have summoned others to his side in time.

I padded through the house all that night, alone and frantic, fearing for him. Latisha Knowles, our cleaning woman, arrived the next morning at her usual time;

Magnus Ritchard rang the front doorbell only a few minutes later.

"There was nothing they could do for Charles," Mr. Ritchard said to Ms. Knowles before he had even taken off his coat. "He's gone—we'll have to call his son." That was how I learned of Mr. Carabas' passing. Whether he ever had the opportunity to broach the subject of my Middle Eastern mission to Mr. Ritchard or to anyone else at the Agency, I did not know.

Maury flew home immediately to take charge of the funeral arrangements. The Requiem Mass was held at the Dahlgren Chapel on the Georgetown University campus, according to Mr. Carabas' wishes, but the majority of mourners chose to pay their respects to his son at home rather than attend the funeral itself. I well understood their reasons for avoiding the service. For such a large contingent of intelligence officers, politicians, Cabinet secretaries, and notorious figures who had been forced to testify at Congressional hearings about Agency operations to show up at the mass might have aroused too much curiosity and attention. Even so, I wished that there could have been more of a crowd, that I might have been present at the rite. Instead, I circulated among the mourners at home, allowing them to pet me and offering what comfort I could mutely, while longing to speak to them aloud about how much Mr. Carabas had meant to me.

Maury soon discovered that his father had failed to apply his considerable intelligence to his own fiscal affairs. The family legacy that had helped to support Charles Carabas was no more. Taxes were owed, investments had failed, considerable debts had accumulated for the purchases of fine wines, cigars, trips to exotic places, and a library of rare volumes. Consultations with Mr. Carabas' executors revealed that nearly everything would have to be sold, including the Georgetown house, in order to cover everything, leaving Maury with what can only be called a modest inheritance.

"Well, little buddy," Maury said to me one late August night, after the bad news had finally sunk in, "I guess it's just you and me now." I was lying next to him, and offered him a few subdued purrs, grateful to realize that he apparently regarded me as part of his father's legacy. "Don't know what's gonna happen, but I'll always look out for you, Angleton. I know how much you meant to Dad."

I rested my head on my front paws as I considered our situation. Maurice Carabas had, unfortunately, not inherited his sire's considerable intellect. Attendance at one of the country's finest preparatory schools had not entirely prepared young Maury for his father's alma mater of Harvard, to which he was admitted only through much covert pulling of strings. He had flunked out of Harvard after two semesters, barely managed to graduate from Georgetown a few years after that, and considerably more string-pulling had been required to get him into a minor southern law school. That he had finally succeeded in earning a law degree was either a miracle or else a function of that particular law school's lack of rigor. How he was going to establish himself in the world without his father's guidance was not a matter I cared to contemplate too deeply.

Yet Maury, I knew, had some potential. He was, as human beings measure such qualities, an extremely handsome young man. His lack of academic accomplishment had been in part caused by a deep devotion to the pursuits of tennis and golf, but such athletic skills would be useful in enabling him to meet people who might benefit him socially. And he was kind and loyal; he had readily accepted his responsibility for me, with no thought of giving me away or consigning me to a shelter.

I knew then that I could not keep my secret from him any longer. I sat up, gazed directly at him, and said, "Maurice, there is something about me that you should know."

"Hey, you can call me Maury," he said absently. A

few moments later, his eyes suddenly widened and his brows shot up. "You can talk?"

"I just did, didn't I? Your father and I used to engage in many long discourses whenever we were alone. I don't suppose I need to explain to you why we thought it best to keep that to ourselves."

He was still gaping at me. "You can talk?" he said again.

"Yes, I can talk, in English and in other languages as well. Je parle français. Watakushi wa nihongo ga wakarimasu. Ich—"

"I get the picture." Maury shook his head. "I always knew Dad was smart, but I didn't think even he could teach a cat how to talk."

"He didn't teach me how to talk. He was as surprised as you were when I revealed my vocal talents. What he taught me was a certain degree of eloquence."

"Maybe some other stuff, too," Maury said. "Like, I always knew he was a spook, even if I don't know much about what he actually did, so I guess he taught you how to keep a secret, too."

"That he did," I said, "and it would be wise of you to keep this one."

"You don't have to worry about that, old buddy. If I told people I had a talking cat, I'd probably end up in the hat factory. Hell, maybe I am crazy, but if it was just me imagining this, you probably wouldn't sound so smart." He sighed. "I guess you know what we're up against, then. Dad didn't leave me a whole lot. I figure it might be just enough for me to go back to Florida and see what I can set up for myself there. There's a couple of guys I knew at law school who might be able to find me a gig in Tallahassee."

"Is that what you want?" I asked.

"I don't know. I always thought I'd end up back here, in Washington, I mean. Never really thought about living anywhere else, but we've got to be practical now." He patted me gently on the head. "I said

I'd look after you, Angleton, and I meant it. I won't leave for Florida without you."

I was moved, even though the prospect of spending my remaining years in the Florida panhandle was less than enticing. An idea was forming in my mind. "But there's no reason to leave your hometown," I said, "and seek your fortune elsewhere. There would be far better hunting for you in Washington than in Tallahassee."

"Maybe," he said, "but I can't afford to live here now."

"You'll have a nest egg after everything's sold. Would you like my advice?" I asked.

"Sure."

"Use the money to stay in Washington, and leave everything else to me. I've learned a few skills that might stand us both in good stead."

"Really?"

I fixed him with a stare. "Just listen to me, young Maury, and you may find out that you have more of a legacy than you realize."

Mr. Carabas' belongings were auctioned off, the house sold, and the taxes and debts paid, leaving Maury with a slightly larger sum than he had expected. We might have invested some of the money, but Maury knew nothing of such matters. I, given the unfortunate example of Mr. Carabas, knew little more than Maury did about finances, but in any case, the plans I had for him and myself did not involve living modestly on a pittance, being bystanders at life's game instead of players. His father, my rescuer, would have pulled enough strings to get his son set up in a suitable position; in his absence, I could do no less.

"We have to move out by the end of this month," I said to him one evening in Mr. Carabas' library. The built-in bookshelves were empty, all the rare books having been sold at auction, and we were sitting on the floor, since the leather chairs and reading lamps had also been taken away by their new owners.

"I know," Maury replied as he fed me an anchovy from

his pizza, "but every place I've looked at has a rent that's too high. About the only place we could afford would be some shithole in a really bad neighborhood."

"Taking up residence in a shithole would hardly improve your future prospects, Maury. I suggest instead that we move to the Watergate complex and purchase some living space there. It's come to my attention that there are some apartments available in Watergate South." I had found that out at the latest auction of Mr. Carabas' possessions, when one of the buyers had mentioned to another that he was planning to move there soon.

"The Watergate? That's way out of our league, old buddy. I can't afford a place like that."

"You have your inheritance," I said. "That could pay much of the freight, so to speak, and you could borrow the rest, and I vow to you that after the move, you'll be launched on a most promising trajectory."

"I don't think you understand." Maury swallowed more beer from his can. "That would just about clean me out."

"Only if nothing else comes along, and you'll be able to sell your place to another buyer in the future."

"Which just might pay off whatever I end up owing by then."

I accepted another anchovy, then sat back on my haunches. "Maury, think of an apartment in Watergate South not as an expense, but as an investment. If you're going to get anywhere in the world, you have to position yourself among individuals who can help you. Living at the Watergate will put you in close proximity to some influential people."

"And what if nothing else comes along?"

"Leave it to me," I said. "You promised to look after me, and I'll do no less for you. Trust me. After all, we're both in this together."

Maury accepted my advice in the end, largely because he couldn't think of anything else to do. I assisted him with his application to the Watergate cooperative board; he easily won approval, since I was able to demonstrate, by sitting quietly on his lap during his interview and allowing the board members to pet me, how well behaved a creature I am.

By the beginning of January, we were ensconced in a one-bedroom apartment with balcony in Watergate South. By early February, with my advice on whom to call and where to submit his résumé, Maury had secured a position on the staff of one of the senators on the Intelligence Oversight Committee, a gentleman who had always treated employees of the Agency fairly and sympathetically whenever they appeared before him. Maury's salary was small, certainly not enough to cover our expenses, but he was now well situated, with his job and his residence, to meet people who could help him to rise in the world.

By late spring, however, I was coming to see that more action on my part would be needed. Maury was not the sort of fellow likely to become a trusted and influential adviser to his senatorial patron; indeed, he often brought work home with him, or e-mailed it to his home computer, so that I could peruse various studies and polls, read constituents' mail, and advise him on the wording of position papers. Instead of making influential contacts, Maury had made the acquaintance of a number of young ladies, most of them Congressional staffers or interns. From them, he seemed to require only that they be fond of cats and possess a quality he referred to as "bodaciousness." I spent many a night lying on his bed while he and his companion of the evening slept, trying to conjure up a plan of action.

"Maury," I said to him one evening when we were by ourselves, "it's time to cut to the chase."

"What do you mean?" he asked, feeding me a scallop from his take-out carton of Chinese food.

"At the rate you're spending money on wining and dining and tennis playing with your young ladies, we'll be lucky if we have enough money in the end to get to Tallahassee with a low-fare ticket for you and consignment to the cargo hold for me."

"But you said I have to make an impression."

"Making an impression on young ladies nearly as penniless as yourself isn't exactly what I meant. You might at least find someone with more substantial assets."

Maury looked abashed. "It isn't as if I'm not trying. I mean, most of the time they're coming on to me, and I don't, like, ask them about their bank balances. You can't exactly expect a guy to say no when opportunity knocks."

"I suppose not, but these weren't the sort of opportunities I had in mind."

"Anyway, it never lasts," he said. "By the time I'm ready to think about getting serious, they're dumping me and going out with somebody else."

"Which means that going on in this way," I said, "with companions who inevitably tire of you, is both expensive and pointless. We have to take more drastic measures."

He quickly agreed to my tentative plan, which was hardly a plan at all. I was hoping only to scout the territory, so to speak, to see if there was any way to bring Maury to the attention of some of the wealthy and influential human beings who inhabited the Watergate complex. I did not expect an opportunity to do so to land right in front of me.

Early the next morning, Maury and I left our building, he on foot and I in my carrying case. When he was certain that no one was watching us, he opened the case and set me loose. Since it was Saturday, Maury would be able to wait for me until I safely made my way back to Watergate South.

"Take care, little fella," Maury whispered after me as I slipped out of my carrier. "You be really careful, you hear?" He was being far too solicitous. I could easily find my way back, having studied a layout of the complex; in addition, I was wearing an ID tag that I had insisted he buy for me, one that had my name, Maury's name, and our address and phone number engraved upon its surface. Maury's father had always spared me the indignity of a collar, but it was best to be on the safe side. If I did get lost, I didn't want to give myself away by having to ask for directions.

I bounded across the grass, reveling in my freedom. Only a few people seemed to be out, jogging on the pathway near the Potomac or wandering off with guidebooks in the direction of the National Mall. Birds twittered in the tree limbs overhead, and I thought of bagging one or two before resuming my reconnaissance.

Then I spied a glittering loop lying under a shrub. I scurried over to examine the object, and found what looked very much like a bracelet. There was no way to tell if the bright stones of this human limb adornment were of any value or were only cheap imitations, but something about the bracelet attracted me. I rolled around, swatting at it with my paws, and somehow managed to get it hooked around my neck.

A short, sharp, extremely hostile sound suddenly interrupted my play. My ears twitched and my fur stood up; even with my lack of experience in the out-of-doors, I recognized the sound of a dog's bark. I turned my head and moved my eyes just in time to see a large beast bearing down on me from the right, still barking, as a man ran after him waving a long leather strap.

The dog had slipped his leash and was on the warpath. I could either stand my ground and rely on my claws, or flee.

There wasn't time to disentangle myself from the bracelet. I ran, expecting the dog to nip at my tail any second, and managed to claw my way up a tree. The dog circled below, howling and barking, until his human being finally caught up with him. I watched, clinging to safety, as the man hooked the strap onto his collar and led him away.

My heart was beating rapidly. I stretched out on the

limb, reluctant to venture forth again. Dogs weren't my only worry; there might also be stray cats in the area. In a desperate situation, I had a chance of intimidating a dog, but no cat worthy of the name would back down from a fight with me.

I shook myself, trying to free myself of the bracelet, then forced myself to be calm. A survey of the area revealed that I was not that far from the entrance to the Watergate complex's hotel, where a limousine was just pulling up to the entrance.

Something moved below me; a woman in shorts and a baggy shirt was jogging toward me. She stopped under the tree and leaned against the trunk.

"Jesus," I heard her say, "Daddy's going to kill me. He's just going to kill me." She sounded quite distressed.

"Mrrow," I said, thinking that I might be able to use a little help making my way down.

She looked up. Young Maury had always brought home attractive human females, but this one far exceeded them in beauty. Her hair was thick and dark, her eyes large and green, and her teeth were white as she smiled at me.

"You poor kitty," she murmured, and then, "Oh, my God."

"Mrrow," I said again as I crept backward along the limb. When I was halfway down the trunk, hands seized me and gently set me on the ground.

"Nice kitty." She showed me more of her teeth. "You wonderful kitty. You absolutely excellent and terrific little kitty." She reached for the bracelet and removed it from me. "You found my diamond bracelet. Daddy would have just killed me for losing it." She scratched my head; I purred, then rolled around in the grass, showing my belly. "Are you sure you'll be all right? Do you even have a home? I wouldn't mind taking you home myself."

I stretched and got to my feet. She knelt next to me and peered at my tag. "Why, you live around here. I think I'd better take you home."

I squinted at her. I was tempted to scurry away, given that I'd had so little chance to explore my surroundings. But my encounter with the dog had dampened my enthusiasm for more adventures, an extremely large male human being seemed to be watching the young lady and me at a distance, and perhaps it was wiser to take advantage of the safe passage home that this female was offering.

I allowed her to pick me up. She insisted on holding me with my head nestled against her elbow, not exactly the most comfortable position, but I was able to endure my discomfort until we reached Watergate South.

The doorman recognized me as we approached, and quickly opened the door for us. Maury was lurking in the lobby, still clutching my carrying case, as my captor entered the building. "Angleton!" he said to me. "Thank God you're safe."

"Is he yours?" the young woman said.

Maury didn't reply immediately. I had a good look at his face from my vantage point; his mouth was hanging open and his eyes were as glassy as they had been when he first heard me speak.

"Is he your cat?" the woman said. "Are you Maury Carabas? The tag says he belongs to a Maury Carabas." I wriggled around in her arms, trying to leap to the floor. "Hello?" she continued. "Anybody home?"

Maury managed to close his mouth for a moment. "Hello," he said at last in a muted voice. "Yeah, he's my cat."

"It's a good thing I found him, then. You really shouldn't let him run around outside, even if he did find my bracelet for me. I was afraid I'd never see it again." Her arms tightened around me. "You should be a lot more careful with this wonderful, beautiful kitty."

"I know, but Angleton has a mind of his own." Maury still had a dazed look on his face. "What's your name?"

"Desirée."

"That's a beautiful name."

This hardly passed as witty repartee, but the young woman was now staring at Maury in the same stupefied fashion as he was gazing at her. "Maury's a nice name, too," she replied.

"I work for Senator Trilby. I'm a member of his staff."

"I'm here in Washington with my father," Desirée said. "He always stays at the hotel here when he's in town."

They continued to stare at each other for a while, while I longed to feed Maury some more eloquent lines of conversation, until he leaned over and opened the top of the case. "In you go, old buddy," he said as he took me from Desirée and deposited me in my container. "Um, I know this is kind of sudden, but after I take Angleton back to the apartment, would you like to have a cup of coffee with me?"

"Sure. I'll wait down here."

I sighed with exasperation as Maury picked up the case. Risking my hide so that he could find yet another young lady to waste his money on was not what I'd had in mind.

"You can come up to my place if you want."

"Better not." She gestured toward the doors. "One of my security people probably followed me here. He won't bother us if I wait for you here, but he'd probably want to check you out before I went off with you."

"Your security people?" Maury asked.

"My bodyguards. It's not my idea, but Daddy insists on it whenever I'm out jogging or shopping or wandering around. The only thing he gave in on is that they have to keep their distance while they're protecting me. I mean, like, what kind of social life would I have if they were standing right next to me all the time?"

Bodyguards, I thought; people of limited means usually did not hire such protection. Perhaps this young woman had more substantial resources than I realized.

"With the crime rate in this town," Maury said, "maybe your dad's got a good idea."

A man came through the entrance. Peering up through the metal bars of my carrier, I recognized the rather large individual I had spotted outside earlier.

"Jeez, Jeffrey," Desirée said to this man, "you don't have to come in here. It's cool. Like, all I was doing was giving this guy's cat back to him."

The man touched the cap over his brow with one hand. "Never hurts to double-check, Ms. Morlock."

"Morlock?" Maury said.

"That's my last name," the young woman said.

"Any relation to Roland Morlock?" Maury asked.

"He's my dad."

I had to restrain myself from rolling around inside my carrier in ecstasy. A lost bracelet and an unleashed dog had led Maury and me to the daughter of the richest and most powerful media lord in the country.

Maury and Desirée were soon keeping company, so much so that the *Washington Post*'s society pages began to take note of the fact. Whenever the two weren't spending time in the Royal Suite at the Watergate's Swissôtel, they were playing tennis, picnicking in Rock Creek Park, working out at the hotel's health club, playing golf in Chevy Chase, attending yet another performance at the Kennedy Center, or jetting up to New York City for a weekend of theater performances and club-hopping. Often I accompanied them on these junkets, packed in my carrier and safely in the keeping of one of Ms. Morlock's bodyguards.

That Desirée and Maury had a certain lack of intellectual prowess in common only seemed to strengthen their bond; however vacuous they might have seemed to many of their former loves, they never bored each other. The two were together nearly every evening, and on those rare occasions when they were not, Desirée called on the telephone and engaged Maury in lengthy if often monotonous conversations. They spent their evenings at Mr. Morlock's hotel suite, where Desirée had remained even after her father returned to New York, or at Maury's apartment, where they could barely restrain themselves from expressing their affection at almost any opportunity.

The young woman's increasing fondness for Maury also encompassed me, the cat who had found her bracelet and had enabled her to meet the man who had, so she proclaimed, become the love of her life. When they were not at Maury's apartment, the two brought me to the hotel suite with them. Whenever they dined on take-out or room service food, they fed me tidbits with their fingers, and because Desirée was always dieting, I had my choice of abundant leftovers.

Even more miraculously, Roland Morlock, upon meeting Maury, took a strong liking to him. I suppose that I can claim some credit for that, as I was careful to rehearse Maury in a recitation of Mr. Morlock's prehistoric political views before he met his love's father for the first time; by repeating Mr. Morlock's various statements or else keeping his mouth shut and nodding while the great man expounded on politics and society, Maury had made a stunningly good impression on Desirée's father. It was also true that Mr. Morlock had grown increasingly distressed at seeing stories about his daughter's nocturnal shenanigans regularly appear in the publications of several of his competitors. Maury, to his mind, was a great improvement over Desirée's past suitors.

Maury's prospects had never been brighter. One of the wealthiest young ladies in the world adored him, and it was increasingly likely that their strong attachment to each other would eventually result in matrimony. Mr. Morlock, during his visits to Washington, often spoke of various executive positions that Maury might some day occupy in one of his companies.

I should have been as delighted as a cat roaming in a garden of catnip, but I had miscalculated Maury's capacity for subtlety. Knowing that Mr. Morlock was extremely wary of young men who were unduly interested in his daughter's financial assets, I had advised Maury to hint that he was a young man of considerable means. "You don't want Roland Morlock to think of you as a fortune hunter," I had told him, "especially since young Desirée, according to a recent article in *Vanity Fair*, has already had a couple of unfortunate and expensive involvements with mercenary young men of dubious antecedents. The only way to convince him that you're not after his daughter's money is to act as though money doesn't matter to you—in other words, as if you have more than enough of it yourself."

"I always foot the bill when we go out," Maury said. "I'm not exactly a cheap bastard."

"True enough," I said, well aware of how rapidly our scanty resources were being depleted, "but we've reached a point where more is required. You're already living as a young man of means might, and you have an eminently respectable family background, thanks to your father, but it wouldn't hurt to drop a few hints about other assets."

"How the hell do I do that?"

I repressed a sigh, which would only have escaped me as a snarl. "You might mention your occasional enjoyment of a good horseback ride in the Virginia hills, thus leading Mr. Morlock to assume that you possess a horse or two, even a stable and a farm. You can imply that your broker was smart enough to get you out of the market just before the dotcom and telecommunications fiascoes. You needn't say anything outright, or make any overt claims that could easily be checked. The trick is to leave a certain impression."

Maury not only followed my advice, but also exceeded it. Four months after meeting Desirée Morlock, he had managed to convince her father that he had a few million salted away in bonds and other investments, that the acreage of his Virginia farm encompassed a county or two, and that he had given up his late father's Georgetown home for the Watergate only because the house had evoked too many painful memories of his beloved sire. Had he been more discreet and ambiguous, he might have been safely wedded to Desirée before her father discovered his true net worth. By then, Mr. Morlock, faced with a happily married daughter, would most likely have overlooked the matter, especially since he would have had to admit to himself that he had drawn his own conclusions too readily from some rather vague statements of Maury's. He was not a man who cared to admit his own mistakes.

But he was also not a man who would allow his daughter to marry a four-flusher. The truth would come out, either through Mr. Morlock's investigations or else in some published item by an inquisitive journalist. Maury, by being too specific instead of ambiguous in his statements, would soon be exposed as an outright liar, and I had no way to avert the disaster that would ensue.

Maury and Desirée had jetted off to Los Angeles in one of her father's Gulfstreams for a week-long vacation before Christmas. They had wanted to bring me with them, but I had explained to Maury privately that I had other fish to fry.

There was much for me to ponder in his absence. I spent a couple of days at Maury's computer, which he had left on for me, distracting myself by researching real estate listings in Tallahassee. At last I removed my paw from the mouse and closed my overstrained eyes.

The truth of our situation could escape me no longer; we would soon be penniless. The longer we stayed in Washington, and the more prolonged Maury's courtship of Desirée became, the greater the chance of exposure, and of Mr. Morlock's parting the two lovers decisively and forever.

It was time for desperate measures. Perhaps if we decamped from the Watergate and headed south, Desirée would be moved to follow Maury there, and would quickly agree to marry him so as not to lose him again. It wasn't much of a plan, but I was hard-pressed to come up with anything more promising. We might be able to scrape together enough to afford one of the modestly priced bungalows in the Tallahassee listings.

As I contemplated this half-baked idea, there was a rattling outside our door. My ears flicked as I heard the almost imperceptible sound of the lock turning. Desirée had left her bodyguard Jeffrey at her hotel suite with orders to come over twice a day to feed me and clean out my litter box, but he had already completed his rounds.

The door opened. The silhouette outlined by the lights in the hallway was much smaller than Jeffrey's large form. Someone was breaking into the apartment.

I leaped down from my chair, frantically looking for a place to hide in the large room that constituted most of our living space. It was unlikely that a burglar would go out of his way to harm me, but I wanted a good look at the miscreant in order to be able to describe him later to Maury before he contacted the police.

"Angleton," the intruder said then; I had heard that voice before. "Angleton, I know you're here." The door slammed shut behind him; heels clicked against the marble floor of the foyer. "You'd better come out."

I slipped under the dining room table, holding my breath, then crept toward our Christmas tree. An overhead light suddenly illuminated the room as I scrambled under the tree's lowest branches. "Come out, Angleton," the man said. "You can't hide from me, I'm afraid I know all about you. Charles told me your secret, just before his death, while we were planning a certain operation in the Middle East. I know all about what your role in that mission was to be."

I saw his face now, and recognized Magnus Ritchard. For such an experienced operative to get past the doorman and our building's security systems and to acquire copies of our keys was probably a simple matter. But why was he here? Perhaps the Agency had

finally given the go-ahead for the obstreperous dictator's assassination, and Mr. Ritchard was here to enlist
my services in that effort.

He sat down on the sofa. "Here, kitty, kitty."

I crept out from under the tree, still apprehensive.
Mr. Carabas would never have confided our secret
to his colleague unless he had trusted Mr. Ritchard
implicitly, yet I remained suspicious. If the man
wanted my help in one of the Agency's operations,
surely he could have contacted me in some other way.

"Mrrow," I said.

"Don't get funny with me, Angleton. I know you
can do more than meow. Charles told me all about
your long conversations and how many languages you
managed to pick up. I know you can understand every
word I'm saying to you."

I moved a little closer and sat down a few feet away
from his feet. "I know all about you," Mr. Ritchard
continued, "and I'm the only one who knows, now that
Charles is dead. There's something I have to discuss
with you, and unless we come to an understanding,
your nine lives will pass very quickly, I promise you."

My fur rose along my spine; he was threatening me.
He would not have had to threaten me to enlist me in
any Agency operation; evoking the memory of Mr. Carabas would have been enough to win my cooperation.
Mr. Ritchard, I feared, was playing another game.

"Mrrow," I said again.

"You'd better listen, you little fleabag. This isn't
about that mission Charles and I were planning. That
never got past a couple of discussions we had by ourselves. This little meeting involves you and that doofus
you're living with, and if you're not cooperative, a lot
of very unpleasant things can happen to recalcitrant
kitty cats and their masters. Nobody else in the
Agency knows about you, either, so don't think you
can go running to them for protection."

I stretched out, still keeping my eyes on him.

"It's very simple," Mr. Ritchard said. "You'll go on
living with Maury, and every once in a while, you'll

report to me. That isn't asking so much, is it? Later on, when we figure out how to make the best use of him, there'll be more for you to do, but nothing as risky as what Charles was planning for you in the Middle East. Once Maury's married to the Morlock girl, he'll start rising in her father's company, and having somebody in place to watch him and maybe to help in using him later on could be very beneficial to us." He paused. "Wouldn't surprise me if you had something to do with getting those two together."

Somehow I restrained myself from hissing at him. Roland Morlock, who never missed a chance to wave the flag either figuratively or literally, would happily have cooperated with the Agency on anything they asked of him, so why all this hugger-mugger? In any case, given Maury's precarious situation, Magnus Ritchard would have to find another way to spy on the Morlock enterprises.

"You'd better start piping up," Mr. Ritchard said, "or it won't go well for you." He glanced toward the glass-covered door that led to the balcony. "I don't think even a cat could survive a twelve-story drop. Especially if I wring your furry little neck first."

I sat up. "Very well, Mr. Ritchard," I said, "but I fear you're too late. Young Maury's marital prospects aren't looking especially good at the moment."

"Holy Christ," he said. "You sound just like Jeremy Irons."

"Not quite. I'm afraid I picked up a fair number of mid-Atlantic locutions from Mr. Carabas."

"What do you mean, Maury's marital prospects aren't looking good? Is that Morlock girl getting tired of him already?"

"All indications are that Ms. Morlock is still besotted with him," I replied, "but that may not matter in the end. Her father's probably already poking around doing background checks on Maury, and when he finds out how impoverished he is, he's not likely to consider him a fit mate for his daughter."

"There's nothing wrong with being broke."

"There is if you've led someone to believe otherwise."

Mr. Ritchard shook his head. "He can't be that broke if he's living here."

"He's living here well over his head, I assure you. Mr. Morlock is well aware that Maury's riches don't come anywhere close to equaling his own—that's not the problem. The problem is that he believes Maury to be far more prosperous than he is. When he finds out—"

"I can guess," Mr. Ritchard interrupted. "He's going to think Maury's a gold digger. He'll make sure they don't get married after all."

"Exactly." I kept myself still and restrained myself from flicking my tail, but my mind was racing. Magnus Ritchard could not be here on the Agency's behalf; he had something else in mind. I didn't know what kind of game he was playing, or who was behind him, but he wouldn't be the first mole or double agent who had infiltrated our intelligence agencies, or the first who had decided a foreign power could reward him more lavishly than his own country.

"That's too bad," he muttered ominously, and I smelled danger. He had threatened me; now that I was useless to him, he might already be plotting how to get rid of me.

"About the most we can hope for," I said, "is that when Mr. Morlock learns the truth, he offers Maury a nice chunk of change to get out of Desirée's life."

"That wouldn't exactly serve my purposes."

"What I meant is that Maury, being the kind of fellow he is, would almost certainly turn the money down. And at that point, perhaps Mr. Morlock would be moved enough by his sincerity to relent."

Mr. Ritchard scowled. "I don't know if Morlock is that sentimental."

"I am sorry to be the bearer of bad tidings," I said, "but whatever plans the Agency might have for Maury may have to be abandoned." Despite my words, I was now sure that Magnus Ritchard was not here on the Agency's business, and kept my eyes on him, watching for any sudden and threatening moves on his part. "It's a pity we can't just magically make large sums appear in his accounts."

Mr. Ritchard was silent for a while. "Is that what it would take?" he asked. "Just making it look like he has a fat wad tucked away?"

I sensed then that I was on to something; maybe I could use this man for my own ends. "Well, yes," I said. "If only Mr. Morlock's background checks could turn up a few million in accounts and investments in Maury's name, we'd be home free. But it's useless to hope. I feel badly about that, Mr. Ritchard, you know that I'd do anything I could for you and the Agency, but . . ."

"I might be able to handle this." He rubbed his chin. "I can get the money wired to me, since it would only be a loan. Maury won't need it once he gets past Morlock's background checks."

"True enough."

"It'd be well worth it to me. I just about promised that I could pull this off, get somebody into Morlock's group. I just didn't tell anybody how I was going to do it. I'll get the money, Angleton, and open the accounts myself, and backdate the records so it looks like Maury's had it for a while."

"That would be most advisable." I stretched myself, then settled down on the floor once more. "And I'll have to verify that those accounts actually exist."

"I'll bring you all of the passwords." He glanced at the computer. "You can go online and check out the accounts for yourself. When you let me know Maury's passed muster with Morlock, I'll close them out. And then you and I will stay in touch on a regular basis, and you'll follow my instructions, or—" He let the word hang in the air.

"I assume," I said, "that I should tell Maury nothing about this arrangement."

"You are a smart little kitty." He stood up. "Just make sure you don't let me down."

"I have no intention of doing so. Maury will be

back in Washington by next weekend. When do you plan to return here with verification that the accounts have been opened in his name?"

Mr. Ritchard thrust his hands inside the pockets of his coat. "I think I can get it settled by Friday."

"Then come back here after dark. I assume that you can find your way in here again."

"See you then, Angleton. Just don't try to cross me. You wouldn't care for the consequences to you and Maury if you do."

I slept restlessly the next day, my thoughts roiling as I tossed and turned on my favorite cushion. Magnus Ritchard had to be in the employ of a foreign intelligence service. That was the only way he could have arranged for Maury to be worth a few million on a temporary basis so quickly; the red tape required by the Agency would never have allowed for such a rapid transfer of funds. Someone wanted to plant an operative at the heart of Roland Morlock's media empire. For what purpose, I did not know, but could safely assume that the purpose was not to improve television news coverage, produce finer motion pictures, or publish only the best of the world's literature.

What could I do to foil Ritchard's plans? I could not reveal my secret to Desirée's bodyguard Jeffrey and enlist him as my protector. Maury, however devoted to me, would also be of little use in solving my dilemma. No one at the Agency was likely to take the word of a talking cat over one of their most trusted operatives, and Ritchard would probably see that I ended up in a government laboratory for my pains. I could pretend to fall in with Ritchard's plans, and string him along for a while, but there would be hell to pay when he discovered my deception; I took his threats quite seriously.

I could rely only on myself. Realizing that plunged me into a deep well of despair and helplessness. I was unable to eat, even when Jeffrey set down my favorite foods, unable to emit even the faintest of purrs while he combed my fur. Magnus Ritchard had as much as said that no one else knew about me, either at the Agency or among his foreign contacts; admitting that he would be working through a talking cat would have done little to establish his credibility.

The conclusion was inescapable: I could thwart Ritchard's plans only by getting rid of him entirely. But if I succeeded in that, I would also erase any tracks that might lead his coconspirators to me and to Maury.

The cloud of despair lifted a little at that thought. I forced myself up and padded through the apartment, working myself up to a run, flexing my muscles. My task was a dangerous one, but surely no riskier than my foray into the Middle East would have been.

After all, I was a cat, and therefore a superior creature, wasn't I?

Magnus Ritchard returned at the appointed time on Friday. He had memorized the passwords for Maury's temporary accounts, had me recite them, then allowed me to sit on his lap while he accessed the accounts on the computer. The figures scrolling up on the monitor revealed that Maury now had a net worth of some nine million dollars.

"That should be enough to satisfy Mr. Morlock," I said as the Windows desktop reappeared on the screen. "If he completes his background checks before Christmas, and if Maury and Ms. Morlock are officially engaged by New Year's, you can close out the accounts early in January."

"It might be safer to make sure they're married first."

"They're likely to proceed to the wedding quite rapidly," I said. "Ms. Morlock is quite impetuous, and her father is increasingly anxious to see her settled." I hopped down from his lap. "If you'd care to toast our new arrangement, there's some Scotch in the cabinet over the kitchen sink. And you might set out a can of salmon for me."

"I think I'd better be on my way."

"Then perhaps you can do me a favor," I said. "I've been cooped up in here all week, and wouldn't mind getting a little air. Could you open the door to the balcony for me?"

"It's December, Angleton."

"Just for a minute or two. Cold weather doesn't bother me, what with all this fur, and I do need to stretch my legs."

"Fine." Ritchard shrugged back into his coat and walked toward the balcony, with me at his heels. He opened the door; I took a breath as we stepped outside. The weather was colder than I had expected, the balcony dusted with a light covering of snow.

I bounded across the balcony and hopped up onto the ledge. "God," Ritchard said as he came up behind me, "it's cold as hell out here." He was close enough to me now; his hands rested on the ledge next to me, and he had leaned forward slightly. I reared up on my back legs, extended my claws, and leaped at his face, aiming for his eyes.

He was too fast for me. His arm came up, swatting me, and then I was suddenly falling from the balcony. A gust of wind caught me from below; I spread my limbs as something hard rushed up to meet me. For a moment, I hung from the bare bough of a tree, until my claws lost their grip. I continued to fall, was briefly captured by another branch, and finally came to rest on a thick wooden limb.

I lay there for a long time, afraid to move, then tentatively stretched my front legs. Apparently I was unhurt; the tree had broken my fall. Relief swept through me, raising my fur; I backed halfway down the tree, then leaped to the ground.

Above me, lights shone from the concave grill of Watergate South. If I circled the building and made my way to the front entrance, either the doorman or a resident returning home was likely to see me, and my tag would tell them where I belonged. I padded over the thin layer of snow, felt the cold against my paws, then thought of Magnus Ritchard.

I had failed Maury, and wondered what would happen now. Perhaps Ritchard assumed that I had met my demise, and had already vacated our quarters. Perhaps he took nothing for granted, and was already looking for me.

In the distance, I heard the sound of many human voices. A group of people bearing objects of light in their hands came around the side of the building. They were singing, and I paused for a moment to listen to their words. "Silent night," they sang, "holy night, all is calm, all is bright."

Then a beam of light shot toward me; I froze, blinded by the light. A second later, a piercing voice called out, "It's a lost cat!"

I narrowed my eyes. "The poor thing," another person called out. The group of singers was coming toward me, and then I saw the shadowy form of another human being rush up from behind them.

"I think that's my cat," the newcomer said, and I recognized the voice of Magnus Ritchard.

I turned and ran, heedless of where I was headed, until I glimpsed a parkway and, just beyond it, the wrinkled dark surface of the Potomac. The sound of the traffic was a muffled roar. I crept down to the parkway, flattening my ears as the roaring grew louder, then looked back.

The singers were small black shapes and patches of light against the serpentine curve of Watergate South. Magnus Ritchard was a large shadow with flapping arms bearing down on me; I hadn't realized he was so close.

"Angleton," he shouted, "you won't get away from me."

Terrified, I fled onto the parkway. Bright circles of light swelled as they rushed toward me; the shrieks and roars of motor vehicles nearly deafened me. Somehow I reached the other side of the thoroughfare unscathed.

Ahead of me lay the river. I looked around frantically for another escape route. An odd screaming sound came to me, and then the sound of a loud moist slap.

I crept toward the parkway. The roaring sound was fading; vehicles slowed, then came to a stop, their eyes of light still aglow. The dark shape of Magnus Ritchard lay in the road, unmoving, looking as though a giant arm had scooped him up and thrown him there.

I was able to make my way back across the parkway and around to the front of our building. By then, I was shivering from both nerves and the cold, and was far too weak to call attention to myself. It was my good fortune that a neighbor of Maury's found me lying there and brought me to the attention of the night doorman, who wrapped me in a blanket and got a few drops of warm soup down my throat before I fell into a deep sleep.

Maury returned home the next day. By then, I had been brought to our apartment, and Jeffrey, summoned there by our building's manager, was nursing me back to health.

"Well, little buddy," Maury said to me after Jeffrey had left us, "I heard all about your adventure. Maybe you can tell me just how you managed to get outside."

I considered how much to tell him. With Magnus Ritchard out of the way, there was no need to reveal the whole story.

"It would be wise of you," I began, "to advise the managers of this complex that their security procedures should be tightened. Somehow an intruder was able to get into this apartment. While searching the place for something to steal, he opened the door to our balcony and stepped outside. Perhaps he wanted some air, or to take in the view."

"Maybe he wanted to listen to some Christmas carols," Maury said. "The doorman said there was a bunch of carolers here from George Washington Uni-

versity last night. I mean, even burglars probably have
some holiday spirit."

"In any case, I slipped outside while the door was
open, only to be trapped on the balcony when the
door was closed again behind me. Knowing that I
would surely suffer from exposure to the cold air if I
remained out there for too long, I forced myself to
leap from the railing, hoping that the trees below
would break my fall. After that, I was luckily able to
get to our building's entrance."

"You're a tough little guy, Angleton." He gave me
a hug. "Got to admit it. I don't know what I'd do
without you. Anyway, it doesn't look like anything
was stolen, not that I have that much to steal." He
hugged me again. "You could have been killed. I
heard there was an accident on the parkway last night.
I'm just glad you're safe."

"Maury," I said, "I urge you to plight your troth to
Ms. Morlock as soon as possible. I think your courtship has lasted quite long enough."

"I think so, too, and Desirée'd marry me in a second. But what happens when her old man finds out
I'm broke?"

"You needn't worry about that," I murmured. "I
predict that he'll welcome you into his family with
open arms after his background checks are completed.
Let's just say that your assets may be greater than
you think."

Maury and Desirée were married that winter, in a
hastily organized but lavish ceremony at St. Patrick's
Cathedral in New York, followed by a reception at
the Plaza. Not long after that, Maury began his mete-
oric rise through the executive ranks of Morlock Enterprises. Although Maury benefited from my advice,
and was soon a well-known public figure through his
frequent appearances on radio and television talk
shows, celebrity-filled social galas, charity events, and
political fund-raisers, it soon became clear to Mr. Mor-

lock that his son-in-law's particular gifts were perhaps better suited to some other occupation than that of managing a media conglomerate.

Which is why now, four years after leaving Washington, Maury and Desirée and I are returning to that city. Much as I've enjoyed our time in Manhattan, with my own suite of rooms in our domicile, I am looking forward to taking up residence on my old territory. As I was Maury's chief campaign adviser, I can claim some of the credit for his victory, although he might not so easily have won election to the Senate without the vast resources of the Morlock fortune to aid his quest.

To celebrate his victory, Maury bought me a handcrafted pair of red leather Italian boots, which may seem a rather odd, even kinky, accessory for a cat. But my back legs have never been quite the same since my terrified flight from Magnus Ritchard, and I find that a soft pair of boots eases my aches and pains considerably. I've grown more solicitous of my health lately, controlling my intake of treats, working out on my treadmill, chasing catnip mice thrown to me by Desirée. With the opportunities that now lie ahead for Maury, I plan to be around long enough to wear my boots in the White House as First Cat.

A FAUST FILMS PRODUCTION

by Janeen Webb

Janeen Webb is Reader in Literature at ACU National (Melbourne, Australia). She is a scholar and critic as well as a writer of fiction. She has won a World Fantasy Award (for *Dreaming Down-Under*) and both the Aurealis and Ditmar Awards for her short stories. Her current series for young adults is *The Sinbad Chronicles: Book 1, Sailing to Atlantis,* and *Book 2, The Silken Road to Samarkand,* are out now. *Book 3: Flying to Babylon,* is in progress. Her current scholarly work is an annotated critical edition, co-authored with Andrew Enstice, of Kenneth Mackay's 1895 scientific romance, *The Yellow Wave.*

JOHNNY Faust was sitting in Romeo's, sipping his usual café latte, when all hell opened up at his feet. The floor split with a hissing sound like a huge espresso machine, and the smell of sulfur leaked into the air. The woman at the next table wrinkled her nose and looked up from her magazine to stare accusingly at him. He blushed and looked down.

The hole was getting wider, and in its depths he could see a Bosch landscape of damned souls in torment—there were crazed creatures wielding pitchforks, cauldrons suspended above licking flames, deep pits of burning brimstone, the whole nightmarish medieval scenario. He turned away politely, and went back to calling his mother on the mobile.

"Hi. Johnny here. Have you thought any more about my proposition?"

"Too expensive, darling."

"Oh, come on, Mother. You know you can afford it. Look, it's a great script. I just need to be in Cannes to put the deal together. Everyone will be there."

"Can't you phone them? Fax them? E-mail them? Hold an online video conference? God knows, there's enough technology in that apartment of yours."

"No. I told you. I need to be there in person to press the flesh, to oil the wheels. It's business."

"Okay. But I still don't understand why you need twenty thousand."

Johnny thought Mother sounded peevish. And she was being so damned unreasonable. He tried again, wheedling. "I thought I had explained. I have to go first class, have to look as if I can afford it. As if I don't need them. As if I'm doing them a favor letting them in on the deal. You know how it goes, Mother. Money makes money. If you look hungry, they'll feed you to their dogs. That's why I need the twenty gees. Think about it. There's the airfare, and the Ritz Carlton is expensive. And I'll need a car, a limousine, and there'll be other expenses: dinners, first nights, casinos, you know the sort of thing. I might have to make a quick trip to LA to see my agent, and if the project is as hot as I think it is, I'll need to be in London and then maybe in Brussels to broker the deal."

"So how come you didn't wrap it up when you were in London last year? That little trip cost thirty thousand, as you'll recall. And you made nothing. Zip. Zero. I had to cancel my own holiday." She paused, letting the guilt register.

It didn't work. Johnny was used to guilt. It didn't bother him.

"Listen, Mother. You know I'll pay you back when I get the film money. We're talking millions here, with a nice little percentage for me. I'll even pay you top interest. How's that?"

"Why don't you sell the Jag?"

"I need transport."

"The beach house at Sorrento, then?"

"Can't. It's in Michelle's name. And she insists on keeping it for the kids."

"Mortgage the penthouse, then. Melbourne real estate is always good for a loan."

"You know it's already mortgaged. Do you think I'd be asking you if there was any other way?" Johnny was getting exasperated. "Just think about it, all right? We can both make a tidy sum, but the film business is not for the fainthearted. Dad would've understood. How do you think he made all that money you spend on clothes and lunches?"

Reverse guilt. It served only to increase his mother's sense of being unfairly used. Her son reminded her, suddenly, of her late unlamented husband in one of his less tractable moods. She hadn't liked him all that much. "Your sainted father has gone to his rest," she said tartly.

"All right, Mother. Point taken. I know you control the purse strings now." His temper was rising. "But I'll be damned if I'll let this deal go. You have to help me."

"I'll think about it, Johnny, but I'm getting tired of throwing away good money after bad on these movie schemes of yours. Why don't you go back to one of those nice television production companies that used to pay you so well? Going freelance hasn't improved your finances or your temper one little bit."

This one hit home. She knew perfectly well that his departure had been so acrimonious that he *couldn't* go back to TV production work, even if he wanted to. Which he didn't.

Johnny sighed. "Very well, Mother. We'll talk later. Kiss kiss."

He cut the connection.

And looked down again.

Now he could see into the very heart of darkness, where a huge dark angel was lying chained to the surface of a great molten lake that burned with black flames. There were muffled shrieks from tortured souls in the background. Lucifer looked straight up at him and winked.

Johnny found himself smiling back, an easy smile of unspoken complicity.

"Excuse me, may I join you?"

The speaker was immaculately dressed. He stood by the pit, brushing tiny specks of sulfur from the shoulders of his dark Saville Row suit, checking the black flame-opal cuff links on his snowy French cuffs.

Johnny felt suddenly underdressed in his Calvin Klein jeans and butter-yellow cashmere sweater. His Gucci loafers looked scuffed beside the polished Ferragamo leather shoes standing next to him. His navy sports jacket was draped nonchalantly over the back of his chair—he wished he'd kept it on, if only for the authority of its shoulder pads.

"Yes, of course. Please do." Johnny put down his mobile phone and held out a hand. "Faust. John B. Faust. Producer."

The man shook the hand. He looked completely relaxed. The pit began to close. "Mephistopheles. Broker. At your service."

He sat.

An aproned waiter appeared at his elbow. The broker didn't miss a beat. "Double espresso," he said. Hot and strong." He looked at Johnny. "Another latte?"

"Sure," said Johnny. "Why not?"

The waiter disappeared once more in the direction of the groaning coffee machine, and Johnny turned back to his new companion.

"That's an unusual name," he said, twisting his napkin in his hands as he spoke. "Must be a tricky one for a broker. Mephistopheles, you said, as in Satan's envoy?"

"The same. Beelzebub, Belial, Abaddon, Asmodeus, Ehlis, Mephisto. Shall I go on? My names are many. Choose any one you fancy. You can even call me Nick, if it makes you feel more comfortable. But my role as broker is unchanged, whatever name you select. And my rates are always the same."

Johnny smiled, suddenly sure that his pals must have set him up. He decided to play along. "Then what are you doing out of hell?"

"Why, this *is* hell. And I'm doing my job. I came at your summons, Mr. Faust. How may I help you?"

Johnny examined his fingernails, as if he was looking for clues. "I must have overdone the dope last night. I can't be having this conversation."

"Why not?"

"You aren't real. And even if you were, I didn't call you."

The coffee arrived. Mephistopheles sipped thoughtfully. "I'm real enough to enjoy a good Colombian blend, Mr Faust. And I beg to differ. You did call me. Often. Most frequently in this past week. Just this morning you screamed at your wife that you'd be damned if you'd let her stand in the way of your future, and I just heard you tell your mother you'd prefer damnation to losing your film deal. You've shown a lot of interest in hell lately, and I judged that you wished to summon me. So here I am. Ready to broker you the deal of a lifetime."

Johnny said nothing. He would not even look at his companion. The man's acrid cologne was starting to give him a slight headache.

Mephistopheles drained his coffee cup. "I'm a busy man, Mr. Faust. If you don't want my help, I'll be on my way. I have places to go, faces to meet. But you might just ask yourself how some of your competitors are getting *their* money."

Johnny pulled his thoughts together. "Look," he said, "I don't believe in hell. Or devils."

"Fine. I'll just be on my way, then, and you can pretend this conversation didn't happen." Mephistopheles gave him a knowing look. "But," he went on, "it's a great pity. My firm has a lot of money to spend, and we're looking for new film projects right now. Your agent sent us your script, and we loved it. We could be talking forty, fifty million here."

Johnny couldn't help himself. If this was a setup, it was damned good. "How do I know you're legit?"

"You can't consult your contacts on this one. They all know me in the business, of course. And if you ask outright, they'll all deny it. The secrecy clause is part of the contract." Mephistopheles shrugged. "But you could just mention my name. If you pay attention, you'll catch them looking shifty and trying to work out whether you've signed on or not. Whether you're part of the club, whether you're on the A list or not. Because if you *are* an insider, the deals are limitless." He glanced at his Rolex. "Didn't you know?"

He stood. "I'll leave a card with you," he said. "If you change your mind, get in touch with my bankers. They'll set up an appointment."

He turned and simply disappeared. His drained coffee cup was still warm on the table, a black calling card sitting neatly beside it.

Johnny couldn't resist taking up the card. Its expensive black matte surface was embossed in red letters: *The Broker's Group.* There was an upscale Collins Street business address, and a single telephone number.

Johnny went back to the business of the morning. But after a couple more fruitless calls to halfhearted financial backers, and a few more brush-offs by movie industry flackers, he found himself looking once more at the black card. It couldn't hurt to make an appointment. Talk to these guys. He prided himself on following every lead. If it *was* a setup, he'd grant his pals their fun. If not . . . well, you never knew when something might turn up trumps.

He punched in the numbers. He was put on hold for a time, then a suave female voice answered his query. "I'm afraid Mr. Mephistopheles is unavailable at the moment, but he is expecting you. He has a luncheon engagement, but is free later in the day. Would three thirty this afternoon be convenient for your meeting?"

Johnny took a deep breath. "Fine," he said. "I'll look forward to meeting you, Ms. . . . ?"

"Good-bye, Mr. Faust. We'll have everything ready for you this afternoon." And she was gone.

Johnny paid his bill, surprised that there was no charge on it for his visitor's coffee. He shrugged, and headed for home. He spent the rest of the morning working on his pitch for The Broker's Group, setting up his presentation folder, printing up a new copy of his script, getting his figures in order. Then he made a few more calls—no one among his consultants and contacts would admit to having heard of the Group, but all of them hinted that it wouldn't do any harm to check them out. Everyone was always hungry in this business. He gave up on the information trail, opting instead for a chicken salad sandwich in the kitchen. Then he padded off to his bathroom for a long, hot shower and some careful personal grooming. He wouldn't be caught out again.

By three twenty-five he was being shown into The Broker's Group Building, right at the top end of town. He didn't remember it being there, but the tower of dark tinted glass and polished black granite looked very substantial. The private offices were on the top floor—the concierge had held a muted conversation before even letting the visitor across the minimalist chic foyer with its glass and steel tables and uncomfortable looking chairs. *Tight security,* Johnny thought. *A good sign.* He checked his appearance in the full-length elevator mirror: a handsome, blond-haired man looked back at him. He was wearing a perfectly tailored Armani suit, crisp business shirt, Hermes silk tie with a splash of color to remind them of his artistic credentials, shiny slip-on leather shoes and a matching Dunhill leather attaché case. The details were right, down to the Mont Blanc pens nestling in his top pocket. Now he felt like the chairman of the board, felt ready to do business, suit to suit.

The elevator chimed softly, and he stepped out onto the luxurious deep-pile black carpet of another, smaller foyer.

A black-suited secretary was waiting, her glossy dark hair pulled back severely from a plain, pale face split by a shocking gash of red lipsticked mouth. She was holding a sheaf of papers. "This way, Mr. Faust," she said, gesturing toward an oak-paneled door. "Your meeting is in the boardroom."

The view was spectacular. He could see clear out to the harbor across the city. The smoky glass was obviously soundproofed: the roar of uptown traffic seemed very far away. The silence was broken only by the ticking of an ornate antique clock sitting on a black marble pedestal in one corner of the vast boardroom. The woman ushered him into a chair, laid the papers on the long oak table, and left.

Johnny was at the window looking around when Mephistopheles was suddenly simply *there*, holding out a warm hand for Johnny to shake. Johnny had not heard him approach.

"Welcome, Mr. Faust," he said formally. "Do sit down. I'm so glad you've taken the time to follow up on this morning's meeting."

"I'm still not sure what this is all about," said Johnny. "But I *am* looking for backers for my new movie, and to that end I'm willing to explore all propositions."

"Quite so," said Mephistopheles.

"I've prepared a proposal for you," Johnny went on. "Script, costings, market research. It's all here. I'm sure you'll find it interesting as an investment avenue."

"Thank you, Mr. Faust." The broker smiled. "But you need not have gone to all that trouble." He waved dismissively at Johnny's immaculate folder. "We've checked you out already, and have deemed you a most suitable candidate for our investment product. Otherwise, I would not have contacted you."

He paused. "As I told you this morning, I can broker

a deal to give you your heart's desire. That's my job. I can arrange all the money you will need for your film, and the next one, too, if that's what you want. I have had all the necessary paperwork drawn up already. The question is, will you agree to my terms?"

"I can't believe this," said Johnny. "How do you know what I'll need?"

Mephistopheles' voice was patient. "I told you, we've checked."

Suddenly, all Johnny's rehearsed arguments were simply irrelevant. He had to ask. "So what, exactly, are your terms?"

"They never vary. I offer your deepest wish, in your case large amounts of money for film projects, and seven years of unlimited access to our brokerage services. In exchange, at the end of that period you render up to me your immortal soul, irrevocably."

Johnny prevaricated. "I told you, I don't believe in all that religious stuff."

"And I do?"

"Yes."

Mephistopheles' eyes narrowed. "Then what's the harm in parting with something you don't believe in? Think of it as a bet where you back your beliefs against mine. If you are right, I'm offering you millions of dollars for something that doesn't exist. You win. If you are wrong, you give up something you didn't want anyway."

Johnny was tempted, but still wary. It sounded too weird to be true. It couldn't be that simple. "If you really are the devil," he said, "why do you look like a merchant banker?"

"What would you prefer? A monk? An archbishop? A creature with hooves and horns? What would make you recognize me?"

"I don't know. I never paid that much attention. I never really believed in hell."

"Precisely. But you do believe in money. You believe in pieces of paper, in bonds and stocks and shares, in bank notes, in contracts. *That's* why I look like this. And I *do* have the money, Mr. Faust. Any amount of it. You can believe in that."

Mephistopheles picked up the sheaf of papers, selected a slim slip, and slid it across the table to Johnny.

Johnny read it, and let out a long breath. "A banker's draft," he said, "for ten million dollars."

"Development costs," said Mephistopheles. "And you'll notice it's drawn on a major city bank. I'll just step out while you phone them."

Johnny's fingers were shaking as he punched the numbers into his mobile. He was put through to the corporate finance officer, who confirmed that yes, the loan had been arranged for him, and yes, he could access it immediately. Johnny was shaking even more as he slipped the phone back into its case.

"Well?" said Mephistopheles. Johnny jumped at the sudden voice behind him. "Do we have a deal?"

Johnny was hooked, already fantasizing about how he would spend the money. "I guess we do," he said.

Mephistopheles smiled. "Then we just have to sign the paperwork." He walked back to the door. "Nurse," he said. "We'll need your services."

The black-suited woman appeared once more, this time carrying a metal dish that contained antiseptic, cotton swabs, a needle, and a small collecting tube. In her other hand was a tourniquet strap.

"Roll up your sleeve, Mr. Faust," she said.

"What's all this?" Johnny was alarmed now.

"Indulge me, Mr. Faust," said Mephistopheles. "It's traditional. To pledge your soul you have to sign in blood. Don't worry, it won't hurt."

"You really take all this religious mumbo jumbo seriously, don't you?" said Johnny.

"Very seriously. It's your choice, Mr. Faust. You can still call the deal off and tear up that check. You can walk away."

Johnny thought longingly of his movie. So close, he could almost taste it. And he could justify this weird setup as pure theater, really. "Well," he said, taking off his jacket, "it's your money."

"It is, indeed, Mr. Faust."

The nurse was very efficient. She located a vein in the crook of Johnny's arm and expertly withdrew a small vial of blood. She taped a cotton pad over the puncture, and Johnny rolled down his sleeve. She handed the blood to Mephistopheles, and exited quietly, her job done. Johnny wondered, briefly, what else she did here.

The broker took out a graceful Pelican fountain pen, dipped the nib into the vial, and filled the capsule with Johnny's red blood. He screwed the top back on, and handed the pen to Johnny. "Read the document and sign here," he said. "Then we have several more pieces of paper to deal with."

Johnny shrugged and signed. By his reckoning, ten mil was ten mil in anyone's language. The soul document of deed seemed to be old parchment, and at first the pen would not write. But Johnny shook it a few times, and the blood spurted forth, blotting the page. "No matter," said Mephistopheles. As Johnny put down the pen, his signature was already drying a crystalline red-brown. The broker took up the parchment, blew on it carefully, and whisked it away out of sight.

Then there were various other documents—bank drafts, letters of agreement, and so on, which Johnny signed in turn with his more mundane black ink. The deal was done.

"A toast, I think," said Mephistopheles.

He turned to the drinks tray on the sideboard, and poured single malt Scotch into two crystal glasses. "To our partnership," he said.

They clinked glasses, and drank. The Scotch was very good indeed.

"Well, Johnny," said the broker, "now that you have your development money, what else would you like me to do to help you with your movie?"

"I'll need a place in LA. Something classy."

"Of course. Anything else?"

Johnny grinned, relaxing for the first time. "Oh, find me the most beautiful woman in the world to be my star. That would do to begin with," he said.

"Done," said Mephistopheles.

He was not smiling.

Next morning, Mephistopheles, immaculate as ever, walked unannounced into Johnny's South Bank city office. With him was the most beautiful woman Johnny had ever seen. She was tall and curvy. She had green eyes and perfect creamy white skin and long dark red hair that curled about her like living flame.

"This is Helena. Your new star," said Mephistopheles. It was a statement. "No doubt you'd like to see the goods?"

He signaled to the woman, who shrugged easily out of her little black Prada dress. She was wearing nothing underneath. She stood in front of Johnny's desk, a statue in scarlet stilettos. Johnny was speechless with desire as she turned a slow circle before him. He could not take his eyes off the red heart of hair between her thighs.

"Well?" said Mephistopheles.

Johnny managed a hoarse response "She's perfect."

"Thank you," she said. Her husky voice vibrated in the room, promising forbidden fruits. She bent to retrieve her dress, and slipped it back over her head, giving Johnny a chance to recover slightly. Mephistopheles looked bored.

Johnny was grateful for the unstructured Gucci suit he'd worn today. He hoped the loose trousers hid the erection that was now tangled in his boxer shorts. He stood stiffly to kiss her lightly on the cheek. "Welcome aboard, Helena."

She nodded, and seated herself on the couch, crossing her long legs. The short skirt rode high on her creamy thighs, hiding nothing. It was an invitation Johnny could not refuse. Did not want to refuse.

Mephistopheles smiled knowingly at Johnny's discomfort. "I always deliver, Mr. Faust. You requested the most beautiful woman in the world to star in your movie, and here she is. Enjoy."

He rose and left the room, soundless as ever in his polished shoes.

Johnny turned back to Helena, his usual patter forgotten. She was the object of all his desire, and he wanted her. Desperately. Still, he tried to preserve the niceties: "Perhaps you'd like me to take you to lunch, then a tour around the city?"

"Later," she said. And pulled him down onto the couch. They kissed, and Johnny felt her lips suck forth his soul. Her lovemaking was hungry, predatory. She bit his ear, and drew blood; her long red-painted nails raked his back, raising long welts. He didn't care. He was lost in an ecstasy of surrender.

They were still tangled, naked, on the couch when the office door opened soundlessly, and Mephistopheles reappeared.

He cleared his throat.

Johnny was mortified. He scrambled for his trousers, draped his crumpled shirt over Helena, who seemed unperturbed. "Christ!" he said. "I'm sorry. I forgot to lock the door!"

She slapped him.

"What was that for?"

"You must not call on Him. Not now. Not ever."

"Who?"

"She means the Son of God," said Mephistopheles. "It's all right, Helena. He meant to blaspheme, not to sue for comfort." He turned to Johnny. "You'll need to be more careful. My people do take our beliefs very seriously."

"Your people?"

"Of course. Helena is my protégée." He grinned. "We provide for all situations." The smile vanished once more. "Well, Johnny," he said, "now that you've had your free sample, perhaps we can discuss terms."

"Assuming that I want her."

"You want her. She'll provide your every darkest fantasy."

"But can she act?"

"She *is* acting. She's playing the part you wanted, is she not?"

Johnny looked crestfallen. "I suppose so, yes."

"And she'll be perfect in the role of temptress. So, I will continue to provide her services, on condition that I remain in attendance as her manager, and that I will be present whenever you are filming."

"Why?"

"She can be, shall we say, extremely *difficult*. We don't want her running wild. She will behave if I am about. She knows her job."

Johnny wasn't sure he liked the sound of this, but he figured he could not risk having her "services" withdrawn so soon. He could always find a way of escape later, he thought.

"Okay," he said. "We'll do it your way."

"I knew you'd see reason," said Mephistopheles. "Drink?"

Johnny loved Hollywood. His old life was far away. He signed off on his divorce without a second thought. An outraged Michelle got the Melbourne penthouse, the cars, the share portfolio, everything. Johnny no longer cared. He'd even stopped calling Mother of late, since she threatened to visit him to see how he was getting along. He didn't need chicken soup and family bickering anymore. It felt absolutely right to him to be cruising Santa Monica Boulevard in his Porsche, the top down and his arm around Helena. Exclusive nightclubs welcomed him—smiling, heavily-tipped doormen admitted him past the lines of wanna-bes and into the warm glamour of the famous and the well-to-do. He adored the Rodeo Drive boutiques, spent his Saturday afternoons spending too much money—diamond baubles, Italian leather this and that, even a vicuna-wool Emmanuel Ungaro driving coat that cost as much as his old Jag. He treasured his stuccoed mansion on its palm-lined avenue, where he had abandoned his previous taste for understated antiques in favor of the whole *nouveau riche* thing. Now he had sunken marble baths with gold dolphin taps; acres of glass and chrome arranged by Georgio, L.A.'s hottest new designer; and even a Hearst Castle-style swimming pool surrounded by Greek statues and broken columns and potted topiary. Johnny gave lavish parties. The stars, unaccountably, attended. It was suddenly *the* place to be invited.

The gossip mills ground quickly. The casting for his movie, *Trials of Galileo,* became the subject of all the Movie News gossip columns. Major stars were signed by Hollywood's newest producer, John B. Faust. No one knew why, unless the astronomical sums he was rumored to be paying had something to do with it. The agencies were coy about details. And then there was the question of this Helena girl, rapidly becoming a star herself, with no previous history anyone could dig up. She was, all at once, just there, looking downright predatory in her slinky evening clothes worn Rita Harlowe style, *sans* underwear. Women hated her. The media loved her. She made the cover of *Vogue*, did a centerfold for *Playboy,* gave carefully scripted press interviews. Nothing seemed to impress her at all. Johnny never expected it to.

But deals were struck, papers were signed, and filming finally began—on the lot at London's Pinewood, and on location in the hills of Tuscany, where Johnny's villa was as fabulous as his L.A. house.

He was a cool two-and-a-half million over budget, and happy as a clam.

Mephistopheles was often on the set. The crew took to calling him "Old Nick," because they had the devil's own luck when he was about. Sequences ran to time; equipment worked without glitches; and Helena, sullen and moody and downright spiteful if unattended, suddenly remembered her lines and delivered perfect work. It was uncanny.

When he was not around, things were less smooth. There was a minor *contretemps* when the assembled extras refused to recite Latin prayers in the monks' procession—Johnny eventually let them process in stately silence. There were rumors of one devil too many in the torture scenes, which were reckoned by the actors to be a touch over-realistic. There was near mutiny among the sound crew when Helena carelessly trod on the hand of a technician running cable near her feet, leaving him with a broken finger and a fierce determination never to work with her again. Nevertheless, three and a half years of work proceeded, and six months after that the film was finally released.

It was, as Johnny had requested, a box office smash.

When the reviews came out, Mephistopheles was kept busy with Johnny's pique at minor slights. A critic who labeled it "overly sentimental" was busted for possession; a well-known commentator had his mortgage called in; a third had his overdraft canceled. The broker was losing patience.

"Wasting my time isn't in your contract," he said. "Petty revenge isn't worth the trouble. Think bigger."

"Okay," said Johnny. "I want an Oscar."

"Done," said Mephistopheles. "That's more like it."

And when the awards came around, there was Johnny, collecting his trophy and basking in his five minutes of fame. "It doesn't get better than this," he said to every reporter who came near him.

He was right. It didn't. Johnny's next years were spent partying, brooding over who said what about his film career, and working intermittently on a new script, his next blockbuster. It just didn't seem to be coming together. Hollywood was as glitzy as ever, but Johnny was enjoying it less. He lost his temper more often, and was now not even speaking to Mother. No relationship was permanent, though Helena was always available on demand to stoke the fires of his lust. He slept late, gained weight, drank too much. The press lost interest, pursuing the latest hotshots, whom he envied in a halfhearted way. But underneath it all he was proud of his achievements, confident of his talents, and he knew he could be back on top anytime he wanted. He only had to ask. Finally, as he was edging up toward a full three years since the film's release, he felt ready to begin casting.

"There won't be time, Mr. Faust," said Mephistopheles.

It was late evening. Johnny was driving home along the Santa Monica Freeway from yet another party when, without warning, Mephistopheles appeared at his side.

Johnny nearly jumped out of his skin. "What the hell . . . ?"

"Precisely," said Mephistopheles. He stretched his fastidiously suited legs, settled himself comfortably in the passenger seat, and said: "Well, Johnny, your time is up. I trust you've been happy with our services?"

"What?"

"This is our seventh anniversary. Your contract expires tonight. Do you have any last words?"

Johnny struggled to comprehend the implications of this. "What exactly do you mean by 'last words'?"

Mephistopheles was all business now. He extracted a rolled parchment from his inner pocket. "Exactly that." He unrolled the document. "I thought you'd appreciate a spectacular death. You'll get to go out in a blaze of publicity."

Johnny balked at the finality of his tone. "Death?" His voice rose. "There's nothing in the contract about my *dying!*"

"Of course there is. You agreed to render up to me your immortal soul. I have your signature on the document right here. In blood."

"Sure."

"We kept our side of the bargain. Now it's time for you to keep yours. You got your dream. In return, I get your soul. Tonight."

"But . . ."

"Did you think I could take the soul without the demise of the body?"

"Why not?"

"It doesn't work that way. I'm afraid you do have

to die, Johnny. At midnight. In one minute, by my calculation. I'm never wrong about these things."

Johnny's mind refused to accept it. "This can't be happening," he said.

"It can and it is. Prepare to die."

"I'll repent."

"Indeed you will. At length."

"I mean I'll turn religious. Pray to God."

Mephistopheles was unperturbed. "You don't know how. You don't believe. But go ahead, try. You'll have to be quick."

Johnny's mind was blank. He tried, without success, to remember his childhood prayers.

Mephistopheles went on. "You know this has to be. You *do* believe in contracts, and yours is right here. Your soul is mine to take." He smiled tightly and went on. "Besides, if you want to be a legend in your business, you have to die young. The brightest lights burn out first. Think about it—Monroe, Dean, Holly, Joplin, Morrison . . . they all had their time."

Johnny, belatedly, realized this was serious. "I'll give you anything, everything. Please . . ."

"Everything you have is mine already. I'm just doing my job. I told you that, right at the start." He tapped the contract.

The petrol tanker loomed into sight, coming up on the outside.

"I'm afraid there is no choice, Johnny. This is what you signed up for."

A fissure opened in the road. Johnny had nowhere to go. He swerved sideways, colliding with the tanker.

The blaze was spectacular. And amid the explosions, the confusion, the traffic chaos, no one noticed the sulfurous pit that opened up beneath the wreckage, or the demented creatures that carried a screaming Johnny Faust into the hotter flames below.

BROWNIE POINTS

by ElizaBeth Gilligan

ElizaBeth Gilligan lives in the San Francisco Bay area with husband, Doug, their children, and an assembly of furred and heavily indulged cats who are all kept under something approximating control by one very intent, peace-loving terrier. ElizaBeth has dreamed of writing professionally since she was very young and spent the last twenty-five years working on her craft. She is the author of several short stories and 2003 saw the release of her debut novel, the first in the alternative-history *Silken Magic* series, *Magic's Silken Snare,* published by DAW Books. ElizaBeth also leads a research list for genre authors called the Joys of Research.

CYBELLA McCready stared, agape, at her beloved Tweedums and Piddunkle, who had been with the family since long before her birth. With the family? No, they—the human family—considered *them* family and gave them anything they wanted, or anticipated that they might want or, at least, asked for. She couldn't understand why they would turn on her on the very eve of releasing the new line.

The situation was too absurd for words . . . and who was Cybella to turn to? She had no experience with

unions and, until one miserable half hour ago, had not
known that Brownies—of all things!—had unions either.

Why had none of Cybella's ancestors ever mentioned this? Nowhere in the various logs handed down
from shopkeeper to son—or daughter, in her case—
had there been *any* reference to C.O.B.B.L.E.R.S.
Union, Local 555 or any other. How could she have
come so far with the family's failing business only *now*
to learn that there was a union for shoemaking
Brownies and other minor members of the elvish
kind?

Cybella picked up the union rep's card again. Thaddeus T. Tadwinkle of the COBBLERS (*C*obblers' *O*rder
of *B*rownies *B*eleaguered by *L*ax *E*mployers [finally]
*R*ealizing *S*uccess) Union was also an attorney-at-law
"specializing in *B*rownies & *E*lves *W*ithout *A*dequate
*R*epresentation or *E*quity."

"You can't be serious," Cybella protested again.

"What is it you humans say now? We are as 'serious
as a . . . heart attack'?" Thaddeus Tadwinkle said in
a solicitous voice, as though he were offering tea instead of trying to tear control of the centuries-old family business away from her.

"Or an IRS audit," Piddy said helpfully. She pushed
the riot of chestnut curls back behind her faintly
pointed and very hairy ears, then turned back to Cybella with the same cheery expression she had greeted
her with every morning since Cybella could remember.

"Tweedums?" Cybella asked, looking to Piddunkle's chubby little husband.

"Nope. Can't think o' anythin'," Tweedums said
thoughtfully. Nimble of fingers he might be, but Tweedums had never been the brightest of his kind . . . or
so he seemed content to let everyone believe. That
had always been one of those things that in her modest experience of Brownies and their ilk Cybella
never understood.

Beyond Tweedums and Piddunkle, Cybella had only
ever met the occasional Brownie, usually some relation of Piddy's, who stayed for a week or two, assisting

with the workload and chattering on about who married who and why "so and so" had been banished. Piddy lapped up gossip like it was cream on a dish. They had been less lively in their conversations around adults, but did not seem to mind the inquisitive child hiding in the wardrobe near their section of the workshop, as though they did not expect a human child to be capable of remembering the oddities of their little lives.

Cybella, on the other hand, had had her own hide tanned more than once for skipping school to eavesdrop and it was as though each spanking cemented in her memory the nattering details of the Brownies and their lives . . . enough so that she managed to understand more than a smattering of their language.

"Well?" Thaddeus Tadwinkle prompted.

"Well what?" Cybella snapped at him, jerking her dumbfounded gaze from Piddunkle. Inwardly, she wanted to cry. She had thought she knew Piddy so well . . . understood the twinkle of mischief in her unblinking eyes.

"So, it's to be this way, is it?" Thaddeus said gravely, adjusting the tweedy lapels of his topcoat and tails. He took off his spectacles and began to polish them with the crisply pressed linen handkerchief in his front pocket. "I had had my hopes . . . considering the kind words the Flitwaters—"

"Flitwaters?" Cybella asked, slumping into her office chair and shifting automatically as it squeaked and rocked sideways ominously. She stared at the shyster, this purveyor of pitiless pressure.

"You see?" Piddunkle said, taking out a tiny lace-lined kerchief and dabbing at her sea-green eyes. "That's how much this family has cared for us!" She sobbed into the kerchief.

Tweedums looked confused and, after some panto-mimed coaching from his solicitor, vigorously thumped his wife's back with his broad, hairy-knuckled hand.

Piddunkle squeaked and twisted away from her spouse's ungentle ministrations. "Don't trouble yourself, Husband, even you can't comfort me! It's too horrible! Horrible!" She moaned into the kerchief.

The kerchief Cybella remembered her own mother making, weaving the silken threads and tatting fine lace to its edge. Gifts of clothing and food were all the Brownies had ever asked from her family . . . until now.

"The Flitwaters are your employees," the lawyer said sternly, perching his spectacles upon the bridge of his pudgy little nose. He rifled his papers—the worn velvet wing chair allowed him considerable space to sit and spread out his materials—and smiled in deep satisfaction. He produced a scroll from the midst of his papers. "Yes, here it is. The Flitwaters came to your family in 1698—"

"If you'll look closer," sniffed Piddunkle, stabbing the paper with her stubby fingers, "I think you'll see that that is a three. We have been with them since 1693 when it was a modest shop run by Zechariah Hasworth MacGregor and he had barely enough leather for a single pair of shoes."

Piddunkle pinched Tweedums, who scowled, pulling his offended paw out of her immediate reach on the overstuffed recliner Cybella's grandfather had long ago rescued from one of his wife's household renovations. It badly needed to be done away with.

"Yes," Tweedums said. He nodded and scratched his own red hair—hair that, for the first time, Cybella noted was different than his wife's and scattered with bits of white. Even the red itself had faded to near golden. He rubbed his hand and kept a careful eye on Piddunkle's quick little fingers. "That's right, Zechariah." He sighed, gazing out the window reminiscently. "He'd taken a wife and we were just wed, too, Piddy, remember?"

"I don't think that's exactly what we're supposed to be talking about just now," his wife said through clenched teeth and pursed lips.

Tweedums nodded and scratched the juncture where his short pants met his knee. Cybella remembered embroidering those little trousers herself for this Christmas just passed.

"Yes," Piddunkle was saying, "we made the shoes. Pretty they were and sold for the cost of any three he'd ever made afore."

Thaddeus Tadwinkle cleared his throat loudly, drawing everyone's attention back to himself. "You will see this document here that records the Flitwaters' joining with the MacGregor Shoe Shoppe."

Cybella McCready picked at the edge of the business cards Tadwinkle had handed her upon his arrival. The cards served no other function than to introduce their presenter, for there was no information on it that indicated how to contact him. They were magical, as well, growing in size to fit her own work-worn hands.

It was not a matter of the Flitwaters—the name sounded odd on her tongue, even though she spoke it silently to herself—handling all of the manufacturing anymore either. The family, her dad, had hired a full crew to man the manufacturing room back in the '70s. They had, unfortunately had no need to hire anyone since, if you did not count Karr's grandson who swept the shop and tried to look busy.

Since they had hired the men to actually mass manufacture the shoes, the Brownies, or, rather, the Flitwaters had been freed to work in the private workshop with her and her father.

In the workshop—off limits to all other personnel—the four of them worked. Cybella and her father designed shoes and boots. They were no-nonsense cobblers, making sturdy footwear mostly for the sportsman. Cybella had learned at her father's knee and then took classes, she even suffered through a class in Fashions, sitting there in her workaday clothes, her fingers stained and nicked, scarred by the work beside the girls wearing the latest dresses, hairstyles, and polished nails.

The Flitwaters—especially Tweedums—had been fascinated with her texts on Engineering and Design, laughing uproariously at some of the concepts. The Flitwaters, since the '70s, had been reserved for making prototypes of the designs Cybella and her father created.

Cybella couldn't help but wonder if Thaddeus T. Tadwinkle had any power within a court of law or if he could cause the troubles most unions did with their sick-outs and picketing.

As though sensing the drift of her mind, Mr. Tadwinkle cleared his throat, breaking into her reverie. "Let's not let matters get that unpleasant—"

"Just 'cause you don't see Brownie lawyers on CourtTV, doesn't mean they don't have their ways, Missy," Piddy snapped.

Her and her TV!

"Ahem!" Mr. Tadwinkle said, clearing his voice loudly. "Yes, this is true. Just because one doesn't traditionally see my kind in the courts of Man does not mean that we do not have our resources."

Thinking hard back on her Business Administration classes at the community college, Cybella pulled the only rabbit out of her hat she could think of—the rules of incorporation. "But when did I ever agree to accept the decisions of this separate court? The business, McCready Shoes, has gone through fifteen name changes since 1693, and was finally incorporated in Delaware late last century. Furthermore, why can't I insist that the . . . the . . . court of Man, did you call it? . . . What if I prefer human court?" Cybella demanded, leaning back in her chair and crossing her arms.

"Ah, well, you haven't had a chance to read the scroll I gave you, now have you? Your ancestor agreed to treat any possible future disagreements between the Flitwaters and his kin in the court of the Fey, it was but part of his meager apportionment for their labors."

"Meager?" Cybella scoffed, staring from Piddy to Tweedums. The first met her gaze boldly while the latter stared down at the toes of his smaller-modeled Globe Trodders—the ankle-high, trekking boots fit for any sport or terrain *she* had worked so hard to design.

The Trodders were to be the culmination of a family's efforts and their way out of the miserable state the family and business were in and into the big markets.

"Meager," Piddy repeated and turned her head away, nose in the air.

With the gesture, Cybella noted again that the Brownie wife's hair remained the deep chestnut red of youth while her husband, Tweedums', seemed to have faded radically.

"Meager," Cybella repeated, again, growing angrier still. "The Flitwaters have been treated as though they were our beloved children, always getting the firsts in everything from food at the farm to cloth for clothing and leathers for shoes and such. We never denied them anything. All they needed was to ask."

"You've been most generous, you have, Miss Cybella," Tweedums offered earnestly.

"Shut up, you idiot!" Piddy railed, brandishing the long leather strap she wore as a belt.

"Now, now, there," Thaddeus muttered sternly at his clients. "This is exactly one of our 'talking points,' you see? Their need to come begging."

"Talking points?" Cybella said. At the moment, she felt as much a dullard as Tweedums let his wife think he was. One would think, after living with a man—or, rather, a Brownie, for the better part of four centuries that Piddunkle would recognize his sly, quiet humor.

Thaddeus T. Tadwinkle smiled. He paused in the polishing of his pince-nez. "There, now," he warned his clients when they began tussling like small children forced to sit next to one another. Still glowering at them, Thaddeus managed to present a paper covered in calligraphy with a distinctive flip of his wrist.

Cybella took the paper, which expanded and unrolled, hitting the floor and heading fast between the chairs toward the door. She could never remember Grandfather's office being built flat, as it should have been. Every corner seemed to head downward. Scanning the list, she wanted nothing more at this moment than to take the shyster and his clients and throw the lot down the rickety stairs, chase them through the private workroom, pelting them with whatever came to hand as they went, until they reached the manufacturing floor and out the huge, rollaway barn doors. Or, she thought, as she grew angrier, there were about thirty ways to banish a Brownie, but, alas, she knew only part of any of them.

Cybella bit her tongue until she could feel the rush of blood in her mouth. She studied the list of complaints: we eat oatmeal now instead of porridge, no racks of lamb with mint jelly come Sunday dinner. The list ran on with its pitiful ravings, but somewhere, perhaps at the point where both ends touched the floor, the tenor of the grievances changed. The Flitwaters were worked seven days a week and never had a holiday free to visit their kinfolk; they were worked night and day, provided only the barest of clothing and vittles as what one might provide a bondsman— Cybella's blood began to boil as she read further contrivances against her family.

"These are not . . . 'talking points' as you call them," Cybella erupted. "From the characterizations of my family, my ancestors, I can find not a kind word to be said. Where, in these papers, does it speak of Charity McCready?"

"Ayup," Tweedums said and dabbed at his eyes. "Can't remember that 'uns given name, but Charity she was."

"Shut up, you fool!" Piddy said.

Cybella threw the document onto her desk in disgust, ignoring it as it unraveled into a pool of long papers on the floor. "These are no 'talking points,' Mr. Tadwinkle, they are an agenda. Come on, all of you, and let us review the living and working conditions that the . . . the Flitwaters have found themselves in for at least my lifetime."

She strode to the door, shouldering it open wide because of the way the New England damp made the wood swell and, thus, grate. Tadwinkle scrabbled his papers together and stuffed them into his black leather satchel which, before all of the ugliness had started, she had been going to offer to fix up for him. Now she hoped the seams burst in a good strong gust of wind as he scurried past her. Piddy followed him close behind. Tweedums ended the lot. He paused on the precipice of the rickety rounded stair, down from the top of the corn silo long since turned into an office.

Tweedums stared up at her and for a moment, Cybella could not be sure if his eyes had gone rheumy or if tears actually brimmed in the periwinkle blue gaze. He sighed and patted his waistcoat. Hesitating, he stood on tiptoe and peered down the arching stair.

"Have a care, Missy Cybella, and don't let your temper get the best o' you or we'll both be miserable to the end of our days."

"Twee-Dums!" Piddy called shrilly from the bottom of the stair. "Where are you, you old fool? Don't be talkin' outta place now!"

They heard the scuff of her leather soles on the lower stairs and Cybella and Tweedums both muttered imprecations under their breath, then paused to stare at one another again.

"Coming, sweetness," Tweedums coughed and hurried to meet his wife as she reached the point in the rounded stair where she could look up.

"See, Mr. Tadwinkle? This is just what I mean! The conditions we live in!" Piddy railed as she stamped back down the stairs. "They've given my poor Tweedy such a cough! It'll give him the ague and take us both in our sleep, if we should live so long!"

At the bottom of the stair, Tweedums turned one last time and tapped a finger to his nose, nodding as he favored Cybella with one of his warmest smiles.

"Now, see here! What's going on?" Mr. Tadwinkle demanded, harrumphing his way back to us.

"She's threatenin' my poor Tweedy!" Piddy shrilled.

"Ms. McCready? Is there a problem?" a deep, masculine, and very human voice called from the other side of the door in the folding wall.

"No, no, Karr, it was just the TV. I—uh—just turned

it on," Cybella called. Pushing through the cluster of Brownies at the foot of the stairs, Cybella ignored the step stool and reached up to turn on the TV positioned for convenient viewing while she and the Brownies worked.

"Really, Miss Cybella!" Mr. Tadwinkle huffed.

"What? It keeps the other humans from wondering about the voices while we're here in the workshop," she replied. Hands on hips, Cybella surveyed the workshop. "This is it, the salt mines where I torture the Flitwaters day and night."

"You see? She admits it!" Piddy caroled, dancing and clapping her hands.

Tadwinkle had to clear his throat loudly several times to finally capture Piddy's attention. "She was not serious, Mrs. Flitwater," he said sternly to his client before turning to Cybella. "I hardly think that you are taking this matter seriously either and I should warn you—"

Throwing caution to the wind, Cybella pulled up a stool at the drafting table. "So, tell me, Mr. Tadwinkle, sir, what exactly can you do to me?"

Tadwinkle jerked up straight like a marionette on a string. "I warn you now to be cautious in your tone, Miss Cybella—"

"You may call me Ms. McCready, sir, and quit taking liberties with my given name."

Behind Tadwinkle's beet-red face, Cybella saw Tweedums grinning at her encouragingly. Piddy had wandered backward bit by bit, toward the temptation of phosphorescent heaven. Tweedums waited for her, sliding her favorite chair under her rump without breaking her concentration on whatever program was on the TV.

"The problem with you is that you fail to comprehend what Brownie-kind can do to you or for you," Mr. Thaddeus T. Tadwinkle sputtered.

"Enlighten me, then, won't you?" Cybella replied, folding her arms again and staring down at the child-sized Brownie shyster. Lawyers, she thought, apparently *did* come in all flavors.

Thaddeus Tadwinkle glanced around the workshop, scowling at the absorbed Piddy and the seemingly uninspired Tweedums, before grabbing a stool for himself.

Cybella knew it was not particularly nice of her to not mention that the lawyer's choice was nicknamed "Bane" by the family Brownies because it was nigh on impossible to get on and at least as hard to get off with any sense of decorum. She watched him try to balance his weight forward and actually stay almost straddled as the stool rocked toward him onto two of its legs. On two legs, the chair staggered about in a half circle and then in another, opposing half circle as the lawyer managed first one leg and then the other. The slant of the workroom floor added to the little elvish man's troubles and carried him farther along the unevenly smoothed concrete floor.

As he wobbled on the stiltlike legs, Cybella did everything humanly possible to restrain her laughter. "Mr. Tadwinkle, perhaps—"

"I want none of your help! None of it, do you hear?" As he pointed at her, he lost control to the stool though not his balance and rode it like a bucking horse around the corner and, before anyone could save him, landed amid the scraps of leather and unsalvageable tools while issuing such language as would make a quartet of mermaids blush. The mermaids, of course, were the source of much of the ill-reputed sailor's foul language.

Piddy broke concentration from the TV, peering over her little spectacles. "What happened?"

"Never you mind, dearie, I'll take care of it," Tweedums said, patting his wife's shoulder. "Let me turn up the TV for you. Isn't that *Judge Trudy* coming on?"

"Yes!" Piddy said, clapping her hands. "The ad says there's gonna be a case of a woman suing two brothers for alimony and child support!"

"What'll humans do next?" Tweedums sighed, meeting Cybella's gaze over his wife's head. He patted Piddy's shoulder. "I'll bring you a cup of tea in just a bit."

"Right, then! The show's comin' on! Turn it up and be decent enough to keep quiet, will you?"

Murmuring acquiescence, Tweedums climbed the ladder, adjusted the volume, and then scurried out of her way before she could start complaining that he was blocking the set.

Thaddeus had stopped his howls of rage and fallen into smothered epithets. Karr's grandson called through the transom to be sure Cybella—supposedly alone—was still faring well. It took several reassurances that it had been a fallen stool, knocked over by the barn cat that haunted the shops to get young Karr off again.

"Methinks he's sweet on you, Missy," Tweedums said, wading into the oddments left over from his labors. "He's of the right age for you. I happened to overhear, he works down city way as a pair of legals. He works here 'cause he's sweet on you."

"Never mind her love life! Get me out of this!" Thaddeus demanded from somewhere in the pile.

"Now's he's gone and shifted again. We'll have to find him all over!" Tweedums said, though he did not look or sound in the least bit unhappy about delaying finding the Brownie attorney.

Together, swallowing back their laughter, Tweedums and Cybella began digging through the heap of scraps of this and thats.

"You can't be serious, Tweedums, no one would work out in the shop if they didn't have to. Besides it's called a paralegal, not 'pair of legals,'" Cybella said.

"Hah! You've admitted as much, then!" came the muffled cry of Thaddeus T. Tadwinkle from deep within the pile.

"I think he's shifted over there, Missy Cybella," Tweedums said, planting his hands on his hips and staring over the expanse which had once been the deep drive-back for produce wagons and was now filled to its very brim with castoffs and other bits.

"Say something, Brother," Tweedums called and kicked deep into the leather.

"Brother?" Cybella repeated, turning to gaze at Tweedums.

"Haha! That's it, Trudy! You tell 'em better!" Piddy cried, clapping her hands madly.

"Aye, but not mine, you understand. It's her that caused this mess—" Tweedums said, jerking his head in the direction of his wife. "He's her kin, not mine."

"Shaddup, you fool, you!" Thaddeus cried from the pile and then let out a holler when Tweedums, rather gleefully, jumped in the general vicinity of his cry.

The Brownie dug a little more and after a moment bent and seized a child-sized foot. "Found 'im!"

Somehow, Thaddeus T. Tadwinkle had wound up upside down and facing the floor. His woolen knee sock had fallen around his ankle. Tweedums grabbed the foot and began pulling, ignoring the blue language emitted by the half-man-sized Brownie, a true member of elvenkind. Cybella doubted that such language would be suitable for either the Court of Man or the Elven Court. The language the lawyer was emitting surpassed blue, which had been named after the deep blue seas where the mermaids lived.

Cybella waded into the pit and, by guess and, by golly, approximated where the attorney's other leg might be. She grabbed it, kicking and jerking about, and as easy to manage as a wet tuna. Cybella and Tweedums pulled as hard as they could, managing to mostly free the diminutive, still spouting attorney.

The door to the main workshop opened and the tall, blond, muscular man Cybella had repeatedly sent away entered. He ran immediately to Cybella's assistance, grabbing hold of both Tadwinkle's ankles and pulling with all of his might—which wasn't exactly necessary since Thaddeus was almost free and easily a quarter of the man's size.

For a brief, golden moment, Thaddeus disproved all claims that elvenkind could not fly as he sailed—wailing like a banshee or one of those screaming rockets that threatened to pierce your eardrums and that you only see every July Fourth—toward the rafters, tangled briefly in some wiring that had fallen loose, and was then swung once more into the air, sailing over their heads and back into the pile from which he had so recently been rescued.

"Is he gonna be all right?" Karr asked no one in particular.

Cybella held her sides and covered her mouth as Tadwinkle spit bits of green suede from his mouth. Her humor diminished before Tadwinkle found his full voice. She noted the casual air with which Karr—James? She remembered paychecks, John Karr—handled the sight of Brownies in the private workshop.

"Um," Cybella mumbled. "You, uh, you don't seem surprised."

"Surprised about what?" John Karr looked up, his green eyes dancing with merriment. "The Brownies? Anybody who isn't an idiot knows the McCreadys have Brownies in the shop and have had for some time."

"Everyone knows?" Tadwinkle squealed, leaping to his feet and immediately beginning to sink again.

"The McCreadys are one of the oldest families around here," Karr said with a shrug. "You think we don't talk downtown?"

"I'd have thought you had more important things to talk about than my family," Cybella replied as she gazed up at John. He really was quite good-looking, though she did not want to allow herself the time to notice.

"Thaddeus? Thaddeus?" Piddy called, finally leaving her television to join the fray of confusion. "What happened here?"

"What do you mean, what happened?" Thaddeus spouted angrily.

"There was a bit of leather I'd left half cut over on the table—"

"Don't you be lyin' to your own brother now," Twee-dums scolded. "You were watching your Judge Trudy."

"So, what's goin' on?" John Karr asked, looking from Tweedums to Cybella with equal familiarity. He grabbed the long-handled broom and stuck it out for the Brownie lawyer to grasp. Facing his employer's chagrined expression, he said, "Or do I go back to pretending I don't know what's going on on this side of the wall?"

"Tweedums said you were a pair of legal—I mean, a paralegal. Is that true?"

Karr nodded.

"When do you have time? You put in eight hours and a lunch break here every day of the week," Cybella said.

John grinned wolfishly and Cybella felt definitely weak in the knees. "Oh, I take freelance work, just enough so I can really pay the bills. I work mostly at night."

"Really?" Cybella's voice came out in a squeak. "And whyever would you do—"

"If you *please!*" Thaddeus T. Tadwinkle blustered. "Our matter was on the table first. I shall be adding charges of reckless endangerment."

John glowered down at Tadwinkle as he began straightening his clothes—from his wheat-gold woolen stockings to his tweed pants and so on.

"He talks like a lawyer," Karr said, nodding toward the Brownie attorney and union rep. "In miniature."

"Yep," Tweedums said with a sigh.

"Then why did you let me pull him out?" John asked. He waved off Tweedums with a grin. "Do you need help, Ms. McCready?"

"Call me Cybella, and, yes, I could use some assistance."

"Make no mistake, I'm no lawyer," John Karr said.

"That's fine," Cybella replied, sighing, "just help me out of this mess!"

"I thought we were going to keep this pleasant and cozy, Missy—"

"Address her formally, please," John said, glowering down at the diminutive attorney. "Missy is the familiar used by a house or family Brownie. Am I correct, Mr. . . . Mr. . . . ?"

"You are correct, but seeing the relationship between the Flitwaters and myself—"

"One you failed to mention before this," Cybella snapped from just behind John Karr's broad back. When, she wondered distractedly, did John have the chance to work out and how could he work in the shoe factory all day and still smell of Old Spice and fresh soap?

"Keep it down, will ya?" John muttered over his shoulder. He thrust his hands into his front pockets. Cybella, despite all of her best intentions, could not help but notice the ripple of his forearms and the way his jeans stretched across his derriere while he fished out a business card. He handed the card to the Brownie Attorney-At-Elvish-Law and waited for the Brownie to return the favor. He perused the card. "I suppose, you notified Ms. McCready of the existence of your union before this? Before you began issuing demands?"

"About five minutes before," Cybella said, "and that's being generous."

"You're out of your league, Mr. Karr," Tadwinkle pronounced as he finished adjusting his clothes with a final tug on the waistcoat portion of his coat. "The Laws of Man do not control us. Brownie and Elvenkind live by different laws."

"When did Ms. McCready ever agree to those laws? She and her business *are* human, after all," John said.

"Good point," Cybella agreed, nodding fiercely at the Brownie attorney.

"Will you let me handle this?" John Karr said, turning to Cybella. *"Please?"*

Cybella nodded and stepped back.

"Let's not be hasty, Ms. McCready," Tadwinkle said. "It's foolhardy in the highest degree to trust a lawyer's helper if you're really going to insist upon representation at all. I was trying to handle this friendly-like."

"Don't trust 'im," Tweedums said.

"Hey, now, that's *my* brother!" Piddunkle protested, her voice rising to a high note.

"Yer right, o' course," Tweedums said meekly, then looked up at John and Cybella. "Don't trust either of 'em."

"You'll have cold supper for a decade, Tweedums Flitwater!" his wife swore.

"That's a'right, then," Tweedums sighed. "It makes better fish bait that way, doesn't it now, John Karr?"

"Is that what you've been using?" John laughed. He turned to Cybella. "I never could figure out what he was using. Always caught the best fish that way."

"So, you've been eating from someone else's stove, have you?" Piddie Flitwater fairly screeched. "Them's grounds for Brownie divorce. Aren't they, Brother Thaddeus?"

"Yes, of course it is," Thaddeus ground out. "But we have the first matter at hand before we go on to other matters!"

Tweedums crossed his arms over his chest. "What were they, now?"

"Don't you trifle with me—"

"I'd never have any of your family's cookin' ever again! Especially the *family* trifle!" Tweedums retorted.

"Don't you be takin' my cookin' in vain, do you hear?" Piddunkle fairly screamed.

"Why not? I prayed for centuries now that it would kill me, but it didn't, it just made me miserabler than I was!" Tweedums retorted.

"She was the best of my mother's students. Of all my sisters, her cookin' challenged even our ma's," Thaddeus said.

"Best two out of three? Boiled steak versus the haggis? No wonder you grew up and became a lawyer, seein' such violence!"

Piddunkle flew at her husband in a full rage of fury and the two of them fell into the leather pit from which Thaddeus had only just recently been rescued.

"I blame this on you, too, Ms. McCready! Causin' trouble between man and wife is a serious charge, then introducin' him to another cook, you'll be lucky if my Piddy doesn't own the wretched business and you work for her!" Thaddeus cried.

"You have no grounds to make that threat come true. You'd have to have standing in the Court of Man where *our* laws apply . . . as well as our proofs," John Karr said. He winced at the nasty punch Piddy threw in the pit.

Thaddeus turned his back to the marital fight. "No grounds, you say? All right, then, we'll go by the Laws of Elvenkind."

"If it's Law, then even in Elvish you have to prove your case," John Karr said.

"Look at 'em," Thaddeus said, jerking his head toward his sister and her husband where mutual blows rained freely amidst bits of suede, rabbit fur, and hard tanned leather. "If nothing else, you've earned the wrath of Brownies. This is the way you've treated them. Brownie marriages are sacred. They work together and these two have worked for your family, *Missy,* for the good of your kinfolk for nigh on four hundred years."

"Three hundred and eleven," Cybella retorted.

"Will you *please* let me handle this?" John Karr asked Cybella between gritted teeth. He turned back to the rumpled, red-faced Thaddeus. "I believe it has only been three hundred and eleven, a good ninety years less than four centuries."

Cybella jabbed a knuckle into John Karr's ribs. "Isn't that what I said?"

"Sort of, but I'm your legal representative," John whispered.

"You take this case so lightly, do you? Do you know what Cobbling Brownies have done to the shoemakers all over the world who have not taken us seriously?"

"Let's make this simple. What do you want?" John Karr asked.

"Yeah, and none of that stupid working conditions stuff—" Cybella began. She bit her lip, smiled tentatively and moved back behind John Karr.

"Half the profit for the Globe Trodder shoes and no further trouble will come to your door," Thaddeus said.

John Karr clapped a callused hand over Cybella's mouth before she could finish her scream of outrage.

"My client finds those terms unacceptable," John Karr said with equanimity.

"Considering the contributions that my clients have made to the design of shoes released by McCready Shoes—"

". . . Missy Cybella's ideas . . ." Tweedums called from the center of the pit, ending his testimony with a howl as his wife bit into his leg and he was dragged back down into the mass of flailing arms.

"Do you think we should stop them?" Cybella asked, wincing as the two wedded Brownies rolled back and forth in the pit like schoolyard toughs.

"I'm not sure," John said, deflecting a bit of leatherwork which was flung from the pit.

"More distractions! You see the weakness in your case," Thaddeus declared.

"We're worried about *your* family members," Cybella said.

"Indeed!" Thaddeus scoffed. He glanced into the pit and shrugged. "There's a need for a couple to have a good donnybrook every century or so. How else could they stand to live together for so long?"

"Point taken," John said.

"Right, then, to the matter at hand. I'll accept nothing less than half the profits. Anything either of the clients have said is under the influence," Thaddeus said.

"Nonsense. It's a 'truthful utterance' in an extreme situation," John said.

"Do you realize the powers you're challenging?" Thaddeus asked. "It's been a while since last we punished a cobbler and it's never pretty."

"Such as . . ." John asked.

"Why do you think the Dutch wear those ridiculous wooden shoes?"

"They're ethnic tradition," Cybella replied and nodded at John.

"Ha! How do you suppose a country that spends as much time snowbound as that would wear wooden shoes that have no tread, into which snow easily gets wedged, making the wearer's socks melt and then freeze again. This is an ethnic asset?" Thaddeus said. "Ha! I say. It was the union. The cobbler there got stingy and we convinced him the shoes were a great idea. He was pelted with his shoes thereafter, but it was a time when there was only one shoemaker and, thus, only one kind of shoe. Why else do the Dutch leave the wooden clogs wherever and take whichever is handy when they come outside again?"

"Ridiculous. Ms. McCready is not about to be duped into selling wooden shoes," John replied.

"Ah! But everyone *loves* a good Italian shoe. Its price is doubled just because it is Italian. There, the shoemaker worked with us," the Brownie attorney said. "And it benefited all his brother shoemakers thereafter."

"He's going to claim the shoemaker was Ferragamo," Cybella whispered into John's ear.

"Of course he was," Thaddeus replied, "how else did you think you would know his name?"

Tweedums pulled himself, scratched, bitten, and bleeding, from the pile and collapsed, breathing hard. He flopped onto his back so that he stared up at the humans and his brother-in-law. "I give her back to you and good riddance, I say!"

"You won't get rid of me that easily, Tweedums Flitwater. I've been your wife for four hundred and nine years and—"

"I have information. She," Tweedums gasped, "could be banished."

Thaddeus scowled. "Is this true, Piddy?"

"I don't know what he's talking about," Piddunkle retorted and then began to cry, tearing at her hair.

At that point, a vague memory inveigled itself and Cybella looked closely at the sobbing, wrathful Piddunkle. Some of Piddy's roots were just as light as Tweedums', while the rest of her hair remained the deep chestnut Cybella had always remembered. It was a familiar color. A shade she knew well. Suddenly, she smiled.

"Mr. Tadwinkle, I have been more than kind to your kinfolk. Your sister has become addicted to the TV that had been originally brought in to muffle the sound of McCready and Flitwater conversations. It's had the effect that we've had to build an addition to the barn here so that your sister had electricity in her home for her own television. She has heat, too."

"You know the pod where my sister lives?" Tadwinkle exclaimed.

"I was twelve and the right size to help build it," Cybella said. She turned and crossed the workroom floor, skirting tables and shoe stands and the other sundries that filled her shop. At the far back wall, where all was as clean and smooth as every other joint, she stopped, looking at the wooden floor. She did the careful steps of a jig on certain boards and then stepped back as the wall raised like a portcullis of old. A bastion of warmth and homey smells—even bad cooking made a house smell homey or so Tweedums testified.

"You see?" John said blithely, as though he had known of the Brownie pod himself.

The look on Thaddeus T. Tadwinkle's face was priceless as he stared from the door to his sister, who began to cry again.

"And there's one more matter," Cybella said. "I'd have never brought it up, but the circumstances are such that I really have to reveal the truth. I'm sorry, Piddunkle."

Piddy sniffed and stopped crying. She looked a mess sitting there atop the pile of leather staring at Cybella nervously. "For what, Missy? It don't matter. We can work this whole thing out, whatever the problem is."

"You didn't give me that option, now did you?" Cybella asked, crossing the workroom again. She ran her hand along the rows of canned leather stain and paused, pulling one out. "Shade 357, isn't it, Piddy?"

Piddy returned to wailing, this time covering her head with her hands and arms.

"What does this mean?" Thaddeus asked looking back and forth between his sister and the humans.

"It means, Tadwinkle, that your Brownie belle is a thief. She's been stealin' what woulda been gladly give, had she asked. She's been takin' stain to prettify her hair," Tweedums said with a laugh. He pulled a larger kerchief from his pocket and dabbed his nose. "It's banishing offense to *steal* from the humans. I won't press it to court, if'n you take her with you and be gone from these domains evermore."

"Tweedums! How could you!" Piddy shrieked.

Tweedums laughed.

"In the Court of Man, we would be discussing the Doctrine of Clean Hands," John Karr said to Thaddeus.

" 'Ceptin' we're not talkin' about the Court of Man, we're dealin' in the Court of Elvenkind. We'll bother you no more," the attorney said. Even as he spoke, he began to fade, as did his surprised and disquieted sister.

Cybella came over to Tweedums and helped him sit up. "Will you be all right, old friend?" she asked.

"Now, that's a nice thing to hear. Friends. And afore I forget my place, Missy, this here is my fishin' buddy John Karr. You might already know him. And, John, I don't think you've ever properly been introduced. This here is Cybella McCready."

Over Tweedum's head, the two humans looked at each other self-consciously.

"Hello," John said.

Cybella tucked a blondish-brown curl behind her ear and offered her hand. "Hello."

Tweedums sighed happily and lay back down on the floor.

AFTER THE FLOWERING

by Janet Berliner

Author Janet Berliner received a Bram Stoker Award
for her fifth novel, *Children of the Dusk,* the third volume of The Madagascar Manifesto Series, coauthored with George Guthridge. In 2000, Janet and
George also released *Exotic Locals,* a collection on
CD-ROM containing most of their coauthored short
fiction. Her latest work is a novel of high adventure
and suspense called *Artifact.* Janet wrote the novel
about a group of daredevil friends with her friends
Kevin J. Anderson, Matthew J. Costello, and F. Paul
Wilson. More detailed and up-to-date information
about Janet's work can be found on the BerlinerPhiles
Web site at http://members.aol.com/berlphil/. Janet's
most recent anthology is *Snapshots: 20th Century
Mother-Daughter Fiction*, which she coedited with
Joyce Carol Oates. Janet served as the 1998 Presi-
dent of the Horror Writers Association and is on the
National Writer's Association Council.

THE sound of the player piano filled the crowded
foyer of the Abelsons' West Side rent-controlled
Manhattan apartment and filtered into the small living
room with the sounds of Gershwin.

Let go, Aaron. I'm tired, Mensch. Give a little.

Frieda watched the first sunbeam of the day creep

onto her chintz curtains, hers because she had made them and washed them and hung them up to dry over the radiator so many times. Yet not hers, not anymore.

Dead people couldn't own chintz. They couldn't own anything. *So why, God, can we be owned? Some bargain.*

She heard the first glug of the top-of-the-stove percolator she and Aaron had rescued from a garage sale in the Village. That and a toaster-broiler. Best five dollars she'd ever talked him into parting with. She couldn't smell the coffee. Why sight was allowed but not smell was another thing she'd have to ask God later on. Didn't seem reasonable. Especially this time of year, when the rampion bloomed. *Campanula rapunculus.* They had given their name to Rapunzel, and Aaron had often given the name to her.

She glanced down at the spiky, blue flowers, alive and sturdy, peeking out of the garbage that covered most of what had once been their tiny patch of garden one floor below. Even now she felt hungry for the salad she used to make out of some of the bulbs, after the flowering ended.

Get up, Aaron. Attaboy. You can't lie in that bed all day.

Aaron rolled over and opened one eye. He rubbed it, and pried open the other one with his fingers. He felt for the eyedrops he kept at his bedside. With their help, and his glasses, he could still see something. Glaucoma. Cataracts. The price of getting old.

He used the drops. As always, they made him sneeze. He reached for a tissue, blew his nose, then stroked the long golden braid he took from one of Frieda's hatboxes each night and laid lovingly on her pillow. Ever since he'd known her, Frieda's golden hair had been long enough for her to sit on. She'd told them to cut it and braid it and give it to him before the chemo.

"When you're better, you'll attach it to a wig," he'd said. "Until your own hair grows back."

"It'll grow back white," she'd said, though he could see in her eyes that she didn't believe it would happen.

He held the braid next to his cheek. It still smelled like Frieda. Like his Rapunzel. *If anybody sees me, they'll think I'm senile,* he thought, as he did every morning.

Time to get out of bed, he told himself. Though the day loomed emptily before him, he dared not disturb the rhythm he and Frieda had followed for fifty-two years.

Fifty-three, Aaron. Get it right.

Fifty-three years, Aaron corrected himself, not quite knowing why he did.

He looked over at the curtains, billowing in the breeze of an early spring day. Soon it would be Passover. Time to wash the curtains. Frieda always washed them before Passover.

With enormous effort, concentrating on the ritual, he placed his hands under his right knee and pushed his right leg out from under the blankets.

Always the right foot first, Aaron. So you should start the day properly. Only when you dance. Then it's left first. One, two, and three, one, two, and three . . .

He glanced at the alarm clock. Two minutes to seven. He had to hurry. By seven he had to be pouring that first cup of coffee. He couldn't change anything or he would lose her.

The phone next to his bed rang shrilly. He ignored it. He was drinking his coffee when the knock came.

"C'mon, Mr. Abelson. Open up."

He sat silently at the small kitchen table.

"I'll get the passkey."

"All right, already. I'm coming."

He pushed his feet into his worn bedroom slippers, shuffled toward the door, and opened it a crack.

"The son of the owner, come to bother an old man," Aaron said. "Go away, Joseph, Junior."

Joe pushed at the door. The chain held. "Open up, Mr. Abelson. We have to talk."

Aaron fumbled with the chain.

Joe pushed open the door, wedging it against the

tumble of magazines, theater programs, and old record albums—78s fercrissakes—that cluttered the floor.

"Person could get killed just trying to come inside," Joe said irritably, moving around the dusty old player piano that occupied most of the tiny entryway. The keyboard was exposed. He pulled at the lever marked ON. "Mona Lisa" emerged from the depths of the piano.

As he walked into the kitchen, he sang along with the melody in a fair imitation of Nat King Cole. "Mona Lisa, Mona Lisa, men have named you. . . ."

He glanced back at the antique metronome, wedged and tilting slightly on the far end of the old piano. It trembled slightly, vibrating to the tinny sound of the old instrument. Valuable collectibles, he thought. If the old boy left the metronome behind, he'd take it. The piano too, if he could drag it out. Must be worth something, like those old jukeboxes they sold down in the Village for half a fortune.

He went into the kitchen, shivered, then leaned over and pushed down the window hard. "You have to heat the neighborhood?" he asked. He looked around the tiny apartment. "You haven't started packing. You have two days left, Mr. A. Two days. I warned you. My father warned you. The building's coming down. You have to find someplace else or you'll be in the street."

"Right before Passover you'd throw me out? An old man?"

"Mona Lisa" segued into Buddy Greco's Philadelphia Jazz piano playing. The old man smiled. He placed his hand over his crotch and rubbed gently.

"You had three months—"

"Frieda hasn't even been gone three months."

The younger man shrugged. "Start packing."

"Coffee?" Aaron moved his hand away from its earlier position and poured from the old percolator into Frieda's special gold-rimmed porcelain cup. Wishing for a dollop of *schlaksahne*—whipped cream—he shook the store brand dried milk container and watched it clot on top of the hot liquid.

"What will it take for you to go?" The young man, used to the ritual by now, pulled over a matching cup and poured himself half a cup of coffee.

"What will it take for me to stay?"

"A miracle, Mr. Abelson."

"They're in short supply just now," Aaron said.

Frieda listened. She glanced up at the heavens. *What is this?* she asked. *A rehearsal for one of those television angel episodes? Come on, Aaron. Get moving. You have to pack. You have to let go of this place. Of me.*

A day passed and the next day began like any other. Alarm clock. Eyedrops. Sneezing. Slippers. Coffee.

The knock at the door.

Only this time it was not Joseph but two burly movers, their T-shirts bearing the announcement that they were ex-convicts, parolees working for the city.

Aaron faced them unblinking.

"Coffee?" he asked.

That's right, Aaron. Ignore reality. It doesn't exist if you don't acknowledge it. Frieda could have sworn her blood pressure rose twenty points, except that of course she was smart enough to know that if you don't have any blood, you can't have pressure. Still that familiar angry pounding in her temples was there, the way amputees felt pain in legs long relegated to the furnace.

"Mr. Abelman?"

"Abelson. Abel*son*."

"Mr. Abel*son*," the younger of the two said, smiling in a shy Sal Mineo sort of way. "I'm William. You can call me Bill." He held out his hand as if to shake Aaron's. "You gotta leave, kid."

Kid? Frieda's anger was replaced by amusement. Aaron a kid! An old fart, that's what he was. Stubborn and old.

He wasn't always stooped and wrinkled, *Mr. William-Bill*. She addressed the thought to the smiling youngster. *He was like you once. Young and handsome and charming. A regular prince.* Nothing but the best for Aaron in those days. Silk cravats and tails, shirt starched and pressed, gold cuff links, engraved to match the pocket watch his papa gave him for his bar mitzvah. Night after night, watching her dance, hands in his lap—to stop himself from rising, he used to say, laughing as he took her in his arms after the show.

She felt a stirring in her groin.

Seventy-three years old, dead and holding, and she was feeling sexy. Horny. Wasn't that what the young people called it these days?

"You gotta leave, Mr. Abelson. They're imploding the building." Bill gripped Aaron's arm. The old man shook him off. "You've gotta find somewhere to go."

"I got somewhere to go. Right here."

"You want us to throw you out so you can die in the street?" Bill looked around. "Look. Let me show you something."

He walked over to the window and pushed aside Frieda's chintz. "Look down there, Mr. A."

Throughout this discussion, the second man was doing something that looked suspiciously like taking inventory. Clipboard in hand, he walked around making notes with a stubby, well-chewed pencil.

"See that?" Bill pointed to a truck that was parked on the street. "We're going to load your neighbor's things and take them away. Tomorrow morning it's you. You'll be left with nothing."

The second man looked up. "If they think I can inventory all this stuff in thirty minutes, they got another thought to come," he said. Absently, he sat on Frieda's chair and poured himself coffee. "Not bad," he said, adding sugar. "Got any cookies, Mr. Abelson?"

Aaron peered outside, cleaned his glasses on one of Frieda's aprons, and pushed at the window latch. The window didn't budge. "Fresh air," he said. "Could you help me open this, Tarzan?" He looked sideways at the man sitting at the table.

"Sure, Mr. A."

The mover lifted the window with ease. He inhaled deeply and coughed. "Smells like shit down there to me," he said. "Like my wife used to say, each to his own, or something. Me, I'd rather keep away from them fumes." He lit a cigarette and held out the pack to Aaron.

"Gave it up," Aaron said. He was lying, of course. Just that he knew Frieda was listening, watching, and he didn't want her to know.

Like I couldn't smell it on you, Frieda thought. *Like I wasn't the one who washed your clothes and aired your coats when they smelled rotten, which was most of the time.*

From down below, an alarm sounded. Three long blasts, three short, three long.

Bill looked at his watch. "Fifteen minutes, Mr. A. and we're outta here. We'll be back before eight tomorrow morning."

"Nowhere. I ain't going nowhere," Aaron said.

"Look. You can leave everything here," the window opener said. "The City'll compensate you."

"I'm not going," Aaron said. *Not nowhere without my Frieda. Not ever again.*

You'll go, Aaron. Call the kids, they'll come and get you. But she knew he'd never do that, with his old man's pride. Tell the truth, she wouldn't have done that either. So what would she have done? Killed herself, maybe? Easy to say now.

The movers exited the apartment, leaving the door ajar. Aaron slammed it shut and replaced the chain. *No more answering the door,* he promised himself. *Or the phone.* He tore the jack from the wall.

The music had stopped. He rewound the piano roll and started it over. The songs belonged to the years of his life with Frieda and just once he was going to listen to all of them from beginning to end.

He sat down in the rocker where Frieda had nursed their children, the son and daughter who lived out on Long Island in their fancy homes and made like they didn't have a father. Not to speak of the fancy pants lawyer son with his house in San Diego.

Covering his legs with his favorite throw, Aaron leaned into the chair and closed his eyes. If he could only turn back the clock. What a dancer she had been, his Frieda. And he hadn't been too bad himself, waltzing her around the grand ballrooms of Vienna, holding that tiny waist in his hand, her heart fluttering against him with the fragility of butterfly wings.

"Dance, Ballerina Dance . . ."

. . . He saw her onstage as the curtains opened, holding an arabesque as if her body were designed to do nothing else. The audience applauded, but his hands gripped the arms of the seat. She began to move and so did he. Embarrassed and in lust, he relinquished his hold on the wood and covered himself with the program.

The next day, he sent her flowers. And the next. And the next. Roses. Carnations. Tulips . . .

Not tulips, Aaron. Frieda had been momentarily caught up in his sentimental journey. Tulips weren't in season.

. . . On the fourth night, Aaron sent violets and an invitation to dinner. He waited outside the stage door, knowing she would not come.

She sent a note with a stagehand. She had pinned a violet to the paper. "Stop with all the flowers. Better you should spend the money on an orphan."

He smiled. Frieda the Dresden ballerina, all frills and fancies on the outside but on the inside pragmatic and tough as nails . . .

So who else was going to be tough, Aaron? You? Not a practical bone in your whole body. What a body it was in those days when it was still in working order. Not like the young people today. For all of their personal trainers and fancy machines, they were soft. Left to their own devices, in two-twos, they were fat again. No discipline.

. . . Engrossed in memories of the first night he and Frieda had made love, Aaron heard but did not hear. He could smell again the scent of *Je Reviens*, hear the susurrus of the waves as they licked the shoreline beneath their balcony overlooking the Baltic, feel the softness of her young breasts as he pressed his body into hers. He imagined Edith Piaff's grainy voice sending its sensual message through the tinny notes of the player piano. *"Je ne regrette rien,"* he murmured. "I regret nothing."

On the player piano, Piaff gave way to Dietrich. Once again, Aaron's memory supplied the words. *"Sei lieb zu mir, Komm nicht wie ein Diep zu mir . . ."*

Frieda heard and remembered. "Be good to me. Don't come like a thief to me." Americans. Pah! What did they know. That blonde, what was her name? The one who recorded "Mean to Me." The same melody, but the words. The words were different. The new ones had nothing to do with her, or with the lover before Aaron, the one she'd never told him about. A married man, stealing into her bed and her heart and her body. Like a thief. Like the song.

Aaron stirred in the rocking chair. "I always knew about him, Frieda," he said. "But what did it matter that I should upset you? You married me. *Me.* Aaron."

Fifty-three years and still he was able to surprise her. Like the last time they'd made love, not all that long ago. Or the time he'd had the player piano delivered, complete with the roll of songs he'd paid a fortune to have put together. Their songs. Frieda wished she had an eyebrow to raise, then recalled that even in life she'd never learned that trick.

The melody of "Someone to Watch Over Me" seeped into Aaron's pores. He clutched at the pain in his heart. When it had passed, he opened his eyes and his zipper and looked down in amazement at his erection.

It still works. Frieda was amazed. Maybe he can find someone new. Plenty of young women go for old men.

She was surprised at how much the idea hurt.

It came back to Aaron, and to Frieda, triggered by

Gershwin's melody—the game he and she used to play, the one they had perfected during the early war years when they were living first with his parents, later with hers. Naked except for her worn toe shoes, she'd do her arabesque, maintaining the position until he called to her. Not with words, but with his eyes and his heart. Then they'd lie together, nothing touching but their souls and the desire to reach orgasm together. Their favorite song on the gramophone, the volume turned up as loudly as they'd dared to cover their moans as they and the song rode toward its climax.

So what did it get us, Aaron? Poor, it got us. Children it got us. Love, it got us, she added, softening.

Smiling at himself and his old man's foolishness, Aaron dried himself on the lap rug.

So close the zipper, already, Frieda reminded him. What if those boys come back? You should look respectable at least.

Aaron tucked in his undershirt, pulled up his zipper, and rose out of the chair. He refilled the coffeepot and was standing there watching it, dreading the emptiness of the day ahead, when the pain attacked again. He staggered into the crowded foyer, picked up the metronome, and held it close to his heart where the pain was becoming unbearable. Opening the small brass latch on the side of the measuring device, he said a short prayer, and spread the ashes he had placed there into the inner workings of the piano.

Frieda was right. It was time to let go.

"I love you, Frieda," he whispered. "May you rest in peace with your music."

He slumped on the piano stool, clutching the empty metronome against his heart. He was too tired to care. He could hear the percolator bubbling, but he could no longer smell the coffee.

Tomorrow, he thought. Tomorrow I'll—

Heat rose from the old radiator in the kitchen and riffled the chintz.

Frieda tried to think of something to say, something

funny and wry to neutralize the wrenching pain that coursed through her whole nonbeing.

Aaron's pain. Her Aaron. Claiming ownership of her in death as he had in life.

She begged for Ayin, the blessed nothingness that she had been promised.

Somehow, Aaron made it through the rest of the day and the night that followed. When the alarm woke him the next morning, he remembered at once that in less than an hour Bill and his pals would be downstairs. Still, he followed his usual ritual, until the pain stopped him.

Holding Frieda's hair next to his cheek, he got out of bed.

With faltering steps, he went to the player piano, flipped the lever. Sure that neither Frieda nor God would mind if he changed his routine today, he returned to bed and settled into his pillows. He wondered vaguely what would happen first, the implosion or the heart attack, and what it would feel like.

Not that it made any difference. The only thing he wanted now was to be with Frieda, he thought, drifting into sleep.

He woke to pain and a loud series of alarms. Squinting, he looked at the clock. It was almost time.

I'm down here, Aaron. In the flowers.

Still holding Frieda's hair, he went to the window and tugged at the sash. This time, it opened easily.

My hair. Use it to come to me.

He placed the kitchen chair next to him, then tied the braid to the sash and tossed it out of the window. Ignoring the pain in his chest, he gripped the braid, eased himself onto the chair, onto the sill, and out into the morning.

Whether it was the implosion or his heart, Aaron neither knew nor cared. All that mattered was that it did not come until he joined her, moving into her the way a shadow gave itself to the noon sun. He was the groom and she the bride.

From far away, the notes of the player piano tinkled.

As one, they danced to the last notes—
Always the left foot first when you dance, Aaron.
Frieda resumed her role in the partnership. Accepting eternally their ownership of one another. Singing softly . . .
. . . *Someone to watch . . . Over me.*

LITTLE RED IN THE 'HOOD

by Irene Radford

Irene Radford has been writing stories ever since she figured out what a pencil was for. Author of the *Merlin's Descendants* series, the *Dragon Nimbus* series, the *Dragon Nimbus History* series, and most recently, *The Stargods* series, she has combined her love of history with a fascination with the paranormal. A member of an endangered species, a native Oregonian who lives in Oregon, she and her husband make their home in Welches, where deer, bear, coyote, hawks, owls, and woodpeckers feed regularly on their back deck. As a service brat, she lived in a number of cities throughout the country until returning to Oregon in time to graduate from Tigard High School. She earned a B.A. in history from Lewis and Clark College, where she met her husband. In her spare time, Irene enjoys lacemaking and is a long-time member of an international guild.

"**D**ON'T tell me you are taking meals to *that* dirty old man!" Melissa, Friday supervisor for Mobile Meals, Inc. said. "I won't let you go there." She shook her head vigorously so that her gray corkscrew curls bobbed. A woman of her age should never try wearing that look.

A thrill of excitement ran through me. I had to fold my red lacquered fingernails against my palm. They seemed to grow longer by the minute. Not so unusual this time of the month.

I was sure everyone in the dining hall could hear Melissa over the clank of kitchen utensils, irate cooks screaming, and the chatter of six dozen hard-of-hearing honored citizens.

"Hush, now, sugar. I volunteered to help wherever I am needed," I replied. "Mr. Jason Hanstable needs a hot meal today. I shall deliver it." I adjusted the drape of my brand new Italian wool red coat so that I would not have to meet her gaze.

"You don't understand, Red."

Everyone called me Red at Mobile Meals, Inc., because I always wore red. Red coat, red leather pumps with a sensible two-inch heel, red print skirt and blouse. They did not know that my undies were also red. Silk. Ever so sensuous and not at all proper. Possibly no one at the city's largest geriatric charity knew my real name.

"The last time a woman took a meal to Mr. Hanstable," Melissa said, sneering in disgust, "he fondled and harassed her so bad she ran away screaming and never volunteered again. We refused to deliver meals to him for two whole years until his doctor and social worker intervened. They threatened a lawsuit actually. He's supposed to be a shut-in and helpless. Helpless he is not."

"Maybe he has learned his lesson." I shrugged.

"Maybe the big bad wolf should meet a real wolf. Then he'd learn a lesson," muttered the color-blind cook's assistant in the corner.

That idea set me to drooling.

"You have no one else to deliver to Hannibal the Letcher today. I shall go," I countered Melissa.

"Let him go hungry for a day. Monday we'll have some extra hands to send someone with you."

"Melissa, sweetie, I am not without defenses. I promise you I will be safe." Safer than Hannibal of the Many Hands if he tries anything untoward with me.

"I've heard that one before. You got a black belt

in karate or something?" Melissa propped her hands on her hips in a good imitation of an indignant den mother.

I'd never let her in my den, but that is another story.

"More likely a 'red belt,'" the black-haired assistant cook muttered. *She was just jealous because she had no fashion sense whatsoever. She always wore a boxy yellow-green sweater over faded sagging polyester slacks in a clashing turquoise.*

"Or something, Melissa. I will be all right with Mr. Hanstable," I reassured the boss. I grinned at Melissa, working hard to keep my canine teeth from showing.

"You know she's not really a volunteer," little-miss-color-blind added. "She's here doing community service. I bet her crime was prostitution. She won't mind at all if Mr. Hanstable fondles her."

I rolled my eyes at Melissa to let her know that guess was totally off the mark. *I would never stoop so low as to accept money for sex. But it was just too unfair of that little lingerie chain, "Victor's Whispers" to jack up their prices so high that I could no longer afford to shop there. I had to have that blood-red teddy and garter belt. No one else deserved it. No one else could flaunt it with the same aplomb as I could.*

Too bad I did not notice their security camera and the burly uniformed officer in the mall before I slipped said items into my red designer tote.

Good thing for the security people that happened at the dark of the moon.

With a few more reassurances that if Mr. Hanstable, or Hannibal the Letcher, tried anything hinky with me he'd get a big surprise, I left Mobile Meals, Inc. with a stack of piping hot meals packed into Keepithot plastic boxes. *These packages really do keep the meal warm. It always pays to buy name brands.*

"Remember it's Friday. If any of our clients complain about the baked fish, remind them that our biggest sponsor says we must not eat meat on Friday," Melissa called after me.

"Friday. No meat. Gotcha," I replied and ducked

into my little red convertible bug of a car. No meat
today! Oh, what cruel and unusual punishment.

Noontime traffic in the city is a nightmare. I zigged
and zagged my way through knots of cars, fender ben-
ders, people yelling, horns honking. One time I even
had to go up on the sidewalk to get through. My little
stack of plastic packages would not have a chance to
chill their tootsies before I delivered them. I take my
volunteer work . . . er . . . community service, very
seriously.

Finally I wended into a familiar neighborhood. Tall
buildings on either side of the road made this a dark
canyon, even at noon. I could almost see the moon
rising full. Here and there a loose brick, peeling paint,
a rickety stair revealed the reduced circumstances of
most of the inhabitants. And the neglect of the land-
lords. I had lived in my share of similar tenements
and felt a twinge of pity for the locals. No more. I
had a better way of life now.

Preternatural sponsors add so much to the quality
of life. Let's not forget the spice as well.

My bright and shiny red car made a welcome splash
of color in the drab surroundings. I parked crookedly,
going the wrong way between some garbage cans and
a faded blue '70 Impala up on blocks. Barely enough
room to squeeze my car in. The left rear wheel
perched atop the sidewalk and the hood of the car
poked out into the street a teensy bit.

I know the value of positioning for a fast getaway.

"Hey, Red!" Three gang members slouched over to
my car. One of them leaned on the passenger side
door, leaving greasy fingerprints.

"You going to wash my car when you finish your
nap?" I asked as I slid out of the other door. I flashed
a lot of leg clad in red mist sheer silk stockings. Another good reason for parking that way.

The gang members opened their eyes wide, hoping
to see a lot more.

While they were distracted I leaned over and picked
up one of the Keepithot packages. This time I kept

one hand modestly over my chest. Didn't want to show these adolescents too much. They might get weird ideas about me.

While my hand was perched atop my breasts, I took the opportunity to scratch. Those nails were definitely longer. A little pink crescent showed beneath the blood-red polish.

"Nice shivs you got there, lady." The closest gang boy gulped at the sight of my nails.

"You watch my car now, boys. Make certain no one steals it, or musses up the upholstery or anything," I said to them, batting my enhanced eyelashes.

Their jaws dropped just a little. One of them drooled.

I also flexed my fingers, flashing more of the blood-red color. A subtle warning to one and all.

Then I sashayed up the patched steps of the stoop and rang the doorbell. It did not work. I had not expected it to. Politeness is important, though, so I had to try. They drilled that into the MM, Inc. volunteers. Then I banged on the door. The screen flopped back and forth, rattling almost as loudly as my pounding.

I thought I heard a faint plea from inside for me to come in. Or stop making so much noise. That was invitation enough for me.

My sensible two-inch heels clacked on the peeling linoleum, letting the world know I was here for business rather than pleasure. Spike heels make a totally different sound and impart a more frivolous attitude. It is so important to dress correctly for the occasion.

Mr. Hanstable's apartment was the third floor rear. Of course the elevator did not work. I hiked up my skirt, flashed some more leg to the drunk asleep at the bottom of the stairs and climbed. And climbed. And climbed. I will need to start working out again if I keep coming here.

Hannibal the Letcher answered my knock with a feeble greeting. I pushed on the unlocked door. It creaked open ominously.

Before age and a life of dissipation took their toll, Mr. Hanstable had been a handsome man. Even now, amid the forest of wrinkles, the sparse white hair, and dark sagging pouches under the eyes, his countenance made my heart go pitter-pat.

His skin was so thin I could see his blood pulsing in his neck.

And other parts. Hannibal of the Many Hands sat in his recliner stark naked and ready. I mean *really* ready.

"I am your Mobile Meals, Inc. volunteer today, Mr. Hanstable," I announced myself. I licked my lips in lust for the man. My breath came so sharp and shallow I had trouble hiding my elongating teeth.

He pried his eyes away from the pornographic beauty contest on the television—or should I say boob tube? Then he pushed a lever and banged his recliner into the upright position. His gaze riveted upon my short skirt that clung in all the right places. Gradually he shifted his attention upward, glanced at my face, and then fixated upon my bosom.

"Well, aren't you a tidy little package," he said, wagging his shaggy eyebrows. Two hairs stuck straight up from each white brow reminding me of an eccentric bird's feathers. My appetite decreased at the image.

"Where would you like me to put your meal, Mr. Hanstable?" I stared at his face and spare frame as openly as he stared at me. My, my, he just might know how to satisfy all of my appetites.

"Right here in my lap, sweet cheeks. You do come with the meal, don't you?"

"How about I put the container on the kitchen table?" I walked to the old green Formica and metal piece between the television and the kitchenette.

"I like to eat pretty young things on the table." Hannibal the Letcher was out of his chair so quickly I hardly had time to form a protest. His hands sought my chest with the accuracy of magnet to iron.

"Not much there, mostly padding," he said squeezing me hard enough to make me wince a little, even beneath several inches of foam. "That's okay, sweet cheeks. It's what's down below that counts."

"More than you know," I replied letting my voice drop to its normal baritone register.

He jumped back in surprise as he fondled my family jewels.

"What kind of tricks are those prudes at MM, Inc. trying to pull this time?" he shouted. He scraped his hand against the upholstery of his recliner as if trying to clean a soiled paw.

"No tricks at all. They needed a volunteer. I volunteered." I stalked him. My blood was up now. I wanted satisfaction. I needed satisfaction. Sprouting fur beneath my padded bra began to itch. My lovely red shoes became too small. I kicked them off.

"Aren't you going to eat your meal? It's Friday. Fish day," I coaxed him.

He continued to back away from me.

"Get away from me, you unnatural pervert!" he screamed. His back was up against the wall by the single window. He groped to the right.

I shed my lovely silk blouse, revealing the purloined scarlet lace teddy. It opened down the front, held in place by three little red bows.

He tried to look away, but the sight of my hips shimmying out of the tight skirt kept his horror-struck gaze upon me.

Then his hand found what he sought. He brought a shotgun up and cocked it.

"Oh, you don't want to do that, Mr. Hanstable," I cooed. Saliva ran thick in my mouth. My body flushed with heat. I itched all over in response to the threat.

"Don't come any closer," he said. "I'll shoot." His hands shook so badly he could not maintain his aim.

"It won't do you any good."

"Wh . . . what?"

"No good at all." My voice began to slur as my appetite began to take control over my body. "Ordinary ammunition can't truly hurt a shapechanger," I purred. "Meet your local werewolf, Mr. Big Bad Wolf," I laughed.

I shed the blood-red garter belt and red mist stockings. They cost too much to risk tearing them. My legs thickened as my joints twisted into new angles.

"I didn't really mean those things, miss, uh, sir."

"Very definitely a sir at the moment," I replied. The teddy landed on the floor next to the matching garter belt. Definitely too small for me in the middle of a change.

No time to neatly fold them.

"You wanted to eat me. I want to eat you. Turnabout is fair play."

One swipe of my redly furred paw sent the shotgun flying. He cowered in the corner, arms over his head.

I closed my maw upon his neck and let my incisors prick his flesh. His blood tasted rancid with old age, cheap booze, and tobacco. I spat it out.

"Eeew! You taste funny." I withdrew and reached for my clothes. The urge to change slid away from me like shedding my silk lingerie. "This is my 'hood, Mr. Jason Hanstable. Mine. I protect it. Think you can refrain from molesting my volunteers from Mobile Meals, Inc., Mr. Jason Hanstable?"

He groaned something incomprehensible.

" 'Cause you see, if I hear about you trying anything funny with one of my ladies, I'll have to come back and finish the job. I protect my 'hood. And I won't return on a Friday."

"Wh . . . why not?" he asked through his tears. A yellow stain spread on the carpet between his legs.

I wrinkled my now human nose in distaste.

"I never eat meat on a Friday, even if it is a full moon. Enjoy your fish, Mr. Hanstable."

Out on the landing, I wiggled into my red clothing. No sense in letting the gang members guarding my car see the real me when the illusion is so much nicer.

Just as I thought, the boys hung around my convertible—now isn't it appropriate that I drive something that changes conformation at will? I kissed each one of them sweetly on the cheek. I let my fingers trail down the arm of the biggest of the boys as I fluttered my eyelashes at him. He looked like such a tasty hunk.

Safely behind the wheel of my little red car, I looked at the list of deliveries. Ah, Mrs. Peabody, two blocks over needs her meal. Perhaps I should detour just long enough to put on the red slacks, silk shirt, and athletic shoes I keep stored in the trunk. Of course if I become the big strong man she needs to do some chores, I'll have to remove my makeup. Oh, well. She's one of the ladies in my 'hood and I aim to please.

EXTERMINARY

by Patricia Lee Macomber

Patricia Lee Macomber has been writing since the age of fifteen, when she sold her first novel. Unfortunately, her parents saw fit to crush her first attempt at fame and the novel was never published. She has been published in various genres, taking time off to marry and have children, win a Bram Stoker Award for her editing of *ChiZine,* and do one term as Secretary of the HWA. Today, she lives in a historic mansion in Hertford, North Carolina, with her two children, Billy and Stephanie, four cats, a rabbit, a fish in a blender, and a pit bull named Elvis. She also shares that leaky old mansion with the love of her life, David Niall Wilson. Life has never been better!

IT was summer, the last bastion of unfettered joy for youth set free from the confines of stale books and moldering desks. It was cool evenings following long hot days, ice cream cones that melted on the hand and ran down the arm, firefly brigades and marching bands, lemonade sipped in the shade of a burgeoning oak. It was the steady whir of bicycle wheels, the playing cards slap-slapping on spokes, soft-scented flowers drawing little girls into fields where daisy wreaths were laced into billowing blonde hair. It was rolling down a hill till you landed at the bottom, dizzy and nauseous, then running back up the hill to do it again. It was rapture.

Dave Conner crawled through his bedroom window with all the grace and agility he could muster. His back scraped the bottom of the window frame, but he stayed quiet. He couldn't afford to get caught, couldn't risk his parents hearing. He pulled down the window, latched it, shut the blind. As he eased in between the crisp white sheets, small jar in hand and pajamas still scented with fresh evening air, he felt his brother shift against him, a soft purposeful movement meant more to garner warmth than to proffer it.

"Where y'been, Davie? I thought you was never gonna come back." The boy dragged his nose along one sleeved arm and sniffled.

"*Were* never going to come back . . . and it's Dave now, remember?" The rule, swiftly enacted and never broken. No boy past the age of ten should ever have a name ending in the "ee" sound. That's how Dave put it.

"Sorry. Dave." The boy let slip a languorous sigh, offered with a sour face and a generous helping of eager squirming. Then his face melted, drifting into that boyish mask, all bright eyes and winsome smile, lit by a shaft of light which had intruded between shade and windowsill, so beautifully lit that in Dave's tired young mind it was nearly divine. "Did you get it?"

Dave watched his brother, all eyes and smile and sweet, sheltered innocence. What a shame that six-year-old boy's cherubic face was a mask, a facade designed and carefully constructed, experience by experience, to hide himself from the world.

Slowly, with a degree of reverence usually reserved for church and for the regarding of dead things, Dave drew his hand from under the sheet. He held the jar aloft, a trophy, prized treasure in the lives of two young boys. A buzz, a spark, and Benji gasped.

"It's bee-u-ti-ful," Benji sang, his eyes locked to that sparking, dancing bit of magic.

"No, it's a firefly." The boys laughed at that, a small

tittering sound silenced as quickly as it had begun, choked back with a tight fist and a worried glance at the door.

"Did you remember to poke holes in the lid?"

" 'Course I did! This ain't no novice you're dealing with."

"Isn't."

"Right."

Dave tilted his head until it rested against Benji's, two identical pairs of eyes riveted to the jar, watching the bug as it hurled itself against the sides, bounced off the lid, each impact drawing a spark of light from the frustrated and worn insect. Dave turned the jar in his hand, always wanting that better view, still marveling at the near mystical power of one small bug. In the darkness of their room, it was no more than a brief flash of chemical light, not nearly bright enough to illuminate even the jar, but magical enough to act as a beacon for two small boys who were searching for lost innocence.

"They were doing it again," Benji stated in a tone so steeped in sadness that it made Dave's heart skip a beat.

Dave's eyes darted to his brother's, catching that last sparkle of light as it dulled behind the veil of that revelation. "They didn't come in here, did they?"

"Naw! But they was up and down the hall. Yelling and all. And Dad had his hand on the knob like he was gonna come in."

Dave shivered, drawing his body closer to Benji's, sliding himself along the cool sheets until his hip met that of his brother. "That settles it. I can't leave you here anymore. What if they'd come in and I wasn't here to protect you?"

"S'okay, Davie." Benji opened his mouth to correct himself, then thought better of it as he watched his brother's face, soft and caring, etched in sadness and regret. "Besides, it's not like they haven't hit me before, ya know."

"Yeah, I do know." There was bitterness in his

voice, hung thick and dripping with anger, sliding down his throat until that last word was nearly a pedal point. He swallowed hard and half rolled across the bed to place the jar on the nightstand. "Time to get some sleep, little bro. We'll set it free in the morning."

Benji grabbed his share of the covers and rolled over, taking most of the blanket with him and turning his back on Dave. Dave mimicked the motion, giving a synchronized tug at the sheet as a small smile stretched across each boy's gentle face. Then they inched backward, pressed tight to one another and shut their eyes.

Behind those closed lids, Dave watched his life, the long parade of adults in and out of it, all the different places they'd lived, the times when there'd been no place to live at all. He had been an only child for six years before Benji came into the picture. During those six years, he had been alone, the sole beneficiary of his father's violence and his mother's drinking. He was ever the most mature person in the house, always the caretaker of his parents and their decaying lives. But then along came Benji and everything changed. Though he was no longer alone in his battle, he was now elevated to the position of Benji's protector.

It was not a role he took lightly, nor one that he would easily give up. Dave loved his brother and would fight to the death for him. Every day brought new changes in his body, in his mind, and Dave helped those changes along every chance he got. One day, he knew, he would be big enough and strong enough that he would no longer fight his parents with just his quick mind. One day, he would be able to overpower his father and show him just how it felt to be whipped like a dog. Dave lived for that day.

In that marginal moment somewhere between sleep and wakefulness, Dave's mind tripped over some long-forgotten memory, carefully sealed in protective emotion and relegated to the back of his subconscious mind. He had the sensation of falling, his small body tumbling through the air as it hurtled toward the ground, where he had landed hard enough to embed his elbow. For a brief moment, Dave had lain on the early spring grass, staring up at the apple tree and his father's grinning face. He listened as his father laughed at him, watched as he pelted his son's broken body with overripe apples. Then Dave passed out.

He still bore the scar of that brutal surgery, cut clean across his uppermost elbow and then taking a sharp jog to the right to trace the crease on the opposite side. Until now, that was the only scar he had borne from the incident.

Dave had learned early in life several rules that were needed to keep small boys from being hurt by their parents. The first of these was to avoid the parents at all costs. The second was never to cry out in the middle of the night, no matter how badly you had been hurt or scared.

He sat up like a flash, his eyelids flipping open like loose shades, blue eyes wandering through the darkness in search of some point of focus. They landed on the jar with its attendant bug in a bleary mockery of true sight. Inside the jar, the bug had stopped throwing itself against the glass, had stopped moving entirely.

Dave picked up the jar with trembling fingers and brought it nearly to the tip of his nose. The bug was alive, all right, though its passion for escape seemed to have waned considerably. As he watched, the bug merely sat, perfectly centered on the bottom of the jar and . . . watched him.

Dave glanced over at the sleeping Benji, who was snoring softly into a stained pillow, oblivious to the world. Then he shifted his eyes back to the bug. A shiver raced up his spine and back down again. The bug had wandered to the side of the jar, two of its legs pressed tight to the cool surface almost as though it were studying him.

An audible moan rushed past his full lips at the sight of that humanlike pose, and as always, survival instinct took over, reaction became reflex. The sound of it so surprised him that he froze in place, eyes darting to check that gap between door and floorboards for the shadows of feet. For long moments he stared, unmoving and silent, watching for those telltale shadows to appear and relieved when they did not.

Secure in the knowledge that he had gone unheard, Dave leaned over in the bed, arm stretching to return the jar to the nightstand before his quivering hand could release it to shatter on the floor. No way he wanted that bug loose in there. No way!

With no small amount of effort, Dave peeled his eyes from the jar and rolled over, landing on the mattress with a disgruntled thud and turning his back on the firefly. Beside him, Benji snorted twice and rolled over, one errant arm bouncing off Dave's ribs.

Dave managed to extract himself from the clutches of his brother, accomplishing that feat without waking him up. But now he faced that bug again, the once-coveted, awe-inspiring firefly. There was no escaping it. The bug was weird. Dave watched as it moved about the jar, apparently with some purpose in mind. It ran one quick circuit of the bottom, then flew to mid-jar and seemed to stick there.

Dave shut his eyes and tried to wrap his mind around the dream. What was it that had really happened that day in the apple tree? Had he fallen? Or had he been pushed? Dave's eyes opened again and locked on the bug, now a mere black speck on the cold, graying surface of the jar.

It was crawling across the smooth inside of the glass, slowly, mindfully. Behind it trailed a thin streak of luminescence, an arc, a dot, a line. Dave screwed up his face and watched, slow steps by tiny legs, the soft whir of wings as the firefly tried to maintain its hold against gravity. *F* . . . clear as day. Dave scooted to the edge of the bed and stared. The letter *F*.

Suddenly, the firefly disappeared, gone, or never there, invisible to Dave no matter how hard he stared. Still, that letter *F* remained, biologically produced, glistening wet and glowing with stolen luminescence.

Then there was a little flash of light, no more than
the glint of a moonbeam as it struck the rim of the
jar, or so Dave thought. With that, the firefly was
back. Only, it wasn't a firefly anymore.

Tiny wings fluttered helplessly in new flight, fighting
the ravages of gravity and weakness of muscles. Small
legs—only two now—protruded from the bottom of
the . . . thing. In wide-eyed wonderment, Dave
watched, taking himself for insane or at least still in
the clutches of a nightmare. What had once been a
small firefly, puny by even insect standards, was now
a tiny woman, haloed in shimmering light and fes-
tooned with wings so impossibly fragile as to deny
flight.

Dave shook his head, praying for a quick end to
the dream. *R.* No more than a simple collection of
lines and yet so profound in its impact on the boy.
The firefly/fairy was spelling something. There was
meaning and purpose behind its actions, no room for
coincidence or randomness.

E . . . Dave began to shake. It started as a small
trembling deep in his stomach and quickly infected his
body. He could remember feeling this way once before, when one idle swing of a baseball bat had taken
down the prized reproduction Tiffany lamp that his
mother had saved from someone's garbage heap and
restored. On that occasion, his father had been
marching toward him, large beefy hands sliding his
belt from its loops as he went. And on that occasion,
Dave had wet his pants. Then, as now, he absolutely
knew for certain that something bad was about to
happen.

Another *E.* Dave shook harder now, near convul-
sions of fear vibrating his teeth as he watched. The
firefly/fairy paused in her work, tiny wings still beating
furiously, tinier-still hands pressed to the glass as she
peered out at Dave. A flicker of that divine light, a
softening of the glow, then the fairy was gone, replaced once more by the familiar bug.

It moved more quickly this time, wings pressed into

service for speed and balance, that tug-of-war with gravity still raging on. Dave's mouth was twisted off to one side, his teeth sunk deep into his lip, nearly to the point of drawing blood. Had all of that been a dream, surely he would have awakened by now, surely the hard pressure on his lip would have drawn him back to reality.

"D," cooed the sleepy-boy voice beside him.

Only then was Dave aware that Benji had been watching the whole process, his chin pressed into Dave's shoulder. He shifted now, the sharp point of his chin grinding against the muscle in Dave's arm and eliciting a small hiss of pain as Dave shrugged him off. "Quit it! That hurts!" Gone was the protective big brother, here now the antagonistic sibling.

"It's spelling somethin'," Benji yawned, dragging a corner of the blanket up under his chin and scooting upward to rest his head against the wall.

"Don't be stupid! It's just a bug." Dave adjusted the sheets in an effort to fend off that creepy-weird feeling of being watched by the bug.

"Nuh-uh! It had legs."

" 'Course it had legs. Lotsa legs. It's a bug, for Chrissakes."

"Two legs. It had two legs. And wings. And . . . and . . . a face."

As if by remote control, both boys swung their heads in the direction of the jar, mouths drawing open to release a soft sigh. In the time it had taken for them to stage their childish argument, the firefly/fairy had completed its work.

Freedom. The word, so ethereal in its concept and so seemingly far from their grasp, sent shivers up Dave's spine.

"It wants out." Benji swiped his nose along one sleeve again and yawned.

"Well . . . DUH! But how can it DO that? It's a bug. It can't spell."

"I tol' you. It's a fairy. And fairies can spell. And . . .

and . . . maybe it's a good fairy and if we let it out, we'll get a wish or somethin'."

"Yea, right! When was the last time YOU saw a fairy OR got a wish?"

"Just now." Benji smiled so brightly and so sweetly that Dave was at once caught up in the magic of it.

There was no way to argue with that kind of logic, no weapon you could use to beat sense through the wall of innocent belief and stolid confidence of that imaginative little head. Dave merely groaned in quiet resignation and threw back the covers. "Fine. I'll let it go."

He swung his legs down from the overly tall bed, warm feet meeting cold floor in a quick stab of shock. Then he stepped to the window and slid open the lock, eased the frame up slowly along its track. As he turned to pick up the jar, he ran into Benji, the smaller boy's nose burying itself somewhere just below Dave's diaphragm. He shoved his brother aside gently and clapped one hand around the jar, swinging it around so that both boy and jar were suspended over the windowsill, dangling into the cool night air and . . .

Freedom. Dave gave his wrist a quick twist, metal scraping against glass and screeching from the strain. He paused for a moment then, all time and thought suspended as the two boys merely watched the firefly/fairy in quiet awe. It was perched at the bottom of the jar, directly in the center and staring upward, as though waiting for something. It knew. Somehow, it knew that it was about to be set free. Dave risked a glance over his shoulder at Benji, his expectant face now fully captured by moonlight and glowing blue-gray in the unsympathetic grasp of it. Then his wrist jerked around, pulling the lid tight again. "I can't."

"What?" Benji slapped both hands over his mouth, too afraid to even look back at the door.

"What if it's a bad fairy? What if . . . it hurts us?"

Benji's hands dropped to his sides and his shoulders slumped in a comic parody of disillusionment. Surely his older brother, most revered and perfect in young Benji's mind, wasn't that stupid. "There are no bad fairies, Davie." One quick glance at Dave's stony face trapped Benji's voice in his throat. "Dave."

"All right, all right! I'll let it go. But I'm telling you, if something bad happens, it's YOUR fault."

Quickly, before the fear could get the better of him, Dave twisted open the lid and held the jar at arm's length, tilting it to allow the firefly/fairy an easier journey to the wide mouth. A bright spark nearly blinded the two boys as the thing took flight, the first quick fluttering of wings bringing on that metamorphosis again. A fairy now flew free, shooting upward in a straight path, headed for the trees and speeding as it neared them. Never a backward glance, never a hesitation, the thing merely took wing and was gone.

"Tol' ya!" Benji chuckled against Dave's back, nearly toppled to the floor as Dave jerked himself back into the room.

Benji took one large step backward and watched as his brother shut the window, flicked on the lock with a near furious flick of his wrist. Then Dave turned, his gaze landing flat on Benji and staggering him backward. "Into bed now. If they catch us awake at this hour, we're dead meat."

Weeks passed, months went by, and never again did the boys speak of the firefly. To become too comfortable in the telling of that tale was to risk telling the wrong person. Then the parents would find out and Papa would nail the windows shut again. If that happened, they would no longer have that high-speed exit, they would be trapped in there when things got really bad and Papa set to smashing things again. Once he was done with the things, he always came after the people.

As always happened when summer draws to a close, the wind turned to sharp blades of steel and the leaves abandoned the trees in favor of the ground. Snow began to fall early and September found the lawn encased in a bitter-white crust of snow and ice. Construction came to a screeching halt, work was hard to find. Now, all Papa had to do with his days was drink beer and watch TV. He made the occasional journey down to the services office to collect his disability and unemployment. Save for that, he was a permanent fixture in the living room.

That unseasonably warm Saturday night, filled to the eyeballs with beer and thinking himself bulletproof, Papa had entered into a disagreement with a fellow patron of the Bow and Arrow Tavern. That's what Papa always called it when he fought with people: a disagreement. It had been a real and true brawl and even the boys could tell he had been beaten as they caught sight of his face from the bedroom window. Silently, in their innocent little-boy hearts, they applauded the man who had gotten the better of their father.

As they had caught a glimpse of their father's battered face, so had he caught sight of them, noses pressed to identical circles of steam on the window. Papa's pace had quickened, his hands had balled into painful fists as he marched toward the house.

There would be one more fight that night and Papa would win. He would redeem himself, prove to his own shattered ego that he was not the beaten and weak man that those leering, laughing men at the tavern had seen as he dragged himself out into the cold.

Dave and Benji dove for the bed, made every effort to simulate slumber. No matter to Papa, though. He could beat on them even in their sleep. They heard the door swing open, jumped inwardly as the knob struck through the paneling. Then they lay still and silent, just waiting to see who would be targeted first.

One huge hand, still encrusted with dried blood and split through from the jagged edge of a bottle, lashed out and yanked Dave from his place in the bed. Benji, his fists locked tight on his brother's pajamas, went along for the ride. Within seconds he let go, frozen stiff by terror and even then soaking through his pajama bottoms.

As Dave hung there, suspended in midair by the simple clutching of chubby fingers, he let his eyes bore straight into his father's, scalding him with the heat of that raw fury. "Go ahead. Get it over with." His voice was dripping with hatred, far too caustic for one so young.

Any other full-grown, thinking, and feeling man would have been hammered into submission with a stark statement such as that. But not Papa. No! He merely drew back his hand and slapped Dave hard enough to send his eyes scrambling for focus and his ears ringing. Then he tossed the boy onto the bed and jerked open his belt.

Dave backpedaled across the bed, crab-crawling until his back slammed hard into the headboard. Benji was there, drawn into a ball and crying against his knees. The second his body made contact with Benji's, the smaller boy flung open his arms and grabbed his brother in a death grip. A small trickle of blood ran from the corner of Dave's mouth, creeping slowly toward his chin. There would be another beating for having ruined his new pajamas, he knew. His tongue lashed out, flicked away that first coppery droplet and dragged it into his mouth. Again, a long lavish lick of his lip and the blood was gone.

Dave was old enough to have learned. He knew what would come next. Papa wasn't taking off the belt to whip him with it, oh no! Papa wouldn't be that kind. Papa knew that the best way to hurt Dave was to beat Benji. Twin pairs of eyes stared at him as he loosened the belt and slid it from its loops, letting the buckle strike the floor for a moment before he reeled it in. The sound of it was enough to drag a dissonant scream from Benji's throat. It had only been done to him once, but that was enough. The memory was rich enough and haunting enough to rip apart his young mind with terror.

Then there came a sound from outside, the soft hum of late-fall bugs as they went about their nocturnal flight, feeding on the last remnants of glorious summer and dragging in the last bit of warmth to savor during the winter. It grew in Dave's ears, a small buzz elevating in pitch and volume, filling his thoughts and pulling them away from the monster at hand.

Benji screamed again, louder, more pathetic. It drew Dave back to reality, threw him into the midst of horror gone wild. Only then did he realize that Papa had dragged Benji from his clutches. The boy was facedown on the bed, his pajama bottoms caught in the tight grasp of Papa's large hand. As far as Papa was concerned, a lesson only lasted as long as the marks it left.

Suddenly, there was a new sound, a tremulous rippling of high-pitched whine against glass. It grew and grew until even Papa's attention was drawn to the window. Outside, where the cool evening air danced with the trees, thousands upon thousands of lights had gathered. They filled the lawn, smothered the trees, making them weep leaves from the pressure. They covered the gas grill and the car, the windows and the siding.

Through the half-open window, Dave could see each leaf on every tree, brightly lit and glowing with a surreal sort of halo. Then the lights left the trees, swarming, filling the sky. The window, covered even now in fluttering, undulating light, rising just a bit more.

In they came, millions of fireflies, commanders of flight and brilliant luminescence. They filled the void near the ceiling and hovered there. Dave watched in complete fascination, his heart trip-hammering inside his chest. All that had happened before was forgotten, all that was about to happen lost. One lone, fluttering firefly fell away from the crowd to alight on Benji's nose.

Benji crossed his eyes and looked at the insect, now more human than bug. Small diaphanous wings provided lift and balance as it perched there, tiny mouth stretched into a smile. Then another joined it, landing on Benji's shoulder. Then more and more until there was nothing to see of Benji but a soft halo of light. They came through the window, from the ceiling, in through the door. From everywhere and nowhere they came, filling the room and covering the boys until not one inch of them could be seen. And then, in silent communion, the glow was dampened, dulled, and the boys were raised from the bed.

Papa stood in the middle of the room, body swaying from the effects of the alcohol, enthralled by the vision of those lights. He watched in something akin to reverence as the firefly/fairies carried off his boys, sweeping them gently up from the bed and bearing them to the window. More of them held the window up, more still protected the boys' backs from that jagged frame. At the last second, as Dave's feet slid through the open window, Papa launched himself at the swarm. His large hands shot out and grabbed hold of Dave's ankles, crushing a goodly portion of the fairies in the process.

For a few brief moments, Papa smiled. Surely, he could best a swarm of bugs. Surely, he hadn't fallen into such a hideous state as to lose to a swarm of fireflies. And then the room shifted. It moved. Fireflies were marching up his arms, crawling up his legs and landing on his face. They filled his vision and crawled up into his nose, blocking his air. In the end, he was forced to release the boy in order to swat the bugs away from his face. In the end, he could not.

Dave and Benji had no idea where they were going, no idea how any of it could have happened. Nor did they care as long as they were away from that place and its accompanying horrors. They refused to watch their Papa as he fought with the insects. Borne by millions of struggling fireflies, the boys drifted away from the house, bobbing and weaving in a slow waltz with gravity until they disappeared over the tops of the trees.

Papa struggled with the bugs for as long as he could. His entire body was clothed in them, hidden from view save for his eyes. Ultimately, he toppled to the floor, thrashing and groaning through tightly pressed lips. He knew what would happen if they got into his mouth, knew how quickly his mind would snap. As he lay on the floor, the last ounce of his strength spent, his body held in place by the force of all those bugs that were not bugs, his eyes went to the window. The boys were safely away, they were gone.

As the fireflies crawled into his ears and nose, as the band of them around his eyes slowly tightened, the swarm guarding the window finally took flight. In one quick motion, that single-minded collection of fireflies simply left. Papa stared at the window for as long as the bugs would let him.

As the fireflies pried open his lips and slipped into the heat of his mouth, cutting off the last gasp of his air, Papa stared at that window and let the impact of it sink into his dying brain. The rest of the swarm had finally gone, leaving in their wake a message that was so clearly etched that it could be seen by anyone from inside or out, so profound in its meaning that it suddenly gave reason for Papa to stop struggling . . .

FREEDOM.

THE NIGHTINGALE

by Dena Bain Taylor

Dena Bain Taylor is a Senior Lecturer at the University of Toronto, where she has taught literature (especially science fiction and fantasy) and writing for over twenty years. Most of her publications are nonfiction—this story is her first fiction publication in the American market and is, she hopes, the first of many.

THE Emperor of Chinatown leaned over the balcony to watch his new model fall. She spun almost into invisibility, then hit the rocks far below his residential suites and exploded in an orange puffball that reflected off the city harbor. The bang echoed upward. *"Hung do!"* he shouted into the damp night. He slammed his hand into the railing and whirled back into the elegantly appointed room; the red velvet of his robe fanned out behind him. *"Ho hung do!"* he shouted again. His six vice presidents cowered. When the Emperor swore like a *t'eel,* a lowlife such as his grandfather had once been, corporate heads usually rolled. Even the Emperor's Head Chef, preparing to orchestrate his dinner from a lacquered buffet, fiddled nervously with the red roses and yellow lilies that framed the display.

"Who's this thing supposed to fool?"

VP-BIT cleared his throat, always hesitant to tell

the Emperor the obvious. "The people who don't tell them to jump off the balcony?"

Fortunately, the Emperor ignored him. "If people want a robot clunking around their kitchens, they'll buy one. If biogenetics and interface technology can't give them something more human, why should they spend the extra money? The personality factor was stronger this time, I'll give you that, but it's still too stupid and it coughs like a puking walrus. Bring me something better than this or you'll be cloning sheep in Patagonia, I promise you!"

One by one, his vice presidents reported on their divisions, and one by one were dismissed. Nothing else got thrown off the balcony, though the new VP of Acquisitions worried when the Emperor asked how she liked flying. But then he said, "I want you in all six cities next week to polish off the shipping merger," and she relaxed a bit.

Shipping was a core piece of the Empire, a natural evolution from grandfather Lee Chen's original business smuggling desperate men from Kowloon, Guangzhou, and Fukien into Toronto. He also smuggled the opium that kept them going, after their illusions of a better life got buried in the winter snows that piled up on sweatshop roofs. The white police, with their British legacy of contempt for the lesser breeds, never interfered, and so Lee Chen became the First Emperor of Chinatown and ruled iron-fisted till the last breath of his long life. His son Simon Lee, riddled with cancer, was dead within the year, clearing the way for his own son to move the Empire into the modern era, legitimize all but the most profitable parts of it, and create a sleek corporate animal.

The last vice president escaped gratefully from the suite, back down to the offices of the Empire that filled the rest of this tower and several others worldwide, and the Emperor sat down to dinner. He called for music; a pianist sat down at the Steinway in the corner and played some gently harmonious Bach. But tonight the Emperor found the music strangely unsat-

isfying and he sent the musician away after a few minutes. He ate in silence, watching the day's market
reports scroll along a plasma screen. And thinking,
thinking always about ways to expand his Empire.

That night, lying in bed with a stack of business
magazines, he came across a list of the world's ten
wealthiest magnates. The name of the Emperor of
Chinatown wasn't on the list. Had never been on it.
Should have been, because he was certainly wealthy
enough, but too many of his assets were still illegal.
The move into the bioconstructs market wasn't enough
to do it.

An idea came to him, grew in his mind, took it over
completely. He spoke into his bedside console: "Get
me VP Multimedia," he ordered and the command
was quickly relayed to a helicopter on the roof. VP
Multimedia soon stood before him, showing no sign
that twenty minutes ago he'd been in a chalet north
of the city having sex with his first assistant VP.

"Do you know why my name isn't on this list?" the
Emperor demanded, waving the magazine in the VP's
face. The Emperor had long arms and hands; the black
shadow he cast seemed to be choking a struggling bird.

"That list is a piece of crap, sir," VP Multimedia
hazarded, not knowing what the Emperor was talking about.

"It's a matter of public record, you idiot. And that's
the problem—I own too much that can't go *on* the
record. I'm changing that, taking the last steps to go
completely legal. I've decided to go for the music."

"Sir?"

"The music industry. Worldwide. I want to acquire it."

"You'd, um, need to liquidate too many of your
legal assets, too, sir. You'd be overextended in one
direction. Look at the Bronfmans. When was the last
time you saw *that* name on anybody's list?"

"Edgar Bronfman wanted to own the entire entertainment industry. I just want the music," he answered. Still,

the comparison made him uncomfortable. Edgar, too, inherited an empire built by his grandfather, who fed Prohibition America's insatiable thirst for Canadian whiskey. Then Edgar risked it all and lost in the merger mania of the '90s. What would he say to the ghost of old Sam if he came to call him to account? Lucky for Edgar, Jews don't believe in ghosts.

At any rate, Lee Chen could rest easy. "I know better than to overextend," the Emperor went on. "I want you to figure out exactly what I need to acquire. VP Acquisitions will do the deals. What I want *you* to do is find me a fresh new voice to launch the final merger. Someone better than Céline or Streisand."

VP Multimedia's testicles shivered up small in a way that would have alarmed his partner waiting in the chalet. An hour later, when the VP told him the Emperor's order, that partner was still more alarmed. He knew VP Multimedia wouldn't hesitate to sacrifice his first assistant—however much he loved him—on the altar of failure. And so it went down the line of the Multimedia division: Find me a fresh new voice! Better than Céline or Streisand! Or *yours* will be the ass in the sling!

VP Multimedia quickly built a talent search apparatus that scoured the planet from Afghanistan to Zeeland, trying to find a voice that would satisfy the Emperor. But to no avail; nothing the Emperor heard was good enough.

In the Starbucks in the tower lobby, a seventeen-year-old former street kid worked mornings. One day, after overhearing one too many panicked conversations about it all, she offered her opinion for free:

"Only fossils in walkers listen to that stuff. You wanna hear Gracie Nightingale. She's the one you're looking for." Like sharks sensing blood, every Multimedia executive within earshot circled in on the Starbucks counter.

"What label is she on?"

"Who's her agent?"

"Where can we catch her act?"

The Starbucks kid shook her head. "No act. She just sings."

"Where does she sing?" they demanded.

"Wherever she is, handing out sleeping bags and meds. She's a street nurse. She sings while she works, and sometimes people sing along if they know the words and sometimes they just listen because it's so amazing. And you don't need to fly to Afghanistan—you just have to cruise around Chinatown at night until you hear her and then head that way."

Word rose up through Multimedia to the vice president. Naturally, everyone he spoke to took credit for discovering Gracie Nightingale and claimed to be on the verge of signing her. VP Multimedia hinted broadly to the Emperor about an impending triumph.

But the Emperor wasn't a man for broad hints. "What've you got?" he demanded. When it turned out that the only person who'd ever actually heard Gracie Nightingale was the Starbucks kid, he gave orders for her to accompany him that night and lead him to this magical new talent.

When she saw his limousine, the Starbucks kid shook her head. "That'll never go where we need to," she said, and he ordered up the small BMW. They drove north on Spadina and east through Chinatown. He activated the external sound system—he wanted to listen for the music without opening his window to the cold night and the rancid smells of cooking oil and poverty. They drove up one narrow alley and down another, and when he heard the first note, angelic even filtered through the speakers, he ordered the window half-open. It rolled silently down and the voice of Gracie Nightingale washed over him like balm from the heavens.

He told the car to follow the sound, and it took them up the next laneway. They edged past a boarded-up fish market and a row of grimy restaurants, until the laneway opened up into a cavernous courtyard. It was ringed with old factory buildings that now housed cheap recording studios, artists' lofts, and warehouses for illicit cargo on its way in and out of the city, some of it no doubt belonging to his Empire. A shapeless mass of human figures, layered in sexless rags, crowded around a parked van in the middle. Without his quite knowing how it happened, he found himself in their midst, riveted to the Chinese woman in a green parka who was singing from the back of the van and handing out packages to the line slowly moving past her.

She had a thin face, with mottled gold-brown skin and mismatched eyes; one slanted higher than the other. But they had a mysterious depth and he nearly fell into them when she noticed him. Her song continued, now drifting like snowflakes, now rolling like thunder, and he didn't realize she'd stopped until he was standing before her, a tear flowing down his cheek.

"Hey, China boy! What you want here?" An elbow in the ribs brought him back to shocked attention, and then naked hands reached past him to take a strip of packaged syringes from Gracie Nightingale's gloved ones.

"Hey, hey, Frederick! China girl says be nice. You still having trouble with those feet? You want some socks, too?"

The bubble burst. She was a decidedly unpretty young street nurse, and he was the Emperor of Chinatown. He hadn't meant to be standing here. He'd meant to tell the car to move on, and have her brought to see him. But here he was. For her part, she was seeing a fabulously wealthy man up close for the first time in her life. Her practiced nurse's eye automatically assessed him. Healthy skin, excellent posture, all the physical perfection money could buy. He smelled spicy, like an exotic garden, but he looked down at her with the arrogance of a well-fed predator.

"You're Gracie Nightingale," he said. "You're very well named."

"You're Charles Lee, aren't you?" she answered, matching the face with the media images she'd seen.

"Can I help you? You need some socks? Clean needles?" she finished dryly.

"I need your voice. I want to record you. Will you come sing for me in the morning?"

Her hands paused in their work and she examined his face, intrigued. Her first impulse was to tell him to move along, she had work to do. But the way he'd watched her while she was singing, with a simple openness that had touched her. . . . Her hands picked up their swift rhythm again and she said, "My songs sound best in the open air. But sure, I'll come see you. I finish my shift at six AM. You receiving visitors then? 'Cause once I hit my bed I'm not up for anybody."

"I'll send a car to pick you up at six, with a hot breakfast."

And with that the Emperor shook the last traces of music from his head and returned to his tower by the lake.

"Try it again, honey," the director cajoled from his sound booth. "This just isn't working."

Gracie Nightingale threw her arms up in frustration. After all she'd seen in the streets, she'd thought nothing could ever make her cry, yet here she was nearly in tears. *Why did I agree to this?* she asked herself. *What was I thinking?* But she knew the answer—it was the Emperor's own tears that first night in the courtyard, the common humanity she'd seen in him. "You're damn right it's not working!" she said. "You've got me dancing around like a chimp in heat and I'm going to break my neck in these high heels. All this makeup runs into my eyes. And the blond guy keeps bashing into me."

"That would be because you keep turning the wrong direction when you start," the director explained with all the patience he could muster. "All right," he sighed. "Take fifteen, everyone! Gracie, we'll see what we can do about the shoes and the makeup, okay?" He keyed the mike off and turned to

VP Multimedia, who'd come in to monitor the progress of the plasmideo for Gracie's launch. "Just how committed is the Emperor to using her?" he asked hopefully.

"Totally," the VP answered. "That voice is one in a billion."

"The voice, absolutely. I've never heard anything like it. But the body is hopeless. I don't know how to put this, but the only thing this plasmideo will launch is your funeral procession."

VP Multimedia smiled the smile of a man who's scaled the heights on top of too many bodies to count. "I think you put that very well. And guess who'll be the roadkill under the wheels of my hearse? Now forget the helpful suggestions and let me think." Time was running out. All the acquisitions were moving along, and soon the Emperor would be ready to launch Red Lotus Music. For months, a battery of experts had worked feverishly on Gracie Nightingale. The world's finest hair stylists could do nothing with her hair. Makeup artists struggled to give a pleasing shape to her features, and she came out looking clownish. Her body was lumpy and bony-thin at the same time. And no amount of coaching and direction could change the fact that she had the stage presence of a log.

If only her voice weren't so magnificent, so compelling! She could sing anything, from jazz and blues to nouveau-Broadway or rock-hop. The Emperor was besotted with that voice, and refused to listen to even a hint that all was not well with her plasmideo. As it was, the Emperor had her sing for him every night, and his servants crowded round the door hoping to hear, hanging on every passionately sweet note.

VP Multimedia had a sudden revelation. "Maybe there's a way out of this, after all," he mused. "Kill two birds with one stone. Even better, make two fortunes with one bird." He smiled down on the director, and the director saw a happy future reflected in his shining eyes.

* * *

Three weeks later the VPs of Multimedia and Bio-genetics & Interface Technology were hunkered down outside the Emperor's bedroom suite. Gracie Nightin-gale hadn't arrived yet, because they'd arranged for her to be delayed. Beside them was VP-BIT's latest bioconstruct. She had black hair cascading down the bare back of her evening gown, almond-shaped eyes, golden skin, flawless features. She was stunningly beauti-ful, graceful as a swan, and she'd been programmed with Gracie Nightingale's voice. Every one of Gracie's songs, every musical inflection, was loaded into her memory, and her state-of-the-art vocal cords could re-produce them to perfection.

"Now, Rose," VP-BIT said and she began to sing.

"Gracie!" The Emperor called from behind the closed doors. "Why are you singing out there? Come in here!"

The VPs hugged themselves with delight. They'd fooled the Emperor. They flung open the door and Rose slunk into the bedroom. The Emperor stared in disbelief.

"What's this? What's going on here? Where's Gracie?"

"Oh, I'm sure she'll be along, sir, if you still want her. But why would you when Rose here has her voice—and so much more! Hit it, Rose."

The bioconstruct's mouth opened again and the music poured out. It was a blues song that Gracie wrote after one of her homeless patients threw himself in the path of a subway train. But the Emperor didn't even notice the words.

"A beautiful voice in a beautiful package," he en-thused when she was done, and all the servants gath-ered at the door applauded with gusto. He got out of his chair and walked around the bioconstruct, viewing her from all angles. "You've done a great job, boys," he concluded admiringly.

"And Gracie Nightingale can't sue us for stealing her voice," VP Multimedia explained eagerly. "We checked with our copyright lawyers—we added a little richness in the upper and lower registers, just enough of a change that we can argue in court that Rose has her own voice. Plus, Gracie's contract with Red Lotus Music gives us complete rights to her songs. We'll win a court case, if she can even afford to bring one!" The two VPs cackled at their cleverness. Rose, of course, would never object to anything—she wasn't smart enough to realize that, like the Harvard mouse stem cells that were her distant ancestors, and the plasma microcircuits that controlled her brain, she was a possession.

"What's going on here?" Gracie pushed through the crowd of servants. "Who's she? Why is she singing with my voice?"

"Your replacement in the plasmideo, my dear. I know you never wanted to do it," the Emperor said, gesturing her closer. "Look at this. A biogenetic construct with artificial intelligence. Isn't she magnificent? So human!"

"Not your voice, though," VP Multimedia added quickly.

"No, no, not your voice," VP-BIT agreed. "It just sounds that way to you. You know how it is, you can never really hear yourself sing."

"Nonsense," Gracie said, "I know my own voice, and I certainly know my own song!"

"Oh, don't worry," said VP Multimedia. "You'll get your royalties on the song."

"But that's not the point. Music isn't just the package that sings it. It's the passion of experience that lies behind it. This is a sham. Look at her eyes, how blank they are! Her skin is perfect only because it's never known the storms of life. No wrinkles on that face, not from laughter, not from tears."

VP Multimedia smiled condescendingly. "So naive! The public doesn't care about any of that—hot looks and a hot sound, that's all they want. Rose has got both. It's that simple."

"It's all right, Gracie," the Emperor interrupted soothingly, but she could tell he'd already dismissed her in his mind. Even as he spoke to her, he was watching Rose. "You'll be well paid. You can do a lot of good in the world—that's why you're a nurse, isn't it?"

She opened her mouth to protest again, but the Emperor had turned away and VP Multimedia was instructing two servants to escort her from the tower.

The Emperor stood on his balcony with Rose at his side, watching the moon rise, it seemed, right out of the lake. For a year now Rose's plasmideos had topped the charts worldwide. The fortune she'd made for Red Lotus Music was helping consolidate his hold on the whole industry, and his BIT division was almost ready to launch mass production of male and female models. A new plasmideo, Rose's fifth, was due for release, and it was the first that wasn't based on one of Gracie Nightingale's songs.

"Sing me your new song, Rose," the Emperor ordered and she launched immediately into it. "Stand farther off," he ordered, vexed by her cowlike stupidity. Gracie Nightingale would have had the sense not to unleash that powerful voice so close to his ears. He listened to the song and enjoyed it, but it didn't stir his soul. But then, he thought, the burdens of Empire buried his soul deeper every year. Perhaps it could no longer be stirred to life at all.

He was just too used to Rose's singing, he decided; surely he'd have felt the same way about Gracie by now.

Still, Gracie Nightingale's voice invaded his dreams every night. He was always Lee Chen, newly arrived in Toronto from Kowloon, sweating in the Junction railroad yard beneath a blazing August sun. There was never a body with the voice. The music was always filled with a deep, pit-of-the-stomach longing for something he couldn't put a name to yet desperately desired. It throbbed into him every time he swung his pick high up to the sky and down into the recalcitrant rubble left by long-ago glacial ice.

Rose finished her song and stood patiently awaiting his next command. He frowned. Had she finished? Or had she just stopped? Somehow the song hadn't felt complete, but he wasn't sure. "Sing it again, Rose," he said, and this time he listened carefully. Yes, when she stopped, the song didn't feel finished; in fact, surely it was even shorter than the first time. "Again," he demanded, and now the song was unquestionably too short. Rose noticed nothing amiss, of course.

The next morning, VP-BIT ordered a series of tests and a day later came nervously, with VP Multimedia behind him for support, into the Emperor's office.

"She's shutting down," VP-BIT pronounced.

"What do you mean, shutting down?"

"Her plasma microcircuits have virtually unlimited capacity for information storage, based on the Hau team's original work on halted light pulses."

"Yes, yes," the Emperor said impatiently. "Move on."

"And of course the human brain has an amazing capacity on its own. But when we put them together, there's an unfortunate effect that has just now, uh, come to light."

"Which is?"

"You know how when people age they lose the capacity to learn at the rate they could when they were young? And you remember the early days of biogenetics, when we still thought cloning would work until we realized that cloned animals age prematurely?"

The Emperor pieced it together. "So what you're saying is that Rose is losing the capacity to learn?"

"Worse, sir. She's lost it. She remembers absolutely nothing she wasn't originally programmed with."

The Emperor vaulted to his feet and paced the office. "This is going to ruin me! Do you have any idea how much of my fortune is tied up in these two divisions!"

"No, sir, no," VP-BIT assured him. "It's just a setback, a little setback. Well, more than a little setback—we seem to have hit the limits of biogenetics and interface technology, but there is a bright side."

"I'm not seeing it," the Emperor said darkly.

"If the bioconstructs could learn, they'd eventually

get to a point where the courts would decide they're capable of free will, and then we'd lose our owner-ship rights."

"You promised me we'd never get into those ethi-cal battles!"

"This way they're more limited, but they're all ours. Don't worry—I promise you won't lose your fortune!"

But the Emperor worried. He watched the value of his Red Lotus Music and Empire BIT stocks plummet when news spread that Rose was just an expensive robot, biogenetic instead of mechanical.

The Emperor fell ill, and lay ravaged with a fever that the best biomedical specialists in Canada couldn't explain. More specialists were flown in from the States and wanted to move him to Dallas for more tests. But he told them to bring their equipment in. Which they did—rooms and rooms full of shining scanners and probes, and rafts of computers to work them all and analyze the reams of results. Meanwhile he lay stiff and pale, his dreams empty of either Gracie's voice or Lee Chen.

When he could concentrate long enough, he watched the market reports and the news, but didn't seem able to muster much interest in any of it. Once he saw a local news report about Gracie Nightingale. She was berating a politician over the government's refusal to build affordable housing, and the Emperor smiled at her passion and the discomfort of her overfed foe.

And still no one could explain his illness. Something we've never seen before, all the biomedical specialists said. Not a virus, but not a defective gene. Not a dis-ease or an illness or a condition, not even a syndrome. None of the above.

"It's a ghost, then," the Emperor of Chinatown said, and he gave a feeble chuckle that turned to a cough.

Sure enough, that very night the ghost of Lee Chen came and sat on his chest. The Emperor felt a terrible weight; he could hardly breathe. He opened his fever-crusted eyes.

"You have not done well, Lee Chiu," his grand-father accused him, using the Chinese name no one else had ever called him by. "Where is the fortune I left you? Where are the children to worship at our graves?" Faces floated in the air behind him, each one an action the Emperor had taken, a decision for good or ill that he had made.

"Remember me?" they swooped down in turn to hiss in his ear. "Remember what you did?" They told him so many things he'd forgotten, had wanted to forget, that the tears poured from him and he called out:

"No, no, not me! I didn't do any of that! I don't want to hear any more!" he pleaded. The spirits glared at him and Lee Chen shook his head in anger. Then they faded away, and the weight on his chest eased. But he was left with a heaviness in his heart, as though Lee Chen had planted a stone of remorse there.

Every night Lee Chen came to accuse him, adding to the weight of the stone in his heart. "In my youth," his grandfather said, "I amassed great wealth, but in my age I lived among my family and did much good in the world. What have you done with your life?"

Word spread that the Emperor would soon die, like a starter's pistol for the race to take his place. Nothing, it seemed, could penetrate the fog he lay in, until the name of Gracie Nightingale caught his attention again. Another news report, another stubborn confrontation with bureaucratic indifference.

That night Lee Chen and the spirits came a last time. The Emperor couldn't bear the weight on his chest or in his heart. He knew it would kill him tonight. The faces whispered their tormenting messages and at every word Lee Chen nodded. The Emperor could stand to hear them no longer.

"Music!" he cried. "Someone bring me music! Gracie, Gracie Nightingale—sing for me again!"

At least two biomedical specialists and one corporate executive were always hovering nearby, and so the search for Gracie Nightingale started immediately.

But Gracie was much easier to find these days and VP Multimedia found her working through the night in a clinic she'd built with the Emperor's money.

"I hold no grudge against the Emperor," she said to VP Multimedia when he delivered his message. "That was no life for me. If he wants me, I'll come."

When she came into his bedroom suite, she insisted all the biomedical specialists and executives leave. She sat down beside the Emperor and took his hand. He was very cold; his blood barely flowed. She ran her eyes quickly over the bedside monitors, knowing their messages too well to have much hope for him, and it made her sad. She couldn't see Lee Chen on the Emperor's chest, though; she could only see the man who once had cried at her music. She began to sing softly, a melody without words, and the stone in his heart grew a little lighter. He sighed with relief.

"Why did I ever send you away? I hurt you for no reason. Lee Chen is right; I have done all the wrong things with my life, and now I must die."

"Lee Chen doesn't know the whole story, then," she answered. *Whoever he is.* "The money you gave me has built a twenty-four-hour street clinic, and I'm arranging to finance cooperative housing for seventy homeless families. I have an office and a staff of three, all former street kids. None of it would be happening without you. Your vice presidents would have cheated me out of everything they could—you made sure I got every cent I was owed."

He found he had the strength to open his eyes, and through half-closed lids watched the ghostly faces smile and fade away. Even Lee Chen's face had softened, and he sat lighter on his grandson's chest.

"Oh, let her keep singing!" Lee Chen exclaimed, though of course Gracie couldn't hear him.

"Keep singing," the Emperor echoed. She stopped and leaned forward to hear his whisper. "Lee Chen says."

"For Lee Chen, then," she said, smiling. She sang about a quiet Chinese garden, blooming with white roses and elder, and it made Lee Chen very lonesome for heaven.

The Emperor's blood flowed faster and faster, and he raised his hand in farewell as Lee Chen rose and drifted in a thick white mist through the glass of the balcony door, and high over the moony lake.

Gracie lived with the Emperor for the rest of their lives, and gave him three children. They used his fortune to do good in the world, and twice a year they visited Lee Chen's grave, to burn incense and money for him to use in heaven.

MEET MISTER HAMLIN

by Bill Willingham

Bill Willingham is the multiple award-losing creator of many popular comic book series, including *Elementals, Ironwood, Coventry, Pantheon, Proposition Player,* and the current urban fantasy series called *Fables.* His novels include the young adult fantasy *Down the Mysterly River* and the modern-day *Beowulf* pulp adventure series. Bill was once arrested for overdue library books and lives (always) somewhere near a poker game.

CLAIRE Warrender hadn't intended to stay for the reception following the concert, and she certainly hadn't intended to visit the hotel room of the wild-eyed flautist who'd audaciously pushed in beside her at the buffet line. It wasn't that she was incapable of marital infidelities—she'd betrayed her husband more than once—but never without first meticulously planning her afternoon adventures. She wasn't one for acting on impulse.

And yet here she was.

"We won't be doing this again," she said, lying with him afterward, in the chaos of twisted sheets. "I can't afford to get caught, and you don't strike me as someone who does anything carefully."

"Except play," he said. And then he added, "My

music," in consideration of the other sort of play they'd just completed.

"You didn't look all that careful then either," Claire said. "You seemed much more energetic than the others."

"It was necessary. The piece called for *agitato*, but the conductor seemed content to sleepwalk through it. That's the trouble with provincial orchestras. They attract only the most timid players who can't see when impertinence is required."

"Except you."

"Only today. I sat in at the last minute for one of their regulars who took a bad stumble down the stairs this morning. They were pretty frantic about finding a replacement—about to start scouring the high schools—when I showed up. After all, we can't have an empty seat in the inaugural concert of the new season. I'll be moving on tomorrow, so you needn't worry about me sniffing around for second helpings. Your marriage—such as it is—is safe, from me at least."

Claire considered getting upset at that. The implied criticism was obvious, and deserving of some sharp remark. But she enjoyed these lazy postcoital moments and decided, after some reflection, that it wasn't worth spoiling the mood. She'd be rid of this disarmingly persuasive vagabond soon enough and for now was content to let herself drift in the afterglow a while longer.

"The problem is I've gotten used to living with my husband's money," she finally said, when the mutual silence threatened to continue too long. "But I've never quite warmed up to living with him."

"So fix it," the man said. What was his name again? She'd been trying to ignore him when he'd first insisted on introducing himself. "Hamlin," she thought—or something like it.

"It's complicated," she said.

"Not if you're willing to settle for half."

"No, divorcing him wouldn't work. I foolishly signed a prenuptial. If I leave him, I don't get anything."

"That isn't what I meant," the man who might be named Hamlin said. "What do you get in his will?"

"If he dies?"

"That's generally when one's will comes into play."

"Everything, of course. We don't have children and he has no other family." Claire was troubled by the strange turn their conversation had suddenly taken. And yet there was also something oddly thrilling about it, like the first time she learned cuss words. There's a special joy that can only come when speaking forbidden things.

"Then your problems are solved," he said, idly tracing a finger across that perfect spot—through the almost invisible down of hair on the downward curve of her belly. "Let me take care of everything. All you have to do is go home and wait. You won't even have to be too patient. I don't waste time once a deal is made. Just remember, when everything's settled, that I get half."

"I wish," she said quietly, almost inaudibly, and felt simultaneously horrible and glorious for having spoken it.

"Just your luck that I'm in the wish-granting business," Hamlin said. Yes, now that she thought about it, she was almost certain he'd introduced himself as Mister Hamlin.

On those increasingly frequent mornings when traffic was snarled on Midland Avenue, Joe Warrender would climb out of his limousine on 24th and cut diagonally across Gardener Park, usually saving himself the better part of an hour by doing so. He didn't mind the walk. It was good that his people saw him hoofing it to work from time to time. It's important to remind them that the boss hasn't gone soft. On this morning, as on the two that preceded it, Joe didn't take much notice of the street musician, a lone pipe player who'd staked out a prime spot in the park. He sat each morning atop the bronze turtle shell—one of a cluster of statues depicting children's storybook characters surrounding the central fountain—and blew a mournful tune into the unseasonably chill June air. Joe especially didn't notice that on this morning he'd started absently humming along with the piper's short and repetitive melody.

Later that day Joe summoned his key people up to the roof—his favorite spot for delivering company pep talks. Once the young VPs and various department heads had assembled, Joe wasted no time getting right to the point.

"Boys," he began, and then with his usual pause and a wink, adding, "Marge," to include Warrender Communication's only female department head, "I'm distraught. I've examined my life and found it empty of anything truly meaningful."

They stood there patiently waiting for the punch line. His opening this time was unusual, to be sure, but his trademark rolled-up shirtsleeves, lopsided smile, and jaunty tone were all standard Joe—"don't you dare call me Josef"—Warrender fare. Some new project was in the offing, and the sooner the boss revealed what it was, the sooner they could get out of the snapping wind.

"Sure, I'm a success story by most standards," Joe said. "I made my fortune early enough to enjoy it, I've got my health, every rich man's toy that's ever caught my eye, and a trophy wife lovely enough that our man Dan makes a fool of himself at every company party."

That got a laugh from everyone but Dan Fowler, who turned a bright crimson.

"But I've just realized that none of that matters," Joe continued, just at the right moment, when the laugher had started to fade. He was a born public speaker. "I'm unhappy. No, it's worse than that. Sad. That's it, I'm sad. Much too sad to go on."

And with that, Joe Warrender stepped up on the ledge surrounding the roof and, with a parting half salute to his men, threw himself off of the fourteen-story building.

                          *   *   *

Almost a year passed before everything was settled.
Despite its bizarre details, there was no question that
Joe's death would be ruled as anything other than a
suicide. There were too many witnesses to rule otherwise. But selling Warrender Communications, along
with his other holdings, took time. Joe's widow made
it clear at the outset that she didn't intend to own a
business, or stocks, or anything else that she couldn't
spend, wear, drive, or live in. Shortly after the funeral
Claire commanded an across-the-board liquidation,
and left to mourn privately in Paris while it took place.
She returned to her—formerly "their"—palatial home
on Sycamore Street only when it was time to count
the millions.

A few days later she was exiting the town's best
jewelry store, when Mister Hamlin gently accosted her
in the street.

"It's time to settle up," he said. She almost didn't
recognize him at first. He was dressed much more
gaudily now than the white tie and tux he wore on
their only previous encounter. For a moment she
thought to pretend she didn't know him, but quickly
dismissed that idea, once she saw the disturbing look
in his eyes.

"I don't owe you anything," she said. "My husband
committed suicide. You weren't even there." At the
curb her driver looked concerned and began to step
toward them, until she dismissively waved him off. Regardless of what actually happened back then, she
couldn't afford to have anyone overhear this whispered conversation.

"You owe me exactly half," Hamlin said. "That was
our deal."

"But you didn't do anything."

"You're putting too much faith in coincidence."

"If you try anything, you'll only make trouble for
yourself," Claire spat back at him. "Do you think anyone will believe any story you try to tell? Since I in-

herited my money, all sorts of crooks and con men have tried to cheat me out of part of it. The police will think you're just another one of them. You'll go to jail if you don't leave me alone."

"I'll be happy never to speak to you again, Mrs. Warrender, as soon as you pay me. My half comes to just over thirty-two million." He said it as if he had no doubt about the amount, and Claire was surprised at his accuracy. "It didn't start with what I did to your husband. I was working to fulfill your as yet unspoken dreams from the moment I pushed that poor bastard down the stairs, to get his spot in that day's performance. Then I played for you—just for you—so you'd be inspired to stay on for the reception. So that we could meet. I earned every penny and you'll regret trying to cheat me."

"Oh? What will you do?" she asked, pretending more bluster than she felt.

"The standard penalty. I take your children."

"Then you weren't paying attention last year. I don't have any children and I never plan on having any."

Mister Hamlin didn't answer, and Claire took his silence as an admission of defeat. Before he could speak again, she turned and stalked away from him, toward the open door of her limousine. She was disturbed to note his smile, directed at her, and continuing to follow her, as her car pulled away from the curb, quickly accelerating into traffic.

The first child to disappear was Peter Fradello, son of the Jericho Industries Fradellos. His father believed in learning work discipline early in life, and so Peter had the paper route that served Claire's gated, upscale neighborhood. A week later Michael Horris never made it home from little league practice, though his coach, Lester Conklin of Plume Books, swore he dropped the boy off within sight of his front gate— right next door to the Warrender property. Within a day of that incident, two Girl Scouts disappeared while selling cookies, door-to-door. The police moved in, in force, locking the community down hard and tight. And yet children kept disappearing.

It was only a matter of time before a pattern emerged from the countless interviews and witness statements. Each child was last seen in the vicinity of the Warrender estate. Claire was immediately and enthusiastically cooperative when they came knocking on her door, insisting that the police search anywhere they like, inside or out.

They did so, swarming over her grounds in great numbers, and discovered the first of the recently-dug graves within minutes. It took them a few hours longer to find her gardening shoes, where they were hidden, deep in the back of one of her closets. They were her size and still had grave dirt and blood spatter on them.

Eight years later, when the last of her appeals had finally played out, Claire was reported to have gone to the execution chamber still insisting that an insane musician was responsible for everything. No record of such a mystery man could be found. The community orchestra had not hired a replacement flautist that day, so long ago. No one named Hamlin ever rented a hotel room that afternoon. Claire's driver, the only man who might have backed up any part of her story, claimed no memory of witnessing any curbside encounter with a gaudily dressed street musician.

Among the many suppositions offered to explain her grotesque murder spree was the notion that Claire, lacking any children of her own, somehow thought to make these neighborhood kids "hers" by luring them onto her property and killing them.

That theory was always Mister Hamlin's favorite.

IF YOU ONLY KNEW MY NAME

by David Niall Wilson

David Niall Wilson has been writing and publishing horror, dark fantasy, and science fiction since the mid-eighties. His novels include the *Grails Covenant* trilogy, *Star Trek Voyager: Chrysalis, Except You Go Through Shadow, This is My Blood,* and the upcoming Dark Ages Vampire clan novel *Lasombra.* He has over a hundred short stories published in two collections and various anthologies and magazines. David lives and loves with Patricia Lee Macomber in the historic William R. White House in Hertford, North Carolina, with their children, Billy and Stephanie, occasionally his boys Zach and Zane, four psychotic cats, a dwarf bunny who continues to belie his "dwarfness," a pit bull named Elvis, and a fish named Doofish.

CHERRYL sat nervously across the smooth oak table from a man who was wearing a dark blue suit, striped tie, and a frown. He had a sheaf of papers on the table before him, and one of them, she knew, was her résumé. Sort of. It wasn't the résumé she'd submitted to ACTEC, the contractor who'd hired her for this.

"Don't worry about it," Bobby Shaw, the hiring agent, had told her. "We do this all the time. The job descriptions are never a match for the employee, and once you're in, you can figure out what we need to train you in that you don't already know, and we'll go from there. Piece of cake." There had been about the same sincerity and truth in Bobby's words that there was in the edited résumé.

Bobby Shaw sat to her right. He didn't have any papers with him, but he had an impressive, dark brown leather briefcase, and a company logo coffee cup he'd brought to leave with the client.

The client, Dean Ratliffe, still frowned. Then, very suddenly, he let the papers he'd been scanning fall to the table, and he turned to meet Cherryl's gaze. Her face flushed slightly, as if she'd been caught at something.

"Very impressive," he said. "We've been hoping to bring someone of your caliber on board. There are some pretty important clients we are courting just now who are looking for high-tech solutions. You think you can help us make that happen?"

Cherryl cleared her throat nervously. She'd been programming for over a decade, but her experience was in legacy systems and older databases. Brownridge & Ratliffe was a fast-paced outfit, working to bring advertising solutions and online marketing to older companies mired in tradition and hopelessly antiquated in their technology.

She nodded her head.

"I think so," she said, fighting the shakes that threatened to rack her frame.

Ratliffe nodded. Cherryl got the sudden and very immediate sensation that, though he'd spent a good twenty minutes scanning the résumé and the paperwork from ACTEC, the man really had no idea what he was asking. Apparently, he was accepting her on face value, without a single technical question that might have caused her to stumble.

Ratliffe stood. Bobby Shaw stood, taking the other man's hand and surreptitiously sliding the very elegant ACTEC coffee cup across the table as he did so. Cherryl stood, uncertain what to do next. She caught Ratliffe glancing at her legs and she breathed a bit easier. It seemed, for better or for worse, that she was in.

The rest was a blur. Introductions to a staff of at least fifty people, none of whom seemed to share a job description came first. Cherryl was signed up for the coffee club, the birthday club, assigned a small office and a photo badge, created for her on the spot by another smiling man.

When the storm had passed, she was seated alone in the small office, her briefcase open on the desktop, which it shared with a computer monitor and keyboard. She had a bookshelf to one side that had been thoughtfully stocked with manuals on such systems as Cold Fusion and Oracle, very modern databases, and a set of the newest manuals for Web developers.

Cherryl placed her few belongings on the desk. She turned to the computer, entered the log on sequence and credentials she'd been issued, and watched as the company desktop splashed across the screen.

There was an inbox, and an outbox—both of which were currently empty. Cherryl opened the e-mail program and found that she had been added to a couple of company mailing lists. She had a notice that her coffee club dues would be collected on the fifteenth, which was payday. She was invited to a meeting with a new client on Thursday of the following week as a consultant.

Cherryl sat back and blinked at the screen. Thursday was a long way off.

Over the next couple of weeks, a pattern emerged. Cherryl came to work, arranged her desk, answered the e-mails that had accumulated in her box, then she made a beeline for the coffee lounge. Here she met with coworkers she was slowly coming to know, exchanged small talk, and finally wound her way back to her office. By then, it would be time to begin arranging her lunch plans, and this would carry through, including lunch, to about one in the afternoon.

At one she reported to Mr. Ratliffe. These meetings, which had started out rather stiff and formal, had evolved into a casual, friendly encounter that Cherryl actually looked forward to. She'd been studying the books in her cubicle slowly, and had actually received one project to complete that had made her smile. It was the conversion of a relatively simple inventory system from an older database program—one she was very familiar with. Her knowledge of the older plan, coupled with a bit of advice she picked up in the coffee lounge from a fellow developer, had allowed Cherryl to make some very good recommendations on the project, and had made the client, a local retailer, very happy. Ratliffe had taken her to lunch, company treat.

In her spare hours at work, she'd begun to experiment with the various programs on her computer. There were a lot of graphics design programs, some decent games, though she could never quite bring herself to play any of these through to the end. The creeping fear of discovery hung over her like an angry nun with a ruler poised over her fingertips. Mostly she played at work.

One afternoon she was working up the courage to actually finish a game of online canasta, when there was a sharp rap on her door. Startled, she minimized the window and straightened her hair.

"Come in," she said pleasantly. She expected one of her coworkers, maybe one of her coffee buddies, waving an empty cup at her and nodding toward the lounge, but what she got instead was a well-dressed man in his early forties, with dark hair with flecks of gray, and deep, intense eyes that flickered with energy. She had no idea who it was, but he barreled into the room, a handful of folders in one hand and two CD jewel cases in the other.

"Are you Cherryl Wood?" he demanded gruffly.

Cherryl nodded, starting to rise. He waved her back into her seat.

"Sorry to barge in like this," he apologized. There wasn't an ounce of sincerity in his tone. "I'm Darius Brownridge. We haven't met, I've been on business in

Europe. Dean has told me great things about you. I'm hoping they're all true."

Cherryl managed a weak smile. "I hope he didn't talk me up too much," she stammered.

Brownridge wasted no more time. He dropped the folders on her desk and held out the jewel cases.

Cherryl stared at them for a moment, then reached out tentatively and took them from his grasp. She looked up at him quizzically.

"Databases," he said simply. "These are in Foxpro—older than dirt. I've been working to get them archived to a format we could read for two weeks. There were two other companies there at the same time, and I think I beat them out the door by about a day.

"These are from a very old firm. They are an ironworks, and their computer system was probably designed in the Iron Age. They haven't upgraded in years, and they've decided it's time to redo everything. Hardware, network, software, the works. I've promised them that we can do what they want. You are familiar with Foxpro, yes? I've read your résumé."

Cherryl nodded, breathing a bit easier. She was very familiar with Foxpro, had, in fact, designed and developed in it for years.

"Good," Brownridge continued. This is big stuff, Cherryl. The kind of stuff careers are made or broken on. I need these converted to Cold Fusion, and I need it by tomorrow at ten AM. I have a meeting with their executive board at that time, and I expect to have something to present to them. I know it's like spinning straw into gold, but Ratliffe says I can count on you."

Cherryl boke out in a slow, cold sweat.

"Ten tomorrow?" she repeated, so softly that she could barely hear herself speak.

"Sharp," Brownridge affirmed. "Is that a problem?"

Cherryl started to speak. She started to tell him about the résumé, and Bobby Shaw, and the books behind her that she'd only just begun to delve into, but she clamped her mouth shut tightly and shook her head. She hadn't even looked at this project. Maybe it would be a simple import function. If that were the case, she was about to throw away the only good job she'd been able to find out of cowardice.

"I'll get right on it," she said.

Brownridge smiled, but there was no warmth in the expression. "I'll leave you to it, then."

He spun on his heel and was gone, leaving Cherryl's door to swing slowly closed.

Cherryl took a deep breath. Maybe it wouldn't be that difficult. New programs were intuitive and user-friendly. She grabbed the first disk and pulled it from its case, sliding it into the CD-ROM drive of her workstation. Lights blinked, the drive spun up quickly, and the database opened in a slightly newer version of Foxpro than she was accustomed to. So far, so good. She scanned the tables, checked headers, and memorized structure as quickly as possible. She checked the export menu, but there was no mention of export in Cold Fusion. Big surprise.

Next she opened the Cold Fusion program and stared at the unfamiliar layout. She found the import utility easily enough, but there was no mention of Foxpro in any version on the format menu. The cold sweat returned.

She returned to the Foxpro screen and checked the options. There were some text formats that might work, and she chose one where the data was separated by commas. In Cold Fusion she found an import function for comma delimited text files, and her pulse quickened. She opened the file in Cold Fusion and held her breath. Tables opened quickly, and a series of windows popped up, asking her about options. She grabbed one of the Cold Fusion books from the shelf behind her and tried desperately to find the answers, but by that time she'd already made several wrong choices. The end result of her efforts was a hopeless mishmash of columns and numbers that bore no resemblance at all to the original database.

She tried again. This time she used the book from the start, and the result was minimally better, but still unusable. She couldn't show it to anyone; they would think she was a fool. She tried again. She failed again. Near tears, she closed both database programs and sat back.

What could she do? Without really thinking about it, she clicked on the big question mark on the menu bar at the top of the program screen. A short, odd-looking little man appeared, and above him, a blank where you could type your question. Cherryl considered a number of formats for her question, but none of them seemed likely to garner any result beyond those she'd achieved on her own. Tears were forming at the corners of her eyes, but she pinched them back. Idly, she typed "spin straw into gold," and hit the enter key.

The little hourglass spun on her screen for a moment, then the little man winked at her. Cherryl sat very still, staring, trying to reconcile this with what she knew of help functions. Then the small animated figure stood up, stretched, and walked forward, growing larger on the screen. He stopped, winked again, performed an odd little bow, and the words "how can I help you?" formed on the screen in a balloon above his head.

Cherryl didn't want to touch the keys again, but the question was too compelling. She typed, "I have to convert an older Foxpro database to Cold Fusion by tomorrow morning."

"I can do it," the tiny man replied in another balloon of words. "What will you give me?" he added.

"What do you mean?" she typed, forgetting for a moment she was talking with a help icon. Then she sat back, distancing herself from the keys.

"Leave that necklace on the keyboard, and go home," he told her.

She stared at the screen. She could not fathom what was happening. Had the system been hacked? Could some programmer from outside the company have broken in, singled her out, and insinuated himself into the machine? Unconsciously, she fingered the necklace at her throat. It was one of the last reminders of a very bad relationship—an engagement that had landed her in the predicament this job had to save her from.

Why not, she thought. *I'm probably going to be fired tomorrow anyway.*

She inserted the CDs with the data into her workstation and copied the files to her desktop where they could be accessed. This done, she slowly removed the necklace and stared at it. A single emerald, surrounded by small diamond chips, glittered back at her.

"Knock yourself out," she said to the computer, feeling foolish. The little man bowed and winked again, and that was all she could take. She rose, grabbed her things, and left the building without looking back.

At 9:00 AM Cherryl sat at her workstation, staring at the screen. Nothing had changed, except that her necklace was gone. Probably stolen by the cleaning crew, she thought miserably. There had been no magic files waiting for her when she came in with her with her coffee. The Cold Fusion screen was as blank as she'd left it. No conversion, no salvation. In less than half an hour, Mr. Brownridge would burst through her door again, and she'd be forced to hand over his disks, his lost contract, and her job without a decent explanation. Tears brimmed at the corners of her eyes, and she wondered how she could have been stupid enough to get herself into such a situation.

Then something flickered at the bottom of her screen. It took a moment to register that it was a rheumy, yellowed eyeball—winking. She waited. The eyeball expanded, then with a very neat animated explosion, complete with sound, became a small doorway. The small, dwarfish figure stepped through, dragging something behind him. Cherryl blinked as he pushed two icons across the screen, out of the program window, and onto her desktop. He turned, winked at her again, and a balloon appeared over his head.

"If it had seemed too easy, you might not be grateful."

The file was in Cold Fusion format on her desktop. Cherryl opened it quickly. What she saw resembled the initial Foxpro database structure, but was much cleaner. The tables were aligned neatly, the views came up crisply when she opened them. Everything seemed perfect.

Her mind was racing. If this was a setup, she was about to be made a fool of in front of her boss. It seemed too perfect. Like magic. Could it be a setup? Could it be a hacker? Some kid in a basement somewhere, logged into the phone line while his parents slept? Did it matter?

There was a sharp rap on the door, and Mr. Brownridge entered quickly.

"Well?" he asked. Cheryl knew she was a mess, hair rumpled eyes red from lack of sleep. She hoped it would look as if she'd been working all night. With a couple of quick flicks of her wrist she clicked on the file and slid it into her network folder. Glancing up distractedly, she replied.

"I have it."

Brownridge watched her carefully. Something in her manner must have alerted him that things weren't exactly as they seemed, but Cherryl knew the proof was in the pudding, and the pudding was in a folder on one of the network servers, ready to be served. She glanced at her screen, but the door, and the little man, were gone.

"It's not exactly like the original," she cautioned. "I had to clean it up a little. I think you'll be pleased."

He continued to stare at her for a moment, then, with a sudden shift of his eyes and the corners of his lips, he smiled, reaching out to take her hand.

"If this is as good as I'm expecting it to be," he told her, "we could be talking major deal here."

"I've put it in my home directory," she said softly. "In the public folder. You should be able to access it from the computer in the conference room."

Brownridge nodded. "Get some rest," he said, glancing at his watch. "I'll be with them most of the day. Be back here by five ready to work."

Cherryl stared at him in dismay. "Isn't that . . ." she hesitated, then plunged on. "Isn't that all?"

Brownridge turned toward the door, laughing. "This is just the tip of the iceberg," he said as he left. "This is how we hook them. All the hard work is done as we reel them in."

Then he was gone, and Cherryl was left alone, staring at her screen. She closed all the programs and logged out, pushing her chair away from the desk. One thing was certain. She needed the rest Mr. Brownridge had suggested, and if she was going to get it and be back to work by five, she needed to get moving. The walls seemed to be closing in menacingly, and suddenly she wanted to be anywhere else but where she was.

At two minutes after five, the door to Cherryl's office opened without warning, and Brownridge stormed into the room, his eyes sparkling with excitement. Cherryl herself had arrived only moments before.

"This," he shook a set of folders at her without explanation, "is brilliant!" he exclaimed. "I wasn't sure what to expect after reading your résumé. You have so many skills that I would almost believe you had to be a magician, or making it all up, expecting us to take them at face value. I was expecting to be disappointed. This, though . . ." He shook his head.

"We are a day away from signing on a client that will mean two million dollars in fees. Two. Million. Dollars. You," he added, "are making that happen."

Cherryl was taken aback, but as she realized he was happy, and that she was being praised, she was so relieved that she nearly cried.

"I only did what you asked," she said.

He stared at her. "You're way too modest," he replied. "I expected a crude import, or a skeletal outline of what we might provide for them. Something I could build on until we had a chance to strengthen it. What you gave me is a nearly complete solution—and in a single night. They were absolutely amazed."

Cherryl managed a weak smile. Perhaps she'd still have a job come morning after all.

"Now we need to show them how to access it," he went on. "What I need, by tomorrow morning, same time, is a Web interface to query this database. I'm counting on you, Cherryl."

Her eyes were wide, and she bit her lip to keep from crying out. If she was weak on Cold Fusion, she was totally hopeless at Web development. When she had begun developing, the "Web" had consisted of a lot of college computer nerds sharing text files through incredibly complex commands typed on green glowing monochrome monitors. Web interface? She didn't even know what was *in* the database, let alone how to access it.

Brownridge winked at her. "I don't want to take up any valuable time," he said. He stepped to the door, pulled it open, and was gone in an instant. Over his shoulder he called. "Don't forget! Ten o'clock sharp!"

Cherryl turned back to her screen, her mouth dry.

It wouldn't do any good to reopen Cold Fusion and click on help. That ship had sailed. She accessed her program menu and clicked on a program called Dreamweaver. This, she knew, was her most powerful Web tool, not that it mattered. She stared at the screen, trembling, then, holding her breath, she clicked on the large question mark that denoted help in almost all her programs.

The screen flickered, and, to her amazement and relief, a small door formed in the center of the screen and the little animated man stepped through, bowing low.

"They loved it," she typed. "It was perfect."

"How can I help you?" appeared in the white balloon over the man's head.

Cherryl was momentarily put off. She realized she'd been conversing with a help icon, and she blushed. It was just that he—it—seemed so real.

She typed "How do I create a Web page to access

the database?" into the balloon, not certain that what had been accomplished in one program, albeit by the same gnomelike help icon, would be applicable to her question in this program.

"I can do it," was the simple answer. Text in a word balloon.

Impulsively, Cherryl typed, "Who are you?"

"That would be telling," the little gnome replied, actually winking at her. "For this, you will have to leave more than your necklace."

Cherryl stared at the screen. Her face was scarlet, and she was trembling hard. Who was she talking to? Where was he? It couldn't be a program—could it? No one could program something like this, and if they could, why would they?

"Who are you?" she typed again.

"That isn't important, but I'll tell you what, Cherryl. You leave me that pretty ring on your right hand, right there on the keyboard, and I'll get to work"

"You can be done by ten o'clock in the morning?" she asked, wishing she had the courage to turn away. It had to be something illegal, or someone stalking her, but the chance to get the work done and keep her job was so important.

"By ten o'clock," the little man agreed.

Cherryl bit her lip. She was scared. Whoever she was dealing with knew way too much about her, and he was obviously dangerously unbalanced. She knew she should call security, or Mr. Brownridge, tell them the whole story and let them track him down, but she couldn't bring herself to do it. She had nowhere else to go for work, and nowhere else to go for help. *Besides,* she thought, *what would I say? That the little gnome in the help icon is extorting my jewelry?*

"Help me," she typed.

"I will," the gnome replied. Then he continued, in a much more recognizable and dangerous vein. "Cherryl?" the little man said, winking again. "While you type, scoot your chair back a little, turn to your left, and spread your knees wider. I may need inspiration."

She blushed scarlet. She started to reply angrily. Then she stopped cold. He might leave, and if he left, she was out. Screwed. Poor and jobless. Even Bobby Shaw and his neon grin wouldn't be able to prevent it, and she wasn't naive enough to think he'd stick with her if she failed, and what could she tell them? Nothing that would make any sense.

"You can't see me," she typed. "You are part of a computer program, so how would you know?"

"You don't know who I am," he replied. ". . . and I'll know."

Her face so red she felt the blood pounding and a sudden heat that shamed her, Cherryl pushed back from her desk, pulled the keyboard up nearer to her hips, and the hem of her skirt along with it, pushing her legs wider. A few moments later, a series of codes began to scroll on the screen.

"I'll create the Web access pages you need by morning. Don't let me down, Cherryl. And by the way, white silk becomes you."

The little man disappeared from her screen, but Cherryl was dizzy. Her panties were white silk, and if someone were watching her, they could see this. She glanced around, trying to spot a hidden camera, anything that could explain it. With nothing else to do, she self-consciously smoothed her skirt back over her legs, slipped her ring from her finger—staring at it for a long moment, then placing it on the keyboard. It was a single diamond, surrounded by tiny diamond chips, a ring that no longer meant anything to her, but that was still valuable. She reflected that it was about time her ex started to pay his debts. She dropped the ring on the keyboard and pushed away from the desk. Nothing to do but go home, try to sleep, and hope for a second miracle.

When Cherryl logged on the next morning, she saw something blinking and glanced down. There was a blue progress bar on her screen, near the bottom. It said, "receiving files." She held her breath.

The little man popped up on her desktop, bowed, and pointed toward the progress bar. A balloon popped up over his head that read, "Put these in the same folder with the database. Put the Cold Fusion files there as well. To access, open your browser and click on the file named index."

She nodded, though there was no one to see. Finally, she managed to get the directory created, and the files in place. Holding her breath, she opened the file.

What appeared was clean, clear, and extremely professional. The database tables were displayed, along with several ready-made views for analyzing the data, and a short form where whoever accessed this page could query the database for more specific information. It was exactly what she wished she had been able to create on her own. It was perfect.

"It's wonderful," she typed.

The little animated man bowed.

"Who are you?" she asked again.

"Your new partner," he replied.

"How can we be partners?" she asked. "You're just part of a program, right?"

No answer.

"Right?" she typed again.

The little man winked at her, and disappeared from her screen.

Cherryl had little time to consider what had just happened, or what might come next. The morning quickly became a carbon copy of her first delivery to Brownridge. He bounded into her office, fresh from a good night's sleep and too much coffee and she told him where and how to access the files. Cherryl had found a small text file beside the series of Web pages, explaining to her how to structure them in directories so that when Brownridge opened them in a browser window, they'd operate as designed.

She had had time to open only the main index page herself. It was slick, professional, and offered every feature that had been requested, plus a couple no one had thought of. She copied the files to her home directory before writing them to CD so she could study what "she" had created and be ready to make up explanations. While she was at it, she copied the database itself.

She hadn't slept much. It gave her the look of someone up late, working, and she let that image stand. She was exhausted. Cherryl lowered her head to her desk, but before she could drift off, she heard a soft chuckle, and she sat bolt upright.

The animated little man was on her desktop again, grinning at her. A voice crackled on her speaker. No little text bubble this time, direct contact. The small net-phone icon on her task bar was blinking.

Cherry pulled her microphone closer.

"What do you want?" she asked.

"I've decided," the voice said in a tone of malicious glee, "that the ring alone won't cut it. I want more, or I'll log in and delete the files."

"The files are already written to CD," she said. "You can't delete them."

"If they come online," he said softly, "I can activate the hidden 'features' I've written in, and you'll wish it was deleted."

"I have nothing left to offer," she said, her voice betraying the tears that were threatening. "I need the job, and I need the money. What can I give you? I don't have much more jewelry, nothing special. Who ARE you?"

There was silence for a moment, then the little man sat down on a mushroom that popped up on the screen, and put his chin on his hand to think.

"I'll tell you what," he said. "I wouldn't want you to think I'm not a gentleman. Here's your deal. If you can tell me my name by tomorrow morning, same deadline, ten AM, the files are yours, I won't ask you for anything more, and I'll go away. If not, I'll leave a list of what I want from you in your e-mail, and I'll expect to collect."

The little man blinked off the screen, and the net-phone icon went still.

Cherryl didn't hesitate. She started with the company directory, working her way through each employee, checking their names, their jobs, looking for anyone short, disfigured, or with any relationship to the programs she was supposed to be working with. After about an hour, she'd combed the entire directory with no luck. She logged on to the chat program. As quickly as she could, she went from room to room, posting the same questions in each.

"Does anyone know a short man who programs databases? Does anyone know someone who would break into your computer within the company?"

Many of the people she met seemed to have suspicions, but no one knew who he was or where he was from. Two men and one woman tried to engage her in sexual conversation, and each time it reminded her of how he'd controlled her. How he'd made her sit with her legs spread and her face flushed as he did her work for her.

With a soft sob, she closed the chat program and sat back. She glanced around the office that she would probably not have for much longer. Brownridge would be back, and she had no doubt he'd be excited about the Web interface, but that was no consolation.

Cherryl grabbed her coffee cup and rose shakily to her feet. Coffee would be little help, but it was something to do, and at that moment, having something to do was all that mattered.

The lounge was all but deserted. Cherryl saw that her friend Karl Tseu was seated at one of the small circular tables, nursing a cup of coffee. Cherryl walked disconsolately to the coffee machine and poured herself a cup.

"Hey, stranger," Karl called out. "Finally stopped in for a fine cup of mocha java, huh?"

She turned to him, near tears, and sat quickly down across the table from him.

"Hey," he said, scanning her face and changing gears. "What's wrong? You look as though you've been promoted to management."

Cherryl gulped back the sob that nearly escaped, and met Karl's gaze. *What the hell,* she thought. As quickly as she could, she outlined her problem, the mess she'd gotten herself into, and the way she was being blackmailed over the solution

"You know," he said, "that's odd."

Cherryl looked up, clutching her untouched coffee. "What?" she asked.

"Well," Karl said slowly, "I knew the guy who had your job before you did. Odd little man. He was always hacking into his applications, changing things, bragging about how good he was. The thing is, the company never found a use for him. He sat in that room and wasted away. Literally. He died right there.

"What reminded me of it, though, was that thing about watching your legs. They found out after he died that he'd been hacking into the security system. He scared a couple of the secretaries half to death, and had one of the vice presidents stripped of her blouse before she got caught. She claimed he was blackmailing her with some e-mail or another . . . it's just odd. But it can't be him, he's dead. Heart attack."

Cherryl could hardly breathe.

"What was his name?" she asked.

"I remember the name because it was odd. Dan Stilts. I bet if he were still here, and knew they were giving you the assignments he was so hot to work on, he'd be pissed."

Cherryl was already moving. She stood and grabbed Karl by the arm. "Thank you," she said, kissing him on the cheek. Then she was gone, racing down the hallway toward her office.

There were two voice mails from Mr. Brownridge on her phone, an e-mail, and even a sticky note on her monitor screen. The client loved her work. Their management was eager to meet with her and discuss minor adjustments, and to get her input on further upgrades. In fact, they wanted to work with her exclusively on this project. Cherryl smiled for a moment, but until she cleared things up, she couldn't concentrate on figuring out how she'd meet those expectations. She had to save her job.

Cherryl quickly located the corporate directory and typed in the name Dan Stilts. The entry was still there, though he'd apparently been gone for some time. She breathed a little more easily. There was a picture of a studious man, short and bespectacled. He was frowning, as if the intrusion of the photographer had taken him away from something important. Stilts had been a senior developer. Cherryl read the short entry on the man, everything that remained, apparently. Satisfied that she knew all there was to know, she logged off, closed up her office, and went home.

For the first time since she'd met Mr. Brownridge, Cherryl slept peacefully.

Cherryl found the small, animated man dancing around her desktop when she logged on. She grimaced slightly at the ease with which he could break through computer security, but then, she remembered that he was dead, or that this was something only partially "him," and that the normal rules obviously didn't apply.

Her speaker crackled, and the same odd voice spoke up. "Hello, Cherryl, sleep well?"

"As a matter of fact," she replied, pulling the microphone closer, though she suspected he didn't need her to do so to hear what she said, "I did. Good morning, Dan. I hope you had a good night, as well?"

Nothing for a long moment. Then he said. "That could be a guess. Dan who?"

"Stilts, of course," she replied promptly.

There was another pause, and Cherryl typed in, "We have a deal, yes?"

"Do we?"

She saw that the copies of the files he'd developed were disappearing from her desktop, but that didn't matter. She'd given them all to Brownridge on CD.

"Now," he typed. "Perhaps we'll start dealing all over again."

"I don't think so, Dan," she said softly. "I have something you want. I know, in fact, what it is that you have wanted all along."

"What is that?" the voice replied, wavering.

"This," she said, waving her arms around the office. She grabbed the files Brownridge had dropped off the day before. "You never got a chance to do this, to show them what you COULD do, did you?"

The screen remained blank for a long moment. Cherryl held her breath.

"You are a very clever woman," he typed at last. "Not much of a developer, but clever."

"And you," she replied, "are a great developer, but one problem, Dan. You're dead. You need me, as much as I need you. Who else is going to believe this?"

The little man seemed to consider this. Then he looked up at her, and he grinned. "It's good, isn't it?" he asked. "I heard what Brownridge said—spinning gold from straw. That's why I chose the Rumplestiltskin graphic."

"That and your name," she pointed out.

"Well, yes," he conceded.

"I won't ever tell them," she said softly. "You can teach me, and we can work on these projects together. You can do all that you ever dreamed, and you'll be here when I grow old, just the same. You'll have what amounts to my firstborn—the first important thing ever attributed to me will have come from you."

His face took on a sly expression. "I really do like your legs, Cherryl," he said with a lascivious wink. "You'll have to humor me from time to time. I was very lonely here."

Cherryl colored again, but then smiled. Nodded. "I'm lonely, too," she admitted.

"Then," the small gnomish figure said, standing and stretching, "you'd better get ready for Brownridge and company. Wow them. Promise him anything. He'll like your legs, too—that's one reason I never got ahead here. They didn't like the way I looked."

He hesitated, then, with a last wink, he said, "We'll make great partners. Take the Cold Fusion book home and read it."

She nodded, but as she did so, the little man disappeared from her screen.

Suddenly, her door opened, and she quickly closed the chat window. Both Dean Ratliffe and Darius Brownridge stood in the doorway. Behind them, beaming over their shoulders like the Cheshire Cat, stood Bobby Shaw.

"We've decided," Brownridge told her without preamble, "to pay Mr. Shaw here a healthy fee for locating you, and bring you on as a senior developer here at the firm. This project will make us millions, and it's just the beginning."

Cherryl stood, taking the hand Brownridge offered firmly and noting that, despite his concentration on business, he finally found time to glance down at her legs. She also noted that the ring finger of the hand he offered was bare.

"Well," she said with a smile, "maybe we should celebrate over dinner?"

He looked at her legs again, glanced up quickly, and his own smile flashed. "Yes," he replied. "*That* is a fine idea."

As she logged off and shut down her workstation, Cheryl could almost see the animated figure of a short, grotesque little man laughing and watching them depart. She grabbed the Cold Fusion book from the shelf and tucked it under her arm.

"Light reading," she said, winking at Brownridge, who smiled back at her.

It had been a very good day.

KEEPING IT REAL

by Jody Lynn Nye

Jody Lynn Nye lists her main career activity as "spoiling cats." She lives northwest of Chicago with two of the above and her husband, author and packager Bill Fawcett. She has published thirty books, four of them in collaboration with Anne McCaffrey, including *The Ship Who Won*; edited a humorous anthology about mothers, *Don't Forget Your Spacesuit, Dear!,* and over seventy short stories. Her latest books are *The Lady and the Tiger,* third in her Taylor's Ark series, and *Myth-Taken Identity*, co-written with Robert Asprin.

THE streetlight opposite the door of Sole Man flickered into brassy life. Rodney Price glanced at the clock.

"Six o'clock, Ms. Southey," Rod said. "I've got to close up now."

"Oh, not yet," the big African American woman pleaded. "I just can't decide between this blue leather and this red one." She turned toward the brown-haired white man, who stood three inches shorter and at least thirty pounds lighter than she. "What do you think?"

Rod scanned the two bright scraps of leather in her

hands and contrasted it with her deep skin tones. "The blue. They'll be a knockout with your hat."

"Okay, baby," Desra Southey said, with a big grin. "Blue. But I want lots of beads. Lots." Rod had picked up his order pad, scratched out 'red' and wrote in 'blue,' the fifteenth change in two hours. She went to read over his shoulder. "When can I pick up my boots?"

"Um," Rod opened the calendar on the counter. "There are two orders ahead of yours. How's two weeks from today?" She nodded. He made a note. "Can I get a deposit? Twenty-five percent. That's a hundred and ten."

Desra laid six crumpled bills on the glass top. Rod pulled the carbon copy off the pad and handed it to her. Satisfied at last, she sailed out into the dimming light. Rod locked the shop's front door and turned the "OPEN" sign around to read "CLOSED." He turned to look at the hides and beads scattered on his broad wooden worktable and made a face.

Another order. A blessing and a curse. With a sigh, he sat down at the table and pulled the latest project toward him.

Rod Price had graduated from the Midwestern Institute of Art that June, and in October, over the protests of his parents, had moved from their home in the well-to-do suburb of Camden Bluff to the heart of the city about a mile from campus. All the time he had been working on his degree, he had been fascinated by the moving beat he could sense beneath the surface of the city. He hoped to capture some of that essence in his art. Despite what his family thought, he didn't mean to exist in some castle in the air, waiting to get rich on sculpture and painting. He intended to make a living crafting custom boots.

He knew he had talent. During his senior internship at Cosway Lewis, a noted fashion house, he'd spent an entire semester apprenticed to a master shoemaker. His were the pumps and boots that adorned the feet of the runway models who showed off the house's fashions at the annual show. An item on the evening news that showcased him assured drop-ins from curious customers from all over the vast city, who almost never failed to make an order. Locals had discovered him, too. Even in a place he thought there wasn't a lot of money for luxuries, people were willing to pay for quality and good design.

The problem was, Rod wasn't as fast as he needed to be to keep himself above water. He might make the most incredible looking boots and shoes, but with each sequin and bead having to be hand applied and each applique needing to be hand sewn, it took him a week to make a $400 pair. If someone went crazy and ordered more than one pair, he couldn't promise when they'd be ready. He was already starting to have a backlog.

When he went home after one AM, he was exhausted. Three pairs needed to be finished all for the same wedding at the end of the week, and the customers weren't letting him off the hook. He had no choice but to stitch, glue, and hammer until he couldn't see straight.

The next day he posted a notice in the shop for part-time help. Everyone who came into the store over the next week read it.

"So what's it pay?" one man asked, as Rod measured his feet for a pair of crocodile ankle boots. "My son, he's fourteen. He's good with his hands."

"About six . . ." Rod measured the skepticism in the man's eyes, "er, ten dollars an hour."

"To do what?"

"Cutting out leather pieces, sorting beads, sweeping up—I can't afford to throw away limited-edition beads or sequins," he explained.

The customer eyed him. "My boy gonna learn anything here?"

"Well, sure," Rod exclaimed, maybe a little too heartily, as he sat back on his heels. "I'll let him observe everything I'm doing. When I get caught up, I'll guide him step by step through the process. I'm sure if he's good with his hands, he'll be fine."

"No, that isn't what I mean," the man said, shaking his head. "If he screw up, you gonna tell him he screwed up?"

"Well, I . . ."

"Forget it," the customer said, waving a hand. "Maybe this ain't the place for him. He'll go to Mc-Donald's, or something."

"But why not?" Rod almost wailed.

But the man didn't answer. He finished looking over the design books and left. A few other people glanced at the notice, but no one asked for the job. Rod took his question to Desra Southey. She had been one of the few people on the street who hadn't immediately blown him off when he had moved in, and who told him outright that the only stupid question was one that hadn't been asked.

"Why did he say that?" Rod asked her. "I could really use the help."

"I don't know if he believes you, baby," Desra told him, as she folded baby clothes on a display. "When you didn't say right out that you'd hold his boy to standards, he wouldn't believe you were keeping it real."

Rod had heard that phrase a lot around the city, usually a couple of street dudes talking to one another as they passed him. Frankly, he didn't really understand what that meant. He looked puzzled.

"They still think you're a rich white college boy who came down here to show off, doing them a big favor by coming down here to live," Desra explained. "They think you won't give them their due credit. People want to see your true face, not exaggerating what you think, and not hiding it either. You're offering too much for the job. It's setting the kids up for a fall."

"But that's not what I meant to do at all," Rod protested.

Desra gave him a tilted smile. "I believe you, but you have to give the right money for the job, not too much—just what it's worth. I know an idealist when I see one, but not everyone wants to go beneath the surface. It's a balance. If you go off like a rocket on some kid because he makes one little mistake, you're acting like The Man, instead of a neighbor. If you don't call an employee on mistakes just because he's African American, you're a bleeding heart, knee-jerk liberal like they talk about in the papers, and you'll be out of here when the wind changes. You want us all to approve of you so bad. We'd like to, but we've been burned before. You've had advantages few of us have, and you can understand that people are jealous. You've got to come to people on a level, tell them the truth, and don't overreact. Keep it real. You haven't been."

"That's not true!" Rod protested. But it was. He did want his new neighbors to approve of him. He wanted them to be happy he was doing what he was doing. "I'm staying. I swear it."

Rod went back to Sole Man with his proverbial tail between his legs. He hated to think of himself as either a big shot or a liberal mouthing platitudes. Honesty forced him to realize that it might be construed as acting like The Man, looking condescendingly at his neighbors to notice that he, a well-to-do suburban white male, had "lowered" himself to set up shop here. Why should he get any more notice than any other shop owner on the street, or, indeed, in the city? He meant to do it right, to genuinely be a part of the neighborhood. If that meant realigning his approach a little, he'd do it. The stuff about being scared was true, too. It made him nervous to think of kicking out his supports and working his way up in the local social structure like anyone else. He was afraid of being attacked. But he genuinely liked the people who stopped in to talk to him, he loved the city, and he loved his work. If he could make his business pay, he would stay. His principles were what mattered, after all.

He knew that if they opened him up they'd find his ideals written on his heart. He believed in supporting the needy, bolstering their self-esteem while they worked their way up to meaningful employment, getting involved with community projects and supporting the efforts of those who cared to better themselves and their communities. That's what he was doing there. All right, so his business wasn't aimed at the very basic people who lived around him, but he had to pay his taxes so his fair share would go to bolster the fruits of his idealism.

In the meantime, he wasn't solving the problem of hiring an assistant. Following Desra's advice he had lowered his offered wage, but word had gotten around of the original quote he had made to that first customer, so the next prospective worker had left in a huff and come back with her father. The father, a man of undoubted means from a dubious source (Rod didn't want to admit to himself that the man might be a drug dealer), threatened to go to the city and have Rod's business license pulled, not to mention that Rod might fall prey to a bunch of other, less official problems that would rain down on him if he dared insult the man's daughter again. The man called him a lot of names, but the one that stung Rod the most was "phony." He tried to protest, but his platitudes and reassurances sounded false even in his own ears. He was on the losing side, and he knew it.

By then the girl had tired of the argument, and pulled her father out of the store. Rod closed the door behind them, shaking. Desra was right: he was out of his depth. But he looked back at his workbench, now covered to overflowing with orders. He snatched up the phone and dialed the outplacement office at the art school.

"I need a couple of interns," he found himself explaining to his old counselor Marian McCuillen. "I can pay them."

The counselor tried to talk him out of offering any kind of salary. "The work is supposed to be what's important. You didn't get paid. Working in a creative environment and learning an art form is all the compensation a student should expect."

"I know," Rod said, sewing beads as he talked. He pricked his finger for the fortieth time. "But I wouldn't feel right. The worker is entitled to his or her hire."

"They'll do it for nothing, you know."

Rod knew. "I'm desperate. I need someone right away."

"I'll see what I can do," Ms. McCuillen said. "When do you need them?"

"Tomorrow," Rod said. "Tonight."

"Okay. We'll post it on the Web site and send you candidates."

Rod hung up and called Cosway Lewis. Cos himself answered the phone.

"Roddy! You're not asking for the moon, or anything, are you?" the designer laughed, when Rod explained his predicament. "I'll see if anyone has a little time they can give you. It's good to hear you're making it down there. Come up and show me some of your work sometime. I might find a place for you."

"Thanks, Cos, but I'm okay," Rod assured him.

He was dismayed, but what did he expect? Who could come to his rescue in the middle of the night? This was Friday. The wedding was Sunday, and two of the pairs of gold leather boots were still not even cut out.

Saturday he didn't even open the storefront, sewing and gluing furiously to make his deadline. He was due at his parents' house at seven for dinner. He'd tried to get out of the obligation, pleading overwork, but his mother refused to hear it.

"You've changed the date eight times. Come tonight. That's all," she had said, and hung up before he could argue further.

By six, his fingers were cramped and his eyes half-closed with exhaustion. He shut off the high-intensity lamp over the worktable and stood up, massaging his aching back.

"I wish someone would hurry up and get here to help me," he said.

"Why don't you come back here and set up a little factory?" his mother tried to persuade him over the gnocchi. "I know manufacturers in the Far East who could be mass-producing your designs—a thousand pairs a week!"

"No, Mom," Rod protested, winding his sore hand around the fork. "That wouldn't be right. My boots wouldn't be works of art if they weren't made with love."

He meant to go back to the store as soon as dinner was over, but the combination of his mother's home-made pasta, fine wine, and a little too much dessert along with the hum of soft music and his parents' good-natured bantering lulled him into sleep on the living room couch.

His eyes sprang open in the dark. He scrambled to his feet, thrusting aside the blanket his mother must have tucked around him. Five o'clock in the morning! He had to get back to the store! The wedding party would be there by seven. Oh, no! He was in real trouble. God knew what the bride's family would do to him if the bridesmaids' shoes weren't ready. He was toast.

He made the drive down in record time, speeding through the silent city, the yellow streetlamps glaring at him like so many pairs of hot, accusing eyes. Why didn't he ask his mom to wake him up by ten?

Rod slewed his car into one of the two cramped parking spaces behind his building. It was always dark back there except for the red emergency EXIT sign—where was that bright white light coming from? Was Sole Man being robbed? Very quietly he killed the engine and crept toward the door, keeping to one side like a cop in a TV show.

He wasn't quiet enough. Whoever the intruder was had heard him. Scrambling footsteps erupted inside.

Rod's heart raced as he felt for his cell phone, but in a moment the building fell silent. Rod counted to twenty, then called 911.

Within ten minutes, two patrol cars with their mars lights rotating but no sirens rolled into the narrow alleyway. Rod waited in his car while the four officers kicked in his rear door, then slipped into the store one by one. He held his breath until one of them came out and gestured him over with a wave of his flashlight.

"No one's in here," the police officer, a burly African American in his fifties, said. "Come on in and tell us what's missing."

"I don't have much anyone would want to steal," Rod admitted, rushing into the building a little ahead of his escort. "There's only about a hundred dollars in the cash drawer . . ."

He stopped in front of the worktable, and blinked.

". . . Look worth stealing to me," the African American officer behind him was saying. "Why don't you count 'em and tell me if any of them are gone."

Rod gawked. Not only was the single pair of gold wedding boots sitting there, but so were the other two pairs. Complete. Whole. Finished. The blue boots for Desra Southey sat beside them. It was impossible. Only a few hours ago they had existed that way only in his imagination, but here they were in the flesh, so to speak, including the added fillip he had thought of just before he left and added to the drawing: the inclusion of a single ruby red bead here and there among the sprays of silver tube beads to startle the eye. And the black, over-the-knee spike-heeled boots he was making for the lady friend of the dangerous gentleman. He stroked the soft lamb's leather of the tan ankle boots adorned with gold buckles and dangling heart beads that ten hours ago had been a heap of components, the uppers not even cut out to the measurements on the order sheet that now rested below the pristine black soles. Eight pairs in all had been

completed to the last stitch. Every single order he had
left behind was finished. How—? When—? But most
importantly, *who?* Who had done this for him?

"Well?"

Rod spun, his eyes and mouth open in shock. At
the sight of the policeman's impatient face, he tried
to gather his wits. "Uh. Nothing's *missing.*" How
could he explain that the vandals that had broken in
had done all his work? He unlocked the cash drawer,
counted out the meager contents. "No, it's all here."

"You musta surprised them before they could grab
anything," the burly officer's partner said, running a
finger along the tan boots. "Real nice."

"Sweet," his partner agreed. "Okay, sir, if you'll
just sign this report, we'll be on our way."

They left Rod alone as the sun rose through the
window of his shop, staring at the impossible.

The conundrum continued to puzzle Rod during the
next two weeks. The wedding party had arrived not
long after the police had left. The matron of honor
was so thrilled with her boots which, by the way, fit
her as if they'd been molded around her feet, that she
ordered two new pairs for herself. Having seen the
bridesmaids' footwear, the bride and groom stopped
by on their way to the airport with a design for his-
and-hers stack heels they hoped Rod could finish by
the time they got back from their honeymoon. By the
time he came out of the daze caused by the bizarre
break-in, he found himself with a worktable piled as
high as it had been before.

As for his mysterious benefactors, no one could
shed a light. Cos Lewis and the school counselor both
said that they hadn't sent anyone. Besides, neither one
would have been able to get past the alarm system.
Rod saw his work beginning to stack up again, and
asked both to hurry and send him help as soon as
they could.

The biggest item on his agenda was a pair of jew-
eled desert boots for a charity auction to benefit the

local magnet school. Rod had solicited donations for the materials, and he was donating his time. Paying work, though, began to take precedence, as Rod's bills started to come due. Astonishingly, electricity, water, gas, and trash pickup all cost twice what they did in the suburbs, and he had to start paying off his college loans.

Ashaka, the girl whose father had threatened him, had come back, sulkily, to request a special order. She wanted a pair of flame-red thigh-high lace-up boots with circles cut out of the leather all along the outer edge, for her upcoming audition on *Young Talent America.* Rod hated to take the commission, foreseeing problems with the family, but worse ones probably awaited him if he refused. He insisted on having a chaperone on every occasion Ashaka came in for a fitting. To his relief, that made the girl feel important, so her temper stayed under control, and "daddy" didn't have to come in to deal with any disrespect.

Unfortunately, the elaborate decorations she demanded made the leather pull away from her legs. Rod found himself having to deal with the charity project and Ashaka's, with time running out.

He didn't go home the final night. He was vaguely aware of darkness falling, the traffic outside his door growing heavier and heavier, then tapering off to the occasional vehicle and the sweep of the police patrol's spotlight as they rolled up and down the sulfur-lit street. He threaded a needleful of gold beads, and realized he could no longer distinguish between one size and another. His eyelids irresistibly heavy, he staggered back to a camp bed he kept near the little bathroom. He set his alarm watch for an hour. A brief nap would refresh him. Besides, he couldn't afford to take longer.

A little noise roused him before the beep of his watch. Rod raised his head. He had been drooling into his pillow, dreaming of an Academy Awards ceremony where he had just won the Oscar for Best Footgear in a Supporting Role. In the darkness he strained his

ears to listen. Humming was coming from the workroom, maybe more than one person. Had the burglars
come back?

He rolled off the cot and crawled on hands and
knees toward the sound. His cell phone was in a
drawer with his car keys. He couldn't call the police,
and he doubted he could open the fire door at the
rear without making so much noise the burglars would
hear him. If he could see what they were doing, he
could find a place to hide until they left.

His own heartbeat as loud as a kettledrum in his
ears, he peered around the doorjamb, and his eyes
almost started out of his head.

Sitting on the worktable in a circle were eight little
dark men no higher than his hip. His unfinished work
lay across their laps as they stitched, cut, glued, and
painted, all to the accompaniment of their thready little voices uplifted in sweet, rhythmic song. As far as
Rod could tell, they were naked, the gleam of the
bright lights shining on smooth, walnut-dark skin.
Their hair was braided into tight little knots all over
their heads, and their faces, lined like wrinkled apples,
were decorated with dark blue tattoos. Rod rubbed
his eyes, then pinched himself to make sure he was
really awake. *Ow!* He was awake. Who were they?
What were they? Should he go out and introduce
himself?

Suddenly, the alarm in his wristwatch erupted in
high-pitched beeping. The singing stopped. The little
men looked around in alarm, leaped up, and dashed
into the shadows. Rod sprang out after them, just in
time to see the last one disappearing through the wall
leading to the tire shop next door. He turned back to
the table. They had nearly finished with all of the
projects he had left sitting out. The boots for Ashaka
were complete in every detail. He'd interrupted the
little man who had been applying high-gloss polish to
the uppers. The charity boots were finished except for
two lines of gemstone beads, which he could easily do
himself. Rod raised the left boot to the light and ex-

amined the work. Every stitch was even, tinier than
he could ever do himself by hand or with a machine.
Every bead was anchored, every sequin flat and perfect. Once he had finished being amazed, he was
grateful.

"I'm in debt to them," he explained to Desra
Southey the next morning. "I owe them. I've got to
give them *something*."

"You leave the Little Workers alone," she told him
sternly, pushing him into a chair in the stockroom behind her counter. She leveled a finger at his nose. "Sit
down there, little baby boy, and let me explain it to
you so you get it, 'cause you don't get it. You look
at me like I'm just an ignorant woman, but you saw
something last night you can't explain. I can explain
it, and there's rules to follow.

"Back in the bad old days, when my ancestors were
slaves, their white masters gave them too much work
to do. And when they didn't finish it, they got hell
beaten out of them, or worse." She looked at Rod
sternly. "Don't try to tell me it's not true. It's history,
and we're still fighting it today. The Little Workers
sometimes came out of nowhere, and saved those
tired, downtrodden slaves from a beating by doing
their work overnight. The masters never knew the difference, and those poor people got a decent night's
rest. You ought to be humbled that the Little Workers
are troubling to notice you. It's like they are welcom-
ing you here, little baby. You ought to be proud."

"I am," Rod said, sincerely awed. "That's why I
want to pay them. They're doing what I can't do.
Their work is so beautiful I want to reward them.
What can I give them?"

"You just leave them alone," Desra repeated. "They
do what they do because it's right. You're not anywhere near a slave, but maybe they're saving you from
a beating. This neighborhood can be rough. But they
do it for free, asking nothing and no thanks."

"It's not right," Rod protested. "They did what I

couldn't do. It's only justice that I should pay them
for it."

"No." Desra was firm. "Not a thing. Don't even
notice they're there. They came because they saw you
were honestly overwhelmed. I think it means they believe you're sincere about staying. If you let them
know you saw them, they'll go away for good. Just be
grateful. If you've got to give to someone, give your
money to the church or one of the charities. Lord
knows, there's too many people around here haven't
got what they need. Don't splash out too much. Give
what's right. Keep people's pride in mind. You'd hate
it if someone lorded it over you. Think about that."

Rod did. Knowing that the Little Workers were
watching him, he did his best to stay on top of his
assignments, not wanting to take advantage of their
incredible kindness. He did spend some time reading
up about them. The only references he could find were
in Civil War contemporary accounts dictated by escaped slaves who had come north to the city.

Word about the Little Workers' visits to Sole Man
spread throughout the neighborhood. Some didn't believe it. Those who did were divided into two camps:
the ones who resented that the Little Workers' toil
should be wasted on a honky, and those who saw it
as a sign that he belonged there among them. It was
among the latter group that Rod started to get a
trickle of business. He was grateful for his neighbors'
acceptance, and wary of the ones who belonged to
the former group. Following Desra's advice, he made
donations to five local churches and three charities
and left the Little Workers alone.

He managed to assuage his growing guilt for a time
as his business prospered. The local television station
did a feature piece on him, and the telephone rang
constantly. Aware that he could fall behind again and
have to rely upon the kindness of the Little Workers
he accepted only the orders he could handle on his
own, with the help of two Art Institute interns and
occasionally his mother, but no system was proof against

human nature. As New Year's Eve approached, he found himself once again in a crunch.

On Christmas Eve he found himself wrestling with yards of silver, mesh-perforated leather when the telephone rang.

"Rod? Geneva." It was the elder and more competent of his interns. "Listen, my brother's in from France and he's having a party at the University Club for his college buddies. He asked me to hostess it for him, so I'll be out the next couple of days. You don't mind, do you? Thanks," she said, hanging up before he could protest. He dropped the skins and grabbed for the phone to call her back, but no one answered. Rod fumed.

At least she had called. Tefi, his other assistant, hadn't been in since the weekend before Christmas, and had not dropped a dime even once to tell Rod where he was. Rod felt a headache coming on.

Sixteen pairs of boots lay on the table in various stages of unreadiness, all of them needing to be finished by New Year's Eve. He didn't want to leave that night, knowing that the Little Workers would move in and finish what he couldn't. But he had to go pick up his girlfriend, having promised to stop in at the Cosway Lewis Christmas party, then drive up to his parents' home for the Prices' annual holiday dinner. He almost piled all the pieces in the car to take them with him, but that would call for too many explanations to his girlfriend and his parents. He didn't want to try to explain a 150-year-old folk legend about little people who made shoes.

He returned early the morning after Christmas knowing what he would find. Rod was surprised how angry he felt on beholding sixteen pairs of completed boots. Sixteen pairs of perfect footwear, as artistic and gorgeous as they had been in his imagination, better than he could make them himself. Sixteen pairs whose owners would love them more than anything they had ever owned. Sixteen pairs that would give rise to orders for sixteen, or sixty, or six hundred more. Rod picked up his leather shears and threw them across the room.

"Why?" he howled at the absent benefactors in his frustration. "Why won't you let me thank you?"

He looked across the street at Desra's shop, open for her post-Christmas sale. He considered going over there to ask her to find a loophole in the Little Workers' credo, but he knew what she would say: *Leave them alone, or they'll go away for good.* But he couldn't. His innate sense of justice demanded that a favor had to be repaid. He had no choice. He owed them thanks, and thanks they were going to get.

When he was a little boy, Rod's mother had read him the fairy tale of "The Elves and the Shoemaker." The gift of clothes had made the elves angry, so Rod ruled out clothing his benefactors' nakedness. They made their own music. But everyone had to eat, didn't they?

He considered ordering an elegant meal from the finest restaurant in town, but Rod didn't want to leave hot food out too long, fearing salmonella or botulism poisoning. Instead, he ordered cold trays from the best delicatessen in town, adding bottles of champagne and beer and a whole Eli's chocolate chip cheesecake, his favorite dessert. He arranged the feast on his worktable. To attract the Little Workers' attention to the shop, he left a pair of his own boots that needed repairing in the middle of the table, and sneaked into his back room to wait.

Night fell, and the street grew quiet. Just before midnight Rod was considering whether he should put the food back into the refrigerator again, when he heard the sound of humming coming from the front of the store. He peeked around the doorframe.

Eight little shadows appeared out of the walls and floated toward the table. As Rod watched in amazement, each cluster of darkness coalesced into a little man with a dark, wrinkled face standing in a ring around Rod's bait. They wore expressions of satisfaction as they looked down at the damaged footwear.

One of them lifted his hand, and a needle appeared gleaming between his fingers. Another one clapped, and a piece of leather just the right size and shape dropped into his palms. A third produced a ball of waxed twine out of thin air. Rod felt as though he was living in a fairy tale as the little men moved together almost in a dance. The ruined boot floated up between them as though suspended from a string. The little men's hands flew as they stitched, the needle passing from one to another as the boot rotated in midair. Their movements were so beautiful Rod felt himself slipping into a trance. Their music sounded like the city come to life. He breathed it in, loving it.

Suddenly the humming stopped. Rod, jerked out of his reverie, watched in horror as a couple of the other Little Workers, who had been observing, pointed out the food on the table to their fellows. The little faces contorted in angry grimaces, and one let out a howl of rage.

What have I done? Rod thought in despair. But it was too late. Instead of eating their New Year's feast, the Little Workers snatched up the food and started throwing it. In fury, they raised the bottles of beer and champagne over their heads and brought them smashing down on the tabletop, the floor, the counter, and whatever else was within range. The floor foamed with liquor. The good smoked sturgeon that Rod had so lovingly arranged on the platter splatted a slice at a time into the display window. The sturgeon was followed by the pastrami, the gravlax, the pate de fois gras and the chicken mousse, until the entire pane of glass was covered with a horrible mosaic. One of the Little Workers took out his anger by jumping up and down in the cheesecake, kicking pieces of it to the walls.

When they were through destroying Rod's offerings, the first needleman cleared a space on the table with his foot, lovingly laid the repaired boots down, and jumped off, turning into a puff of smoke as he went. The others followed without hesitation, vanishing into the walls, gone forever.

"No!" Rod cried, leaping out of his hiding place. "Come back!" But he knew they wouldn't.

It took him the rest of the night to clean up the store, kicking himself the whole time. Not a bite of the feast remained that was fit to eat. He dumped the last of the ruined food into the trash cans at the rear of the store, and went out to eat scrambled eggs at the diner on the corner. The man who owned it was in the "waste it on a honky" camp, but he seemed to sense something was wrong. He served Rod's breakfast with an almost sympathetic glance, and went back to jawing with his regulars at the counter.

Sooner or later Rod was going to have to admit to Desra what he had done, and, fortified by eggs and six cups of coffee, he decided sooner was better than later. Her reaction wasn't exactly what he expected.

"I never knew anyone who shot himself in the foot on purpose!" Desra howled, wiping tears of laughter from her eyes. "You're gonna be a legend of your own one day, a man who was too honest to take a gift. I knew you couldn't accept nothing for free."

"I know," Rod said glumly, sitting in the chair with his hands clasped between his knees. "I feel like the dumbest man who ever lived. I'm sorry I did it. Well, I'm not sorry. But I am."

"Well, it might turn out to be the smartest thing you ever did," Desra corrected him, with a friendly pat on the back. "You're gonna have to make it here now on your own, with no magical backup. People who resented you getting help from the Little Workers are going to respect you because you kept going on your own. If you stay," she added, with a questioning lift of her brows.

"I'll stay," Rod promised her. "My success wasn't real before, because it wasn't all mine, but from now on it will be. I'll keep it real if it kills me."

"Now, that," Desra said, pleased, "I'll believe."

THE ROSE GARDEN

by Michelle West

Michelle West is the author of a number of novels, including *The Sacred Hunt* duology and *The Broken Crown, The Uncrowned King, The Shining Court, Sea of Sorrows, The Riven Shield,* and *The Sun Sword,* the six novels in *The Sun Sword* series, all available from DAW Books. She reviews books for the online column *First Contacts,* and less frequently for *The Magazine of Fantasy & Science Fiction.* Other short fiction by her appears in *Sirius: The Dog Star, The Magic Shop, Sorcerer's Academy, Assassin Fantastic,* and *Villains Victorious.*

ONCE upon a time doesn't cut it here. Fairies? Dragons? Evil wizards? Knights? Gone. Long gone. The vast forests in which men came of age are tame little gardens, fenced in by naturalists and big city environmentalists, with their placards, their slogans, their angry words.

He lived in one, once.

Was proud, in one. Arrogant. Even that word doesn't mean what it once did; words are shades. They have no power. He's got some.

Because he's what's left. He and the dozens of dwindling demimortals, cursed by old power to linger. Forgotten, they're clearly not dead, and they certainly haven't been freed.

281

Not, at least, in the traditional sense. He left his forest at the turn of the century, when he realized the boundaries that kept him trapped there were withering like waterless flowers. Trees—normal trees, dwarfed and stunted and with only a hint of true grandeur—overgrew his cage of a ruined kingdom. If kingdom was a word that could describe the empty, small space that remained of his serfs, his peasants, the men and women who labored in droves in the finery of his shadowed castle, shunning his presence, shunning all sight of his face. Even the form that he was chained to was forgotten; it drifted past as the cities grew across the landscape. As cars replaced coaches, and enlightment replaced romance. He was here.

It's at least a century since he was forced from his forest home; since the prison bars were bent out of shape and the magic of containment fled. He didn't know what had killed the old witch who had cursed him, but he could guess: There's a steel here that knows no life and responds to no magic. Instead of swords, men have guns, and the guns are often too heavy for a single one of them to lift.

He never had that problem. He was doomed to be trapped in the form of a raging beast until the spell at last ended, and he joined the war. The men couldn't see him for what he was; the spell was *that* weak.

The war was fought in trenches. It was fought with gas, with guns, with the unfashionable bayonets given to the less valuable soldiers when armaments were in short supply.

He survived, but he knew he would. He made no friends, but at least he had comrades—people who trusted him to guard their backs. Trusted him to survive. He had ordered men to their deaths at his leisure as a noble, and once or twice, he'd made an entertainment of it.

The war was less entertaining. Perhaps because the men who died in it—boys, really—didn't deserve death. They hadn't thwarted his will. And they didn't complain about a man who looked as if he would have been more at home on a Viking warship, although they did complain about his stench.

After the war—and the medals that were somehow significant in that diminished age, he drifted for a couple of decades. He had money, and he knew that money was of value because he had *always* had money. He used it wisely, and it grew.

He joined the second great war as well, and his ferocity and strength were again tested, as was the witch's curse. Both held true; he didn't die. But he lost most of the men assigned to him on a beach somewhere in Europe; he walked among the carnage, thinking that monsters were no longer something to be feared. Not when men alone could do so much damage.

And again, for surviving—and killing—he was given medals and decorations, and he was paid. The money grew. The respect grew. He used both sparingly, because he had not yet left the forest entirely behind, and he knew what he was: The Beast.

But in time, the forest at last left him, and the captivity left as well: he was a free man. The witch, he thought, was certainly dead, and good riddance. He bought a house. And when he found the neighbors too persistently *friendly,* he sold that one and bought another.

The only thing of value he had left behind in the ruined kingdom of his forgotten youth was his garden. And as time passed, he missed it. In the city, with postage stamp backyards, there's not a lot of room for rosebushes. He began to grow them anyway, changing their color and the folds of their leaves with time and patience; making them diminutive or giant when the whim took him. Other men took such flowers to hothouses across the continent and won prizes for their supposed mastery of their craft. He didn't want to share. He never had.

He was no longer the Beast. The name belonged to some muppet in a children's show that played drums. But even memory of that began to fade, with time

and fashion. He lost dirt and hair. Everyone in the
city he chose as his home showered at least once a
day; sometimes more in the summer months. Far be
it from him to stand out, although the transition was
harder than the one that had given him an earned
home: the guns and the noise and the screaming
deaths were gone, and their echoes teased memory.
He let them.

He remembered the day his hair fell out. It fell
out in clumps. He looked more pathetic than chemo
patients, because he was tall and his shoulders were
linebacker broad. His teeth, praise whatever gods
lived in the electronic age, didn't go the same route,
but they blunted and shortened, losing edge and
sharpness. They were still too yellow, but he disguised
that fact by the simple expedient of smoking. Smoking
fell out of fashion, though. He indulged anyway. The
confederacy of smokers was growing as small as the
forests that once kept salvation at bay.

He had been a prince, in his kingdom. And he had
offended a powerful witch. He no longer remembered
how; witches were easily offended, and they didn't
usually bother to offer an explanation if it provided
their victims any comfort. But the covenant between
the cursed and the curser still bound her, and she was
forced to tell him what the rules of his confinement
were; forced as well to tell him the key that would set
him free. It had something to do with roses and
women. That's right. He had to earn the love of a
woman while trapped in the form of the Beast, and
he would be a man once again.

And on this particular day, he thought of that old
curse with something approaching rage—a rage that
had died with the death of Hitler, with VE-Day, with
the end of that war.

Something about the war had scarred him. He
couldn't say what. Others did, and at leisure, over the
decades. Psychologists. Veterans. The children of the
men who had died, unknown, upon those distant fields.
He hadn't. Maybe he suffered from survivor's guilt.

He couldn't say. But for the first time in two wars, he *wanted* to.

So he started the roses again, and he began to look for a woman. Somehow they would cure him, and he could let go. Age would creep in, and death, but he'd seen death and youth, and he could *still* see it, whenever he closed his great, round, animal eyes. The senselessness of it. The rage. Not even as the ruler of his beleaguered kingdom had he seen such carnage, and for the first time since he'd escaped his captivity, he regretted the loss of those old magics. There wouldn't have been war, that's for sure. A lot of useful curses, but no war.

But the witch was demonstrably gone, killed by lack of belief, by boredom, by technology. Her curse remained, and he set about lifting it with a vengeance.

He met his share of women. In the fifties, it was difficult. But later, in the decades to follow, things changed. In the seventies, and the eighties; in the nineties and even at the turn of the millennium. When the wars, and the fear of wars, were gone. The women weren't shy, they weren't often young, but they had a raw energy—a visceral bestiality—that he found attractive. They didn't simper. They didn't plead. They didn't get thrown out by their families if they happened to lose their virginity. That took him a while to get used to. The lack of weeping and wailing. The lack of fear.

But the thing is: they were all the same. They wanted sex, not love. They sometimes confused the two. Sometimes he confused them.

Still, sex brought him a certain sense of skin comfort, and he accepted the exchange of pleasure for moments without any memory other than scent and touch. He became content to be the Beast in this city. He changed his name. He changed his house. He mowed the lawn, and he found neighbors that wouldn't pry too closely into his private life.

He didn't choose a poor neighborhood to live in, and it sort of grew up around him, a forest of cement and wood and aluminium, of shale shingles, and asbestos, things neat and orderly in the hands of men. The advantage of living in an upper middle class neighborhood was this: No one was home during the day. They worked long, long hours. They went to cottages or vacation condos on the weekends. Or skiing, when the season was right for it.

Raccoons became more of an enemy than the men with sharp swords used to be. They picked tiles off his roof. He could hear one of them now, tearing the vines off the garage that hemmed in his little green space to the north. They'd even chewed a hole in the siding on the remodeled back end of the house, which really annoyed him. Had he still had the teeth and the jaws of a beast, he would have eaten them with great satisfaction. But he tried, once, and he ended up getting rabies shots as a result. It wasn't pleasant, and it didn't keep the little bastards away.

He had a car. Not a little one; a little one didn't fit. He had as much food as an army of serfs could produce, two blocks away, in neat aisles, stacks of tins and boxes, labeled with color and content. He had no need to hunt or kill.

Perhaps the loss of the need for sustenance and survival caused the melancholy.

When he first left the forest, when he first made his home here, he looked like a hairy barbarian. Now he looked like a civilized man, just one side of his prime. The mirror didn't recognize the changes, but it didn't matter; no one else saw the Beast.

Which seemed, to the only man who could observe the *truth*, to mean that he could never actually be free of the curse itself.

Then again, what harm did it do these days? He was going to live forever. He would never age. He had everything a mortal man claimed to want in this age of youth and beauty.

And he was tired of it all. So he continued to grow his roses. He made a shrine of his tiny backyard. He watered them, fed them light, fed them nutrients. He tied their branches up in place while the bushes themselves matured, and he tended them whenever he could. Thinking of salvation.

He tended his roses in the day, and when the day was done, he dressed up and went out for the evening, looking for salvation. There were a lot of people who hit the bars looking for salvation, and he had as much reason as any of them did.

He never found it.

There was a time when he thought he would. In those days, relationships could last months. One even made it past the crest of a year before it fell apart, in tears and accusations. And the accusations—something to do with fidelity—were entirely true. He wasn't. It wasn't in his nature. It never had been.

He wasn't dishonest about that. Honesty was less costly than the stressful web of lies and deceit. *Everyone* lied, these days. It was the fashion. Sometimes the lies were big, and sometimes they were small. Sometimes they referred to wealth and money, sometimes they referred to age. Sometimes they referred to love, but usually in those instances, the lies were like double-edged, forgotten swords: they cut both ways.

They weren't for him.

Because he was no longer quite the Beast. Sure, he prowled. He prowled as much as the next guy. But he wasn't required, by his curse, to kill.

Which was a pity, at this particular moment, in this time. He didn't speak much. When he did, his voice was low, a growl of a voice. A bear's voice. A Beast's voice. It was the only thing that truly remained, and he hoarded it carefully.

Usually. But today? No. He couldn't contain his outrage, and he *roared*. The leaves in his garden trembled at the force of a sound they were never subjected to. He thought the roses might wilt, and that lent his fury strength, sustaining it. Hope wasn't much, but apparently when there was little of it, it was vastly more valued.

"How the hell did you get in here?"

The subject of his anger was as white as the whitest of his flowers—if you didn't count the dirt and the weather-beaten look of skin too long in the sun. Hair that made his early hair look *clean* by comparison grew around a gaunt expression like an oily, greasy frame. Dirt was smeared like makeup across the face that met his, caught in the motionless O of surprise that was rapidly turning to fear.

He took a step forward, and the interloper took a step back, crying out when the roses caught the dirty sweater. A girl's voice. High and fluting, wordless.

"Answer my question!"

Which, of course, produced no response. Well, not no response. Her hands clutched the stem of the flower she'd snapped from the bush. And her teeth bit her lip, the way thorns bit her dirty skin. How *dare* she touch his flowers?

He pulled a cell phone from his jacket pocket and waved it in front of her, like a gun. "I want to know how you did it. I lock the damn garage, and you didn't come in through the house. My yard is a greenhouse; it's domed by expensive glass, and heated year round. There are no gates. The only way in is through the garage or the house. You didn't get in by the house."

She said nothing. Nothing at all. But blood seeped between her fingers, tracing lines around her small knuckles. Shaking hands. Foolish girl.

"I'm going to call the police."

The police were useful. They owed their allegiance to no king, no kingdom; they weren't soldiers. They had guns, yes, but their uniforms were meant to be trusted, and if you had money in a well-off neighborhood, trust was easily invested.

"Oh. You don't want me to call the police? And why not? Look at you. Your jeans have holes in them. They're a size too large. No, two sizes too large. And they haven't been washed in two weeks. Your sweater is two sizes too small. You stink."

She swallowed. Her hands were red, and the blood

made them seem white as ivory. Small hands. Too thin to be strong.

Her fear seemed to eat away at the edges of outrage. But it didn't still his voice.

"What did you come here to steal? You can *see through the damned glass*. You've got eyes. You're an ugly little urchin, you're probably three different kinds of addict. You might have AIDS. You think the police won't cart you off and stick you where you deserve to be?"

But it was clear that she thought they *would*. She should have run. Then again, the garden was all of fifteen feet long; there weren't many places to run *to*.

"And your hand is *bleeding*. Did you think roses don't grow without thorns, you stupid child?"

She spoke for the first time, her voice so soft he had to strain to catch it. "I know all about thorns," she said bitterly. "And bleeding. You want your damn flower back? Here!" She held it out. But it didn't roll down her open palm; the thorns went deep, and they anchored themselves to her dirty skin.

He might be able to save it. He might be able to graft it to another bush.

He took it from her, and she cried out; he wasn't particularly gentle. But he had to stow the phone away in a pocket to do it.

Yes, he thought, calming slowly. He *could* save the flower. The prize of his collection, black rose. Night blossom.

"Why this flower?" he said bitterly, the softness of his words a wolf's growl.

"I meant it as a gift," she replied, just as bitterly. "It's a flower. You've got so damn many, I didn't think you'd miss one."

"I'd miss this one," he snapped. In spite of himself, his nose wrinkled. The *stench* of the girl was overpowering.

He reached for the garden hose and turned it on her face. And then, when she gasped and floundered, he snorted in disgust and picked her up by the back of her neck. She wasn't very heavy. She kicked him. She scratched at his arm. But she didn't bite. Good thing, for her.

He dragged her, cursing and swearing, into his house and he dragged her up the stairs to the bathroom. There, he turned on the bath, and let the water run until it was hot. He shifted the switch, and rain poured down from the metal casing. Into that manmade storm, he thrust the girl, handing her soap as he did.

"You can clean yourself," he said, "Or I can." It was a threat. It worked.

She slammed the glass door shut on him, and he watched her for a while.

"Take the clothes *off,* " he growled.

"Not while you're here!"

He considered his options with growing disgust, and then snorted and walked out, slamming the door. From behind its closed surface, he said, "You do know how to *use* soap, right?"

And she swore a lot, the words muted by the fall of water.

But the time he lost in taking the girl to the shower was the rose's time, and when he returned in haste to the garden, he saw that the stem itself was too dry. His anger returned, and he brought the flower into the house, and set it in a vase. He added sugared water. The bud would blossom; he would have at least that much of it. But it was already dead. Like so many people, it simply didn't know it yet.

The water fell silent.

He touched, as delicately as he could, the rose's petals, and then he pushed himself up from the table and bounded up the stairs, three at a time.

The girl, dressed still in clothing that reeked of the streets, had sidled out of the bathroom, her bright hair dripping. It was a deep shade of brown, and it took him a moment before he understood why it seemed so familiar: it was the color of his coat fur in bygone ages.

Her face was whiter than it had been, but her

scent—the scent of soap—was lost to the unwashed clothing. His sense of smell was acute; she was overpowering.

"You-will-take-those-off," he said, wanting to kill her. Wanting very much to kill her.

"I don't have any others," she replied, taking a step back. She dripped water across his carpets. No fine halls these, but they were still *his*.

"You can wear mine."

Her brows rose. The difference in their size—he, widened and strengthened by fury—was apparent.

He said, "The doors are locked. If you attempt to leave before I return, I will kill you."

Just that, but the promise in the words was plain, and she swallowed and nodded, still nursing the hand that had clutched the rose's stem. He walked into his room and took an older shirt from his closet; this he threw at her as he entered the hall.

"Wear this," he said.

"But the pants—"

"It will look like a dress. You are not the first woman to spend time in this house. If I am lucky, you will spend *less* time than any other; you will certainly have no enjoyment from it."

She clutched the collar of his shirt, retreating to the bathroom; humid air escaped in a rush before she closed the door. He waited, listening, and after a moment, she returned. She looked younger, in a shirt that dwarfed her frame.

"Come," he said, as if he were still a ruling lord.

She followed, subdued. Afraid.

He led her to his kitchen, the brightest of the rooms in his house. There, the flower, bud closed, stood in the vase that would be its last home.

"Do you see?" He said, shaking.

She nodded, her eyes dark with fear. And wonder. "It was just one flower," she said, but weakly now. "I'm sorry."

A drunk driver might apologize to the family of his victim in just such a tone, and with just as much effect.

"You're *sorry*?" he roared.

She lifted thin hands to her ears. Tears welled in her eyes; he knew the look. He'd seen it so often on the faces of other women. But she did not shed them.

Instead, he leaned toward her, meaning to intimidate her with his size and bulk. He did. "Why did you take it?"

"I told you—for a friend."

"And how will you pay for what you have done, you stupid, stupid child?"

"I don't have much money," she said at last.

It was the wrong thing to say. He slapped her.

She fell. She fell back, traveling the length of the kitchen's gleaming floor.

"Don't speak to me of *money,* " he roared again. "You have taken from me a flower, and I have done *nothing at all* to merit its destruction."

"It's just a—" The word fell away as she rubbed her jaw, rising slowly, risking that much.

"And to whom would you have taken it?"

She said nothing, and then, with a bitterness that her years could not possibly have earned, she said, "A dying friend."

Death had so much more meaning in this world than it had in the previous one. Although his anger and his resolve did not lessen, he gentled his voice. Which made it a growl. Her reaction indicated that it was not, in her mind, an improvement. He reached for his phone again, and held it front of her, like a threat.

"I'll work," she said quickly. "I can work. I'm good at it."

"You are *not* good at it. If you were, you wouldn't have come in that sorry state!"

Her head hung low; her hair, thin, was already drying. Her eyes were blue, a gray blue, when she lifted her face. And they were also reddened.

"What work?" he said.

"I can do you," she said at last, with a hint of unease. "For free."

" 'Do me'?"

"You know. Do it. Here."

He laughed. It was harsh and unpleasant. "I assure you," he said coldly, "that I have no shortage of companionship, and I do not have to purchase it." His gaze made clear that she was in no way attractive to him. It must have made other things clear, because she straightened her shoulders, and although her cheeks were now red, she said, "Don't look down on *me*."

"You killed my rose," he said darkly.

And her brows rose in anger and confusion. "You care about that more than you care about people?"

"Much more."

"It must be nice."

He stopped.

"To have so many people in your life that you can be so careless. Look at this place. Look at this *kitchen*. It's probably worth a small *house*."

"If you had just stolen money," he told her with contempt, "I would have let you go."

"Money won't help," she told him, her voice quavering.

He almost slapped her again. But he had no control over his own strength, and he knew that killing the girl here would cause him trouble. With the police. With the neighbors.

But he could not just let her leave. She had to pay. "Where is this friend?" He said at last.

Her lips compressed. The line was thin and unpleasant.

"She is not the author of your misfortune. I will not hurt her for *your* crime." He held out a hand. In the bright light of the kitchen, it looked almost pawlike, the fingers short and stubby, the nails hard. A man's hand.

Her eyes rounded, but she understood there was no request in the gesture, and she put her own in his. It was dwarfed, insignificant. And it trembled. "Why do you want to see her?" She stopped. "And how do you know it's a she?"

"I have difficulty believing you'd steal my roses for a man."

"I wouldn't do anything for a man," she snapped. She made fists of her hand, and he saw that the one was still bleeding.

With no grace whatsoever, he led her to the kitchen cupboard in which he had placed bandages and ointment. "Give me the hand," he said coldly. "The injured one."

She did as she was ordered, and he brought out the tube, squeezing its cap off. With rough care, he tended her wounds. He'd done it before; no doubt he would do it again. When he finished, he bound it carefully.

She was staring up at his face. "I don't understand," she said at last.

"No, you don't."

"Why are you trying to help me?"

"I'm not. But I don't like the smell of blood. And I don't like the smell of old sweat and urine. I don't give a shit what you do with your life—it'll be short and messy, no doubt. But while you're in my presence, you will *smell* like a person."

"I can leave."

"No," he said, voice shading into danger. "You can't. Not without me. Take me," he added, dropping her hand, "to this friend."

If she was surprised at his car, she didn't show it. She was meek and quiet by his side. She strapped herself in, fastening the seat belt; her whole hand was pressed against the window, slender fingers splayed wide.

"Where?"

"Casey House," she said quietly.

He wasn't surprised. He started the car and they drove.

But the traffic was bad, and they were forced to start and stop. Road repair did that to the city; it clogged the arteries, arresting movement.

"Where do you live?" he asked her.

"None of your business."

His hand brushed her shoulder and then settled there in a ferocious grip. "I don't live anywhere."

"Where *did* you live?"

She shook her head. "Doesn't matter," she told him, and her eyes were now entirely gray. "I'm not going back."

"You haven't been on the streets long."

"Long enough."

"You're what, eighteen? Nineteen?"

"Sixteen. Seventeen in four days."

"School?"

She shrugged. "Who the hell needs school? People with houses. People with cars. People with families."

"People who want to someday *have* those things," he growled.

"What are you, a parent?"

"No."

"Then spare me the lecture. I don't want any of those things."

"What *do* you want, besides the destruction of my roses?"

"To help a friend," she replied darkly. "The only friend I have left."

"They're not magic," he snapped.

She raised a dark brow. "Nothing is. Can I smoke?"

"No."

"Why not? You do."

"Because you're underage."

He could hear her grinding her teeth. He stopped speaking to her at all as the traffic began to move.

The woman in the bed was old. Old enough that he couldn't easily tell what her actual age was. She had hair, but it was patchy; her skin was covered in a rash, and it was clear she had bedsores. Her mouth, when she opened it, hid fungus, things that grew in damp places. She tried to smile when the girl walked into the room.

But frowned when he instantly followed, hand on the girl's wrist.

"Trina," the young girl said, trying unsuccessfully to free herself. She smiled gently, and it softened her angular face in a way that he couldn't describe.

"Cassie. Who is that with you?"

"A man I met."

"Where?"

"In a rose garden."

Trina, if that was her name, shook her head. "A rose garden? Which one?"

"Not a public one," the Beast said coldly. But something about the pathos of this woman stilled anger in an unexpected way. "You like roses?"

The woman nodded quietly. "Before I ran away from home," she said, as if running away from home were a simple part of growing up, "I used to tend them. Our neighbors had them. The old woman there loved them. She loved the buds; she loved the blooms; she loved it when the petals fell. She'd gather them and soak them and boil them in her kitchen. Smell of roses," the woman added, in a sweet, cracked voice. She held out a shaky hand, and Cassie took it and pressed it between her palms, as if she were a book and the hand, a flower that she intended to preserve forever. "That was my real home," she told them both, her pupils widening. "With Mrs. Grayson. She loved roses. She taught me to love them." She turned toward the window. He thought she wanted a moment to gather her expression, but when she started to cough, he understood that she meant to spare Cassie the pain of her decay.

"What do you know of roses?"

She began to tell him. And listening, he understood that she had made a story of the growth of thorn and blossom; that she had made a legend of their names, the way they were grown, the amount of sun that they needed, the cruel emptiness of their branches in winter. He thought words had no power, but he was wrong: there was power in her cadence, and terrible desire. For comfort. For the things that she had lost.

He touched Cassie's shoulder.

"Why are you wearing that?" Trina asked, when she saw the gesture."

"My sweater fell apart," Cassie lied. "And he offered me a shirt—"

"You haven't started to—to work again?"

"No, Trina. I promised."

"Good. Don't end up like me."

Cassie shook herself free of his grip and bending, kissed the woman's brow. "We're in it together," she said, and her voice was as steady as rock.

"She gave me a place to stay," Cassie told him, staring out the window of the moving car. "The first time she found me, I'd been badly beaten," she added, as if she were speaking of a stubbed toe. "She took me to the hospital. And then she took me home. She took care of me."

He nodded, but absently.

"She's dying," the girl added dispassionately. "I can't stand to see it. But I have to go. She was there for me."

"And you don't have a place to live now."

She shrugged. "She lost her place when she couldn't work. But it doesn't matter. She's got one now, and she won't be leaving it until they find a box that'll fit her."

He said nothing.

"The black rose," she continued, looked at light through the veined hand across glass. "I wanted it for her. Because I've never seen one growing before. She would have liked it."

"She didn't grow roses?"

"Not in a small apartment, she didn't."

He nodded again. But he did not speak until they arrived in his garage and the door had slid shut on its rails.

"How did you know I grew roses?"

She shrugged. "I was casing the neigborhood," she

said at last. "People work a lot. They go out. It's easy enough to smash a pane of glass, run in, grab a few things. I can sell them."

"And not your body."

"I'd sell that, too," she told him bitterly. "And more easily. I look like a kid. Men like that."

He didn't.

"But she wanted to work for the both of us. She made me go back to school." She swallowed air. "She made me promise that I wouldn't work. Not that way."

"You offered me—"

"That wasn't work. That was restitution."

"Big word."

"Fuck off."

He caught her chin and held it. "Never say that again."

Swallowed more air. She couldn't nod; not with his hand on her face. But after a minute he let her go, hoping he hadn't bruised her chin. Wondering why he cared.

They entered the rose garden. Passed through it while he eyed her suspiciously. At last, he said, "I will let you work here."

"I told you—I promised—"

"Not that work." He opened the back door of his house, and entered the kitchen. "You made a promise. You'll keep it."

"What kind of work?"

"The hardest kind," he told her. He took his phone out of his pocket. "But for now, you can clean the kitchen."

"It's already clean."

"Then practice."

She shrugged and entered after him. He closed the door on her, and stood in the garden, fingers against the rubber numbers of the keypad.

The ambulance arrived that evening.

"Do you know how to cook?"

"Some. I learned a bit. In school."

"You can cook."

"I told you—"

"For us."

"What do you mean, us?"

"You," he said severely, because she needed food. "Me. And Trina."

"What?"

The doorbell rang. He rose. "I'll get it."

"What did you mean, Trina?"

But he passed her by without a word, and answered the door. He followed the ambulance attendant out, and when he returned, he carried Trina in his arms, as if she were a child. "I'm not your Mrs. Grayson," he said quietly. She was coughing and shaking. "She was a nice old lady. I'm a mean old man."

But she didn't answer him, because he had brought her to the table. The bud's outer leaves were beginning to curl away from the rose's heart. She reached out in wonder—in obvious wonder—and her fluttering hands caused a petal to fall. He caught it carefully and placed it in her palm.

"Do you like the light?" he asked her gently, ignoring Cassie's open mouth.

Trina nodded.

"Good. I have a guest room. It has a large bay window, and the bed there is high; you'll be able to see the sun and the trees on the lawn."

She clutched the petal as if it were a talisman.

"But first," he continued gently, "I thought I would show you my garden. Cassie, open the door."

And Cassie, wordless, did exactly as he told her, her hands shaking as she pulled the door handle down. He carried Trina into his small garden, its glass dome distorting the pale face of the evening moon.

He showed her his roses. His arms did not tire beneath the woman's weight; she felt precious to him, although he could not say why. Perhaps because she understood roses. Perhaps because she found, in their growth, hope or comfort.

*   *   *

When Trina was at last asleep—and it didn't take long—he turned to Cassie. Cassie still held the old woman's hand in her own; those fingers were her petals. "Cassie," he said quietly.

Cassie raised tearing eyes, and she quietly set Trina's hands upon the coverlet before she rose and backed away. "Thank you," she said, meaning it. "When will the ambulance come back?"

"When she's dead."

"W–what?"

"It won't be long," he continued, almost enjoying the young girl's confusion. "She doesn't have long at all. But while she lives, she can spend some time in my garden."

"Why are you doing this?"

"Why am I doing what?"

"This. For her. Being nice."

"Honestly?"

She nodded, and her expression was bleak.

"Because she loves roses," he replied. And he studied the girl for a moment with careful eyes.

"But I killed the black one."

"Yes."

"And you hate me because of it."

"Yes."

"But—"

"I don't hate *her*. She didn't kill my flower." He looked down from a height. "While you were sitting with her, I laundered your clothing. The sweater—I'm sorry—shrank. But the pants, unfortunately, didn't. Put the pants on, Cassie."

"Why?"

"We're going to the mall."

In the mall, surrounded by brand names as dense as any jungle, he found clothing for her. She didn't choose, and he made it absolutely clear that if she tried to five finger discount *anything,* he'd let the police throw her in jail. What there was left of her.

But she didn't protest when he pulled out a credit

card, and she didn't protest when he signed the bill. He handed her the bags and said, "We'd better get home."

She clutched them to her chest a moment, and then said, "You want to, you know—"

"No. Never. Not with you."

"Why not?"

"I don't like children."

She shrugged. "I have a schoolgirl uniform. I had one," she added, her face falling. "Some men like it."

"Cassie." He caught her arms more roughly than he intended.

But she met his face, and hers was a mixture of steel and fluff. A young face. "What?"

"I am not one of those men. I told you, I don't lack for companionship. And I don't think that anything I *pay* for is going to be worth what I pay *with*."

She nodded, and as they made their way to the parking lot, he added, "You'll go back to school."

Her lips thinned. "I won't."

"You will. It will help your friend."

Mutinous, she said nothing at all.

But she went. She looked clean, but the wariness in her eyes made her seem a hunted creature. It did not suit his nature. He wanted to hunt her, then. Instead, he practically threw her out of the car. "I'll be back," he told her roughly, "at three fifteen."

Trina woke several times during the five hours Cassie was gone, and he was aware of her each time she did. He carried her out to the garden, lifting her as if she were an infant, and cradling her, unconscious of the movement, to his broad chest. Because he took her to the roses, and let her talk and ask questions until her strength failed, she seemed to forget that he was one of those despised creatures: a man.

But when she wearied, and she also did this quickly, he returned her to her room.

"I don't know your name," she said, when he had rearranged the coverlet and pulled the curtains wide.

The phone rang before he could answer her. He answered it instead, with a momentary relief. But the voice at the other end of the line was just another one of his conquests, and he was brusque as he rid himself of the call.

"Does it matter?" he asked her, surprised to see that she was still awake.

"I don't want to call you Mrs. Grayson," she told him, with just the faint hint of a wry smile. Thirty-five, he thought her. Or forty. But aged so badly by her life and her dying, that the truth of those numbers was buried.

"Don't call me anything."

"What were you called?"

"When I was in the war?"

"What war?"

He shrugged. She was drugged, and in pain, but still sharp. "The Beast," he said at last.

She laughed, coughing before the laugh could die a natural death. "Beast," she said. "It doesn't really suit you."

"You didn't see me in the war."

Cassie was waiting for him. She got in the car and he drove home, letting her out in front of the house. "Sit with Trina," he told her. "I'll go shopping."

Shopping for three—for two, if Trina's appetite were taken into consideration—was different. He realized as he pulled produce from its bins and tins from their shelves, that he was purchasing things almost blindly. That he hoped that they would like food that he didn't normally eat.

On the other hand, he decided that one night of Cassie's cooking was enough. He cooked.

She came downstairs while he was busy, and she watched him from the safety of a bar stool tucked under the breakfast counter. "I'm not doing much work," she said quietly.

"You are," he told her. "You're comforting the dying."

She hung her head. "I don't want her to die."

"No."

"Can you—do you think there's anything—"

"No." He turned the stove down and removed his apron. "But, Cassie, I understand now why you killed my flower. I can almost forgive you."

She was silent; he looked up and saw that she was watching his broad back. "I don't understand you," she said at last.

"That makes two of us."

He wasn't much impressed with the marks she got on her first test, and he let her know it; he growled. She flinched.

"Cassie," he said, "you aren't a stupid girl. What is *this*?"

She shrugged. "Math."

"Look, your job here is to comfort a dying woman. Do you think that *this* is comforting?"

"I don't think she'll care."

"Then why don't we ask her? Come on; she's awake now. I can hear the television; it just went on." He held out a hand, and she swore at him in two different languages. This time, however, he didn't slap her.

"You told me that she sent you to school. You told me that she—"

"All right, you stupid, interfering bastard. Enough."

Trina lasted longer than he expected. Although she didn't improve, and her bedsores still lingered, she kept pace with the slow blossoming of the dark rose. He gathered petals for her, one at a time, and carried them to the room, placing them between the bowls of liquid that were the only food she could keep down.

"Beast," she said quietly, one afternoon.

"Trina?"

"Cassie told me."

"What? About the flower? I've already forgiven her."

"Not the flower. I wouldn't have seen her cut it," she added, with genuine regret. "But if she hadn't, we wouldn't be here."

"Then about what?"

"She told me that she offered to pay you."

Ah. That. He was cautious when he met Trina's sharp eyes.

"You didn't take her up on her offer."

"I took her to school."

"Why?"

Because Trina was not a child, and because he knew she was tiring rapidly, he gave up as gracefully as he knew how. "She has the body of an anorexic."

Trina frowned. Clearly this was not the answer she wanted.

"She's too young," he added. "And I don't find her at all attractive."

"Liar."

He raised a brow.

"Why didn't you take her up on that offer? You get around enough. I've heard the phone calls."

"I'm not lying. I don't find her attractive."

"You're lying about your reason."

He shrugged. After a moment, trusting death to keep his secrets, he said, "She killed my flower. I can have sex any time I want—it's meaningless. The flower wasn't."

"I know. I've seen you with your roses. They're the only thing you seem to care about."

"Oh?"

"You come alive when you talk about them."

He laughed. "So do you."

"I don't want to sleep with her either."

"Well, then," he said, rising, his eye on the clock. "Let me go and pick her up."

She nodded, but as he reached the door, she said, "She can't repay you."

"No."

"What will you do with her?" *When I'm dead.*

He had no answer for her. None at all.

*   *   *

Cassie cooked. She *insisted* on cooking. The Beast took refuge in Trina's room, his face fixed in a scowl that was almost affectionate.

"Let her. It'll make her feel useful."

"I don't think she cares all that much about being useful."

Trina's sharp eyes narrowed. "It's all she does care about. But the type of use most find for her doesn't sustain her. It wouldn't sustain anyone."

"She'll ruin the meat."

"So?"

"You only say that because you can't actually *eat* any of it."

Trina smiled. It was a pain-filled smile. He thought about morphine; thought that it was almost time for it. But he said nothing. Because he thought the morphine would dull her wit and her tongue, and he found that he wanted to keep these for himself for as long as possible.

"You trying to be a knight in shining armor?"

"No. I never found a suit of armor that wouldn't crush me."

"Or a horse that you wouldn't break the back of?"

He laughed out loud. "I had one or two that were big enough," he said. "When I wasn't eating them."

She thought he was joking, and she laughed, and he let it be. He also forced himself to eat Cassie's meal, and found that it wasn't as hard as he'd thought it would be. When he finished, she started to clear the table, and he lifted a hand and gestured for her to sit. "You cooked," he told her firmly. "I'll clean up."

"But I—"

"Trina hasn't seen you all day. She wants your company. On the stairs, you'll find a bag; it's full of books. I wasn't certain what she would read, and what she would throw away. But you can find something there to read to her."

Cassie pushed her chair away from the table; it fell over as she left it. She was almost out of the kitchen at a run, and he knew why: beneath the hall light, her cheeks were glistening.

"She had a hard adolescence," Trina told him quietly.

"She's still an adolescent."

"She is that. But she's still had it hard."

"Harder than you?"

Trina shrugged. "Maybe. I was too old, when I found her. Too old to change. Already dying. I didn't know it then."

He nodded. "And now?"

"She's all scarred. Scared because of it."

"Scared of what?"

"Of what happens when I die." There. She'd said it. And because she had, he couldn't ignore it.

"She's tough enough."

"She's not. That's the point. She's not. She isn't afraid you'll turn her out into the streets—she expects that. But she loves the books." The old woman's eyes narrowed. "Harry Potter? You told her you bought that for *me?*"

"You chose it."

"I thought she'd like it enough to keep reading it on her own."

"You were right." He reached out and gently laid petals across the erratic movement of her chest. Black petals all. "It's almost in full bloom," he told her gently. "And when it is, you'll see the color of its heart. I never thought it would last this long. And I never thought I'd be grateful just to share its beauty with someone that understands how much it means. She gave me that. It's a gift."

Trina coughed for a long time, her shaking hands scattering the petals. But she caught them at last and held them in a shaky cupped palm. "She's afraid of the end of this."

"Not your death?"

"That, too. But no. She's . . . almost happy here. I've only ever seen her like this once."

"When?"

"When we first met."

He nodded. "She won't tell you this because she can't—but she loves being able to clean. This room. The room you gave her. The kitchen. She's trying to learn how to cook. She wants to—" coughing destroyed the sentence; pain destroyed the thought.

He caught her hand in his, just as Cassie so often did. "She'll be home soon," he told her softly, rising.

He picked her up. "You should have a license," he told her quietly, as she got out of the car. She stopped a moment, her shoulders bunching together, her neck falling.

"I won't need it," she said at last, choosing defiance and anger with which to answer him. "I won't have a car for much longer." She ran into the house. He had stopped locking the door, which was foolish.

The next day, he brought her a key. He gave it to her, and she looked at it as if it were a magic wand. "I can't take this," she told him. "I don't live here."

"You are living here."

But her gaze fell to the blossoming rose that graced the empty table. The last of its petals were opening now, and the stem was drooping and wilting.

"Not for long," she told him, bitterly. "Look. It's almost done." As if she believed that Trina's life and this rose's were intertwined somehow.

Why shouldn't she? He believed it as well. He stared at the dying rose, and he shuddered at the passing of beauty. Then he lifted the vase with care and took it to Trina's room.

That night, he called a doctor, and the day after, the morphine drip was installed.

But with the cessation of pain, Trina didn't simply disappear in the soft folds of narcotic embrace. She sat up when he entered the room. And she pointed, almost wordless, to the flower: the last of the petals were open, and the heart's center at last laid bare. It was red.

He nodded. "Cassie didn't want to go to school today. Will you stay until she gets back?"

"I'll stay."

"And after?"

Trina shook her head. Her smile was pleasant, and it was calm, but it was also shorn of illusion. "Beast," she said quietly, "what will you do with my girl?"

I can't keep her here, he wanted to say. But he found that she, like the thorny roses that were his first hope, had grown round him. She cut him in ways that the roses had, when he had not yet learned to navigate their sharp points, their hidden edges.

"I'll never sleep with her," he said at last.

"Good."

He nodded.

She said, after a pause, "She'll never trust you again if you do."

And to his great surprise, as if knowledge were blossoming with the rose, he said, "I know. I knew it the first day she offered."

"You still don't find her attractive?"

"I find her beautiful," he replied quietly.

This time, it was the right thing to say. "So do I."

That night, with Cassie reading by her side, Trina closed her eyes. She would never open them again.

He knew it; he caught the scent of death well before Cassie's cry dragged him up the stairs. He had been staring out the windows at his garden; he longed for the roses, but he also knew that if he were outside, he might miss Cassie's cry. And he was right. Because it started out so quietly, he could almost mistake it for intense conversation. He took the stairs at a run, and opened the door to Trina's room.

Cassie was on the ground by the bed's side, her hands clutched tight to Trina's. Trina's were slack and gray; her face, mottled by sores, was also gray. Her chest was still, but a blanket of petals adorned it.

Black petals. Red heart stood in the window upon a drooping stem—all that remained of his flower.

He caught Cassie by the shoulders, as he so often did, and when she was still, he said, "Her pain is ended, Cassie."

"She's *dead!*"

"Yes. But sometimes that's the only way that pain does end."

She turned and began to hit him, her flat open palms becoming fists. They were so light that they fell like heartbeats on the outside of his skin, and he let them rain down, sharing, in them, some part of the loss he had never expected to feel.

He let her rage. He let her leave him for a moment to throw books across the room. He let her scream at Trina, and at him, in a rising alternating frenzy, until she was suddenly spent. And then he carried her to her room, and he tucked her into her bed. "In the morning," he said quietly, "we can decide on funeral arrangements."

But he had already made his decision.

And because he had, he almost lost Cassie for good. He was outside, digging up the part of the garden in which no roses grew. He didn't hear the door of Cassie's room swing open. He didn't hear the light tread of her footsteps. Didn't see her with her school satchel, stuffed with clothing, as she made her way to the front door.

But he saw her, because he looked up at the moment, and she was a shadow just beyond the bright glow of kitchen lights. He dropped his spade then, and he ran.

Caught her as the front door opened, his hand upon her arms. "What do you think you're doing?" he shouted, roaring as he had not done since he had first laid eyes on her.

She was afraid; he saw that in an instant. It robbed him of his voice, and his voice was the last thing, beside the roses, that was left of his old self, his old life. But he saw more, besides: he saw that she was not afraid of his anger, not afraid of his question. She said, "The rose is gone," in a little girl voice. The only time he had heard that voice was while she read Harry Potter aloud.

"Trina is gone," he told her. "But I wanted to bury her here, beneath the garden. She'll be happy here. You can still come and read to her."

"She won't hear me." The little girl voice hardened; the street returned to the cadence of those harsh syllables.

"I will," he told her quietly. So quietly. All rumble gone from his voice, all growl.

"I don't care about your stupid roses. I only wanted them for *her*."

"I know."

She shook her head, and then she turned to face the kitchen that she had made half her own. Her face had grown less gaunt with food and shelter. She was not beautiful.

But she was. Oh, she was.

She said, flatly, "Let me go." More in the words than his hands could cause. He trembled as he removed them.

She opened the door. Stepped out.

"You have the key," he shouted after her retreating back. "I'm not about to change the locks."

She stared at him for a minute, and then she turned and ran. And he let her go.

Three days, he waited. He counted them, counted hours and minutes. Counted the times when he could not drive her to school, and the times when he could not retrieve her. He ate very little. Too little. The bulk seemed to vanish from his frame; he was shrinking in on himself, drooping as the black rose had, trapped in its slender vase.

He walked up to Trina's empty room, and he stood a moment in the doorframe. The phone was ringing, but he ignored it; it was just another call, and he didn't feel like fending off a stranger whose body he happened to know.

On the fourth day, he slipped into Trina's bed. The smell of death was there, but it was faint; roses lingered instead, for he'd cut them and he'd placed them in the window whose light the old woman had loved. He closed his eyes and slid into delirium.

And woke to a familiar face, familiar small hands slapping him, a familiar high voice screaming, *screaming* in his ear.

"Don't you do it!" she shouted. "Don't you leave me, too!"

It made no sense. He looked up at her, and thought that she had grown, or that he had diminished. "I wasn't the one who left," he said at last. No roar in his voice. Just the quiet of words.

She lifted a key in trembling hands. "I came back," she said at last. "And I'm making—I'm making dinner."

He closed his eyes as she left the room. His face was wet, and he raised a heavy hand to brush those tears away, never noticing that his fingers were longer, his palms smaller.

But when he didn't come down to join her, she made her way up with familiar bowls—soup bowls. Trina's bowls. She tended him, as he had done with Trina, all the while crying.

"I want to stay here," she told him, when she had control of her voice. "I want to live here. I want to read those books, in that garden. I want to—" And she cried again.

He reached up and brushed her tears away. "You have to go to school," he told her quietly. "Because Trina's still here. And you can't work," he added, "because you promised."

"She's *dead*."

"You aren't. And it was your promise."

She fed him soup, ignoring his words for a long

time. And then she offered him a tentative, a terrified, smile. "You'll hate living with me," she told him. "I'm impossible. Even Trina said so."

"I have been living with you," he answered. "And I don't hate it."

"You don't want *me*."

"I don't want something meaningless from you. I don't want sex with you. I want—"

She held her breath.

"I want to see you grow," he said. "Thorns and all, little Cassie. I want to see you blossom. I want to see—"

"I'm not a rose."

"But you are," he said. "More precious than the black rose. I know you're afraid of me. I would be. But I want you to stay. Will you stay?"

And she said, "Yes. Beast."

He felt the curse lifting as she said the words, and he almost laughed. Because she would never say it, and he would never say it, but they were bound by it anyway: she had learned to trust him, in a few short weeks. And she had learned to love him.

It was not what he had been searching for, in those crowded bars, in his isolate bedroom, in the lives of those countless women.

It was more.